**Welcome to Gold Valley, Oregon,
where the cowboys are tough to tame, until they
meet the women who can lasso their hearts.**

Cowboy Christmas Blues (ebook novella)
Smooth-Talking Cowboy
Mail Order Cowboy (ebook novella)
Untamed Cowboy
Hard Riding Cowboy (ebook novella)
Good Time Cowboy
Snowed in with the Cowboy (ebook novella)
A Tall, Dark Cowboy Christmas
Unbroken Cowboy
Cowboy to the Core

**In Copper Ridge, Oregon, lasting love
with a cowboy is only a happily-ever-after away.
Don't miss any of Maisey Yates's
Copper Ridge tales, available now!**

From HQN Books

Shoulda Been a Cowboy (prequel novella)
Part Time Cowboy
Brokedown Cowboy
Bad News Cowboy
A Copper Ridge Christmas (ebook novella)
The Cowboy Way
Hometown Heartbreaker (ebook novella)
One Night Charmer
Tough Luck Hero
Last Chance Rebel
Slow Burn Cowboy
Down Home Cowboy
Wild Ride Cowboy
Christmastime Cowboy

Look for more Gold Valley books coming soon!

For more books by Maisey Yates,
visit www.maiseyyates.com.

MAISEY YATES

Cowboy to the Core

HQN™

ISBN-13: 978-1-335-50497-5

Cowboy to the Core

Recycling programs
for this product may
not exist in your area.

For my readers. Thank you for loving this series.
You're the reason it exists.

Cowboy
to the Core

CHAPTER ONE

"I ain't afraid to love a man. But I ain't afraid to shoot him, either."

—Annie Oakley

"GABE DALTON, YOU shouldn't be handling a horse like that."

Jamie Dodge was firing on all cylinders right now, her adrenaline hopped up from the punishing ride she'd just taken with one of the mares, out on a trail behind the Dalton ranch. She'd pushed the horse and the horse had pushed back, more fire in her system than anyone had suspected.

It made Jamie happy to feel the old girl exhibit so much spirit. A great many of the horses that had recently come to the ranch were—according to Gabe— old and burned out, or abused.

Gabe Dalton had been in the process of turning his family's ranch into something of a sanctuary for horses that had come to the end of their usefulness, either in the rodeo or with their previous owners. He'd hired Jamie to lend her expertise to the endeavor, and today was her very first day on the job.

A rodeo cowboy, Gabe had told her it had been so long since he'd handled horses out of the arena, he'd wanted someone who had experience working with older animals.

Jamie had been doing just that on her brother's ranch for the past year and a half. Finding horses who were slow and gentle, and good for the beginners they often took out on rides at Get Out of Dodge, the guest ranch she worked with her family.

But when Gabe had offered her a chance to flex her muscles and work with him, to gain a little independence and make way more money than her brother was paying her, she'd jumped at the chance.

Gabe Dalton was a legend, who theoretically made women swoon across county and state lines. She had been told—by a breathless woman in the feed store who was clearly a rodeo fan—that Jamie working *under* Gabe made her an object of pure envy.

Jamie had fought to keep from rolling her eyes.

Gabe was perfectly symmetrical. And muscular. If you were into that kind of thing. And she was...well, she had other things on her mind.

Today had been perfection in many ways. She'd been feeling increasingly lost on the Get Out of Dodge ranch. Not because the work wasn't great. It was. She loved leading trail rides for the guests at the ranch.

It was...the surrounding part of it. Everyone had paired off.

It was like springtime in an old cartoon. Her brothers were all married or engaged, her best friends were in relationships...

And Jamie felt a little bit lost.

But not here. Not right now. And not when it came to horses.

Animals made sense. And to Jamie, horses made the most sense of all.

"You have a problem, Jamie?"

She was doing her best to keep her spiked adrenaline under control. To be…nice. She'd been told, on a few occasions, that her direct manner of communication was off-putting sometimes.

"I just feel," she said, searching for some tact somewhere inside her, "that perhaps you could handle Gus a bit differently."

Gabe looked down at her from his position on the horse, his eyes shadowed by the brim of his cowboy hat. His large, weathered hand pulled back on the reins and he dismounted, muscles in motion from his forearms down to his denim-clad thighs.

He made for a striking visual, that was for sure. His horse there in the center of the arena, the white fence and manicured arenas, encircled by the bright green lawn, a stark contrast to the wildness that hemmed in the ranch itself.

Thick groves of pine trees that bled up the sides of the jagged mountains that closed in all around them.

It was a familiar sight, in every single way.

And for just a moment, her confidence faltered.

He was familiar in every way. A cowboy like the kind she'd grown up with. But when his eyes clashed with hers there was an unfamiliar echo in her stomach. It made her feel hot underneath her skin, and shaky down in her center.

She didn't like it at all.

Jamie Dodge wasn't a woman who wasted time on insecurity and uncertainty. She'd had to grow up fast, and she'd had to grow up tough. Living in a house populated entirely by men meant learning how to meet them on their level.

And so she'd done that.

Her father had been a man with a ranch to run and four kids to raise, with no wife to help him. Her brothers had been older. Gods, in her estimation, or something a little bit less perfect but no less unbreakable.

She'd wanted to be just like them.

There was no doubt about it; her older brother Wyatt wouldn't be standing there like a guppy, staring at Gabe Dalton just because the muscle in his forearm had twitched.

It was normal to appreciate something like that. He was—she thought—a bit like a quality piece of horse-flesh.

Muscular. Agile.

But that was just a little visual appreciation. Nothing more, nothing less. Nothing at all to get wound up about.

"He's sensitive," she said, planting her boot against the bottom rung of the fence. She gripped the top rail, launching herself up over the top, jumping down into the fine arena dirt, a small cloud rising up around her.

One piercing blue gaze wasn't going to turn her into a giggly feed-store girl. Giggling was for other women. Women who didn't have goals of getting themselves into the rodeo by next season.

Women who'd grown up with mothers with soft voices and soft embraces. Who could afford to take risks because they knew they had a safe place to land if they fell.

The only thing Jamie knew she could count on was

that if she fell—no matter how hard the ground—she'd pick herself back up.

From the time she could remember, when she had fallen down and scraped her knee, she wiped the blood on her palm, and wiped her palm on her jeans. Gone on with her day, not letting a single tear escape. She learned to suck it up and to buck up.

"I know when it comes to riding saddle bronc and dealing with horses who have a lot of fight, you're one of the best. But trust me on this. I know these kinds of horses. This one is skittish," she said, approaching the horse slowly. "And handling him like you are is just…" She did her best to find some words that weren't overtly confrontational and it was damned hard.

She'd been raised by a man who didn't mince words.

There hadn't been a whole lot of softness in Jamie's life, and that was fine by her. The fact was, she preferred direct methods of communication. Often things like this seemed unnecessary to her. But he was the boss and she was the employee. So she had to figure out some kind of way.

"Horses like Gus, who have a lot of trauma and a lot of years behind them, need a different kind of intuition. It's not just which way they'll move. It's why they're moving that way," she said.

"He was doing fine for me," he said, looking at the old gelding that he'd been riding only a few moments before.

She shook her head. "He did a lot better with me this morning. He's balking. Pulling against your reins. He doesn't like it." Really, there was no point mincing words here. "He doesn't like you."

"All right, what's the problem?" He crossed his arms,

and her eyes flickered to his forearms. They were streaked with dirt and muscle, and there was a cut right next to his elbow that was just beginning to heal.

She returned her focus to his face. She could see his eyes, now that she was closer. Along with the hard, square cut of his jaw and the firm, set line of his lips.

He was not happy with her.

Too bad. She wasn't happy with him.

"He's got a soft mouth," she said. "You need to be more sensitive to that."

"Horses are big-ass animals who don't need to be babied."

She fought to keep her eyes from visibly rolling back in her head. "In general, I agree with you. But we are getting horses from all different backgrounds, and some of them will need to be babied. I have a firm hand, and I lay out expectations with my animals. But you also have to know when you need to be a little bit more forgiving. And Gus here needs forgiveness."

Also, a rider who doesn't have his head up his ass.

Biting her tongue through that last part was a personal victory.

"Why is it you think you know better than I do?"

"You're a rodeo cowboy," she said slowly. "What you do is a specific thing. Your type… I know all about your type."

Gabe snorted, pulling his hat off his head and running his hand through his dark hair. "Really?"

"I was raised in a house with cowboys. Believe me. I've had enough exposure to make me immune to your charm, and also give me enough insight to know that a lot of times you're leading with your ego."

"You don't think I could possibly just have a different take than you on what Gus needs?"

Her patience frayed, then snapped. "If so, it's the wrong take."

"Little girl," he said, his eyes going hard, his mouth firm. "I hired you to work for me. I hired you to assist me. I didn't hire you to tell me what to do."

She didn't apologize, because she knew Wyatt wouldn't have. Because she knew it was how he would have talked to someone in this situation. Straight up.

Wyatt wouldn't have ignored being called *little girl*. But Jamie figured since he was her boss, she'd let it go. "You've taken on a lot here."

"You don't need to tell me what I already know. But between the horses I had already agreed to take in that were retired from the rodeo, and the horses that came from that farm Bea told me about, I didn't have much choice. I wasn't going to turn them down. They didn't have another place to go."

"And that's real sad, but we have to make sure we can do good by the horses, too. I understand that your goal is to make it so they can go to families. Less experienced riders who need gentle mounts. But we are going to have to make gentle mounts out of them."

"Yes," he said dryly. "I am aware of my goals. And that is why I hired you."

"I'm the best you're gonna find," she said confidently.

She didn't have any trouble claiming her expertise. That was the thing. If horsemanship was only about training, then she supposed people could assume that at twenty-five she didn't have the necessary experience to back up her confidence. But it wasn't about age or experience, not alone. So much of it was about instinct and a connection to the animal. About having a good sense for how to work with each individual horse.

Her experience had come from barrel racing, from years working the family dude ranch, where she had managed finding and training new horses for experienced and inexperienced riders alike.

From where she was standing, it looked to her like Gabe Dalton only knew how to do one thing. He knew how to ride bucking broncos. Hard and fast. She didn't think he knew how to sense the different personalities of the animals he was working with. Not intuitively.

"Let me ask you a question," she said, crossing her arms and cocking her hip to the side. Her tank top bunched up at the front, her shapeless jeans stiff against the movement.

Her friend Bea often gave her grief for buying unisex clothing at a farm supply store. But Jamie found that it was serviceable enough. Except for some reason, standing there in front of Gabe, it all felt a little bit ill fitting.

"Why do you want to do this? Why do you want to work with horses like this? I mean, obviously you can ride."

I guess. For eight seconds at a time. If you're lucky.

"I think you and I both know luck is part of it." His words so unerringly mirrored her thoughts for a moment she was afraid she'd said it all out loud. "But since you asked, I am a damn good rider, thank you very much."

"A certain kind of riding," she said. "This is different. I have a lot of experience with training horses who are older, and who need to be made into safe mounts. A lot of it isn't training so much as an evaluation. You have to know who has the temperament. And they all won't. Some horses are just a lot more hot-blooded than others. A lot more skittish. Now, there are still things we can do with them…"

"You're right, Jamie. I don't have experience with that. But it could be argued that there is some intelligence in knowing that, and in the hiring of you."

"Well," she said, approaching the big horse, Gus, that Gabe had been on. "I think that Gus has a pretty good chance at being made into the perfect horse for someone older. Kids could ride him, I guess, but he's big, and that will be difficult for them, and I imagine parents will be naturally leery of a horse his size. He is skittish, but I think that's circumstantial, more than his temperament. The fact that he has a soft mouth means that he is responsive. And that will also be good for an older, less experienced rider. Actually, when we're through training Gus, I think that we could use him at Get Out of Dodge."

"Is that so?" He was like a wall. Totally unimpressed with her. And also totally not intimidated by her.

She didn't know what to do with that.

"Yes. We get a lot of people coming to the ranch who don't necessarily have experience with horses, but want to learn. A lot of people later in life who've never been on one."

"It must be an interesting job that you have over there."

She blinked, unsure of what to do with the way he'd taken the conversation and turned it to her. He sounded sincere—that was the weird part. Not like he was mocking her, and all things considered, she'd have expected mockery.

That was how her brothers would have behaved.

But not Gabe, apparently.

"It's fine." It was a job that she was going to be taking a break from in the next year. After she'd saved enough money to get herself on the road with the rodeo. After she'd found the right horse, and done all the work she needed to do in order to not…humiliate herself barrel racing.

Wyatt was a rodeo legend. A bull rider who'd won the championships four times.

Jamie wanted to make her own mark in the rodeo. Oh, she knew barrel racing didn't command quite the enthusiasm from the crowd the bulls did. But she wanted to succeed on her own. On her own merit.

She wanted to get out and do things on her own. She *needed* to.

She'd been in Gold Valley all this time. The most distance she'd gotten from her family was working at a Western-themed store in town called The Gunslinger. Otherwise, she lived on the ranch, worked on the ranch.

Her life revolved around it. Around them.

She knew that her father and brothers all felt like they took care of her. Right down to Wyatt being completely and utterly disapproving of her taking a job with Gabe Dalton. He'd been on her about it ever since Gabe had approached her about the job a few months earlier, which was ridiculous. He'd given them plenty of time to sort out schedules. Really, it had been overly planned. Which seemed to make Wyatt even more obnoxious.

As if Gabe was planning to seduce her or something.

As if he could.

Hell, she'd grown up in a house full of men just like him, and those men had brought their friends around. Had brought other rodeo cowboys around.

They smelled. They left the toilet seat up. They hit on everything that moved. She'd spent her life picking around men's underwear in the clothing baskets, had been rinsing whiskers out of the sink with great distaste since she was ten.

Between her father and her older brothers, men had been pretty thoroughly demystified.

Body odor, constant swearing, jockstraps, asshole behavior...

Gabe was watching her while she mused, his lips tipped up slightly as if he could read her mind.

"Does Wyatt give you a lot of freedom?"

She snorted, the action loosening some of the tension in her chest. "Wyatt doesn't give me anything. I work at our family ranch. Otherwise, I do what I want."

Cowboys were not her type. Not at all. She supposed that in order for them to be interesting at all, their behavior had to seem romantic.

And to her, it just wasn't. But then, Jamie wasn't a romantic. She was a practical kind of girl. She was well aware of the way the world worked, well aware of the way cowboys worked.

Her desire to get back into riding had nothing to do with cowboys, as a matter of fact. She was always much less interested in a man on the horse than she was in the horse he was riding.

If she was going to be interested in a man—and someday she supposed she'd find one—it wouldn't be one like that.

Gabe Dalton was exactly the kind of man she was immune to.

But Wyatt worried.

What Wyatt didn't understand was that she had always taken care of herself. But until she wasn't right at home, he was always going to feel like that was his responsibility.

Jamie had learned early on how to be self-sufficient.

Babies didn't *choose* to be born, and they definitely didn't choose the manner in which they were born.

Jamie certainly hadn't chosen to cause a blood clot that led to her mother's death days later.

But the fact of the matter was her mother had essentially traded her life for Jamie's.

The boys and her father had lost her, and gained Jamie.

In return, Jamie had done her best to be tough. To be like them.

Maybe that was the real reason cowboys didn't hold a lot of appeal or mystery to her.

She hadn't just been raised by them. Hadn't just been surrounded by them.

She'd learned to become one of them.

Tough as nails and confident in who she was and what she knew.

"My work at the ranch is definitely interesting," Jamie said. "But I'm looking forward to this. To a change."

"To getting Wyatt out of your hair a few hours every day?"

Jamie bristled. "My brother is the best man, and the best cowboy, out there. You could probably learn from him." It was one thing for her to think uncharitable thoughts about Wyatt, but she would be damned if she would let Gabe Dalton say anything.

"He's a bull rider," Gabe pointed out.

"Yeah, and he can ride both."

"There's a reason I chose not to," Gabe said. "First

of all, I have a brain in my head. Second of all, I like horses."

"I thought you chose to ride saddle bronc because that's what your daddy did." She hadn't meant that to come out quite like it had. Yes, Hank Dalton was a famous rodeo rider, who'd had celebrity status that had transcended that thanks to endorsement deals. But Gabe had fame in his own right. And she was actually pretty annoyed with herself for making the comment. Given that she was fighting against that concern herself.

Wanting to join the rodeo, not wanting for everyone to think she was there because of Wyatt.

Something shifted imperceptibly in Gabe's expression. As if he'd injected his face with granite. The whole thing had gone firm, solid. "I chose to do it because that's what I like to do. But that's not what this is about. What I'm doing here has nothing to do with my life in the rodeo."

"Well, you're off to a good start."

"I thought you thought I was off to a bad start?"

"I meant with hiring me. The rest... I'm not so sure."

He crossed his arms, his eyes taking on a mocking glint. "All right, Jamie Dodge. You going to show me how it's done or what?"

"Gladly." She stuck her left foot in the stirrup and swung herself up onto the back of Gus. "Watch and learn, Gabe Dalton. Watch and learn."

CHAPTER TWO

GABE COULD ONLY marvel at the way the little brunette handled every animal she came into contact with that day. He supposed he could marvel at the way she talked to him, but that was something else. Jamie Dodge didn't seem to have much in the way of fear. Or common sense, though she didn't seem to know it.

He'd never met such a hardheaded female in all of his life. And that was saying something.

His own mother had smashed in the headlights on his father's truck with a baseball bat back when he'd been a kid. At another stage, she had lit a different truck on fire. Literally.

And he respected the hell out of that. She was a tough woman who didn't take any shit, and while she'd been more than willing to seek redneck justice when necessary, Gabe felt protective of her.

Just because she could handle herself didn't mean someone shouldn't try to protect her, too.

High-spirited women—or rather, just women with a strong sense of fairness—had been a fixture in his life since he was a boy.

Jamie was something else entirely. If little girls were supposed to be made out of sugar, spice and everything nice, he imagined that Jamie was made out of star thistles, grit and the total willingness to skin a man alive if it came down to it.

She was also absolutely the best he'd ever seen when it came to dealing with a variety of temperaments in horses.

There was something about the way she connected with the animals that reminded him of a piece of himself he'd lost years ago.

But she could obviously use a lesson on dealing with people. He could go toe to toe with her, show her who was boss in that most basic of fashions. Berate her until she saw things his way, and until she internalized the fact that he was the one who was in charge here.

He watched men do that kind of thing all the time. Try to use their size, their power, to force other people to respect them, which Gabe had always thought was a weak move. Only men who were afraid they might not have any power had to act that way. At least, that was his take on it.

That was what men did when they were secretly concerned their power didn't have any teeth. And Gabe didn't carry that fear about himself, in secret or in public.

But he imagined that most men—most people— who went toe to toe with Jamie Dodge gave as good as they got.

Men didn't like being challenged, especially not by women.

And he imagined she wouldn't be expecting someone to sidestep.

He grinned. "I'm happy to have you show me how it's done, darlin'."

"I… You are?" She blinked.

And suddenly, the pit bull looked a whole lot more like a harmless kitten.

"Sure," he said, keeping his tone casual. "You're right. I hired you for a reason. Look, I haven't worked with horses in this capacity. Not for a long time, at least. And the whole point of having you here is to make it so that I don't have to be here."

There had been a time when he'd wanted her job. When he'd wanted that life. Working on a ranch. Working with horses.

He'd let that go a long time ago. He'd had to.

And he'd found something else. A tarnished kind of glory that he'd managed to get lost in for years. On the other side of it, he didn't know who he was or what he wanted.

But he could get the ranch up and running. It could do some good whether he was here or not.

"Well," she said. "I don't know how long-term I can necessarily…"

"You're the person that I need to get things going here. I never made you give a certain commitment time frame. Don't worry about it."

"Right," she said.

"Show me how it's done."

She urged the horse forward, and horse and rider moved in one fluid motion together. Jamie's connection with the horse was instant. And it was damned impressive. She struggled to get him to make some changeups, but eventually, he would comply. And she was right. It took significantly less pressure on the bit than he'd been giving. When she came back around and dismounted, he nodded.

"That was a damn fine ride," he said. "You're going

to have to give me a rundown of your take on the horses we have so far. It would be helpful if we were on the same page."

"I...I could do that."

"Great. Why don't we get Gus squared away?"

He didn't make a move to take the lead rope, and Jamie grabbed hold of it quickly, turning toward the barn and walking in that direction. He was happy to allow her to think that he was following her lead. Just like the horse was. When they walked back into the barn, Jamie began to remove Gus's tack.

"Let me get that," he said, stepping between her and the horse and taking care of the saddle himself.

She gawked at him, her brown eyes wide, her lips dropped open slightly. "I can get it," she said finally.

"Sure," he said. "But I can, too."

"I work for you," she said, elbowing her way back in and seeing to the rest of the work.

She knelt down, lifting Gus's foot and checking his hooves, digging out any rocks that had lodged there with the pick. "I'm fully capable of lifting anything around here that's going to need lifting. Ranch work is kind of my thing," she added.

"But there's no reason I shouldn't carry something heavy for you if I'm here," he said.

"Sure is. I don't need you to. You'd do the same for one of your brothers?"

He shook his head. "Well, no. Because they're my brothers. And they're assholes."

"*I'm* an asshole." She treated him to a mulish look.

He chuckled. "Also a lady."

Her face went scarlet, from the roots of her hair, down to the collar of her tank top. "You didn't hire a lady to work on your ranch, Gabe Dalton. You hired an expert with horses. That's how I expect you to treat me."

Very interesting.

And obviously the exact right track to take with her. Because he hadn't seen her flustered, not once. Not any of the times they had interacted away from the ranch, and certainly not since she had set foot onto the ranch today, her first day as an employee. She'd been all piss and vinegar.

But suddenly, she was flustered, and that was a damned interesting thing.

She moved on to Gus's other foot, her motions jerky, filled with irritation.

"Are you making commentary on how I treat my staff?"

"Just on how you should treat me," she said. "I'm not a fragile flower. I've done every single chore at Get Out of Dodge that my brothers have done, at least once. If not more. I was raised by my father, just the same as they were, and the same things were expected of me. I'm not here to be treated differently. I'm here to be treated the way I deserve to be, based on my skill level."

"Me lifting a saddle for you is not underestimating you. It's just polite."

"To you. Not to me."

She continued on checking hooves, a strand of dark hair falling in her face, her slender arms rippling with muscle every time she moved them. She was small-built, slim, but definitely fit. Obviously someone who was used to working hard, and with her hands.

When she was through, she got a brush and pushed her hand through the strap and began to work it vigorously over Gus's back. "So you're going back to the rodeo?" she asked.

"Yep," he said. "Skipping this year, obviously, but afterward I'm getting back in."

"Why are you skipping this year?"

He shook his head. "A whole lot of things. McKenna came a bit ago and that changed things. Now my dad has me working on the ranch. It's just not a great time to be gone for eight months."

His half sister was only the beginning of the different changes that had taken place in his family recently. His dad was getting older, and he wasn't able to work the land the way that he once had.

Hank had retired from the rodeo some fifteen years ago, and that had been hard enough for him. But he'd been the old man of the circuit at that point and he hadn't been winning. Then he'd come home and found his wife ready to walk out the door, and that had been the beginning of something more than toxic fights.

The toxic fighting had been the status quo for his parents. His mother faithful while his father wandered the country being a bastard, and then the inevitable explosion when it all came out into the open.

But when Hank had come home for good, Tammy had issued an ultimatum.

And Hank hadn't wanted to lose his wife. Not when it came right down to it.

So he'd been on the ranch. Working the land, behaving himself.

But he couldn't work the land quite as well as he once could.

That had been true for a while, and there had been hands working on the place for a while now, but it was only recently that Hank had admitted just how much he was struggling to keep up with all aspects of the ranch, and had asked Gabe to take on the charge of it.

You're my oldest. Caleb and Jacob, they've got fire-fighting...

And I have the rodeo.

I know better than anyone that it isn't going to last you, Hank had said. *It's why I wanted you to go to school, instead of wasting all the good years your body had on the back of a horse.*

Right. Because you did it. And it wasn't good enough for me?

I did it so that my kids wouldn't have to.

I'm supposed to believe that you did it for anyone but yourself, Hank? That it wasn't about your own glory ever? Just about you wanting a better life for us?

Believe what you want, his father had said. *But the fact remains, I always knew that the rodeo wouldn't last you. It can't. You break down, and then you don't have anything. Well, you have this.*

And Gabe had swallowed down his rage and agreed to taking it on as an undertaking.

But it gave him an opportunity to use the facility the way he'd always wanted to. To get horses into a place where they would be cared for, where they would be safe in their retirement years, and even get a new lease on life.

Much like a rodeo cowboy, a rodeo horse had a lot of years left in them once they were done competing.

The question was what you did with the rest of that life.

He'd known once. But that had been lost along the road. And somewhere in there he'd taken a turn and started feeling like he not only understood his old man, he was also damn close to being him.

But he could get this started. He could make it happen without being the one running it day to day. And in a few seasons, maybe he'd settle here.

"I have a few years left in me." He echoed his own thoughts, a little bit uncomfortable at the parallel he was drawing, even if Jamie wasn't aware of it.

"You think so?" She straightened and faced him head-on, her brows lifting, creating a slight crease in that smooth skin of hers. Smooth skin that reminded him she was just in her early—maybe mid—twenties, compared to his midthirties.

"It's not like I have one foot in the crypt," he commented.

"You're about Wyatt's age," she said, tilting her head to the side. "He retired a couple of years ago."

"I'm *younger* than him." For God's sake, the woman was acting like he was elderly.

"Not by much," she said, giving him a critical eye.

"Well, maybe I'm just in better shape."

"Well, it's probably also the difference between bulls and horses," she mused.

"I like horses," he said. "That's the real reason saddle bronc is my event."

He didn't really like to talk about that, because feelings were his least favorite subject, down very low on the list somewhere after poisonous snakes and getting kicked in the balls.

"Well, maybe we can find common ground with that." She dusted her hands off, leaving faint handprints on her jeans. "He's ready to go," she said. "If you want to I can get Lola out."

"No," he said. "I think you can call it a day if you want."

"Really? It doesn't feel like I did anything."

"It was your first day." He looked around at the stalls that were still empty, conscious of the fact that by the end of the month they were going to have a full house. "This is kind of the calm before the storm, so to speak. Then we're going to be busy, rotating horses through as best we can."

"Well, all right."

"I'll take those notes, though. If you can bring them tomorrow. Your take on all the horses, and then you can go ahead and keep that up-to-date as we get more."

"I can do that."

"You know, that's another reason that I might offer to lift something heavy for you, Jamie. I can hire anybody to blockade. You're the only one that knows horses like this. And you're the one that I want for that specifically. So you don't need to get all testy with me, girl."

She looked slightly uncomfortable at that compliment.

"Okay, I guess I can accept that."

He smiled. "I don't recall giving you a choice."

She started to walk toward the barn door, and he moved in front of her, holding it open. She paused and blinked, her expression one of almost comical discomfort.

Her lips twitched. "Are you doing that for me because I'm a lady, too?"

"No," he said slowly. "I'm doing it because I'm a gentleman."

She didn't seem to know what on earth to say to that,

and her dark brows knit together, her lips pursed for a moment, before she clearly decided that standing at the door making an issue was more trouble than simply walking through it. She breezed past him, kicking up dust as she went, and Gabe took a moment to enjoy watching her retreat.

That woman was all prickles. And even so, her ass looked mighty fine in a pair of Wranglers. He tended to prefer his cowgirls covered in rhinestones, but there was something more than a little bit compelling about this one covered in dirt.

And if you hired her on and screwed her, no one would be that surprised. Because no one would expect any different from Hank Dalton's son.

Hell, no one would expect different from you. Your reputation stands on its own.

Yeah, he'd earned it. Even if not everyone knew the half of it. He'd made some dumb-ass mistakes in his life, and when he'd gone into the rodeo, even though it was on a path marked with Hank's exact footsteps, Gabe had thought his own clear-eyed view of who he was would make it different.

But years on he'd woken up one morning, his last night out on tour, and realized as he lay in bed, with a stranger and a hangover as companions, that he was an apple flourishing right beneath the shade of a tree he had hoped to roll far away from.

At this point he had a feeling the roots were too damned deep to do any different. He'd started to wonder if the vision he'd had of becoming Hank was the wrong one, after all. If he'd just been born him.

Hank's bringing him back now, asking for his help

on the ranch like it might be some atonement or home-coming for both of them, felt too little too late.

Hank had known exactly what Gabe had wanted when he was a teenager. He'd been so invested in the horses on the ranch. He'd wanted to train horses then. Maybe breed them for the rodeo. He'd wanted to run the ranch and work it with his hands.

And Hank had put an end to it then.

He'd wanted Gabe to go to college. To make a better life for himself when Gabe hadn't been able to imagine a better life than one spent outdoors.

But the ranch was Hank's, and what happened on the ranch was Hank's choice.

Hank couldn't stop Gabe from going into the rodeo, though. That was out of his control. A big middle finger from Gabe.

And after all that his dad wanted him back here on the ranch, where Gabe had wanted to be back in another life, a life he wasn't sure fit him anymore.

Even so, he was having a hell of a time keeping his eyes off Jamie Dodge's ass.

He really needed to keep his eyes off her ass.

It wasn't so much about what was said about him. He already knew full well what he was. But he didn't want to have that particular fight with Wyatt Dodge. Or any fight.

He didn't have a death wish.

Jamie looked over her shoulder, and even though he didn't take her for the kind of woman intuitive enough to know when a man was looking at her ass, there was something sharp in her dark eyes.

And he had to laugh to himself.

He was thinking about Wyatt killing him if he

screwed around with the man's sister. But the honest truth was, if he messed with Jamie Dodge, she would be first in line to him.

Truth be told, he respected the hell out of that.

And he was going to keep his distance.

CHAPTER THREE

"How was work, Jamie?" Wyatt asked the question so casually that Jamie had to conclude that Lindy, his wife, had threatened him within an inch of his life, and commanded that he not be a dick.

Everyone who'd worked on the ranch that afternoon—which today had been Bennett, Kaylee, their son Dallas, Grant, McKenna, Wyatt and Lindy—was seated in the private family dining area that they built out behind the main house.

A Very Lindy Touch that had been added to the property recently. A large paved area, covered by a hard-top gazebo with lights woven through the rafters, picnic tables and benches, a barbecue. A place for the family to gather no matter their configuration.

Jamie had to admit, it was a lot nicer than the dirty firepit area they'd sometimes occupied, or than trying to eat at odd hours out behind the mess hall that was reserved for guests.

"It was good," she said, shifting uncomfortably as she thought back to her interactions with Gabe that day. In hindsight, she didn't really know what she had been thinking, coming at him like she did, yelling at him about the way he was interacting with Gus, but his response hadn't been what she expected. And she kind of would've rather he behaved in a way that was expected.

She had figured he would be the kind of guy to come right back at her if she went at him. That he would yell and puff out his chest, and be all...

Well, the way that Wyatt acted with her.

She got on Wyatt's nerves, and he went straight for hers. It was what she knew. And she had figured that Gabe and her big brother were cut out of the same cloth.

They were, after all, oldest brothers and rodeo cowboys, so it seemed fair enough to make that assumption.

And in her experience there were only a couple of different kinds of men.

There were the responsible ones—the space under which she filed her brother Grant. Less so her brother Bennett, who had certainly turned into a responsible adult but had made a few mistakes in his youth, one of which resulted in a secret son he had only found out about a couple of years earlier. Still, in his thirties, he fit the bill of Responsible One.

Then there were the laconic whores. Like their family friend Luke Hollister, who was quick with a smile and had a whole lot of easy charm that Jamie thought was about as transparent as a glass-bottom boat.

Gabe was a charmer, and women liked him, but that was the same with her brother Wyatt, and he wasn't what Jamie would call easy. No, far from it. He was hardheaded, stubborn as a mule and infused with too much pride and testosterone to be able to cope with anything.

Her sister-in-law had done a pretty good job of taming Wyatt—the gazebo being a fine exhibit of this—

but she had a feeling if she said that, he would have to go out and punch a tree or hit a wasp nest with a stick, or something else that would prove his unending masculinity.

Yeah, she had imagined that Gabe Dalton was more like that.

But when she'd come at him, he had done something totally unexpected. He had smiled. And he had... He had acted completely undaunted by her. And then he had gone and done all that chivalry bullshit.

Lifting the saddle, opening the door. Talking about how he was a gentleman. For the first time in living memory, she'd felt at a loss. And she hadn't had a clue what to do.

Her face had gotten all hot, and her skin had felt kind of prickly. It had been the strangest thing, and she didn't like it. And was not looking forward to a repeat performance. Ever.

"Fine," she said.

"Just *fine*?"

She snapped her fingers. As if she'd just remembered something. "Oh, yeah. Except for the part where he slapped me on the ass every time I walked past him."

Making that joke was a lot like firing a black powder revolver and getting her hand in line with the cylinder gap. She might have gotten a shot off, but she'd been left with a burn of her own. She ignored the heat in her cheeks and tried to focus on her steak.

She didn't know why she was letting that man get in her head. He hadn't even done anything. That was the thing. All Wyatt's warning her away from Gabe, and he had been completely appropriate. She would have been ready for two things. To have to fend off lecherous advances—not that that had ever happened before—or for him to grouse and get all sour at her for yelling at him.

He had done neither.

"Don't even mess around like that," Wyatt said. "I don't want to go to prison unless I absolutely need to."

She rolled her eyes. "It was fine. It was a workday. How are things at the ranch without me? Did everything fall apart?"

"*Wyatt* is falling apart," Grant commented, a smile curving his lips.

It was a good thing to see her brother smile again, and the source of that smile was sitting right next to him. His fiancée, McKenna, had absolutely transformed him. Had brought him out of the grief that he'd been mired in since the death of his first wife and given him a life that Jamie hadn't imagined he could ever have.

"I'm *not* falling apart," Wyatt said.

"You're a little testy."

"Because I care," Wyatt said, leaning back on the bench he was seated on and taking a bite of steak with him.

"Because the sins of his past are flashing before his eyes," Lindy said. "And all he knows is what he would have done if he hired a beautiful woman to come and work for him."

Jamie recoiled. "I do not think that's what's happening here."

First of all, she wasn't a beautiful woman, though she wasn't going to get into that. Mostly because she didn't want her sisters-in-law fluttering and petting

her and trying to reassure her that of course she was
pretty, because everyone was beautiful in their own
way, or whatever. Her saying that had nothing to do
with insecurity, and she knew that they wouldn't understand that.

She was fine with who she was. She had accomplished everything she wanted to in life, and she was
on the path to accomplishing more. She didn't want or
need to be soft and pretty, didn't make it an aim to be.

She supposed she could wax various parts of her
body, or put makeup on, or change the way that she
dressed, but she didn't want to.

She was happy the way she was.

And it suddenly occurred to her why all of this was
so off-putting.

She had never been treated much differently than
her brothers. Not at all growing up, and suddenly,
Wyatt was treating her like she was different. Suddenly, the fact that she was female seemed to be at the
forefront of his mind, and consequently of *everyone's*.

She'd felt agitated by it for the past couple of months,
ever since Gabe had approached her about potentially
taking this job on. It had been under her skin the whole
time, but she'd simply attributed it to the fact that she
didn't like to be told what to do, and Wyatt was trying
to set a record for how many times he could tell her
exactly what he wanted her to do in a single breath.

But it wasn't just that.

"Let me ask you this," Jamie said, kicking her legs
out in front of her and leaning back in her chair. "Why
are you suddenly so fixated on the fact that all he's
going to see is a woman when he looks at me? No one
ever has. Everybody knows that I'm Quinn Dodge's

only daughter. That I'm basically another son. That I am good with horses, and good with my hands. I am another Dodge boy, as far as the entire town is concerned."

The expression on Wyatt's face shifted. "What?"

"Come on," she said, slapping her knee. "No one in the history of *ever* has treated me like a delicate flower, and all of a sudden you're obsessed with the fact that Gabe only sees me as a pair of pants he can get into."

"You don't really think that, do you, Jamie?" It was Bennett who spoke, his expression grave. "That everybody thinks of you as another Dodge brother?"

"Hell," she said. "I know they do."

"I don't think that's true," Wyatt said.

Her brothers exchanged looks that held no small amount of pity, and Jamie felt like she was missing out on something, and she hated that feeling.

She had felt it occasionally when she was younger, and the men would share a joke that went over her head. She had always done her best to act like she hadn't even noticed, even though she did.

"Jamie, I don't think anyone ever saw you that way in town," Grant said gently. "People felt sad because you lived with all of us. Because there was no woman around to…"

Jamie was only vaguely conscious of making the decision to stand, shoving her chair backward with her boot heel. "Don't you fucking tell me that people felt sorry for me."

"They did, honey," Kaylee said softly. "Not to be mean, but because you lost your mother…"

"I don't even remember her." Jamie cut her off. "They should've felt sorrier for *them*." She gestured toward her brothers. "I'm just fine. I had everything in life that I ever needed. And I... Now you're telling me that everyone sees me as a charity case?"

"Not a charity case," Wyatt said, his tone maddeningly placating.

"When did I ever act like I needed someone to feel sorry for me?"

She hated this conversation; it was awful. It made her feel stupid, and small, and she couldn't even bear it. How dare anyone feel sorry for her. She had Quinn Dodge, the best father anyone could ever ask for. He was gruff, and he was a little rough around the edges, sure.

He had taught her how to be tough. He had taught her how to work with horses, how to work with the land. He loved the land and he'd taught her to love it, too.

And he'd had a couple of girlfriends when Jamie was younger, before he married his current wife, but Jamie had never had any use for them.

She hadn't needed them.

She had her father, and she had her brothers. As annoying as her brothers were, they were everything she needed.

And what Jamie hated most of all was that hearing people thought...those things about her...forced her to imagine a small, lonely little girl, sitting by herself, aching for the soft, loving arms of a mother. And that wasn't Jamie. She never wasted a moment crying over what she lost. Crying over what she didn't deserve to feel the loss of.

"Well, you all should know me better than that," she said, her tone fierce. "He hired me because I am the best horsewoman around. I can sure as hell put my boot in his crotch if the occasion calls for it. I don't need you to act like a posturing ape about it, Wyatt Dodge. I don't need anyone to sit around talking about me, worrying about me. I know what I'm about. Just because you don't…that's not my problem."

She turned on her heel and walked away, shaking with barely repressed energy.

How dare they?

All of them.

Her brothers and the whole town.

She felt angry and tangled up.

It was dark now, the sky a handful of diamond dust surrounded by black velvet. The moon was yellow and swollen, appropriate, since Jamie felt round with indignation. Absolutely full of it.

She wasn't even fully conscious of where she was going or what she was doing, but as soon as she opened up the barn, and the familiar smell of damp shavings, dust and hay hit her nose, she felt home in a way that she hadn't sitting around that table with her family.

She loved her family.

But all of that just underlined the fact that what she was doing was the right thing. That not telling them she was doing it was the right thing, too.

She needed to get out of Dodge, finally enough.

Off the ranch, out of this town.

To figure out who the hell she was untangled from it all, and she could've done it years ago. But…

They'd needed *her.*

That was the other thing that stuck out in her mind as she pictured the scene she had just left.

She wandered over to the stall where her horse Lilac

was, reached out and smiled as the horse pressed her soft, pink nose to Jamie's knuckles.

They didn't need her anymore.

Her father had married Freda, and moved away to New Mexico.

Wyatt had Lindy. Bennett had Kaylee, and his son Dallas.

Grant had McKenna.

And Jamie...

Jamie had herself.

Fundamentally, that was what she'd always had.

It was what she could count on. That her own shoulders were broad enough to carry whatever got sat down on them. That her own legs were solid enough to support her.

And it would be true when she left.

When she went out on the road with the rodeo, and figured out if she could get her own kind of glory barrel racing, away from Wyatt's influence and reputation.

One thing she knew for certain was that she didn't want to be poor, motherless Jamie Dodge.

And if she had to leave to figure that out... Well, then she would.

CHAPTER FOUR

"How is your new hire working out?"

Gabe looked across the table and at his brother Caleb. They were sitting smack in the middle of a very crowded Gold Valley Saloon. It was midweek, but the local crowd didn't much mind what day of the week it was.

Around here, the nine-to-fivers were rare. There were shopkeepers who worked weekends, mill workers who worked all hours, ranchers who never took a day off.

It didn't need to be a Friday night to hit the bar. The beer just needed to be cold.

"She's fine," he responded. "A little on the mean side."

Mean. Spirited. Compelling.

And the heat between them could start a damned campfire.

At least on his end.

He wouldn't be surprised if all Jamie felt for him was annoyance.

Caleb chuckled. "She's a Dodge. What did you expect?"

Yeah, he supposed Caleb had a good point. Not that the Dodges were mean so much, but they had stubborn streaks, and they were pretty notorious for it.

"Glad you could make it out," Gabe said.

Caleb stretched in his chair. "Yeah, I think we're

getting sent out to Montana in the next couple of weeks. The wildfires over there are picking up already."

"Where's Jacob?" he asked.

His brother had been noncommittal about coming out when they'd talked earlier, but he'd figured Caleb might have some success dragging his ass out.

Jacob and Caleb had always been close. They were Irish twins, both younger than Gabe and hell on two legs from the time they could walk.

His brothers had gotten into fighting wildfires after their short careers in the rodeo, and as great as he thought it was for them, it didn't hold the same appeal for Gabe.

Maybe because as good as his brothers had been at bronc riding, they hadn't risen to the top the way that he had. They hadn't had the passion for it. He had no doubt that if Jacob and Caleb put their minds to it, and decided they wanted to really compete with him, they would have.

But they didn't want to. The same way he didn't want to camp around fire lines in burning wilderness for a month at a time.

"You know…brooding or whatever."

"Damn." Gabe shook his head and took a long pull on his beer. "How long is he going to carry this?"

Caleb shrugged. "Clint was like a brother to us. And he left behind a hell of a lot more than either one of us would have. Jacob carries that. He can't let go of it."

"He takes living with guilt to another level," Gabe commented, shaking his head.

It shocked Gabe that Jacob had responded to Clint's death the way he had. Not because it wasn't a tragedy, but because Jacob had taken living life with no responsibilities to a whole other level.

Gabe knew people thought rodeo cowboys were adrenaline junkies—and they were, no doubt about it—but Jacob was something else.

He'd been a paramedic, a rodeo rider and then a firefighter. Rodeo hadn't had the life-or-death stakes Jacob seemed to look for.

But then Clint had died in a helicopter crash during one of the wildfires, and Jacob had changed. Completely.

His brother pushed his baseball cap back on his head, a black one emblazoned with a logo for the Logan County Fire Department.

"Clint was another Dalton brother, as far as I'm concerned," Caleb said, his voice rough. "He meant the world to me, and to Jacob. Having to tell Ellie what had happened…" Caleb shook his head. "That was the damned worst thing I've ever had to do. I miss Clint. I hate that he's gone. But I think Jacob feels responsible. Responsible for getting Clint hooked on the firefighting. And because he was supposed to be at that fire…"

"Sure, and if he'd been in the helicopter *he* would be dead. And we wouldn't even have a kid of his to remember him by. I miss Clint, too." Clint Bell had spent every day after school at their place, running around in front of their house, in the fields. Everywhere. He ate at their table almost every night, and slept over whenever he could.

He truly had been a Dalton in many ways. The lack of him now was something Gabe felt every time they sat down to a holiday dinner. Every time they had a barbecue.

He'd never lost a person he'd loved before, and the

gaping hole it left in everything sometimes took Gabe's breath away.

When Clint had married Ellie, she'd become part of their family, too, and she still was.

Jacob and Caleb were the closest brothers, and they'd always shared everything. They seemed to have split their pain over Clint's loss in half. Jacob bearing some kind of burden of responsibility that had turned him into a gruff lone wolf. And Caleb doing everything he could to care for Ellie and her daughter.

"Yeah, I know." Caleb took another drink. "But you have to let him do it his way."

"Well, I guess that's fair enough. He isn't going to just up and do it our way because we tell him to. He's just like you that way."

"How do you know that?" he asked.

Gabe looked at his younger brother and managed to, somehow, not laugh his ass off at him. They all looked alike. Hair differing shades of brown, eyes the same Dalton blue.

"Because *I* wouldn't. None of us would. We are all just a shade too stubborn for that bullshit."

"Tough to say if we get it from Hank or Tammy," Caleb said, shaking his head.

"I expect we split the difference between the two. Tough news for anyone who has to deal with us."

"I suppose McKenna might be a little more even-tempered than the rest of us as a result. Since she's only got Hank's DNA."

"Who the hell knows what her mother was like," Gabe said, reluctant to think about his half sister right now. Which was stupid. He had felt a connection to her pretty instantly when she had shown up at the ranch the first day Jamie had stopped by to get a tour of the place. McKenna had come along and dropped her bombshell, and Gabe had done his very best as the oldest brother to pave the way for his younger half sister. To try to set up a meeting with Hank and feel out the situation. And then Hank had been a dick and told her that he didn't want his wife to know about her. Had given her money and sent her on her way.

Gabe and his father had not had a fight like that since Gabe was in high school. If they'd ever had one quite that vicious at all.

Gabe had been ready to blow the whole thing up himself, and ultimately, it was that threat that had seen Hank calling a family meeting and confessing his sins to their mother.

That had been a fight. One that Tammy had never let McKenna see evidence of.

Tammy was everything you could expect a good redneck woman to be. She was tough, and she was fierce, but she was also fair.

When she got angry, she directed it at the person who deserved it, and no one else. But boy, when she was pissed the woman breathed fire.

Gabe could remember one time his mother had been the inspiration for a country song, out of their driveway with a baseball bat, sending their dad's new truck to an early grave.

But after the explosion of anger, sadness hadn't been far behind. And Gabe had been the only one she'd ever shown that vulnerability to.

She'd needed a protector. And Hank had never been that.

In some ways, Gabe felt that as long as he protected

his mother he was finding some way around that stamp of sameness Hank Dalton had left in his blood.

Tammy hadn't lit anything on fire when she found out about McKenna, so there was that. But he supposed that you could only be so angry about a mistake that was obviously twenty-seven years in the past.

It wasn't as if Hank's philandering was news at that point, anyway.

He truly did believe that ever since his mom had made her ultimatum, Hank had been as faithful as promised. Mostly because Tammy was a bloodhound, especially after years of being betrayed, and at this point, she would have not only found out, she would have made sure the entire town of Gold Valley knew about it, too. So there was no way anything had happened that Gabe and his brothers didn't know about.

Still, with all of that, McKenna, her appearance and her existence, shouldn't be a negative to Gabe in any way, and mostly it wasn't.

But she did remind him. Of what his father was, what he'd always been.

"Yeah, she seems pretty scrappy to me," Gabe said, taking a swig of his beer.

"What is your plan with the ranch?" Caleb asked, the sudden subject change throwing Gabe for a loop.

"To take on the rodeo horses. Get them rehomed. There's no reason not to. And anyway, it's something that… Dad used to talk about it. All the horses that ended up without a place. I figured… It's as good a time as any to get that up and running. But I want someone else to manage it. I've still got some years left in me on the circuit."

"And you still like it?"

That was an interesting question.

He was *good* at it.

That was kind of the bottom line. He had known what he didn't want. He hadn't wanted to do what Hank had asked him to do. He hadn't wanted to knuckle down and study more and go to school. Hadn't wanted to make better of himself in the way that his father thought he should.

He wanted to be a rancher. A cowboy.

And when his dad had made it very clear he wasn't going to support that, Gabe had refused to let his dad manipulate him in that way. It had come together perfectly in many ways. He'd gotten a petty kind of revenge on his dad and he'd made a real living out there riding saddle bronc. Had bought himself some independence.

He was damn good at it, too. A champion.

He'd done better than most men had, and even without his father paying him to run the ranch stuff these days, he was well able to afford a venture like that.

Plus, the house that he lived in away from his father's property. His own, much smaller parcel of land.

He wasn't sure what he wanted mattered so much as what worked. And right now the rodeo worked. So he might as well chase that.

"I'm going to want the money later," he said, lifting a shoulder. "And don't lecture me about safety, or my body breaking down, or any of that shit. You jump out of helicopters into infernos."

Caleb laughed. "I'm not about to lecture you about any of that. Hell, I'd try to recruit you, if I thought you would go for it."

"Why do *you* do it?"

"Something to do," Caleb said. "Something that's not Dad's."

Gabe shook his head. "Yeah. Well. Maybe if I do it enough people will think of me instead of him when they hear our name tied to saddle bronc." He shook his head again. "I love that old bastard. But he…"

"Yeah, it's complicated," Caleb said. "He's the best and the worst all at once. I've never known anyone who could make a group of people laugh so hard. And if you need a fence fixed or a barn raised—"

"He's there. And he probably gave money to help."

"He's also a tool."

"Hell, yes."

Hank Dalton was complicated. A selfish man who seemed to act to satisfy his every appetite. Who seemed to conveniently forget he had a wife and kids when a woman flashed a smile at him.

He was also charming. Funny and irreverent. Generous with time and money. His lack of class and over-the-top sense of style—evident in every gaudy corner of the family home—a testament to the fact that you could take the man out of the trailer park but you couldn't take it out of the man.

He was gold-plated and down-to-earth all at the same time. A bastard and an angel.

"I think we are justified in deciding we want our legacy to be something a little bit different, don't you?" Caleb asked.

"I guess so."

"So your aim with Jamie is to have her be the… manager?"

"I don't know if that's what I'd call her. But she'd be in charge of the horses. She's great with the animals.

I've never seen anything quite like it." It reminded him of something he used to be. Or maybe something he could have been. But time changed people. And he didn't think he could ever be that idealistic kid he had been. There were too many years and bad decisions standing between him and that boy he'd been.

It made him wonder what the hell he was now.

"Well, best of luck to you."

"Thanks," Gabe said, shaking his head, mostly at himself.

He drained the rest of his beer and figured he had time for another one. Even if he had to have his brother drive him home, it would be worth it.

He was antsy to get out of here. That was the problem. Badly wanted to be back out on the road, where he could drink hard and ride hard. Where he could find an endless supply of anonymous women to fill his time in his bed.

There was a restlessness in him, and he didn't know what to do with it.

He often wondered if it was the same restlessness that lived inside Hank Dalton.

It made him understand. And the last thing he wanted to do was understand his old man. That was too close to sanctioning his behavior, and Gabe could never imagine doing that.

"I want another drink," he said, standing up.

"Am I your designated driver?" Caleb looked disgusted.

"If you have a problem with that… You should yell at Jacob for not coming."

A smile tipped up the corner of Caleb's mouth.

"Yeah, I suppose so. Though we could also see if we can ferret him out to get him to play designated driver."

"Now, that," Gabe said, slapping his hand on the table, "is a good idea."

There was a buzzing sound, and Caleb leaned back and pulled his phone out of his pocket. "Dammit," he said.

"What? Is there a fire you have to get out to?" Gabe asked.

"No," he said. "That would come over the radio. It's just Ellie. Amelia is sick," he said. "Ellie was just wondering if I was able to go out and get some pain reliever." He typed a response then waited a moment, shifting in his chair. "I'm just going to get her some."

"We just got here," Gabe said.

"I know," Caleb said. "What exactly do you want Ellie to do? Drag Amelia out to the store when she isn't feeling well? So that I can sit here and drink as late as I want? That would be an asshole move."

Gabe sighed. "Yeah, okay, fair enough. I'll hold that drink."

"Sorry," Caleb said. "But you know...she doesn't have him. She should."

"Don't tell me you feel responsible for it, too," Gabe said, shaking his head.

"No," Caleb said, his voice rough. "I feel responsible for her."

"All right, then. Let's get going."

They stood and Gabe settled the tab on the way out. And the whole way back to Caleb's truck, Gabe wondered.

What it must be like to have such wholehearted dedication to *something*.

Jacob had his guilt. Caleb had Ellie.

Gabe was caught between a career he'd never loved and a ranch that he still didn't control.

And that was starting to feel unacceptable.

CHAPTER FIVE

WHEN JAMIE ARRIVED at the barn the next morning, Gabe was nowhere to be seen. But there was a list of assignments left out for her. The first of which were easy enough. Take Gus and Lola and ride them around. Take Gus up on a trail ride and see how he fared.

Then there were a few ranch chores that she was a little bit less experienced with. One of which included replacing the motor on one of the automatic gates on the property. The part was next to the instructions, and she squared her shoulders.

"Just figure it out," she said out loud to only herself.

He was treating her like a ranch hand, the way that she had asked to be treated. And Wyatt and Bennett and Grant were wrong.

People *didn't* see her as a lost little girl.

Gabe wouldn't have left a motor and minimal instruction for a lost little girl. He wouldn't have even done that for a lady, she didn't figure.

So whatever had happened yesterday with him opening the door and all that… It didn't matter. It didn't matter because he was wrong.

She frowned, moving first to Lola's stall and nickering softly to get the animal's attention. The pretty gray mare lifted her head, and Jamie smiled. She was a beautiful horse. Dappled and lovely, with kind eyes and an easy disposition.

Jamie could hardly imagine the horse being used in the rodeo. She just seemed too mellow for the bursts of energy required.

Jamie didn't have a problem with the way the animals were treated in the rodeo. She knew that they were expensive and valued, if not just for their monetary worth, but because the men and women who cared for them, who rode them, spent more time with animals than they did with people. There was a deep appreciation for them, and a whole lot of pressure to keep them healthy and in top form.

That was the good thing about taking on animals like this. At their age, though they'd led athletic lives, they had also been given vitamins and vet checks, and a great many things that horses left out in fields often didn't have the benefit of.

She allowed her thoughts of Lola to push the conversations from the night before outside of her head. Allowed her jaunt around the arena to fill her senses. The breeze in her face, the dust in her nostrils.

She didn't need to keep replaying that conversation over and over.

None of her brothers had come after her. And no one had said anything to her about it this morning.

Due in large part to the fact that she had scampered out of her house early and eaten in the mess hall, making sure to avoid Wyatt and Lindy as she did.

She didn't regret it.

She lived in a small cabin on the property, the one that McKenna had lived in before she and Grant had gotten married. It made it pretty easy for her to come and go as she pleased, and if she wanted to go unseen, it wasn't that difficult.

Not that she ever had occasion to be sneaky, really.

She finished up with Lola and moved on to Gus, getting a little kick of exhilaration as she took him up away from the property and up the winding trail into the mountains. It was what she'd been craving last night, but she had decided that not going out riding in the middle of the night was probably the better part of valor.

Gus was a dream horse, in Jamie's estimation. He was so responsive and in tune with the rider, which was one reason he was bound and determined to fight someone like Gabe.

He was a horse who needed the trust of his rider, not a rider who wanted to control him overmuch. Far too soon, she was finished making her loop with Gus, and it was time to move on to the other tasks. She started with cleaning out water troughs, which was fine, if a bit boring, but she had told Gabe that she could do any of the work, and so she was going to.

The motor in the gate she saved for last.

Finally, it could be put off no longer, and she found herself standing in front of the giant metal beast, the motor out of the box and in her left hand, red toolbox at her feet. She could do this. She could figure it out. She shifted her shoulders, bunched them up by her ears and let them fall.

There was a slim slip of paper in the box that seemed to contain instructions, one side in English, and Spanish on the other.

Both completely foreign to her in this context.

She rooted around in the toolbox until she found

some that seemed to match the picture, and stared at it. She supposed that she had to start first by dismantling the motor that was in there. And to do that she had to…

She checked the instructions. "Disconnect the power," she muttered, finding a line that ran up to a box by the gate and examining it. There was a place where it seemed to connect, and she couldn't see why simply pulling it out wouldn't solve her problem.

So she yanked on the cord and hoped for the best. It came out easily, and she assumed that was that portion of the job done.

And then came the job of unscrewing a zillion fiddly screws.

By the time she had been working on it for at least fifteen minutes, she had sweat rolling down her face. And it was making her enraged. Because the motor was hung up on something, or attached somewhere where she couldn't see it, and she couldn't get the damn thing out. There was no indication on the instructions where this piece might be. And she would have thought that if it was attached, she would see the source of said attachment in the instructions for installing the new motor.

Except that she didn't.

She gritted her teeth, urging herself to keep going, not allowing herself to let out a primal scream that would alert everyone around her to just how annoyed she was.

Thankfully, she still hadn't seen Gabe around all day.

The last thing she wanted was for him to see her struggling with this. And she had the passing thought that perhaps her struggling with this had been his aim in the first place.

But she would be damned if she would be defeated. If she would let him treat her like anyone else. She was… She was going to figure this out. Blast and damn, she was going to figure it out. She growled ferociously, ignoring the fact that the muscle that ran from her neck along the top of her shoulder was starting to feel like it weighed a thousand pounds. "This is stupid," she muttered, jerking and twisting the motor, moving her head to the side and trying to see what she was missing.

"Everything okay?"

She turned around sharply, so very aware of the fact that her hair was plastered to the front of her face, that her cheeks were probably red, and that she had sweat beaded up on her forehead. And there was Gabe. Looking pristine and perfect in a white cowboy hat and a black T-shirt that seemed far tighter than was necessary.

She wasn't sure that she had ever really noticed a man's chest muscles before. But in her defense, this particular man was basically wrapped in a second skin posing as a T-shirt. It looked so solid.

He looked so solid.

Clearly, fiddling with tiny screws out in the boiling sun had fried her brain.

"I'm fine," she said, not making a move at going back to her work, because if she did, then he would only realize that she was in fact having difficulty. And she didn't want him to know that.

"Just a little… A little motor," she said, waving her hand that was clutching her screwdriver. "That's easy. No big deal."

"Yeah?"

"Yep."

"Well, I needed it done today, and I figured I would assign it to you, seeing as you are just like all my other ranch hands."

"You're right about that. The other thing is, I know how to read instructions. Pretty groundbreaking, I know, but I'm damned awesome at it."

"It looks like it."

"Yep," she said, backing up slightly.

"Aren't you going to keep going?"

"Don't you have somewhere else to be?"

"Oh, I've got nowhere else to be," he said, his lips working up into a smile. "Nowhere at all."

She swallowed hard, then turned her focus back to the task at hand. And she couldn't hide the fact that she was struggling for more than a couple of seconds. She grabbed hold of the motor again and gave it a twist, and still it refused to budge.

"Oh, yeah," he said. "There might be a trick to that."

She turned around to look at him. "Are you kidding me?"

"No. Why would I kid?"

"There's a *trick*?" she asked, aghast.

"Yeah, if I remember right."

She narrowed her eyes. "Well?"

"I thought you didn't need help," he said, lifting a shoulder.

She took a step forward, shaking her screwdriver in his face. "Gabe Dalton, I will skin you with this."

"Is it that hard to ask for help, Jamie?"

"I wouldn't need help if there wasn't a trick."

"Sometimes in life it's not all in the directions,

honey. It's not going to kill you to ask for a little bit of advice from someone who knows what he's doing."

"You set me up."

"Maybe I did." Those blue eyes locked on to hers and somehow it felt like he'd put his hands on her. "Maybe I didn't. But you're not going to find out if you don't ask."

"I would rather drown in a sea of beetles," she said, lowering her brows.

"That seems extreme."

"What is this? Some kind of Mr. Miyagi ranch hand thing? Are you *wax on wax off*-ing me?"

"No. But the thing is, I'm your boss. And if I assign you to do something, I expect you to do it. And if it's not in your wheelhouse, I expect you to let me know. And then I expect you to ask for help. If you can't handle that, we have a problem."

"Fine," she said, blowing out a breath. "Show me your trick."

"The thing is," he said, leaning in, "when we installed it, the housing ended up getting bent, and we folded part of it over and put an extra screw through...

"Want a hand with the screwdriver?" he asked. He was so close now, his scent filling her nose, his big body right next to hers. She could feel...something like a vibration in the scant air between them and it made her skin feel itchy. "I can show you."

"Why don't you tell me?" she said, refusing to hand the screwdriver to him.

"If you insist." He wrapped his hand, rough and calloused, around hers and guided it back behind the motor.

Her body jerked forward, and her heart lurched right along with it.

He let go of her, but she was still trying to catch her breath even as the screwdriver butted up against what felt like the head of the screw.

She swallowed hard. "Thanks," she said.

"No problem."

She started to unscrew it quickly, trying her very best to ignore the extreme sensations his touch had created in her body. It was ridiculous. And stupid.

Except, she couldn't remember when the last time was she'd been touched like that by a man who wasn't family.

Never. Pretty much never.

But this wasn't about him touching her hand. It was about him being a butthead, who had given her this task knowing that she wouldn't be able to finish it without this little bit of intel. She arched her shoulders back, bumping into his, not on accident, and then finished undoing the screw. After that the motor came out easily.

She scowled at him, then turned around and looked on the ground for the replacement part.

"Do you need help with that?"

"That depends," she said. "Is there a trick to that, too? Something that you booby-trapped?"

"I promise you I didn't set out to sabotage you. But I did assume that if you needed help you would ask."

Oh, he'd totally planned this and she would never believe otherwise. She gritted her teeth. "Well, I haven't seen you around all day. Where exactly have you been?"

"I slept in for a minute," he said. "And had to take care of a little bit of admin work."

"Slept in?"

"I went out last night," he said, a lopsided smile on his face.

Those words, combined with the roguish expression, made her stomach curl. No. He wasn't different or unusual or unpredictable.

He was everything she'd always thought he was.

He'd hooked up with some poor, unsuspecting woman last night who probably hadn't realized all his sweet whispers were damn dirty lies. And now he was wandering around like everything was just fine and dandy.

And in his world, it was.

"That doesn't seem responsible," she said, her tone stiff. "You know, seeing as you're the boss and all."

"I am the boss," he said. "Which is just one of the reasons that I get to do it if I feel like it."

She gritted her teeth and returned to the task at hand, bound and determined to get the rest of it done without his help.

Without him touching her again.

He was still worrisomely close, and now that she had been close enough to smell him, it seemed like it was all she could do. Smell him. He didn't stink. No. Instead, he was like cedar and dirt, a little bit of sweat, that was somehow enticing.

She had been smelling dirty, sweaty men her entire life, and why this one man's sweat should make her want to get closer instead of recoil, she didn't know.

It shouldn't be different.

He wasn't different.

She put all of her focus on installing the motor, ignoring the fact that Gabe was still standing behind her. She knew that it was taking her probably twice as long as it would take him to do. Even if she could figure it out, it still wasn't her forte. But she managed to get it in, and when she reconnected the power, she sent up a small prayer that the thing would actually work. When it actually did, her breath left her body in a rush of relief. Thank God.

"There, that went pretty well. After you asked for help," he said.

She shot him her deadliest glare, which she had on pretty decent authority was quite deadly.

"Well, if you need any motor installed in the future, obviously I'm your person."

"Eventually, there will be too much horse business for you to see to for any of that nonsense."

"I mean, here's hoping."

"Yeah, I guess so," she said.

"Do you need a drink?" he asked.

She was tempted to say no, but she was hot and thirsty and he'd certainly made his point that if she found a way to be stubborn for the sake of it, he'd make her suffer. "Some water would be good."

"There's water in the office. Just come this way." She knew that there was an office space in the barn, but as far as she could tell, it was rarely used. He opened the door for her on their way into the barn, and she didn't think to protest, and then he did it again when they stepped into the office space, and he led her toward a mini fridge that was filled with soda and bottled water.

"Oh," she said. "That's nice."

"Feel free to help yourself whenever you're out here working. Sorry. I should have shown you that on the first day."

"Well, since today is only day two, I think I'll get over it. So what was today about?" she asked. "Really."

Considering the discussion she had last night with Wyatt, Bennett and Grant, she honestly did want to know. What exactly he was doing. How he saw her. She didn't want to do anything quite so vulnerable or sad as asking him how he saw her, but she was curious about a few things.

"Honestly, I think you're great with the horses, Jamie, but I think you have an issue being told what to do. And the reality is, I'm in charge, and I'm going to need you to take orders sometimes. And I need to know that if I leave you in charge when I leave, you're going to be able to get everything done. Not just by doing it yourself, but by getting the right kind of help if necessary."

"Yeah. Okay. I can do that."

She didn't want to do it. But this was one of those weird, unwinnable discussions. If people were concerned about her—her performance at work or her feelings—they would hover more. And what she didn't want was that hovering. That feeling she needed to be looked after.

But she also didn't like asking for help.

She still hadn't made a move toward the fridge, and he suddenly leaned down, reaching past her, so that she took a whole breath of him.

All that skin and sweat and *man*, in a way she hadn't quite thought of *man* before.

Then he took a bottle of water and held it out in her direction.

She opened the bottle and took a step back, suddenly becoming conscious of just how hot she was when the cool liquid slid down her throat. "Is there anything left you want me to do today?"

"I was actually wondering how you would feel about another trail ride. I know that you took Gus out earlier, but I'd like to see how Gus and one of the rescue horses I got a while back do on the trail together. We can save it for tomorrow if you want…"

Jamie's only real option was heading back home, and since she wasn't really eager to hang out with her brothers after last night, she was ready to jump at Gabe's offer of riding, even though it would mean more time in his company.

Right now it was preferable to dealing with her family.

A little shiver settled in her stomach, rippling through her body.

Time spent with Gabe. It made her feel such weird things.

Weird and not entirely unpleasant.

Maybe she was a little interested in feeling more of that, too. It was better than feeling the same old things all the time, anyway.

"A trail ride is just fine by me."

"Great," he said. "I'll pack us up some sandwiches."

"Sounds good to me."

CHAPTER SIX

GABE FELT LIKE a fucking dolt for asking her to go on a ride, particularly after the way his body had reacted to being so close to hers when he'd helped her out with the motor.

That had been a dumb-ass move, too. He shouldn't have touched her.

His reaction to her didn't exactly make sense. She was pretty, it was true, but she was young, and she was a tomboy. He tended to be a little bit more of a magpie when it came to women. Attracted to the obvious and the shiny, rather than the simple and down-home.

Jamie was a down-home girl, that was for sure.

Gabe had never put much thought into his type of woman. He had roots that were low-class as hell, and he figured his taste went right along with that, and he didn't much care.

He liked what he liked. Big hair, a lot of makeup, rhinestone jeans.

Nothing wrong with that.

But then, in all reality, his body was probably just enjoying the kick of arousal it got out of proximity to a woman at all.

There was a thrill to it. Meeting someone he'd never been with before and wondering what might happen next. Knowing that whatever it was, it wouldn't be permanent.

Wouldn't have any lasting consequences or emotional entanglements.

It was bungee jumping. A little thrill, but you knew you wouldn't fall straight to the ground.

Relationships were jumping off a cliff. And he had no earthly interest in that.

He liked the thrill without the risk. Without the promise.

Without the chance of failure.

Hooking up was tough to do in Gold Valley, mostly because he knew a lot of the women, and was sure to see them again after an encounter, which was not his favorite thing.

That was all.

He was just being a basic bro. She was a woman, and so his body was searching out whether or not she was possible. She wasn't, and that was the end of that story.

Basic or not, he had roast beef sandwiches and Diet Cokes, and he figured that was a decent enough offering. By the time he got back out to the barn with his pack full of food, Jamie was standing outside the barn with the horses prepared.

She had redone her braid, which had been escaping in great chunks after the fight she'd had with the motor. She was wearing a black cowboy hat, with no adornment whatsoever, and holding the reins for both horses, one in each hand, her hip cocked to the side.

Usually, she looked pretty straight up and down, given the shape of everything she wore, but now that tank top she was wearing was clinging to her curves, sticky with sweat from earlier, and putting him in the mind of all the ways a woman might work up a sweat.

"You ready?" she asked.

If she could read his mind right now she'd shove the reins down his throat.

"Hell, yeah," he said, moving away from his moment of admiration. A moment was fine. Anything else was pushing it.

"I'm letting you have Gus," she said, her expression very serious. "But be aware that I'm going to give your ass a hard time if you don't handle him well this go-round."

"My ass feels duly notified," he said dryly.

She nodded once. "Good."

She dropped the reins, and Gus stood steady. Gabe approached slowly, putting his hand on the horse's neck, a strange, familiar sensation overtaking him as he did.

The truth was, riding bucking broncos was similar to this in a lot of ways. He always took that moment. That breath. When he was on the back of the animal straining underneath him, and the gate was still closed.

To try to get a sense for his rhythm. Of his mood. To really feel the connection.

A lot of riders missed that. And to his mind, it was the thing that separated out the champions. His brothers, great though they were, didn't have the patience for it. They couldn't do stillness. And while he didn't like it in abundance, he always took that moment. Where he let the crowd fade into the background, the clanging of the gates and the noise around him, the horses kicking against the fences, all that. He let it fall away.

He learned this as a boy growing up on the ranch.

It had just been a long time since he'd used it in a quieter context.

He hadn't been allowed to.

He'd known every horse on the ranch as a boy. He'd spent all his free time outside. Riding, exploring. And he'd known it was in his blood.

Waking up one morning to find that his horses were all being sold had been like losing a piece of his soul.

He knew even now that Hank didn't understand that. That his connection wasn't about liking to skip out of school or ignore his homework.

That it had been something deeper.

Something that had been damaged in a deep and real way that day. He'd spent years after waking up on a ranch with no horses.

And at that point the rodeo he'd never really wanted to be part of had looked pretty sweet by comparison. Bonus points for pissing his dad off.

For proving to him that he couldn't win.

Still, in moments like this when Gabe realized how long it had been since he'd truly connected with one of the animals, he wondered if Hank had won in a more profound way than he realized.

"You a horse whisperer?"

He looked over at Jamie, who was watching him with amusement, her arms crossed, that sassy mouth of hers quirked up to one side, a groove there deepening.

"You're not the only person who knows how to find a connection with an animal," he said.

"Then why weren't you doing it the other day?"

"I don't know," he said. Lying.

He knew why. This whole thing was uncomfortable,

this fit back into the ranch, when he wasn't really here. When his plan was to leave.

When he had so intentionally put off the desire to do this. When he had so intentionally run headlong into the thing his dad hadn't wanted him to do.

His version of revenge, he supposed.

Become a rodeo champion.

It was complicated in a family like his. His father wasn't an irredeemable villain. He might have done underhanded things, but when it came to his kids, he'd done it to try to give them what he'd thought would be a better life. He had the subtlety of a damn sledge-hammer, but his motives were often good. Hank Dalton loved his kids, and they loved him. He was charming, and he was fun. And he provided a lot of the very important pieces that made Gabe who he was.

A lot of important pieces. A lot of shitty ones.

"Well, you better find some intuition today." She swung her leg up over the horse in one fluid motion, firmly in her element again and with all her cockiness right in place.

"Is that so?"

"Yes."

"You giving out the orders now, Jamie?"

He mounted Gus, moving alongside her. And suddenly he could see that lost little girl in her eyes. The one he'd glimpsed earlier when she'd been battling with the gate.

"I'm just…just…"

"You've got a hell of an attitude, little girl. And someday it's gonna get you in trouble."

"How do you know it hasn't already?" she asked, lifting a brow.

It took him a minute to decide what she meant. If she was talking in innuendo or not. He decided ultimately that she wasn't.

"Because you'd have learned," he said.

"I'm a Dodge. We never learn the first time."

She urged her horse forward and headed down the trail, and he did the same, allowing her to lead the way. Not just so he didn't have to listen to an extensive critique on his form, which he imagined Jamie wouldn't hesitate to give.

But because he enjoyed watching her. There was something fascinating and innate about the way that she worked with different horses.

"So you're fixing to leave?" he asked.

"In a couple of years," she said.

"That long from now?"

"I'm not sure I'm in competing form for professional barrel racing, not just now. Plus, I have to go through the process of turning pro and all that."

"Sure. Familiar with it. Gotta get your card."

She laughed. "Yes, and not embarrass myself. And also have the money to get started."

"So that's why you took the job with me."

"I love working for Wyatt, but the pay is shit."

"And does he know that you're looking to get into the rodeo?"

"No," she said, whipping her head around to look at him. "You can't tell him."

"I'm not that close with your brother. I'm not going to go talking about your business."

"Good."

"I think you overestimate the connection men have."

"I don't think so. Things come up. Why wouldn't you mention it? I just need to make sure."

"Why don't you want him to know?" Gabe knew a fair amount about family expectation, but he was curious to know why, at her age, the influence of her older brother meant that much.

He'd been young when he flung himself into the rodeo headlong, and angry at his dad. Angry at the way the old man had tried to take control of his life, determined to prove that he couldn't.

He was the oldest, so he'd considered that act to be a trailblazing one. One that would hopefully make it easier for Jacob and Caleb.

Now, his ideal rebellion would have been to buy a ranch and do what he'd been wanting to do on his father's ranch there. But he'd had no money.

Still, he understood those angry impulses coming from somebody with no real power or understanding of the world. Someone fighting against a parent. He understood it less in context with her life.

"I don't want his opinion or his interference. I don't want him to make any phone calls to make it easier for me. I don't want him spending his money on…a new horse trailer or giving me a bunch of money for hotels."

"Yeah, what kind of monster would do something like that?" Gabe asked.

"You don't get it. I could have joined the rodeo years ago. I have access to all the knowledge, and I have connections. I don't want to be Wyatt Dodge's little sister. I don't want to be Quinn Dodge's daughter. I want to be Jamie Dodge. And I want to see if I can do it on my own."

He nodded slowly. "I can understand that. You

know, as Hank Dalton's son." He cleared his throat. "But as a warning, even if you do it on your own, no one's going to remember it."

"Why?"

"As the voice of experience, I can definitely give you some whys. My father did not want me joining the rodeo, Jamie."

"He didn't? But you did exactly what he did. I would just assume that you were…taking after him."

"That's what everyone thinks. Which is kind of my point." He chewed on his next words for a moment. This wasn't something he talked about. Not with anyone. "My dad wanted me to go to college."

Jamie let out a sound that was somewhere between a laugh and a hoot. "Sorry. It's not that I don't think you could… I mean…"

"Go ahead. Laugh. I did. I wanted to be a rancher. My dad didn't want me to be. He said that he didn't work as hard as he did for a son of his to end up in the same damn place. He got money so that I could have it better. So that I could choose what I wanted. And when he said that…what he meant was so I had something that he wished he could choose, but hadn't been able to. I just wanted to be a cowboy. Can't say as I particularly wanted to be in the rodeo, but it served a dual purpose. Pissed my old man off, made me money."

"So basically what you're saying is that no matter what I do, people are going to assume I got there because of Wyatt?"

"Yep," he said. "Some people. The question you have to ask yourself, Jamie, is what it means to you."

It was a damned hypocritical thing, him talking to her like this. Lecturing her. Asking her what it meant to her, when he knew what it meant to him. But then, he had spent a lot of years avoiding deep thinking. And he wasn't sure that was a bad way to do things.

He'd been happy enough, out on the circuit, and that was why part of him was eager to get back to it. Being around here… It made him think. It made him think about every time he'd wanted to run when a real man would have stood and faced life.

Made him feel even more like Hank Dalton than he did when he was out walking his boot steps in the rodeo.

The trail dipped downward, the trees seeming to close in overhead, giving a dark, cool space that felt like it was closed off from the rest of the world. And Jamie looked…well, she looked at home. Out here beneath the pines, on the back of a horse.

Those clothes she wore seemed right here. Not ill fitting at all. He'd thought of her as plain initially. A little brown wren in comparison to the kind of women he was used to. Her hair straight and always tied back, her face scrubbed clean, her clothes more serviceable than decorative.

But there was an ease to her here, on the back of that horse, out in the wilderness. Not the brash, bold woman who seemed to be spoiling for a fight half the time, or the lost girl he saw haunting her eyes other times.

It was still enough out here that it was easier to really see. Quiet enough that you could really hear. When he'd been younger this was where he'd found his peace, and also where he'd done his thinking. Where he'd been his strongest and most vulnerable.

He could see it in her now because he knew what

this place, what these mountains, did. Broke down your walls. Made you feel small.

Not small in a way that made you easy to crush. Small enough to find shelter in these trees.

"I wouldn't mind a change of scenery for me," she said finally.

"Oh, yeah?" he asked, thinking it funny she'd said that since he'd just realized how well she fit into the scenery.

The trail carried them upward again, moving in a zigzag pattern at the side of a mountain.

"Yeah. It's just…they don't need me now."

"Who?" he asked.

Gus decided to pick up the pace, bringing him in close to Jamie's horse, who startled and took a step backward, kicking toward Gus.

"Whoa," he said. "Whoa, whoa." He backed Gus up slowly while Jamie's horse continued to twitch and experiment with the idea of bucking.

Jamie hung in, patting the side of her horse's neck with firm movements. "Ah, ah," she said. "Shhh."

The horse crossed her feet, moving sideways back down the mountain for a couple of steps, but not startling anymore.

They stopped for a moment as Jamie's horse settled. "She's okay," she said. "But apparently, she needs Gus to keep his distance when the terrain gets a little bit uncertain."

"Apparently."

"Did he spook?" she asked, her trainer voice firmly in place.

"No, he just took a step back. No bucking. Didn't seem startled."

"Good. I think Gus is going to be ready for trail rides for just about anyone pretty quick. I think he'd be good for an inexperienced rider. Doesn't take a lot of pressure or much strength to get him to go where you want him to."

"Yeah, that was my real problem with him the other day," Gabe said, grinning as they moved forward on the trail. "Just a little bit too strong."

"Spare me," Jamie said. "All that chest pounding doesn't impress me."

"Who said that I was trying to impress you? I'm just stating a fact."

"Right," Jamie said, huffing a laugh. The trail merged with the dirt road that was cut into the side of the mountain, and brought them to a lookout point that gave them a view of the pines and mountains before them, plus the patchwork of fields down below. They could see the main street of Gold Valley, and beyond that, the dark green, rolling grapevines. He identified Grassroots Winery easily enough, but there were a handful of others he wasn't that familiar with.

The explosion of new vineyards in the area was about the biggest change to the place he'd seen.

He'd traveled a lot of places with the rodeo over the years, and he'd watched main streets shift and change, and sometimes die. He'd watched some towns undergo overwhelming expansion. Places like Bend that had transformed from a small community into one of the trendiest, most sought after places in the state.

But Gold Valley remained much what it had been when he was a boy. Oh, the businesses on the main street had changed over the years, but the shape of things had stayed pretty much the same.

"Ready for lunch?" Jamie asked.

It occurred to him then that she hadn't answered his question. About who didn't need her. He didn't know if she'd forgotten or if she was avoiding it.

She still had that soft look in her eyes. That one that hinted at vulnerabilities she'd rather chew nails than admit to.

He'd let her have her avoidance.

"Sure," he said.

He moved off his horse, then went over to where Jamie was, extending a hand.

She looked down at him, her dark brows knit together, the corners of her mouth turned down into a frown. Then she launched herself to the ground, dust kicking up around her boots. "Mighty fine of you, cowboy. But I'm more than able."

He shook his head, laughing. Jamie was truly something else.

"Will you allow me to unwrap your sandwich for you?"

She huffed a laugh. "If it's the only way I'm going to get it. Otherwise, I can unwrap my own sandwich."

"Because chivalry is not dead," he said, reaching into his backpack. "I will unwrap the sandwich for you."

She shook her head. He did exactly what he'd said, and handed the roast beef sandwich to her, along with a can of Diet Coke.

Jamie looked around and found a large rock, plopping down on the top of it and taking a big bite of the sandwich.

"You did a good job quieting the horse," he said,

unwrapping his own sandwich and taking a bite. "It was impressive."

"I thought she might get testy and try to throw me," Jamie said. "But I could tell that if I squeezed too hard with my legs she was only going to panic more. Fight against me. That's the hardest part. Doing what's counterintuitive as a person. When you want to just cling to them for dear life and really... Really, you just have to listen to them. Well, I guess the thing is you have to know when to listen to them, right? Because sometimes you have to be the boss."

"No, I know what you mean," he said.

For a brief second he felt a strange flash of something. An ache as he thought about what might have been if this had been his life. It was Jamie's life, and she was running from it. Quiet, on the trails. Working with horses.

After the strange intensity that had come with his childhood—the way his parents fought with each other, the drama that always seemed to surround them—he had wanted something different.

Something quiet.

Yeah, well, you're choosing to leave it, too.

The truth of the matter was, the idea he had now wasn't enough to sustain him. Even with as much money as he made. He would need something else. Something more.

Even as he thought it, he resisted it.

He was doing the horse rehabilitation. He cared about that. It was something.

It could be enough.

"I'm not sure you need the rodeo to tell you who you are," he said.

She looked over at him. "It's not so much about the rodeo telling me who I am. It's wanting to figure out how that might be different if I'm not surrounded by… all the same things."

"Well, apparently, you're more than able to install a motor and a gate," he pointed out.

"Yes," she said, smiling slightly. "As journeys of self-discovery go, that's a little bit of an anticlimactic one, but I suppose I'll take it."

She smiled at him, and he held her gaze for about thirty whole seconds before she quickly ducked her head down, a little bit of color mounting in her cheeks.

He turned his focus to his sandwich. And he was going to forget that happened. Not that they locked eyes like that, but that it had made her blush.

It was not the kind of thing he needed to think on.

Jamie Dodge had already given him a few too many things to think on today.

He was not going to add the way looking at him had affected her to the list.

JAMIE WAS OVERLY HOT, flustered and cranky by the time she was in her truck and headed back to Get Out of Dodge.

The trail ride with Gabe had been… Well, it had been nice. She had enjoyed spending time with him, and she enjoyed watching the way that he worked with horses. He was more relaxed out here in the mountains than he'd been that first day. And she could see his ease with them.

But then he'd lectured her about what she needed to do and didn't need to do to get to know herself. And then there had been that moment when he'd looked at her.

There had been something in those blue eyes she couldn't read.

But that hadn't even been her first thought, trying to decode that. Oh, no. Her first thought had been… *wow, his eyes are* so damn blue.

And that just felt…not like her. But no matter how unlike her it was, she couldn't seem to shake the thought, or the response.

Her little escape had turned into something sharp and edgy and she just wanted…something comfortable.

The horses weren't it. Not now. Not thanks to Gabe.

She needed her family. The familiar.

She might be annoyed with them, but they were her constant.

It was a little late, but she imagined everyone would be in the mess hall. Unless they had other plans, they usually ate there after a long workday. She figured they'd be finishing up, but she should be able to grab a plate and some company.

But by the time she got into the mess hall, all the lights were off, and it looked like everything had been cleaned up and put away.

Jamie let out a feral growl and stalked back out of the room, heading toward her brother's house. When she arrived, she tromped up the front porch, and then knocked, feeling hungry and impatient. And unaccountably wounded that something else was not the way it should have been.

It took a few moments, but Wyatt finally appeared, looking freshly showered and overly happy.

Happy.

She wasn't happy.

"Hey," he said. "What brings you by?"

"I'm starving," she said. "And everyone seems to have eaten without me."

She sounded whiny as hell but she felt…off. Tender and maybe a little bit bruised and she had no idea why.

"It's seven o'clock," Wyatt said. "We finished eating a half hour ago."

"Well, I didn't," she said. "Nobody thought to leave me anything in the kitchen?"

"I'm sorry," he said. "I would have assumed that you have eaten already, on account of the fact that it was late."

"Well," she said, "I didn't. And if you and everybody else feel so sorry for me, it seems to me that you could translate that into something useful, and feed me. Poor, motherless Jamie Dodge, who is incidentally starving to death because her asshole brother didn't save any dinner for her."

Why was she freaking out at Wyatt? She didn't know. She'd never been like this. Never been…emotional. She'd always kept her feelings on lockdown, and when they did escape they took the form of anger. Right now her voice was shaking and it was perilously close to being on the line of something other than anger.

"Hey," Wyatt said, "I thought you were covered. You didn't tell me that you needed dinner."

"Well, you're useless," Jamie said, turning on her heel and stalking down the stairs.

"Why don't you come in the house and I'll find you something to eat."

"No," she said, waving a hand. "I'm sure that I have an onion and a bottle of beer in my fridge."

"Jamie, I don't know what the hell your problem is, but if you want to be treated like an adult, maybe don't slide into acting like a child whenever it suits you. Either I need to feed you every day, or you're a strong, independent woman who can handle her own self. But you're going to have to make up your mind on that."

"It's not about being strong or independent, jackass," she said. "It's about expectation. Which is that we would eat together, since we always eat together."

"Not always," Wyatt pointed out. "Anyway, Lindy and I just brought food back to the house tonight. Bennett and Kaylee never even came by today. Grant and McKenna worked their shift and then they went back to their house. We don't live in each other's pockets these days, and we don't have to."

"No," Jamie said, "of course not." She felt deflated, and more than a little bit irritated.

"Are you still mad about last night?"

"Yes," she said. "I'm mad. Because you can't have it both ways, either. You can't treat me like I'm independent and tough, and then like a lost little girl. You can't talk about how everyone feels sorry for me and then expect me to just get my own dinner."

"Jamie, I'm confused as to how these are part of the same fight."

"You know," she said. "It doesn't matter."

"It mattered enough for you to come up here guns blazing and get in a fight."

"Well, how would you feel if you found out that… nobody actually thinks you're a great rodeo rider? And everybody just thinks you're kind of a sad, delusional sparrow that they're humoring?"

"Jamie…" His voice softened. "It's not a bad thing to have people feel some sympathy for you."

Except it *was*. And he wouldn't understand. Because it was useless damn sympathy. No one had… No one had offered her any help. No one in the town had given her anything to assuage their guilt over her status of sad half orphan. And she was questioning every inter-action she'd ever had with anyone and she didn't like it. She didn't like it at all.

More to the point, it made her feel…

Lonely.

Which was a strange reaction to the whole thing, and she knew it. But that she was doing one thing, while so many other people seemed to think some-thing else, while her brothers knew something else… it was really isolating. And she was already feeling…

Left behind. Extraneous. Useless.

She'd always been the only girl. She'd done her best to close that gap by being as tough as possible.

Now everyone was a couple. And she was the *only* in another way.

She was alone.

She looked at Wyatt, standing there with the porch light on behind him, and for the first time she was struck by how different the house looked all of a sud-den. There was a wreath hanging on the door, and there were little potted plants everywhere. New covers and cushions on the seats that sat beneath the windows.

It was so very much not the house she had grown up in. Not anymore. Wyatt and Lindy had a life. They had a home.

So did Kaylee and Bennett.

Grant and McKenna.

Luke and Olivia.

Her friend Beatrix and her fiancé, Dane.

Everybody had a life except for Jamie.

Sad Jamie, who was apparently pitiable, and not a competent, tough Dodge woman like she had always imagined.

She felt like she was standing outside her life, looking at herself, and there was a strange and horrible clarity to it that she didn't like at all.

And she didn't know what she was angrier about.

Everything that Wyatt had said to her last night, or the revelation of why it all bothered her so much.

Of the fact that she was…

Not *jealous*. She didn't want to be paired off with someone, not necessarily. But it was impossible to ignore the fact that she was the only single person left in her family. In her group of friends.

Her stomach tightened, a strange metallic taste in her mouth.

Fear.

She'd ridden a horse up a mountainside today. Had weathered the animal getting spooked, and hadn't even felt the slightest lick of nervousness.

But for some reason now she was afraid.

Realizing she didn't fit. That there was no place left for her anymore.

"Look, whatever," she said, shaking her head and trying to get a handle on the strange feelings rioting through her. "I'm going to go…make some nachos. And maybe…maybe we could sit together?"

Wyatt rubbed the back of his neck and looked toward the house. "I'm, um… I mean we're…"

Of course.

Of course he wanted to spend time with Lindy. And of course it wouldn't occur to him that Jamie was feeling low because they never talked about things like that and she never asked for him to take care of her, or baby her or anything like that.

If she said she needed him he would probably set aside how much he wanted to fool around with his wife. But she wasn't begging her brother for attention. No thanks.

"Never mind," she said.

She waved Wyatt off when he took a step toward her, and got in her truck, turning the key in the ignition.

And as she drove out toward her cabin, she felt some foundation in the deepest part of herself crack, shift. She had always felt like she knew who she was. Certain of her place in the world around her. And now she felt like she was looking inside at something she couldn't understand, her face pressed against the glass.

People saw her as sad, apparently.

Everyone around her was involved in relationships, and she'd never been in one.

She'd never even wanted to be.

But right now all of that just made her feel rootless, adrift and very not like herself. Or maybe that wasn't even the problem. Maybe the problem was it made her not want to be herself at all. And it made her feel a whole lot closer to that sad, motherless girl than she had ever wanted to be.

CHAPTER SEVEN

EARLY THE NEXT morning Gabe's phone rang.

It was Beatrix Leighton, and it didn't surprise him that it was regarding an animal emergency.

"Do you have room for another horse?"

"Sure," he said, shifting his phone from one ear to the other, looking around the stable at all the empty space. "What's the story?"

Bea filled him in on the details, which involved an injured barrel racer who'd needed money and had sold her horse to pay medical bills. The horse had ended up at a farm, which had numerous animals that had been abused and neglected for years. Thankfully, the horse hadn't been there long and was in decent shape.

"Well, this would be a good place for her," Gabe said. "And I've got one of the best trainers out there working for me."

There was a smile in Beatrix's voice. "I know. I almost called Jamie directly, but I don't know about the space at Get Out of Dodge, and since you're actually running a rescue, I thought I would just go ahead and give you a call. Since I knew that Jamie would end up riding the horse, anyway."

"Where's the horse right now?"

"Right now? Gem's in my field. But if you want to come by and get her, I'll have her ready to go."

"Will do." He hung up, wondering when he should head out, and if he should wait for Jamie. He knew she'd want to be involved in the situation, but he also figured time was of the essence here.

As if on cue, Jamie Dodge's truck pulled up to the barn.

"I have an unexpected mission for us this morning," Gabe said as soon as Jamie's boot hit the gravel.

"What's that?"

"We have a new acquisition. Beatrix Leighton just called me."

"Yeah?"

"A former rodeo horse, apparently. Not retired. But one that's been in a rough situation for the past month or so. A whole bunch of animals were just removed from the home. The horse is in better shape than the others. Beatrix is managing the rest of the animals, but she figured that we might do the best with the horse."

"Well, then, let's go," Jamie said, immediately gung ho.

This morning she was wearing that same black hat she'd been wearing yesterday, and had a long-sleeve flannel over the top of a white tank top. It completely obscured her figure, but now he had a much better idea of what it looked like after yesterday. So his mind did a good job of filling in the blanks.

She was toned and slender, strong from all the hard work she did. Her breasts were small, but they were a thing of beauty. And her ass was perfection from lifting, squatting, riding and everything else she did on the ranch.

He shook his head and opened the truck door for her. She stopped and stared at him.

"What?" he asked.

"You don't need to open the door for me," she said.

"We could save a lot of time if you didn't protest my being polite."

Her lips twitched, and she climbed up into his truck, settling into the passenger seat and buckling herself in.

He closed the door behind her and rounded to the driver's side, climbing in and starting the ignition. "Would you guide me while I hitch up the trailer?"

"Sure," she said.

A few moments later they were around the back of the barn, and he was getting into position to back up to the trailer. Jamie hopped out and waved him along, and in pretty much record time they were ready to go.

It was a quick drive through town down to Grassroots Winery, where Beatrix's animal sanctuary was. There was a private access to her portion of the property.

"I'm still surprised that Lindy was able to relinquish enough control on this place to let Bea open her sanctuary," Jamie commented as they turned down the gravel drive that would take them to the barns.

"I don't know Lindy well enough to be surprised by it, I guess. She seems nice to me. Like somebody who would be completely on board with an animal rescue."

"Well," Jamie said, "she is. But she's, you know… she's fancy."

He laughed. "Okay, yeah, she's a little fancy." The sleek blonde Wyatt had married definitely had a lot more sophistication than he did.

Jamie looked over at him, her eyes shifty, like she was about to let him in on a deep secret. "Did you come to the Christmas party she threw?"

"No," he said, "I didn't. I think I wasn't invited because the situation with McKenna was complicated at the time."

Last Christmas was right around the time his father had told McKenna that she should take a payout and leave, rather than being a part of their family. At that point McKenna had been involved with Grant Dodge, who had understandably not taken kindly to the whole situation.

"She served tiny little chickens," Jamie said, her voice rising up half a step in incredulity. "And mini pies."

"Tiny chickens?"

"Cornish game hens," Jamie clarified. "Or so I was told."

He laughed. "And that offended you?"

"I wasn't…offended. I just think that kind of thing is mystifying. If you like steak, why not have steak on Christmas, too? Why be fussy?"

"Some people get enjoyment out of a little fancy, Jamie."

She shifted in her seat, her shoulders going all indignant. "I prefer to be practical."

The way she said it. As if the idea of anything other than pure practicality was an affront in some way. Or like it scared her.

It made the strangest urge roll through him. To give her something more, something deeper than practical.

"Practical is pretty good for every day," he said. "But don't you ever just like to indulge?"

He wasn't going to think about the kind of indulging he liked to do. Not here. Not now.

"No," she said, her voice tight.

"My family likes comfort. Though it's straight trailer park fancy. But then, the Daltons have never worried about looking sophisticated a day in their lives. It's part of our charm. Or something."

The decor around the family home seemed to prove that well enough. It was tacky, and over-the-top, and it was one of the things that Gabe had always appreciated about his parents.

They were who they were.

It was also the thing that often bothered him about his parents.

Because who they were was…flawed.

Especially Hank.

And there was a whole trail of pain he'd left in his cheerful, selfish wake that Gabe had gone out of his way to not put too much thought into. Something that galled him more and more the older he got. The more he realized what it said about him.

Hank had a whole heap of consequences for his actions he'd avoided having to contend with.

And Gabe could have done something to make his father pay. But he hadn't. Because when it had come down to it, he'd wanted to keep his mother safe from them. He hadn't wanted to destroy it all.

And part of him, a part he'd hated, had understood.

Because when he'd been seventeen and he'd faced down his own unintended consequence, all he'd wanted to do was run.

He could still see his girlfriend's tearstained face when she'd told him she wasn't pregnant, after all. And he'd been entirely made of relief, and she'd been devastated. The resulting fight had put Tammy and Hank

Dalton to shame, and at the end of it Gabe had been left with a lot of hard truths about himself.

The one girl he'd ever cared about and he'd failed her. He'd gotten to know her in study hall. Had become obsessed with making out in cars and then later sex in cars, because of her.

A high school boy's dream. Love at only seventeen and nothing but the future in front of them.

He'd thought with all the feeling between them they could have made something. Something that could have lasted forever.

But oh, he'd been wrong. And he'd seen how stupid you could be for a feeling you told yourself was love.

He'd seen it explode right in front of him.

And he'd failed spectacularly.

And what the hell would have happened if she had been pregnant?

What would he have done?

He wanted to think he'd have done the right thing. But the fact of the matter was, when the going got tough in his life, he seemed to behave like Hank Dalton.

When they arrived at the barn, Beatrix was already out front with the horse ready to be loaded into the trailer. Her curly red hair was tumbled-looking, and she had a wide grin on her face. And the source of the smile stood behind her, her fiancé, Dane Parker, Lindy's younger brother.

Gabe knew Dane pretty well, from their years riding together in the rodeo, though Dane rode bulls like Wyatt Dodge. He had also been horrifically injured a little over a year ago, though he seemed on the road to recovery now both mentally and physically.

Jamie smiled when she saw Bea, and when he parked she got out of the truck and greeted her friend enthusiastically. It was definitely a different kind of reception than he ever got from Jamie.

He followed behind slowly, and gave Dane a nod, extending his hand. The other man shook it. "Long time, no see," Dane said.

"Yeah, I think the last time I saw you, you were drunk," Gabe said.

"Uh, no," Dane said. "I think the last time you saw me I was doing the walk of shame out of Bea's cabin."

"Oh, right," Gabe said.

That had sure been a moment. Dane and Bea had gotten caught fooling around by her former sister-in-law, Wyatt and Gabe all at the same time. How could he have forgotten that?

Maybe because seeing Dane Parker doing the walk of shame was less notable than seeing him sloppy drunk over a woman. Which was frankly what the evening they'd spent together drinking had been about.

Dane's feelings for Bea and attempting to not act on them.

"I forgot about the drinking thing," Dane commented.

"Of course you did. Because you got hammered."

"When did he get hammered?" Beatrix asked.

"That was quite a few months ago," Gabe said. "I think he was drinking to forget a woman."

"More accurately," Dane said, "I was drinking to keep myself from going after a woman that should have been off-limits."

"Oh," Beatrix said, looking delighted. "That was me."

"Yes," Dane said. "Yes, it was."

"Obviously, the alcohol didn't work," Gabe said. "Congratulations, by the way."

Beatrix lifted her hand and a ring sparkled on her finger, but not as brightly as her smile. "Thank you."

Dane looked...well, happier than Gabe could ever remember seeing him. Even when they'd been in the rodeo together. *Happy* wasn't the right word for him then. There had been a drive and intensity beneath all his careless charm. Like he was always trying to prove something.

Come to think of it, the same was true for a lot of the men.

Gabe knew what that was like. That need to prove something about himself. He'd been trying to prove to himself that he could make a life he hadn't been manipulated into by his father.

What Gabe couldn't imagine was...this.

This slow slide into domesticity Dane had made. Getting engaged.

But all the same, Gabe couldn't help but wonder...

If he hadn't gone into the rodeo, would he have gotten married? Would he have married Trisha, even after the pregnancy scare and the fight?

And would they have just been his parents in the end?

As it was, he hadn't done that. He'd left Trisha behind, and he knew he'd broken her heart at the time. But he'd always figured if they'd stayed together he'd have broken it worse.

Now he might sleep around, but he always used condoms. He might sleep around, but he didn't have a wife back home waiting for him. Not even a girlfriend.

Gabe had made the conscious choice to be responsible with his irresponsibility.

He'd never been destined for a position as a saint, but he could certainly aim to be considerate in his debauchery.

"We have a whole bunch of other animals to deal with," Beatrix continued, sounding as brusque as she ever did. "I really appreciate you taking the horse. I gave her a medical check, and everything seems great. I'm glad that we found these people when we did. Otherwise, things could have been really catastrophic."

"I'm glad, too," Gabe said.

They took some time loading the horse into the trailer. Jamie providing some tough encouragement and Bea cooing and apologizing for all the commotion as if the animal could speak English.

"So this is your new project for the day," Gabe said, looking over at Jamie.

"I'm definitely ready for this. She's not even old," Jamie said. "I bet she could get back in fighting shape really quick."

"You know," he said, "maybe this is the answer to some of your problems."

"What problems?"

"Weren't you just saying that you needed some time with the right horse to get on track with your barrel racing? Maybe Gem is your answer."

"Oh," she said. "Yes. But I'm not sure that… I don't know if I could afford a new horse, not with the way that I'm trying to save up."

"Obviously, I would give her to you. At least use her. I'm not planning on keeping any of these horses, and I'm not looking to turn a serious profit here."

"Really?"

He wasn't really sure why he was offering the horse to Jamie, except that...

Jamie had a passion for all of this that he couldn't seem to find in himself. And it made him want more. Want more in a way he'd avoided for a long damned time.

He...wanted to feel.

That was a shock. But seeing Jamie, that fire in her, it reminded him of what it had been like to really want something. To really care.

To live a life that went past just being lost in a haze of the roaring crowd, strong whiskey and easy touch of the newest buckle bunny who'd set her sights on him.

To want something bigger. More.

"Let's get the horse secured into a paddock, and we'll give her a few hours. Then why don't we do some evaluation."

"Sounds good to me," Jamie said.

When they got back to the barn, Jamie took responsibility for their new acquisition, and Gabe went off to see to some of his own chores. He was sitting in the office, making some phone calls regarding potential incoming horses, when the door opened.

He didn't know why, but he was half expecting it to be Jamie, so when it proved to be Hank, he was surprised. "Can I help you?" he asked his father.

"I figured I would come out and check on your changes," Hank said, stuffing his hands in his pockets and leaning against the door frame.

"I didn't think you would care much about the changes I'd made."

"Why do you think that? I'm the one who asked you to take the helm around here."

"Sure," Gabe said, "but this isn't what you wanted me to do."

"You're in your thirties now. It's the kind of work you do, whether or not I wanted you to do it back then. There's no fight to have about it."

Gabe gritted his teeth. "Sure."

He regarded his father for a long moment, and the older man leaned back and crossed his arms. It took Gabe a moment to realize he was leaned back in his chair, his arms crossed in just the same way.

He relaxed his posture and rested his hands on his desk.

"I wish you'd stick around here."

"Well, I'm probably not going to," he said, looking at the computer screen and not at his dad, very much on purpose.

"What are you waiting for? Are you waiting for a career-ending injury? The right woman?"

"No. But you're right. The rodeo is what I do. I made my choices, and I might as well see them through."

He'd done it to hurt Hank back then. To prove to him that he couldn't control his life, and to prove to himself that he could do something valuable.

His mother had wanted him in the rodeo. Hank hadn't.

The choice had seemed clear to him.

But along the way he'd lost that clarity. The reason he'd gone into the rodeo in the first place.

He'd become a rodeo star, and he'd found ways to revel in it.

"Trust me," Hank said, "you hang in there too long

and all you end up doing is being a shadow of your own glory days. It's not the most exciting way to burn out."

"I think I'll skip the lecture, thanks. I'm not sure you're the best person to go telling people when to quit."

"Do you have something to say to me?"

His father seemed put off by Gabe's hostility, and Gabe supposed that was fair enough. It wasn't like they had ever had the most contentious relationship. The protectiveness Gabe felt toward his mom had always made it thorny with his dad. But more or less, Gabe kept it civil when the two of them were together.

"I don't have anything to say."

"I saw your new hire out there working today. She's a pretty thing."

Immediately, the blood in Gabe's veins turned to ice. "That's not something you should be noticing."

"I'm sorry. You noticed her first, I take it?"

"No, Dad. Because unlike you, I don't fuck around with women that I hire. I don't fuck around with women when it isn't appropriate, and whether or not I want to doesn't come into it. I hired her because she's qualified to work with the horses. No other reason."

Hank raised his hands in a defensive gesture. Like somehow Gabe was the asshole. "I've been faithful to your mother for the past fifteen years. I wasn't stating intent."

"Oh, I'm sorry. I didn't realize that I was supposed to trust you had indeed kept your vows after so many years of not doing it."

"Is this about McKenna?" Hank asked. "I'm doing the best I can to do the right thing. I can't change the past. But it was a mistake that I made twenty-seven years ago, Gabe. And I never claimed to be a saint before then. It's not like you didn't know."

If only it were just McKenna.

If only his dad's inability to control his damn self weren't such a formative part of Gabe's life. But it was.

And of course Hank would never realize that. Because he never really seemed to understand how deep his harmless little *oopses* cut the people who loved him.

Who depended on him.

"No, I knew. You are who you are," Gabe said. "And I can't hate you for it. If I could have, I would've started a long time ago."

And I'm too damned much like you for my own peace of mind.

But he didn't say that last part. And he wasn't. He did have control. Gabe hadn't gotten married. That was the bottom line. While his dad had gotten married to his mom when he'd never seemed to want to keep any of his vows.

"Don't think I haven't noticed that it's been different over the past couple of months."

"I'm just finding my feet, trying to do what you asked me to do."

"I'm not going to be around forever," Hank said. "So whatever you think I'm doing to you, whatever you think I'm playing at…it's not that. It's just that this place is going to be yours someday."

"Not Jacob or Caleb's? Not McKenna's?"

"They'll get a piece of it. But you're the one whose heart is in it, Gabe. Don't think I don't know that."

"No," Gabe said. "My heart was in it about twenty years ago, but you made sure that I learned some hard lessons about that."

"So you don't want to? You want me to sell?"

Anger clutched at Gabe's chest. "No, I don't."

Whatever he didn't know, he knew that. This conversation was like physical therapy for his soul and he wasn't sure he liked it. He'd shut down that part of him that loved this place. Now his dad was exposing it, digging it up again. Offering it to him like he wasn't the one who'd killed his dream in the first place.

Maybe in Hank's world this was an apology.

But in Gabe's it wasn't enough.

"I'll keep the ranch going," Gabe said. "And you stay the hell away from Jamie Dodge."

In the end, he wasn't sure if he'd said that last part to his father, or to himself.

CHAPTER EIGHT

JAMIE WAS ANTSY to work with Gem.

Gem.

It was about the perfect name, as far as Jamie was concerned. Since this horse definitely had value to her. An unexpected gift in the middle of everything she was striving for.

In the end, she decided to skip lunch and see how Gem was faring.

The horse seemed content in the paddock, well-fed and happy. And when Jamie got her out and started to put a bridle and saddle on her, she acted like it was routine.

She paid close attention to whether or not the horse was jumpy, or nervous, and she seemed to be neither.

She let her out into the arena, and walked her in a circle, letting her familiarize herself with the area. Then she led her around the barrels that were set up, letting her get familiar with the pattern. Jamie wasn't going to try to all-out race her immediately, but she figured she could jog the horse's memory.

Theoretically, this was what she used to do, so there was no reason that it would bother her now. It wasn't at the hands of her former rider that she had experienced any kind of maltreatment.

After she was confident in the horse's state of mind,

Jamie decided to mount. The horse took a couple of steps, like she was acclimating to something she hadn't experienced for a while, but then steadied.

"Good girl," Jamie whispered, patting her on the neck.

She began to walk her in a circle in the arena, then gradually increase the pace.

And the barrels were tempting. So very tempting.

She maneuvered her around one first, then another, going slowly. A grin broke out on her face. The horse's movements were sure and smooth, and Jamie was feeling positive.

The second time through, they increased the pace.

She could feel the horse's energy, pent up and ready to go. She knew this. They both knew this.

She tapped the horse twice with her heels, moving her into a gallop. They went around the arena into circles, before Jamie moved her into the barrels, going quickly around each one.

Out of the corner of her eye she caught movement down in the dirt, a digger squirrel that was skittering through the dirt, the little bastard.

And the horse responded.

Gem rose up on her hind legs. Jamie squeezed tight, almost managing to keep hold, but then she lifted her back legs and bucked up hard. The sudden, sharp burst of energy surprised Jamie and unseated her.

She fell inelegantly to the side, scrabbling for purchase and not getting any. Then she fell down hard onto the top of a barrel, her hip bone connecting hard with the edge of the metal drum.

She cursed, and found herself facedown in the dirt.

She rolled away from the horse, doing her best not to

take a hoof to any part of her body on top of anything else. Her hip ached, and slowly she became aware that her shoulder blade did, too.

"What the hell?"

She turned and looked up, seeing Gabe barreling toward her, his expression like a thunderstorm. He knelt down beside her, reaching his hand out and dragging his fingertips down her jaw on either side, and she couldn't tell anymore if she was dizzy from the fall or if it had something to do with his firm, sure touch. His hands were rough.

And for the life of her she couldn't figure out why she'd notice that, or why it made something resonate deep inside her.

"Are you okay?" His voice went softer, gruff still, but there was no anger in it now. His blue eyes were blazing, and she felt an answering heat ignite in her stomach. His thumb was rough as it skimmed over her cheek and she felt it resonating through her body.

He was looking at her. Not that he hadn't looked at her before. But not like this. Not this close. "That was a hell of a fall, honey."

Honey.

The word filtered through her veins just like that. Sticky and sweet.

Her head went funny. All light and airy and she wondered if she'd hit it when she'd fallen. But she didn't feel any pain there.

When was the last time someone had asked if she was okay like that? When had someone worried about her over a fall?

She was tough-as-nails Jamie Dodge. Her brother

didn't even realize she was lonely and needed his company for dinner.

And Gabe was… Gabe was acting like she might be fragile.

Her throat dried, her heart feeling even more bruised and tender than her hip.

"I'm okay," she said, more desperate to get away from him than she was certain that she was okay.

She tried to stand, but her hip ached, the stabbing pain making her wobble.

Gabe grabbed hold of her arm and held her suspended, up off the ground, but not quite on her feet.

"I can stand up," she said.

He ignored her. Strong arms bracing her as he brought her to her feet, and held her firmly. She winced, pain shooting up through her hip.

"I think it's just going to be a seriously nasty bruise," she said.

"You got hit really hard," he said.

He reached out and put his hand over her hip right where she had connected with the barrel. The gesture shocked her so much she stood frozen. But his expression was neutral, and his touch was clinical in nature. He pushed against her as if he was waiting for her to cry out in pain, or something.

But she didn't.

It hurt. It hurt badly and the pain rang through her bones like they were a gong that had been hit, but she wasn't going to react.

"I'm okay," she insisted.

"Good," he said, releasing his hold on her and taking a step back. "Jamie, you need to be careful."

"She seemed fine," she said, gesturing to the horse.

"Actually, she was fine. It wasn't her fault. A stupid ass—" Jamie waved her hand and made a skittering motion with her fingers "—squirrel ran out under her feet. Any horse could've freaked out like that."

"Jamie." Those blue eyes bored into hers all serious, and she couldn't breathe. "You don't even have a helmet on. You could have been seriously injured."

"I don't wear a helmet when I barrel race," she said.

"Not even with a new horse? Jamie, you have to take precautions. The dumb-ass bull riders even wear face masks nowadays. There's no point putting yourself at risk when you could take a small step toward keeping yourself safe." He still wasn't mad. His voice was shot through with concern and that only made her angry. Though maybe more than that, she was angry at herself for wanting more. More of the tenderness. More of his touch.

"Hey," she said, "it was just an accident. And it happens. You can't tell me you've never been thrown from a horse."

His jaw firmed. "I ride bucking broncos. That's kind of part of the deal."

"I ride," she said simply. "It's part of the deal there, too."

She turned away from him and limped over toward Gem.

"What are you doing?"

"I'm getting back on, jackass. That's what you do." She felt prickly and uncomfortable, and like her skin was too tight for her body. Combined with the pain, it was a damned annoying sensation.

She gritted her teeth and touched the horse's neck before putting her foot in the stirrup and launching herself up onto her back. They rode a quick easy loop, with Gabe's gaze on them the whole time, and then she dismounted before leading the horse back to the barn. She ignored the fact that Gabe was following her, still clearly irritated.

"I'll put her away," he said.

"No," she said. "I'm going to put her away. I'm going to finish my work. I'm fine."

He didn't seem to take that as his cue to leave. Instead, he leaned in the doorway, muscular arms crossed over his chest, his blue eyes like ice as they appraised her every movement. Like he was waiting for her to crumble to the ground and swoon like a maiden from an old movie from all the pain at any moment.

"It's just pain," she said. "There's a big difference between being in pain and being injured, Dalton. Don't tell me you don't know that."

He didn't say anything.

"You make a pretty good doorstop, I'll give you that," she said. "But you could also go do anything else."

"You're a potential liability," he commented. "I need to make sure you're okay."

"I told you that I am," she said, fierce.

"Next time you ride one of the new horses, one that no one has ever ridden, you make sure I'm out there."

"Oh, that sounds like a great idea. Had you been out there would you have gotten down on your hands and knees and intercepted the squirrel before it got into the arena? Because that's what you would have had to do to prevent this."

"I could have appraised the situation."

"*I* appraised the situation," she said. "If the horse hadn't been startled it wouldn't have been a situation."

She patted Gem on the rump and sent her into the stall, closing it behind her.

"It doesn't matter what you think," Gabe said. "That's the new rule."

"It's not necessary."

"It doesn't matter. I'm your boss. And I say that's the protocol now."

"You're being ridiculous and you're treating me like a child. I'm not a child, Gabe."

She moved to walk past him, and he reached out and grabbed hold of her arm. Those same rough hands connecting with her skin. "If you have a problem with the order, Jamie, you can take your things and go, and don't bother to come back tomorrow."

Just like that, she saw everything she was working toward evaporate into dust. Those blue eyes were still boring through her, right through all her shields, and she couldn't catch her breath, much less find it in her to defy him one more time.

That strange sensation that felt like a shimmer of heat over hot pavement was coursing through her. An intensified version of what she'd been feeling in his presence ever since that first day of work.

She hated it. She kind of liked it.

She had no idea what to do with it.

She just needed some distance.

She needed him to not be touching her.

"No," she said.

"No, you're not going to take the order, or no, you're not quitting?"

"I'm not quitting," she said.

She stared at him, not breaking eye contact, stared until the air seemed to vibrate between them. And he finally released his hold on her arm.

"When you ride Gem tomorrow, text me. And let me know that's what you're doing. I want to be out here."

She bit her tongue to keep from arguing, and instead she nodded.

"Go home," he said. "Put some ice on your hip."

And it hurt badly enough that she wasn't going to argue with him about that. But she collected her things without saying another word and got into the truck, starting the engine and beating a hasty retreat from the ranch.

And it wasn't until she was out on the highway that she realized she was shaking. And she didn't think it was from the fall.

CHAPTER NINE

GABE WAS MADE of pure agitation by the time the evening rolled around. He kept seeing Jamie, tumbling off the horse and hitting the barrel.

It played in his mind over and over again. And then, worse than that, he kept on reliving the moment he had knelt down in front of her and touched her face. Realized how soft her skin was.

He didn't know what in hell had possessed him to do that. To act like he was a nurse, when he was the furthest thing from it.

But all that, mixed with the conversation he'd had with his dad earlier in the day, had driven one thing home for him. He needed to get a grip on himself.

Because what he'd said to his dad was true. He didn't forget who he was or where he was. He didn't forget what his obligations were.

Those were his dad's excuses. That he was in the moment. That he had just kind of forgotten that he had a wife and children waiting for him at home. That a pretty little thing smiled at him and he just couldn't help himself.

He could well remember his dad trying to excuse himself with words like that after screaming fights with Tammy.

He remembered the time his mother had taken a bat to his father's truck out in the driveway.

Gabe had been fourteen at the time.

And Hank just smiled and laughed.

I made a mistake, he'd said. *I can't say it more than once. She's left me before, but she never stays gone. She knows how I am. I don't mean to. I don't want to hurt anyone. But you know... Think of how stupid you feel sometimes when a pretty girl looks at you. That's just how it is. Some of us are a little weaker than others.*

He had given him a conspiratorial grin like Gabe was supposed to understand. Like it was just how it was for men like them.

And then, God help him, he'd proved he was just like that.

Seventeen and on fire for Trisha and not taking time to use a condom. Her late period had ended up being nothing at all, but it could have been. And it was enough to prove he actually did understand just what his dad was talking about.

A pretty face, a pretty body. And everything else turned to dust.

He'd thought it was love. He truly had. But he'd failed at that first hurdle, and he'd seen exactly what he was made of.

Gabe hated it. He hated understanding it, and it had made him double down on the protective feelings he had for his mom. Because he was determined he wouldn't be like that.

He would protect the women in his life.

And when it came to relationships, he just wouldn't make any promises.

And he would keep his control.

There was something easy about the kinds of hookups he'd found in the rodeo. He played the part of cocky cowboy while the woman played the part of insatiable buckle bunny.

And both of them had real lives outside those choreographed encounters, but neither of them shared them.

He'd done it for so many years, being that character was easy.

But he couldn't be that here. He had to be engaged. He had to take his responsibilities seriously.

Jamie was a responsibility in a lot of ways. Wyatt wasn't a close friend, but Gabe knew that Wyatt was worried about Jamie, and Gabe had told Wyatt he could trust him. That Gabe didn't have any designs on her. He'd hired Jamie and assured her of the same.

And that meant going out and dealing with himself.

He toyed with the idea of calling his brothers. But he figured he was better off dealing with it on his own. He took a quick shower, put on a pair of jeans and a T-shirt. Put three condoms in his wallet, because he was feeling optimistic.

And as he got in his truck to head out toward the Gold Valley Saloon, he did his very best not to think of the last woman he touched.

Because he couldn't think of her that way. He couldn't think of her while he thought about condoms, or anything else.

And he wouldn't.

What he wanted to do was go into his dad's office and throw the condoms down on his desk and say: *This is what real men do. We think about our actions and the consequences of them.*

But he wasn't going to do that, because it was a little bit too dramatic for him. And also, as much as Hank Dalton might be comfortable elbowing and winking and implying things about his sex life, Gabe was not.

So instead, he started his truck and tried to convince himself that this particular brand of responsibility would be a pleasure and not a chore.

In the whole ten-minute drive to town, he couldn't seem to convince himself.

He just had to hope that when the right woman showed up, it wouldn't take much convincing at all.

CHAPTER TEN

"LET'S GO OUT," Beatrix said.

"Oh, yes," McKenna agreed. "We should go out."

Beatrix had come over that night to talk about the horse, and had been round-eyed and overly concerned about the fall that Jamie had had. McKenna had stopped by Jamie's cabin, too, and for a moment Jamie felt content. Like maybe life wasn't so different and difficult, after all.

"Out?" Jamie wrinkled her nose.

"Yes," McKenna said. "I've gotten domesticated. And I'm getting married in five months. I have to get out and enjoy my freedom while I can."

"Me, too," Beatrix said.

And just like that, Jamie's stomach curled in on itself. "Well, I have endless freedom stretching before me. So I feel no particular pressing need to go out to a bar. But if you really want to…"

"I do," Beatrix said, nodding.

"Fine," Jamie said. She picked up her flannel shirt she'd been wearing earlier and shrugged it on. There was a little bit of dust on it, but otherwise, it was fine.

"Is that what you're wearing?" McKenna asked, her tone absent of judgment, but the fact that she asked the question at all impressed upon Jamie the judgment all the same.

"Yes," she said. "You have a problem with it?"

"Well," McKenna said. "It's just that you mentioned your endless freedom. And perhaps, you could be *less* free if you…"

"I am not dressing up to try to get a man's attention," Jamie snapped. "If I wanted a man, I could go out and get one."

Men were simple, after all. She'd seen it over and over again. It played out all the time in her family.

She flashed back to Gabe, the way he'd looked at her when she was down on the ground, and she pushed that image to the side.

"Okaaayyy." The skeptical word came from Bea, and Jamie bristled.

"What?"

"I'm just… You don't… Okay. I love you, Jamie, but you don't actually know anything about men."

Jamie frowned. *"What?"*

"We've listened to you talk like this for months. You tried to give us both advice on our relationships," McKenna said.

"I was helpful," Jamie insisted.

"You meant well," Bea offered.

Jamie huffed and McKenna went on. "We let you talk. No one wanted to hurt your feelings. We still don't. But now we need to have a real conversation here because you're about to bite off more than you can chew."

"I literally grew up in a house with all men," Jamie protested. "I know more about men than any one woman could want to. I helped you out with Dane."

Bea and McKenna exchanged a glance that turned Jamie's blood to lava. "No offense, Jamie," Bea said slowly. "But no. You didn't. And no, you don't. You know about men as brothers. You don't know anything about… You don't know anything about sex."

Jamie's whole face felt like it had been lit on fire. And she wanted to push against this. Against this feeling of being lost and of not knowing. "I know about sex," she said.

McKenna frowned. Deeply. "Oh…Jamie."

"Don't! Don't *Oh, Jamie* me like I'm a sad kitten. I am completely fine. I'm not envious of your relationships or your…your…carnal knowledge of men's bodies, okay?"

"I didn't say you were," McKenna said, holding her hands up in a defensive pose.

"No, but you're acting like I don't know anything and—"

"Jamie, it's not like anyone is calling you out. But it wouldn't kill you to acknowledge that maybe your friends who are in relationships might be more up on men and sex than you are."

Bea, being Bea, was beginning to look concerned. Probably that she might hurt Jamie's feelings. But Jamie wasn't hurt. She was annoyed.

Jamie held up her hands. "Tab A. Slot B." She made a rude gesture. "I'm aware of how it works. And if I want to know more, I'll go on a fact-finding mission all on my own. Now, do you have any more comments on me, my clothing or all the things I don't know, or can we go and get a drink?"

Her friends stared at her.

"You look good," Beatrix said finally. "Let's just go out."

"Good," Jamie said.

They piled into Jamie's truck and headed down to the Gold Valley Saloon.

It was packed out tonight. Always busy any day of the week, it got a little bit of an extra influx on the weekends, especially during this time of year, when there were tourists hanging around on the edges of town to tour wineries, go on white-water rafting trips and use the hiking trails that wound around in the mountains beyond the town.

And once all that outdoor activity was done, it was definitely drinking time.

Jamie was always somewhat bemused by the injection of people, but their favorite table in the back corner was available, so she didn't feel the need to complain.

She also still felt plain uncomfortable after the conversation at her house. They'd done their best to make conversation on the ride over but Jamie had mostly stewed.

"Drinks?" Jamie asked once they deposited all their things in the chairs.

"I'll get them," Beatrix said.

"No," Jamie said, conscious of the fact that Beatrix could be overly generous if you didn't watch her, and she would end up paying for everything before anyone had realized it. And even annoyed with her, she didn't want that.

"All right. I'll have a…a beer," Bea said.

"A beer?" Jamie questioned.

Bea shrugged. "I live with a rodeo cowboy. I've acquired a taste."

The change in her friend—tiny though it was—hit Jamie funny.

She had acquired a taste for beer because of Dane.

Bea had always been a sugary alcohol drink or soda kind of girl, more than a beer drinker. She wondered if Bea and Dane sat around in their living room drinking beer now. And then she wondered what that would be like. To have your life so wound around someone else's that it changed what you drank.

"What about you?" she asked McKenna.

"Beer," McKenna said.

That, at least, was normal for McKenna, as far as Jamie knew. It wasn't like she had known McKenna all that long before she had gotten together with Jamie's brother. But they had formed a friendship somewhat separate of her relationship with Grant, when McKenna had first come to the ranch to work.

"All right. I guess I'll be back with three beers," Jamie said, turning around and heading off toward the bar, while Beatrix and McKenna took their seats.

When she approached the bar, Laz, the bar owner, flashed her a grin, and then walked down to her end. "Hi there, Jamie," he said. "What can I get you?"

"Just three bottles of beer. Whatever's good and cheap."

"I think I can figure that out," he said. He turned away from her, headed toward the cooler.

Jamie leaned against the bar, resting her elbows against the scarred wooden countertop, then turned and looked over her shoulder.

McKenna had her hand extended, held in front of Bea, who was studying McKenna's engagement ring.

Bea smiled about something, then placed her own hand at the center of the table, pointing to something on her ring.

Jamie blinked, grappling with that sense of isolation that had walloped her suddenly the other night.

She turned back toward Lazarus, who was headed toward her, beer bottles in hand.

"On your tab?" he asked.

She tried to force a laugh. "I don't suppose I could put it on my brother's tab?"

"You could," Lazarus said. "But I don't really want to have to answer to why later."

"All right," she said, slapping the bar top. "You can put it on mine, then." Jamie nodded and transferred the bottles of beer to her own hand, turning and heading back toward the table, setting them down a little bit too firmly, breaking up the engagement ring conversation.

Neither of them said a word about rings after Jamie sat down.

"How is everything going at work?" McKenna asked.

"Good," she said as casually as she could. "Other than the fall. Probably going to have a mother of a bruise."

"What happened, anyway?" Bea asked. "Was it related to Gem?"

"It wasn't her fault," Jamie insisted. "It was a squirrel."

Bea nodded sagely as if the fact that a squirrel might be at fault for some kind of trouble seemed eminently sensible to her. Not long after, Bea launched into a story that explained her reaction, involving Evan, her pet raccoon, and a fight that he had with a digger squirrel not that long ago.

Jamie took a sip of beer and turned her focus across the bar, and suddenly, Bea's voice faded into the background.

She was about to open her mouth and say something. To complain about the weirdness of it all. Because right across the bar from her was Gabe Dalton, and what were the odds he'd be here, when she had just spent the entire day with him.

Except the words stuck in her throat, and her eyes felt glued to the scene in front of her.

He wasn't alone. He was leaning against the back wall, a jukebox shining brightly between him and the woman he was talking to.

Jamie felt like she was observing a ritual right out from another culture. Something she didn't understand. Something she never wanted to understand, really. But for some reason right now she found herself captivated by it. The woman had big blond hair, and Jamie wondered how in the world you got your hair—especially when it was straight like that—to stand out from your head with quite that much of an effect.

Hers certainly didn't do that. She took it out of her braid at the end of the day and it fell limply down past her shoulders, usually one kink about an inch before the end. It certainly didn't defy gravity and make a little frame around her face.

And then there was her dress. The kind of thing that Jamie would never be caught dead in. It looked like she'd wrapped herself in pink tinfoil, the shiny gown clinging to her curves like another skin.

And Gabe was looking at her.

Intently.

The same way that he had looked at Jamie earlier. Except… No, it wasn't the same.

Jamie tilted her head to the side, transfixed and unable to redirect her focus.

Gabe chuckled, shifting and leaning in, reaching out and running his fingertips along the other woman's jaw.

And something inside Jamie burned.

The place where he touched earlier tingled, and she fought the urge to reach up and touch her own face. The woman tossed back that shimmering blond mane and treated Gabe to a big smile.

And Jamie couldn't help but think of the way that she had reacted to him earlier. Angry and irritated and like a porcupine ready to shoot quills into him.

Are you okay, honey?

He'd called her *honey* and now he was talking to this woman.

Said woman took a step toward Gabe, and he reached out, placing his hand on her hip this time, just the way he had touched Jamie earlier. Except this wasn't clinical. And the expression on his face didn't have any anger or irritation.

And suddenly, she just felt suffocated. By this. By everything. By a crushing sense of…being lost. Being ignorant.

Of not knowing anything about sex, just like Bea and McKenna had said.

She'd never experienced this feeling in her entire life. It was so intense that she couldn't breathe.

She'd just been thinking how simple men were. How basic the interactions between men and women were. And yet right now, looking at this and comparing it to what happened earlier, it all felt anything but simple. And she didn't feel like she understood it. Not even the tiniest bit.

Jamie had always been confident in herself. Because that was what it took to stand on her own two feet.

To make sure that she fit in with her family. That she wasn't needy. That she wasn't a burden. She prided herself on being no-nonsense. On being tough. On being a pragmatist, which made certain things self-evident.

She'd been raised with brothers, with her father. She *knew* that men were motivated by sex, and that they often had it indiscriminately, that they went to great lengths to get it, even. She understood that with a kind of detached certainty.

But there was a whole language here being spoken between Gabe and this woman. And suddenly, those feminine accoutrements that Jamie had always thought unnecessary seemed like an essential part of speaking in this language. Communicating in this nonverbal way that Jamie didn't understand.

She had never once in all her life envied another woman.

She had always felt like she'd chosen to be what she was.

Like the fact she was plain, the fact that she didn't wear makeup or pay attention to clothing, was a choice she made. A skin she could shed at any moment if it ever grew too tight.

But it was too tight now, and she couldn't breathe. And she couldn't change, either.

She didn't know how. And she felt like she was drowning in that fact.

Like there was a piece of herself that was missing.

Not *makeup*. But this innate understanding. This sense of being a woman.

McKenna had been half-feral when she'd come to the ranch, and even she seemed to understand it. Bea was very light, delicate and tough all at once, petite and with bouncy curls that drew the attention of any man in the vicinity.

And then there was the…this…this *sex bomb* that was detonating across from Gabe right now.

She had always written these things off as silly, frivolous.

And now she just felt like they all knew something that she didn't. That she couldn't even hope to understand. And worst of all, she felt envious.

Envious of the way those too-blue eyes looked at the blonde. At the way his hand moved over her hip.

She felt like an ache had opened up inside her, and it had nothing to do with the bruise she had sustained earlier. Nothing at all.

But that bruise hurt. That bruise right on her hip, right where he'd touched her earlier.

Where he was touching this other woman now.

Gabe moved, his head turning toward Jamie, and his eyes clashed with hers. His dark brows lifted upward.

Jamie looked away quickly, and saw that McKenna and Beatrix were looking at her intently.

"What?" She nearly growled.

"We lost you for a second there," Bea said softly.

"I just…"

"You saw Gabe?" McKenna asked, her tone knowing. And right now the knowing was about to send her over the edge.

"Yes," she responded through gritted teeth. "I didn't realize he'd be here. Kind of a buzzkill to see your boss when you're trying to hang out and have a good time."

"Yeah," McKenna said, her expression strangely tender.

"I told you," Jamie said, feeling itchy.

"What did you tell us?" McKenna asked.

"About Gabe. About the fact that he's just like every other rodeo cowboy. *She* couldn't be more of a buckle bunny if she tried."

She was trying. And succeeding, it appeared.

"He seems to be looking at you now," Bea said, her tone such a false kind of casual that Jamie didn't even think she was trying too hard to fake it.

So Jamie didn't bother to pretend she wasn't interested in what Gabe was doing. She glanced over again, and saw that Gabe actually was looking at her.

The blonde was looking at *him*, and Jamie could see that she was a little bit irritated to have lost some of his attention.

Something uncoiled in Jamie's stomach that she didn't have a name for.

The woman grabbed hold of Gabe's face and redirected his focus back to her. And immediately following that, pressed her lips to his.

Jamie felt like someone had struck a match on her scalp and then thrown the lit flame into her hair.

The kiss only lasted a moment, and when it was over, the woman looked at Jamie. Right in the eyes. And she had a little smile on her glossed lips that said she knew she'd scored a point in a game Jamie didn't know the rules to.

And before Jamie could even think about what she was doing, she stood up.

"Jamie…" But Bea's voice faded into the background as Jamie squared her shoulders and strode across the bar.

Jamie Dodge didn't run scared. It wasn't in her. And she sure as hell didn't let women in high heels think they could intimidate her with a wink and a little bit of lip gloss.

"Hi," Jamie said, crossing her arms and standing squarely between the two of them. "How's Gem?" She directed the question at him, ignoring his companion completely.

Gabe blinked twice and looked her up and down. "Good."

"Good," Jamie said. "Just wanted to make sure. You know, since we haven't talked for a couple of hours. My hip is fine, by the way. Thanks for all the…all the attention you gave it."

"Good to know," Gabe said, tension biting off the end of every word. The woman was looking at Jamie now, and suddenly Jamie felt like she'd scored a point.

A point in a game she didn't know the rules for, but a point was a point.

She wasn't exactly sure what it was about what she'd said that had perturbed the other woman, but she wanted to chase that.

"I took her temperature," Jamie said. "Gem. Before you came down earlier. Just to let you know. I know Beatrix said she gave her a veterinary check, but I just wanted to make sure everything was good." She nodded, mostly to herself. "It is."

The other woman blinked, clearly unsure of what to make of Jamie at this point. Jamie wasn't quite sure why that comment didn't land the same as the other one.

"Jamie," Gabe said, his lips curving upward. "Can I talk to you for a second?"

"We're talking," Jamie said, planting her feet firmly on the wood floor and widening her stance.

"Not here," he said. He turned to the woman. "Crystal, can you wait just a second?" He hooked a hand around Jamie's elbow and led her toward the front door of the bar. And right outside into the cold.

"Hey," Jamie said. "What are you doing?"

"I think the question is what are *you* doing?"

"I saw you over there. I thought I would come say hi."

"That's not what you're doing. You have the need for a fight written all over your face, and I don't know what your problem is, Jamie, or why you think every encounter we have is an opportunity for you to wage war, but it's got to end."

"I didn't know there was anything wrong with coming over and saying hi to my boss," she said.

"You're not that naive," he said. "I'm not having a pleasant conversation with Crystal. I'm trying to hook up."

Why did that make her feel like he'd hauled off and punched her in the stomach? Like he'd knocked the wind out of her?

"Well, I know that," she said, admitting it to herself at the same time she did to him. "She looked at me like she had something to prove, so I figured she could prove it to my face."

"Why? Why do you feel the need to do that? Like you need to get in there and face everybody head-on and be right all the time."

His words felt sharp and strange, particularly given everything she was grappling with at the moment. Way too sharp.

"I don't need to be right all the time," she said.

"Yes," he said. "You do."

"No, I don't. And this isn't me trying to be right all the time. It's just me being right about myself."

He snorted. "You're like a live firecracker waiting to go off at any minute, and damned if I know why."

"You're just… You're wrong. I don't… I'm not challenging you. I'm not trying to make a fight. I just came over to say hi."

"Is that why you looked like you wanted to light Crystal on fire?"

Jamie sputtered. Her heart was pounding so hard it was making her dizzy. A lot like when she'd fallen off her horse earlier today.

"She started it," Jamie said. "She kissed you. *At* me."

"I see," he said. "Or maybe she just kissed me because she wanted to."

Jamie laughed. "No," she said. "That is what she was doing. Believe me."

And Jamie didn't know for the life of her why any of it mattered or why she felt invigorated to have him outside with her. To have his hand on her elbow.

He was touching her now. Not Crystal. And why that was a victory, she didn't know. She didn't know what she wanted. But she knew being near him made her feel alive in a way she hadn't known she could.

"The way I see it," Gabe said slowly, "you're competing for attention."

Jamie leaped away from him, her heart thundering. "I'm not."

"If you want the kind of attention that I'm giving to Crystal, I suppose we could work something out, but you have to be prepared for what that means."

He took a step toward her, and this time, when those

blue eyes burned into hers, she felt something different in that heat.

She didn't know if *it* was different, or if *she* was.

"I don't want that," she said, taking a step away from him.

"How else is a man supposed to interpret the way you're behaving?"

"I don't know," Jamie snapped. "Maybe you could quit trying to interpret *me* and go back to your date."

"Is that what you want? You want me to go back in there and close the deal?"

She didn't. She felt strangely and unaccountably like whatever link she had to him, whatever thing was keeping her grounded right now, would vanish if he went off with that woman.

It was something strange and mysterious that she couldn't get a handle on.

It was sex.

That was what it was.

The strange sense of isolation that she had around her family, around her friends, and even in this interaction with Gabe and that woman, came down to the fact that she didn't understand that kind of relationship. That she'd never had one before.

And the not knowing made her feel so small and lost and vulnerable and weird. And she hated it.

"Don't," she said.

She felt like she'd been cracked open, and she didn't like it. Like that admission was revealing something about herself. But it shouldn't. Gabe was being open about the fact that he wanted sex. That he wanted sex with that woman. She knew it. He wasn't hiding it. Why should she? Why should she hide the fact that she…?

Did she *want* to have sex with Gabe?

It was a strange thing to consider. Especially since she never even kissed him.

She wasn't ready to answer a definitive yes to that question. The only thing she knew was that she didn't want him to be with that other woman.

"Don't what?"

Jamie scrunched her face up. "Don't leave with her."

The silence was sickening. Horrible. Jamie didn't like being embarrassed. She supposed nobody did. But she... she just didn't have a lot of experience with it. Which maybe said more about her and her self-confidence than it did about the situations she'd been in before.

But right now her need—it really felt like a need— for Gabe to not leave with that woman, to not get naked with her or touch her or kiss her, overrode everything.

"Why not?" Gabe asked, crossing his arms.

"I..." The words teetered on the edge of her tongue, words she'd never spoken before in her life, about an emotion she didn't think she'd ever felt. At least, not one that she ever indulged in. "I'm jealous," she said.

"Jealous?"

She clamped her teeth together, doing her best to speak around them. "I don't know. Whatever the thing is when you don't want someone to touch someone else. That thing."

"Jamie," he said, his voice rough. "Do you have any idea what kind of invitation it seems like you're sending out?"

She lifted her chin, gritting her teeth, ready to stand in defiance. "I didn't know a conversation was an invitation."

Then Gabe did something she didn't expect. He

reached out and cupped her chin, his eyes intent on hers. And he moved his thumb over her lower lip. A shiver went through her body, all the way down. "Don't play games with me. Honey, this is serious."

Honey.

He'd called her *honey* again.

Like she might be sweet or something.

Like she might be special.

And…and maybe she should make it an invitation. She wasn't…innocent. Not really. She might not have practical experience with sex but she knew what it entailed.

Though the events of tonight made her question that.

She had always felt surrounded by sex in the way that she was surrounded by the rodeo itself. She might not ride bulls, but she understood the sport. She'd observed the way her brothers behaved with women they were interested in. Hell, she'd seen them waving hookups off early in the morning. She was sure they'd figured they'd gotten away with it, but Jamie had known what was happening in her house.

But suddenly it all seemed so mystifying and unknowable to her now.

She clasped her hands behind her back and twisted them together, making a knot with her fingers. "Serious how?"

"You need to know what you want. If you call me away from a woman I'm interested in, you better know what you're doing."

He was so…large and so very…male. And that had never once been something that seemed foreign to her. She'd grown up surrounded by big, masculine men. But

Gabe seemed like another species right then. Something she had no experience with, and when he got in closer to her, the proximity made her dizzy.

"You don't have a clue what you want, do you?" he pressed, those blue eyes like shards of glass, embedding themselves beneath her skin and making her feel hot all over.

"That's bullshit," she said. "I...I know what I want."

"And what is that?"

"For you to tell Crystal to go away."

He arched a brow. "So that you can take her place?"

A wave of heat rolled over her face. "I don't know about that part yet," she snapped.

"Jamie Dodge, do you *not know* something?"

"All right, maybe I don't know everything. But I know enough to know that whatever I decided to do, it'll all be fine. I know what I want, in the sense that I know that I want to go pro in the rodeo. I know that I want to get out of here. I don't want what McKenna and Bea have. I don't want to sit there and compare wedding rings and whatever. I'd like to live a little, though."

"Are you propositioning me?"

His eyes were intense and blue, and they cut straight through her armor, and there was an answer she wanted to give, but it scared her.

"I don't know," she said, making as good of friends with that word as she could.

She felt frozen and unsure and she hated it. So very, very much. But she wasn't brave enough to say anything more.

"Get back to me when you do."

And then Gabe Dalton turned and walked back into the bar, and for the first time in her memory, Jamie Dodge stood frozen, unsure of what she wanted, or how to get it.

CHAPTER ELEVEN

GABE WENT BACK into the bar and walked right up to Crystal.

He'd had every intention of proceeding with his plan when he'd left Jamie standing outside. Never mind that what he had been attempting to do had felt a whole lot like trying to force himself to eat broccoli when what he really wanted was cake.

And it was a damn thing, because honestly, very few men would look at Crystal and see broccoli. But for some reason, his entire world felt like it was standing on its head and…

He wasn't even all that pissed off about it.

Not like he should be.

Because Jamie was *interesting*. She had a passion about her, and it had touched something inside him he hadn't accessed in years.

And she'd gone and made him feel. Made him feel things about the ranch, the horses, about the life he'd left all those years before.

And then she'd done this. Walked up and broken into his routine. And it was a routine, no doubt about it. The same kind he'd performed out on the circuit. Crystal was just his type. Game for a good time and playing a part, just like he was.

Not Jamie.

Jamie had walked right up and started talking about taking a horse's temperature.

He'd had to take her outside and be real with her, and he couldn't seem to find his way back into character now.

He'd…he'd almost kissed Jamie Dodge. And now her face, her mouth, was all he could think about.

He bit back a curse as he faced Crystal. "I think we both know this isn't going to work out."

Crystal frowned, the expression more of an adorable pout. Of course it was. She was the kind of woman who could make a sulk pretty. Not a boot-stomping terror.

And yet.

"Because of that horse girl?"

"I think so," he said, knowing his tone sounded about as defeated as he felt.

She lifted a shoulder. "Everybody has their kinks, I guess," the woman said, looking him up and down.

Then she turned and walked away, clearly pissed off. He looked over at the table where Jamie had been with her friends and saw that it was still empty.

He could still see her standing outside the bar, her arms crossed over her chest, her head bent low.

And right about then something snapped inside him. Then a fire began to blaze. One that was unlike any he'd felt in far too long. It wasn't just sex. Not just attraction.

It was a spark. Interest. Intrigue.

She made him *want*.

It had been a long damn time since he'd wanted.

It had all started with her. Her and the horses. Her on the ranch.

Just her.

Jamie Dodge had brought something to life inside him, and she was the one who had to manage it now.

And he didn't think much beyond the next step he took, and he didn't let himself think beyond the next one, or the next. He threw the door open and went back outside, and Jamie looked up, her ponytail whipping around as she did.

"What?" she asked.

He looked up and down the street and saw that it was mostly empty. Then he grabbed hold of her arm and pulled her around the corner, pushing her up against the brick wall of the saloon.

"You sure like coming up to me guns blazing, Jamie Dodge. Just saying whatever it is that's on your mind. No concern for the fallout of it. Well, all things considered, I'm pretty sick of keeping myself on a leash."

He cupped her face, and in the dim light he could see that she was staring up at him, her eyes wide. And then, without letting another breath go by, he dipped his head, and his lips crushed up against Jamie Dodge's.

They were soft.

Good God, she was soft.

He didn't know what he had expected.

Prickles, maybe.

But no, her lips were the softest, sweetest thing he'd felt in a long time. It was like a flash of light had gone off and erased everything in his brain like all his thoughts had been printed on an old-school film roll.

There was nothing.

Nothing beyond the sensation of her skin beneath his fingertips, the feel of her mouth under his. She was frozen beneath his touch, and he shifted, tilting his head to the side and darting his tongue out, flicking it against the seam of her lips.

She gasped, and he took advantage of that, getting

entry into that pretty mouth so he could taste her, deep and long, and exactly how he'd been fantasizing about.

Oh, those fantasies hadn't been a fully realized scroll of images. No. It had been a feeling.

An invisible band of tension that had stretched between them in small spaces of time.

In the leap of panic in his heart when he'd seen her fall from the horse earlier today.

It had been embedded in all of those things and he hadn't realized exactly what it meant he wanted until the right moment. And then suddenly, it was like her shock transformed into something else entirely.

She arched toward him, her breasts pressing against his chest, her hands coming up to his face. She thrust her chin upward, making the kiss harder, deeper. He drove his tongue deep, sliding it against hers, and she made a small sound like a whimpering kitten. The smallest sound he'd ever heard Jamie Dodge make.

He pulled away from her, nipped her lower lip and then pressed his mouth to hers one more time before releasing his hold.

She looked dazed. He felt about how she looked.

"I thought about it," he said. "And I realized I couldn't let this one go. I let you criticize my riding, question my authority, but I wasn't about to let you get away with cock-blocking me, telling me you're jealous and then telling me you don't know if you want me. So I figured maybe I'd give you something to think about."

HE HAD KISSED HER. With his lips. His teeth. His tongue. Kissed her in a way she hadn't really understood kissing could be done. And by the time she'd fully realized *she was being kissed*, it was over. And she really didn't know what to do, or what to think.

Gabe was gone, but she hadn't seen if he'd gone back into the bar, or if he'd left entirely. And she really wasn't sure exactly what she hoped. If she wanted to push him. If she wanted to see what might happen if she chased him down. If she found him. Or if she wanted to run and hide like the sad, *ignorant* little virgin she suspected she might be, after all.

Her lips burned. Her body burned.

Kissing was *not* like she'd thought it might be.

His whiskers had been rough; his hands had probably left bruises behind where he had held her.

And frankly, she hadn't understood why a person would *want* someone else's tongue in their mouth. No matter how many times people had giggled about French kissing in the halls at school or she'd seen Bea get all dreamy over a passionate kiss from Dane…she just hadn't understood.

Not until Gabe.

And then she had felt…like if he really wanted to consume her that way, he was welcome to do it.

Her whole body felt overly sensitive, lit up. From the inside out.

She ached for more. To have Gabe put his hands on her. *All over her.*

And actually, that was an exhilarating discovery.

Kissing hadn't been at all like she'd thought.

It was better.

So much better.

Yes, it had been proved that she didn't know everything about sex, but she had to concede now that the idea of it was a hell of a lot more fun than she had imagined it could be.

She'd often thought of sex from the point of view of men.

After all, that was what her life was full of. A whole bunch of men.

And while she knew that a lot of women liked that, a lot of them seemed to not like it so much, and she had always suspected that there was some kind of...trade happening with it. Like they were agreeing to do it just because they wanted the guy around, and maybe they liked the attention. And Jamie had kind of imagined none of that would be a good enough reason for her to get naked with someone.

But she felt...

Right.

Her breasts were heavy, her nipples tingling, and she was wet between her legs.

She'd never felt this before. Ever.

She knew what it meant but she'd never experienced it. And she'd never had...had these urges before.

She had wanted to...to strip his clothes off right then and there. To do things that she had never thought she'd be into at all.

Her head buzzing with these revelations, Jamie peeled herself off the brick wall and headed toward the saloon on unsteady legs, trying to avoid the uneven patches in the sidewalk and wondering why more drunk girls in heels didn't fall down out here.

She pushed the door open and made her way back over to the table. Beatrix and McKenna turned to her with a comic attention, their glittering hands clasped on the table. If they'd had antennae, they would have been standing straight on end.

"What happened?" McKenna asked, leaning in, her eyes keen with interest.

"Nothing," Jamie said, her eyes wide.

"He dragged you out. Then he came back in, but *you* didn't come back in. Then he went out. But you came back in, and he didn't," Beatrix said, gesturing toward the door with each *out* she spoke, and back with each *in*.

"Did he not come back in?" Jamie asked, looking around.

And Crystal was still here.

Jamie wiggled in her seat, a friction of satisfaction moving through her body.

"No," McKenna said, "he didn't."

"Well," Jamie said, "there's nothing to tell."

"He kissed you," Beatrix said, her eyes wide, the word injected with shock.

Jamie's whole face felt like it had been pressed against a branding iron. "He did not," she said.

"You have whisker scratches on your cheek," Bea said accusingly.

McKenna nodded sagely. "You do."

"Really?" Jamie put her hand on her face. She forgot to be cool about it because the very idea was so... fascinating.

"Yes," McKenna said, sagely. "And I'm an expert on that particular subject."

Jamie wrinkled her nose. "I'm not sure if I hope you mean my brother, or I hope that you don't."

"Well, he's the only beard that's going to give me a rash for the rest of my life. I should think that you would wish us well."

"I do." She blinked.

"I want kiss details," McKenna said.

Jamie's whole body felt like it had been dipped in hot wax. She burned. All the way down through her skin. "I…I can't… I don't…"

"How long was it?" Bea asked.

"The kiss or…or… I didn't take his clothes off."

McKenna howled. "How long was the kiss? Was there tongue?"

"Long enough and…and yes," Jamie said, her cheeks burning. "Don't say anything. To Wyatt."

McKenna winced. "I'll tell Grant not to say anything. But I don't keep things from Grant."

Jamie pulled a face. "But I'm his sister. You're really going to tell him that I kissed some guy outside a bar?"

"Do you think it will bother him?" McKenna asked.

"I don't know. I think, of any of them, Grant would be the most reasonable." She thought of her brother, of his life and his experiences. "Yes, Grant would definitely be the closest thing that I would have to an ally. But mostly, it was a kiss. And it doesn't need to be a thing. I mean…Gabe is my boss…"

McKenna shrugged. "Grant was my boss. Things happen."

"You and Grant are not me and Gabe. Gabe and I are not…" She squinted. "Relationship people."

"Are you sure about that?" Bea asked, her tone soft and careful. She had that look in her eye like she often got when she was looking at wounded animals.

"I am sure," Jamie said. "Anyway, Beatrix." She very carefully enunciated Bea's full name. "You sat in this very bar and told me all about how fun sex with Dane was. Now you're being prudish about me?"

"How did we get from a kiss to sex?" Bea asked.

Well, they hadn't. But that was the next step on this particular path. It would have to be, really. Otherwise, it would always feel like a loose end.

"I would think you'd know all about how a kiss goes to sex," she said. "I thought I was the one who didn't know anything."

"Someone has to worry about you, Jamie," Bea said. "You think you're bulletproof, and I'd rather you didn't go testing that."

"I just want…the fun thing you were talking about. I like him. I think he's hot. Why shouldn't I do it? Anyway, he's the last man on earth I'd ever want to…end up with. I'm very realistic about cowboys."

Bea laughed hollowly. "The problem, Jamie, which I learned, is that what starts as fun can turn into other things. And that's the real problem."

Jamie took a breath. She could see she wasn't going to convince Bea unless Bea knew Jamie had a plan. "I want to go compete in the rodeo. I have some work to do before I can get myself into competition shape, but that's what I want to do. I'm not even close to wanting to settle down. I doubt I ever will. So…"

McKenna shrugged. "Well, why not? Have some fun."

Jamie gestured wildly toward McKenna. "See? Fun."

"Yes. You know, you've been telling us both for ages that you know all about rodeo cowboys. And you're a rodeo cowgirl anyway, so you don't want a relationship. You know that he doesn't. He's a good-looking guy."

Jamie couldn't say she was thrilled to be in this conversation. She didn't want her feelings for Gabe talked about like it was simple and easy. And this was way too public.

But that just made her feel contrary. Because she had been annoyed when they'd all been talking about something she hadn't had access to. And now that she had some, it felt too personal to have a conversation about it all.

And that was just one kiss.

"I kissed him. That's it. I don't know if it will be anything more." But the thought of it not being made her feel hollow and sad.

"Okay," McKenna said, shrugging. "I don't need to know if you had a fight. I need to know what spurred the kiss!"

"I might have made commentary on…that woman."

"Jamie," Bea said. "Are you jealous?"

Jamie felt magnified all of a sudden. Like she'd grown large in her seat. "I was a little. But I got better. I am better."

"Crushes are a whole thing. Especially when you're working with a good-looking guy," McKenna said. "I promise I'm not being ironic or anything. Not referring to me and Grant. I'm serious. Sometimes you have moments of insanity, but then you pull it together."

"Well, and sometimes crushes are serious," Bea said, looking even more worried now.

"You really are just talking about yourself," McKenna said.

"Thank you," Jamie said crisply. "But I can handle it. I can handle Gabe Dalton. It's not a big deal. But I would like to talk about something else now. Anything else."

"Well, Bea and I can talk about wedding plans."

Jamie treated them to an overly fake smile. "Okay, maybe not *anything* else."

Beatrix smiled happily and started plaintively discussing Dane's objections to trying to train Evan the raccoon to be a ring bearer.

And Jamie was completely fine with the long, ludicrous story, because she loved that about Beatrix.

And she gave her a chance to take a breath.

To clear her head and decide what she was going to do next.

CHAPTER TWELVE

AFTER ANOTHER HOUR Jamie drove Bea and McKenna back to their respective homes. She dropped Beatrix at Grassroots Winery, where she lived with Dane, and then headed toward Get Out of Dodge, where both Jamie and McKenna lived.

McKenna took the opportunity of the two of them being alone to put in another endorsement for Jamie to have a little fun.

Jamie stretched her shoulders back, shifting her hands on the steering wheel.

"Bea worries," McKenna said. "She's soft."

The implication, of course, being that Jamie wasn't soft. And she wasn't. She had never thought of herself as soft. Never.

"Well, if I decide to," she said, giving her future sister-in-law a long look, "I'm not going to tell you, because you'll tell my brother."

McKenna pressed her hand to her chest. "Ouch. I feel wounded."

"You've earned it. Why don't you just go get some beard burn from my brother," Jamie said, pulling up to the cabin that McKenna and Grant shared.

"A mighty fine idea, Jamie," McKenna said, getting out of the truck and stumbling a little bit, reminding Jamie that her friend was slightly tipsy.

She imagined that would translate to a good time for Grant.

It didn't even gross her out. It just made her feel oddly morose.

Jamie pulled away from their cabin after McKenna was safely inside. Then she drove slowly back to her house. She pulled in, feeling restless and antsy.

Both of her friends had obviously gone home to get busy. And Jamie...

She could. She could be with a man she wanted if she felt like it. He put that on the table. Had kissed her until she couldn't breathe.

And yeah, maybe putting first kiss and first time into one night was a little bit of a tall order, but she was twenty-five years old. She didn't think it was past time, or anything silly like that. She didn't think there was a *time*.

But there was no reason to wait, either. She was a woman who knew herself. Who knew her mind. She was attracted to Gabe Dalton.

And suddenly, she realized that a lot of the strange resistance she'd put up to him had been about that. Had been some kind of weird protection, in case he wasn't interested in her. Because it had honestly never occurred to her that he might be.

She was...well, plain-Jane Jamie Dodge.

Good with horses. Good at a whole lot of things, but not especially accomplished when it came to seducing men.

She had always imagined that men like him would go for the women like Crystal. The buckle bunnies. And yeah, maybe a little bit of her hostility had been down to that. To pretending she didn't want something she didn't think she could have.

Well, she could have it.

Could chase all those wonderful, physical feelings he'd ignited inside her when he kissed her out behind the saloon. She turned around in her own driveway, headed out down the highway.

Her heart was thundering hard, her hands feeling a little bit clammy.

She felt...

Not nervous.

No. It reminded her of when she was sitting on her horse, the barrel set up in front of her, ready to go. Reminding her of what it was like to launch into the most wonderful, exhilarating thing she knew how to do.

She'd never been to Gabe's house, but she had a vague idea of where it was.

It had been pointed out to her several times by Wyatt, Bennett and once by Beatrix, when they had been driving down the highway. But then, that was common enough in an area like theirs.

Rural directions.

You didn't give street names so much as talk about something being two miles past Gabe Dalton's place, around the corner from the big field of cows and past that big red totem pole on the left.

That meant it was essential to know where people lived. And it was proving to be handy to her now.

Even in the dark, she could find the red mailbox and the big, natural wood arch that stretched over the end of the driveway.

And the metal sign that said *Dalton*.

It was difficult to tell in the dark, but she had the

sense that his father's place—which was ornate and nearly overwrought in its detail—was completely different to Gabe's.

She was proved correct when she pulled up to the house. Two stories and made of logs, like her family home, with a large front porch, and one light on shining through the window.

She realized, obviously a bit too late, that what she was doing could be construed as a little bit creepy. But it was kind of too late to worry about that.

Because she was here.

She was here, and she had made up her mind already. She swallowed hard and got out of the truck, and had planted one boot on the bottom step when she realized she was wearing a very plain pair of underwear.

She had never given much thought to her underwear, since no one had ever seen it.

She had never worried about how frilly anything was. Or whether or not it matched her bra.

She liked sports bras, which kept everything kind of locked in and had generous elastic bands around the bottom.

She imagined a sports bra wasn't considered hot lingerie by men, either.

Oh, well. She was here. She was here, and she was committed to doing this.

Plain white cotton panties, lime-green sports bra and all.

She took a breath and charged up the steps. And then she knocked. Firm. Sure. She heard footsteps, and then saw the top of his head through the window on the entry door.

It opened, and her stomach did a free fall down to her feet when those blue eyes connected with hers.

Gabe leaned against the door, his muscular forearm propping him up. "Under most circumstances, I wouldn't have to ask a woman what she was doing at my house at this hour. But with you, I feel like I do have to ask."

"Well, since I impacted on your ability to get laid earlier, I thought I would stop by and let you know that I'm available."

There. She'd said it. About as open and honest and matter-of-fact as she could possibly be.

She was not going to play the part of blushing virgin. That just wasn't in her. It wasn't who she was.

Gabe had given her a taste of physical ecstasy up against that brick wall, and she wanted the rest of it. No need to be wobbly voiced and embarrassed about that. Especially not when she knew the guy was into her.

"Come in," Gabe said, stepping to the side and allowing her entry. "Couple of things. You have to understand that this never had anything to do with your job. You don't have to be here, Jamie. And you don't owe me a damn thing."

"I understand that," Jamie said. "In any case, if you'd tried to hold my job hostage for sex I would have told you to go fuck yourself, because you certainly wouldn't be fucking me."

A smile tugged at the corner of his lips, and she had a feeling that she had said something right. "Fair enough."

"What's the second thing?"

He frowned. "What?"

"You said you had a couple of things. That was one thing. What's the other thing?"

Something about his demeanor changed. His smile going laconic. His posture intentionally relaxed. "I'm not a relationship guy," he said. "I like to have a good time, and nothing is off-limits in the bedroom for me, baby. But outside that I don't have anything else, understand?"

She laughed. "Okay."

He looked stunned. "Did you just roll your eyes at me?"

"You made that grand announcement like I might have thought something different about you. Like maybe I was going to be disappointed? Gabe, if I wanted to get married and have babies I would hardly be aiming to start a professional career in barrel racing. And if I wanted to get married and have babies, I sure as hell wouldn't be here with you. Like I said. I know about your type. I know about rodeo cowboys."

"Jamie…this is just physical. I only have tonight, but I can make it count."

"Do you have this all written down somewhere? Like a big speech you give?"

"What?"

"This sounds rehearsed. Like you're… You sound weird."

He frowned. "I'm trying to be charming but honest."

"I already know you're not charming. And as for honest…well, you were more honest with me out by the bar. More honest with me on the trails when we were out riding. I like that Gabe, even when he pisses me off. I don't need this one."

"I…" He laughed, but it wasn't full of humor. It

sounded more surprised. "I don't remember how to be that Gabe during sex."

"What does that mean?"

"I hook up a lot, Jamie. And I like to make sure the women involved know the score."

"Okay, are they all stupid?"

"I… Maybe. I don't get to know them."

"You know me," she said, feeling annoyed and stubborn and she didn't know why. "You know me, so you don't need to play a part. I don't want you to. If you're going to act like someone different I'd just as soon find someone different."

He firmed his jaw up, a muscle there jumping. "I'd rather if you didn't."

"Good. Well. I'd rather not. Honestly, I didn't see the appeal of cowboys until you. Mostly because…to me…it's not that exciting. I mean, other women might get het up over some guy flinging himself around the back of an animal. But basically, every man I know does that."

"So you don't find me exciting?"

"Not particularly. I think you're sexy, though." Saying that made her cheeks heat a little bit, but she did her best not to let him see.

The corner of his mouth lifted upward. "You're not so bad yourself."

"I'm not a blonde in a skintight dress—that's just a fact. But I'm not afraid of dirt or sweat or sore muscles. So I suppose that might work in my favor."

She could see him debating something for a moment, and then it was like a switch flipped. That light, easy glint in his eyes went hard. Feral.

And she liked it. Liked this version of him much, much better.

"You bet your pretty ass it does," Gabe said, reaching out and wrapping his arm around her waist.

All the air was sucked from her body. It was still such a strange thing, to be close to him like this. To be held right up against him like this. He was so big and hot, so incredibly arousing.

She was already aching between her legs again. And he hadn't even kissed her.

And when he did… When he did, she felt like she'd caught fire.

They weren't in public now. Weren't on a street in Gold Valley, where anyone might be able to see them. They were in Gabe's house. Alone.

No chance of interruption.

It made her feel so…strong. And like so much of a woman. In a way that she never really had. She could be here, she could do this. Nothing and no one could stop her.

And this man… He wanted her.

She wrapped her arms around his neck and returned his kiss, parting her lips and sighing with pleasure when he slicked his tongue against hers. She really liked it when he did that.

But then he surprised her, moved his big hands down, over her butt, down her thighs and lifted her up off the ground, wrapping her legs around his waist as he kissed her and held on tight, walking them both away from the door, and up the stairs.

She pulled her lips away from his, and he pressed his mouth to her neck, down her collarbone. "What are you doing?" she asked, feeling dizzy.

"Bedroom," he said, his voice husky, the word thick with pleasure.

Bedroom.

Her heart slammed into her breastbone, excitement fizzing through her.

She was going to Gabe Dalton's bedroom.

She was completely okay with that.

He kicked open the door and carried her inside, kissing her mouth again as he sat her down at the foot of his bed.

He smiled, those blue eyes hot. Hotter than they'd been looking at that pretty blonde, and Jamie felt the most extreme sense of triumph that she'd ever felt in her life.

Better than getting a great score barrel racing.

Better than blowing up milk jugs with a .30-06.

Then he grabbed the hem of his shirt, and pulled it up over his head, exposing that incredible body to her.

She hadn't even known.

She was around men who were in great shape. Had had a fair exposure to muscles all of her life.

But this was different. This wasn't her brother, or a man who might as well have been her brother like Luke Hollister was.

This was Gabe Dalton.

Half-naked in front of her, with hard, cut abs, well-defined pecs and a sprinkling of dark hair over his skin.

Gabe Dalton, the man whose bedroom she was in, alone. The man she could do anything she wanted with.

She tilted her chin upward, grabbed the hem of her top and lifted it over her head. She was about to apologize for the lime-green sports bra, but Jamie didn't apologize for much. So she was hardly going to apologize when she was presenting herself about a quarter naked to a guy she was going to have sex with.

He didn't deserve an apology from her. No matter what her underwear looked like.

Anyway, he didn't look like he required one.

His eyes only went hotter, and he closed the distance between them. He dragged his hand along the line of her jaw, and she closed her eyes for a second, luxuriating in his touch, the way she had wanted to do when she'd fallen off the barrel.

Today. That had only been today.

It didn't seem like it. It felt like another lifetime ago. Maybe another body ago.

Because this one knew all kinds of things the one from eight hours ago hadn't.

Knew all the ways that Gabe's hands could make her feel good.

Hell, scratch that. She only knew maybe half the ways. She wasn't even close to all.

But she was ready.

He pushed his hands beneath the elastic band on her bra, and then pushed the bra up, bringing it over her head in a fluid motion, one of the little straps snagging for a second on her hair tie, sending her ponytail swinging.

Her breasts weren't anything to write home about. She could honestly say she had never given them much thought. They were small enough that they didn't get in her way. And that was about all she required out of them.

But they ached now, beneath his gaze, her nipples going impossibly tight as he looked at her, hungry, and his eyes filled with masculine appreciation.

So maybe it was all right that they were small.

Gabe seemed okay with it, anyway.

He closed the distance between them again, but this time, when he drew her up against his body, they were skin to skin, her bare nipples to his bare chest. The hair on his chest was so rough, and the stimulation against her nipples felt…amazing.

She felt dazed, drunk on the scent of him. On the feel of his body.

She lifted her hand and pressed her fingertips against one pec, dragging her hand down low, skimming it over his ab muscles.

The fact that men's and women's bodies were different was something she had known like anything else.

In that distant, inexperienced sense that she had confused with knowing.

But it was like now she understood the purpose of it. Of the way his strength could make her feel.

His size.

The way those big, confident hands moved up her back, and around to cup her breast, the way his thumb skimmed over her nipple.

She gasped, her head falling back, a pulse starting to pound between her legs.

He growled, his lips crashing into hers, his kiss savage.

And Jamie submitted to it. But it didn't make her feel weak. It made her feel strong. That she was created—at least it felt like it—to withstand the force of this man's desire.

It was no small thing. He was beautiful.

So very beautiful.

Her hands were trapped against his chest, his heart

raging beneath her palm, and he lifted her up off the ground with ease, one arm wrapped around her waist, and deposited her back on the bed, their denim-clad legs tangling together. And she could feel the hard ridge of his arousal against her stomach.

She'd made him hard.

She'd made a man hard.

Not just *any* man—Gabe Dalton. Who'd had his pick of soft, pretty women likely since he'd reached sexual maturity.

It made Jamie feel like an Amazonian goddess.

He kissed her neck, her collarbone, and then he moved his mouth to her breast, his tongue sliding over one tightened bud. She cried out, lifting her hips up from the mattress, bringing her into more firm contact with his arousal.

He used that wicked mouth on her in ways that she hadn't known a man could.

He moved his hands down to the snap on her jeans and flipped it open, moving his big, calloused hand down beneath that fabric, beneath the fabric of those cotton panties she'd been bemoaning earlier, and pushed his finger through her slick folds.

She couldn't hold back the hoarse cry of pleasure as his fingers lit a fire trail across her body. Pleasure so hot and reckless, it wasn't like anything she'd ever known.

He chuckled, and her eyes flew open, watching his face as he teased her beneath her fully clothed lower half. He spread his fingers wide, pressing down on either side of that sensitized bundle of nerves down there, teasing and tormenting her, moving his fingertips to the entrance of her body, and toying with her there. Not giving her what she wanted.

She shifted, pushing her body against his hand, trying to force him to increase the pressure, trying to force him inside. She ached. Felt hollow. And she couldn't even say for certain she understood why she instinctively knew what she needed.

"Impatient," he said against her lips. "Somehow I should've known that you were impatient, Jamie."

"What does that mean?" she panted.

He chuckled. "It just means I could tell that…from everything about you, sweetheart." He removed his hand, grabbing the edges of her jeans and her underwear, and tugging them down her legs, leaving her completely naked beneath him. He settled back between her legs, the denim rough against her thighs, against other parts.

"That isn't fair," she said.

"What isn't?"

"I'm naked," she said. "And you're not."

It surprised her that she was so completely fine with it, too. She wasn't embarrassed to be naked. How could she be? Gabe appreciated it so much.

"I can fix that," he said, rising up on his knees, his hands going to his own belt.

Okay, right in that moment she felt a little bit self-conscious. Because she was spread out in front of him, and he was looking down right at the most intimate part of her.

But as had been the case with everything else, he seemed to like what he was looking at.

He pushed his own jeans down his lean hips, and Jamie's throat dried.

Okay. She'd seen a whole lot of male bodies in her life.

Men wandering around her house half-naked, at all hours, for all reasons. But she had never seen an aroused, naked man before.

And this wasn't just a generic, aroused, naked man. This one was interested in her.

There were no barriers between them.

Well, there. *There* were some virginal nerves that she had been hoping to avoid.

She took a breath. There was nothing to be concerned about. People did this all the time. Women pushed babies out of there.

Of course, historically, they made that seem like it didn't feel too good, so she had some concerns about how it was supposed to be pleasurable, but it was *possible*. She knew that.

She could handle discomfort. As long as she wasn't an abject failure.

But she didn't have to worry about it, because Gabe didn't seem to be done. He leaned forward, bracing his palms on either side of her body, pressing a kiss between her breasts, down her stomach.

He paused then, turning her to the side, brushing his fingertips over that big, angry bruise that bled over her skin. "Damn, baby, that looks like it hurts."

"It's…it's fine," she said, her voice shaking.

The way his fingers moved over her body now wasn't clinical or medical at all. There was fire in his touch.

He lowered his head and licked her hip. Her bruise.

She jumped. "I can kiss it better," he said, his voice rough as he pressed his lips to the edge of the bruise, then went gently around the perimeter. It was so soft. Such a tease.

She gripped the bedspread, trying to tamp down the restlessness in her body. She had no idea what to do with this. With this torture.

This beautiful torture.

And when he was through with her hip, he went down farther.

"Gabe…"

Theoretical knowledge of sex had not prepared her for this. For what he intended to do. This moment.

This wasn't Tab A into Slot B. *This* was extracurricular.

But Gabe was intent, and far be it from her to interrupt the expert.

And oh…he was an expert.

He kissed the inside of her thigh, then moved to her center, his tongue unerring as it slipped right over her sweet spot.

She reached down, gripped his hair and held on as he teased her. As he tormented her.

She felt like in the past few hours she had learned a very key thing. Men had magic tongues.

She had thought tongues were for talking, for helping you chew, for sticking out at your annoying brothers.

Apparently, there were a whole lot more things you could do with the tongue.

And Gabe was very good at all of them.

She shifted, and then he pressed a finger against the entrance of her body. She winced as he pushed it inside her. The invasion was unfamiliar, but not unpleasant. She began to relax, and by the time he added a second finger, she was arching toward him, basically begging for more.

He pumped his fingers in and out while he continued to tease her with his tongue, and then he closed his lips over her and sucked, pleasure breaking over her like a wave.

One she hadn't seen coming.

She cried out, clenching her legs, digging her knees into the side of his head, pulling his hair, as her orgasm rocked her.

When she caught her breath, when she came back to earth, Gabe was looking up at her, those blue eyes filled with smug, masculine triumph.

And Jamie felt...

Well, she felt profoundly naked.

But she didn't have a moment to ponder that, because Gabe was kissing his way back up her body and reaching over into his nightstand, grabbing hold of a condom and tearing it open.

She watched, unable to tear her gaze away as he pressed the latex against his length and rolled it down over himself with great efficiency.

Speaking of all the experience that he had, that she absolutely did not.

But then he was kissing her again, and she had a hard time thinking when he kissed her. His hands were all over her body, holding her hips, as the blunt head of him pressed against her. As he slid into her slowly.

Filled her.

She gritted her teeth, waiting for sharp pain, because she'd heard that there was pain.

There wasn't really. It just felt weird. A little bit tight and unlike anything she'd felt before.

But then he flexed his hips, and that brought him up against that wonderful place again, and pleasure sparked through her like glitter. And with him deep inside her like that, it went further. Felt more all-encompassing.

This wasn't Tab A into Slot B, either.

Not in the way she'd imagined it.

It was elemental, but it wasn't simple. It was physical, but that wasn't all.

It didn't just affect her body.

And all the knowledge of rodeo cowboys in all the world couldn't make it something that touched her body and not her heart.

He withdrew, and then pushed back in, not breaking the kiss as he did. As he established a rhythm that brought her closer and closer to another release.

But then, then, he seemed to lose his own control, his mouth growing ravenous, kissing her mouth, her neck, down farther, capturing a breast again as he bucked against her with no finesse at all.

And that made her lose her mind. She rolled her hips against his, pushing back, enthralled by this thing they were creating between them. Man and woman.

A deep, unending pleasure that couldn't have come from anything else.

Something she couldn't have found alone.

Maybe not even with another man.

Something that she and Gabe uniquely made together, with their particular combination of need.

His advance to her retreat.

His hardness to her softness.

She never appreciated her own softness before. It

had seemed like a failure in many ways. Because she wanted to be hard, because life had asked it of her.

But not now. Right now she gloried in it. Because it had given her the gift of Gabe.

He lowered his head, his forehead pressed against hers as he growled, thrusting into her one last time, his big body shaking, shivering, driving her over the edge to another release, her orgasm blooming inside her and spreading out through her body, pleasure radiating from her center on out, down to her fingertips.

And when she looked up again, she saw his eyes. And then he kissed her. Slow and tender. Still buried deep inside her.

And Jamie Dodge did something she hadn't done in longer than she could remember.

She burst into tears.

CHAPTER THIRTEEN

GABE WASN'T SURE what he was supposed to do now.

Jamie wasn't an easy lay. And she wasn't someone he could go on autopilot with. He'd been different with her. Different than he could ever remember being. She ignited something in him. She called him on his crap. She'd asked for the real him.

Now she was crying, so he had to wonder if it was because he'd done something wrong. But Jamie wasn't talking. She was just crying.

So he just held on to her, because he figured, if a woman burst into tears in your arms, the only thing to do was to keep on holding her.

He'd never had a woman cry after sex with him before. And if he was going to take a guess on which woman might be the most likely to do it, his guess wouldn't have been Jamie. No. It would not have been.

He said nothing. Instead, he held her while she shook and cried, completely silently, tears tracking down her cheeks in large, wet streaks. The intensity of her silence, the way she bit her lip, made him seriously question which one of them was more horrified.

He had a feeling it was her.

So he held her, stroking her hair back from her face, moving the strands that had fallen from her ponytail during the act.

"Are you okay?" he murmured finally.

She nodded. Still not making a sound.

"Do you *always*…cry?"

Sex was a release, after all. It was entirely reasonable to think that some women just cried afterward. Maybe even some men did.

Not *him*. But he could understand it.

The sex had been so good between the two of them, he could understand weeping with gratitude over it. But he'd barely had a minute to enjoy it, given that she had burst into tears, and now he was terrified.

Throw him on the back of an angry, bucking horse and he was right at home. Give him a soft, naked woman, weeping after an orgasm, and he had no clue what to do.

Yeah, he was pretty damn terrified.

She shook her head. Great. So it was just *him* that made her cry. That made him feel like a real winner.

And somewhere in that tangle of feelings, his stomach hollowed out. Because now he wondered if she had really wanted to do this. If somehow, he had been too hasty. If he'd been selfish.

His dad had said that about himself more than once. That he turned off his conscience sometimes when a beautiful woman threw a look in his direction. That he was so focused on getting what was good, he didn't think about what was right.

After Trisha, Gabe had intentionally made sure that there was no one in his life he was beholden to. He'd never been in a relationship since. And that meant he was free to take up what was on offer without thinking about it too deeply. He never went to bed with women who weren't excited to go to bed with him. And he'd never betrayed a woman back home.

He hadn't had emotions tangled around him after sex since high school.

Since Trisha and all that rush of hormones he'd thought was love.

And it certainly hadn't felt this complicated to be with someone since that day he'd found out she might be pregnant.

Why Jamie's tears made him feel quite that off balance, he didn't know.

"Do you want to—" he winced "—talk about it…?"

"No!" The word was broken, desperate.

He shook his head and rolled out of bed, heading to the bathroom and disposing of the condom before coming back into the room.

"Do you want me to get you anything?" he asked.

She shook her head resolutely. Stubborn as ever, even with a fat tear gleaming on her cheek.

And Gabe decided he was going to ignore her.

He hunted around and looked for his boxers, heading out into the kitchen and fishing around for a mug. He heated some milk up on the stovetop. Then took a package of wheat bread out of the cupboard and untwisted the top, taking out a piece and putting it in the toaster. When the milk warmed, he poured it into a mug and added a hot chocolate packet.

Right as he finished stirring, the toast popped up. Gabe slathered it with a generous amount of butter that had come straight from Laughing Irish ranch in Copper Ridge, right next door.

It was the kind of thing his mom had always made him when he didn't feel well, and for some reason, he thought crying after sex might fall under the header of *not feeling well*.

He walked back into the room and saw Jamie, out of bed, pulling her sports bra over her head, her white cotton panties already in place.

She froze.

Her face was red and blotchy, her eyes watery, miserable.

"Get back in bed," he said, gesturing toward the mattress.

"I should go," she said firmly.

"You are not leaving while you're crying. Get in bed, have some hot chocolate and toast." He set both items down on the nightstand and made a more insistent gesture.

"You can't…force-feed me snacks."

"I can. And I will."

He didn't suppose pointing authoritatively at the bed was forcing her to have snacks at all, but he decided not to comment either way.

"Take those panties off," he added.

She frowned, and did no such thing, getting back under the covers and pulling them up midwaist, tucking them resolutely around her hips.

"Are we going to have a talk or what?"

Jamie bent her knees beneath the covers, the blanket tenting over her lap. She picked up the toast and bit into it fiercely, her expression sullen.

"So you're going to be difficult today?" he asked.

"I'm difficult every day," she said grumpily.

"Jamie, I asked you if you were sure. You're not acting like a woman who was sure at all. And I need to know… You wanted this. You came to me."

"Yes," she said, her voice sounding scratchy. "It's not like I knew I was going to cry. I would rather put tacks on my saddle for a barrel racing run than cry in front of anyone. I don't cry."

"Well, no offense, but you could've fooled me. You look like you cry pretty good."

"I don't know what my problem is," she said, wiping at her nose.

She set her toast down and brushed crumbs from her hands, then from her lap. There was a crumb on her cheek, but he decided not to say anything.

She picked up the hot chocolate mug, curling her fingers around it and tapping them against the ceramic. Then she took a long, slow sip.

"My mom used to make me this when I had a cold," he said. "No real science to it or anything. My mom doesn't cook. So…canned chicken noodle soup, packaged hot chocolate and toast was like luxury. It always made me feel better."

Jamie looked up at him, the expression in her eyes confused. She blinked slowly. "Nobody brought me anything when I was sick."

She looked back at the hot chocolate and took another slow sip.

"What?"

"Oh, my dad was always really busy. He worked the ranch every day. My brothers were usually in school. I used to go hunt around and get myself saltines and bring them back to bed. I didn't get sick much. It was not fun."

"Being sick isn't fun," he pointed out.

Except, he knew what she meant.

Having a cold was never fun, but he had been one to eke a sniffle into a whole day lying in his room, because he knew it meant his mom would be back and forth with goodies and cool, caring hands. That he would feel safe and nurtured, and have Popsicles and TV shows and all kinds of attention, which, growing up in a house with three rowdy boys, was incentive enough.

In general, Tammy Dalton was of the opinion that her boys ought to be self-sufficient. But when they were sick, she softened right up. It was all Campbell's and Otter Pops.

She had been there for him when he'd needed it. And he'd always felt he needed to be there for her, too. It was the way of things. His mom had protected him, taken care of him when he'd been small and vulnerable.

And now that he had the broader shoulders, he did the same.

It was a choice he'd made. To act the way he felt a man should.

Real men protected the ones they were supposed to love.

"If you were really sick…" he began.

"It's not like my dad didn't check in on me," Jamie said, her expression stormy. "He's a good dad. And you know, he's never been the warmest or softest man, but he cares. And you can see it in how he works the ranch, works with the horses. It showed me what mattered, and he shared it with me. He made me who I am. I didn't need toast."

Gabe thought about his own dad, and how he'd treated Gabe's desire to get involved with the ranch. The way he'd taken the horses from him.

"He gave me everything I asked for," Jamie continued.

"You never asked him to take care of you," Gabe said.

"Nope," Jamie responded, setting her hot chocolate down and trading it for the toast again.

"Well, I don't know how to tell you this, Jamie, but my mom didn't need to be asked."

A sheen of tears welled up in Jamie's eyes again, and guilt lanced Gabe. He shouldn't have said any of that. He was just feeling sharp because she'd reminded him of the differences in their fathers.

Fathers were a weird thing. Hank wasn't taciturn or distant. He was gregarious and laughed loudly. He hugged his sons often.

He'd cheated on his wife for years, and often went on the road for weeks at a time.

He was willing to take pretty drastic action to get his way when he had to.

Then tell a boy holding back humiliating tears he wouldn't let himself cry, his fifteen-year-old shoulders shaking, that he'd be better off without the thing he loved most.

And he'd said it all with a smile. Because ultimately, Hank had thought he was right. And nothing could shake his certainty in himself. He'd been certain Gabe would see it his way.

But Gabe never had.

"Maybe you don't have to ask moms to do that kind of thing. But my mom was dead, Gabe. I didn't have one. I don't have one. And everyone else in my family had to make do with that. So did I. I don't waste time crying about it. I didn't even know her. You can't mourn what you never had."

Gabe shook his head. "I don't think that's true, Jamie. I think you can mourn things you never had."

"What's the point?"

"No more point, I guess, than mourning anything."

None of his tears, his curses or his anger had brought the horses back from where his dad had sold them off to.

And horses weren't even people. There wasn't reason to cry for them.

The event had changed the landscape of his life. His goals. Him.

He hadn't had work to do on the ranch anymore, but he hadn't worked any harder in school. He'd gotten involved with Trisha and discovered sex, and he'd been happy to take that as a distraction for a while.

It had given him a chance to really see what was happening in his parents' marriage.

And at that point Hank was the villain in his world. Simple as that.

Once his mom had been sure she'd seen it his way, she'd leaned on him. Confided in him.

Every dark family secret, and Gabe had set out to shoulder them.

It had all come to a head after Trisha's pregnancy scare. Gabe's whole life had felt fractured. His view of himself.

And his mom had given him one last Hank Dalton secret.

Gabe had felt like he was staring into his own future. So when his mom had suggested he get out of town and get revenge on his dad, all at the same time...

He'd taken it.

"Thanks for the toast either way," Jamie said. "And the orgasms. Those were pretty good, too."

He could see her starting to gather her brave Jamie face. Trying to get into that space where she forced everything to shed off her, like a particularly aggressive duck bound and determined to get that water to roll off her back, dammit.

Even when it was determined to try to soak in.

He wondered if Jamie had ever let someone take care of her.

"Thank you for the orgasm," he said, sitting on the edge of the bed.

"Are you going to keep me here all night?" she asked. There was nothing suggestive in her tone; he had a feeling it was related to the fact that he had ordered her back to bed only a few minutes ago.

Still, his body began to stir.

Great, you asshole. So great to get wood over a woman who just cried in your arms. Maybe give her a break.

"Whatever makes you feel better."

She let out a shuddering breath. "I think I should go home."

"Okay. You sure you're okay?"

"I…" She popped the last bite of toast into her mouth and chewed over the top of what would've been her next words, likely giving herself a chance to pick some new ones. "It was more intense than I expected it to be," she said after she swallowed. "It was like… You know, when you finish riding a bronco. After that eight seconds is up. You can't control the shaking. Doesn't mean you're scared. Doesn't mean you won't do it again. It just…"

"Physical," he said.

"Yeah," she responded. "It's a physical thing."

"Okay."

"I'll see you Monday for work, I guess," she said, lifting the hot chocolate up and draining that quickly.

Obviously, Jamie was done. A little bit of a carb injection and some sugar, and she was ready to scurry off into the night.

"Okay."

"My brothers can't know this happened."

"Yeah, funnily enough, I was not going to call them up and let them know."

"Okay."

"Jamie…" He didn't quite know what to say.

She nodded as if she knew what he'd intended to voice. Which was funny, because he didn't even know.

"See you Monday," she said.

He nodded. "See you Monday."

Jamie collected her clothes and dressed quickly, and Gabe sat up in bed until he heard the front door slam behind her, until he heard her truck engine start. Then he stood up, pushing his hands through his hair.

He wasn't totally sure what had just happened between them.

The sex had been extraordinary.

What had happened after had knocked him for a loop.

He knew what to do with a woman *physically*.

Hot chocolate and toast was the best he had *emotionally*.

Family was one thing. You were bonded by blood with family. This was different. To feel an obligation to someone just because they'd gotten naked.

Though maybe that was a sign he wasn't as broken as he'd worried he might be.

That meant it was time for him to figure some things out.

There was no excuse for a man to take himself to a place he didn't want to be, when he had the power to stop it.

CHAPTER FOURTEEN

WHEN JAMIE EMERGED the next morning for breakfast with her family in the mess hall ahead of her Saturday trail rides, she felt sore, gritty-eyed and extraordinarily tender somewhere down deep in her chest.

Apparently, there were other side effects to sex beyond the major ones that were typically advertised.

Yes, she understood pregnancy and STDs were the big ones that people went on about, but she thought somebody might have mentioned this. That you might feel like there was crushed glass embedded somewhere deep inside you that you couldn't get to. That when you breathed, it hurt a little bit.

That you might feel like you'd traded part of yourself when you took another person inside your body.

She shivered beneath the pale morning sunlight as she crunched across the gravel-laden driveway toward the rustic building where they took their breakfast.

The Dodge family ate hours before the guests typically did, getting together to establish a game plan for the day.

It had been a little while since Jamie had taken guests out on a ride, with Kaylee and Dallas taking turns with her now.

She was eager for this morning. Because it would feel a lot like her old life.

Like before changing.

Before last night.

Before the past few months.

She sucked in a deep breath, before pushing the door open, and when she walked in all the hope that she'd just been imbued with drained out of her system. Because her family was sitting there, just like they often did on such mornings. Dallas, Bennett and Kaylee. Lindy and Wyatt, even, since this was one of the mornings when Wyatt didn't cook her bacon. Grant and McKenna.

And Jamie didn't feel like she had yesterday morning. She still felt different. Still felt changed.

She hated it.

"Good morning," Jamie said.

She was greeted by a chorus of good-mornings, and a slightly slower good-morning from McKenna.

Jamie shot her friend a look, and felt like McKenna could see straight through her. Jamie looked away, choosing instead to focus on Wyatt.

"Good to have you with us this morning," he said.

"Yeah, good to be here."

"You know, since we missed dinner the other night."

She had a feeling this was as close as she was going to get to an apology from her older brother.

"Yeah," she said.

She really hadn't appreciated how horrible this might be. She had been such an idiot last night. And she had done her best not to think about it too much this morning when she woke up. She'd been so exhausted when she'd gone home that she'd fallen into bed, curled up into a ball and forced her mind into a blank. Tried to ignore the fact that her body was still pulsing, that her skin was still burning from all the places that Gabe Dalton had touched. And, since that was pretty much everywhere, it meant her whole body felt like it was on fire.

And now, for some reason, she couldn't stop thinking about it. The fact that she had...

She had *cried*.

She'd had sex with Gabe, and then she had cried like a baby. It was the most horrific, awful thing she could even think of. And yet it was her life. It was what she'd done.

And she had no one she could confess that to.

It would require having so many other conversations she didn't want to have. Thankfully, everybody finished breakfast pretty quickly. On Saturday mornings there wasn't much time to dawdle. It was high season, and weekends were always packed out at the ranch these days. Jamie had a ride starting soon, so they could beat the heat. But when everybody dispersed, Wyatt held back.

"Is something going on?" he asked.

"Why do you...? Why do you think that?" she asked.

"You've been moody."

"I'm not moody," she said, realizing that her protest sounded a bit moody indeed.

"Look, I'm sorry about the other night. I told Lindy what happened, and she said that I was being a dick. I didn't realize that you wanted to hang out."

"Oh. I didn't really. It was fine."

"No," he said. "That's what I thought. I thought you were being a brat, and throwing a fit about dinner. But that wasn't it, was it?"

"Look, Wyatt, it's not a big deal."

"I know things have changed a lot around here," he said. "I know that with Dad leaving, and Lindy and I getting married…"

"I'm happy for Dad. Freda is great. She's been awesome for him. Even though they're in New Mexico and we don't see them very often, it matters to me that he's happy. I'm happy for you. I'm happy for Bennett. I'm happy for Grant."

"Jamie, I'm not saying you aren't happy for us. But it's changed things. And it's easy for me to get so wrapped up in being married…"

"You should be. At least, I think maybe you should be. Wyatt, we didn't grow up with married people. How would we know? We just had what we had. I am happy for you. And you don't need to placate me."

"I don't want to placate you. But sometimes… Sometimes, Jamie, I think you're bulletproof. At the same time, sometimes I'm so aware that you're my younger sister. Twelve years younger. That's a lot of years."

She wondered exactly how much older than her Gabe was, and what Wyatt would think of all that.

She decided she didn't want to know the answer to either question.

"I think that's why sometimes things can be difficult between us. Because I think I overprotect you sometimes when I shouldn't, and don't protect you at all when I should. The other night is a good example of that. I can't be acting like you can't go out and handle a job with Gabe Dalton, and then ignore the fact that you're obviously feeling a little bit lonely."

"I'm not lonely," she said, drawing back, feeling snappish and exposed, mostly because she felt raw, anyway, and to have Wyatt get up in her face about her feelings right now was truly the last thing she wanted.

"Well, whatever it is," he said, "I'm sorry for the part I played in it. I'm going to try to… I'm going to try to figure all this out."

"You never had to be a parent to me, Wyatt."

"Sometimes it felt like I did. Dad was pretty checked out for a lot of that time. And I have my own issues with him. God knows I love him, but you know we didn't have an easy relationship and…"

"Yeah, I know."

"Quinn Dodge is a man made out of granite. I think losing Mom cracked somewhere deep. And I think he felt like he had to be harder to keep himself together, to keep us together. But I'm learning that it doesn't have to be that way. Lindy… Loving her has changed things for me. Dad raised us Dodges tough. But I've learned that being strong doesn't mean not having feelings. Hell, I think it's a strong damn thing to let yourself have those when you've been hurt so badly. Look at Grant. He's not weaker now that he has McKenna, is he?"

"Yeah, I know." She sighed. "Okay," she began, her throat tightening up. What was it with her? Why was she being such a ridiculous…girl? "I was upset. I wanted to spend time with you, but it isn't because you haven't paid attention to me, or because you made it so I'm lonely. The problem is just that things are different. And I clung to making Get Out of Dodge my foundation for an awfully long time. I felt safe here. It's my home. It built me. You built me, Wyatt. And all those changes you mentioned… It's shifted the foundation. And I'm working at the Dalton ranch… And…" She gritted her teeth. "I'm gonna leave."

Wyatt looked shocked. "You're what?"

"I'm going to leave. I've taken steps outside here a few different times. When I worked in town. But not… not seriously. I need to do this, because you can't be responsible for me for my whole life. You can't drop everything and eat nachos with me because I'm feeling unsettled."

"The hell I can't," Wyatt said. "I can do that if I damn well please. If you need me, Jamie, I'm going to drop everything to help you out."

"That's nice. But we both know it isn't true. You're going to have babies with her, aren't you?"

"Yeah," Wyatt said, his voice rough. "Yeah."

"And Grant and McKenna will. And I'm going to be so happy to be everybody's favorite aunt. But things are just going to keep changing, and everyone is going to have their own life. And I can't make myself your responsibility. It's not fair."

"Jamie, I don't see you as a responsibility. You're my sister. And I love you."

But she was the reason that Wyatt had to be tough. She was the reason that her dad was cracked around the center. And no matter how much her rational mind told her that a woman dying in childbirth wasn't the baby's fault, she felt it.

She felt it in her soul.

And standing in front of Wyatt when he said things like that just drove it on home.

"Wyatt, I love you," she said. "But you know I need to find something else for me, too."

"What are you going to do?"

"Barrel race." She barely suppressed a smile.

"Wow. You know, it's hilarious that I was worried

about you working with Gabe Dalton. And now you're going to go right in the rodeo around all those pricks."

"Yeah," she said, her stomach turning. The color flooded into her cheeks when he said Gabe's name. But she knew it was there. She felt hot. Unsettled.

"I'm sorry," Wyatt said. "For everything."

"No. Thank you," she said. "For everything. I think that's a lot better."

"I don't know about that." Wyatt drew her in for a gruff hug and kissed her on the forehead. She pulled back, wrinkling her nose and rubbing out the spot.

Wyatt shook his head. "All right, get on your trail ride."

Jamie did, and she enjoyed her group. A family of four who had come from Portland, a couple who was on their first weekend away together, and three friends having a girls' weekend. They were chatty, and the kids were fun, and Jamie enjoyed their squeals of delight and exclamations of awe as they traversed the terrain, heading up to the top of the mountain where they could enjoy the magnificent views.

But it gave her too much time to think.

They all kind of chatted softly among themselves, listening intently when Jamie would point out an area of interest, but not asking further questions of her.

And so she was stuck replaying memories of last night in her head.

She had been so focused on the humiliation of crying that she had lost a bit of what had transpired.

The heat. The insane, glorious heat that had fired up between them.

She shifted, feeling embarrassed to be dealing with

an intense tingling between her thighs while she was in front of people.

But the very thought of him was intoxicating.

And she had to wait till Monday to see him again.

She nearly groaned. She wasn't even sure she wanted to see him again. Well, she would see him again, so it was kind of a moot point. She made it through her three groups without going completely insane. Thankfully, group number three had an incessant talker. One who wanted to make pronouncements to the entire crowd, and not just to their companion. Ordinarily, she found those people a little bit irritating, but considering she wanted a vacation from her brain, the mind-numbing commentary from the man helped.

She finished up with her duties and headed back to her house, and when she got there, she stopped.

There was a truck in her driveway. A familiar truck.

She pulled up to the side of it, looking through the driver-side window to where Gabe was sitting. Her heart lurched, jolting into her throat, rattling her entire body.

"What are you doing here?" she said before she realized he probably couldn't hear her through her glass and his.

She turned the engine off and got out of her truck. Gabe did the same.

"What are you doing here?" she asked again.

"I figured I'd better check on you."

"You couldn't have called?"

"I actually did. You didn't answer."

Jamie reached into her pocket and pulled out her phone. Well. She had a missed call.

"I didn't feel like I should leave things the way that we did last night."

"Well…come in."

Jamie edged into the center of the room, feeling for the first time ever like her cabin might be too small. Certainly too small to sustain this man's presence.

Jamie had always loved her little house. It was homey, and different from the cabins that the guests stayed in at the ranch. The kitchen area was small, with the woodstove for cooking—which Jamie never used—and a lovely, solid oak pantry at the back of the room lined with jars that contained nothing, but were lovely to look at all the same.

There was a small living room area with a love seat and chair that Jamie had claimed from the main house when her father had left and Wyatt had brought in his own furniture, that was less than twenty years old.

The only new thing in the whole house was the large rug she had put underneath the coffee table. It covered the scarred, pitted wood floor. A dark red with green stripes, and pine trees and black bears in a pattern.

She liked it because it reminded her of the outdoors. And even when she was inside, it was the thing she preferred to be thinking of.

Gabe was so big, so devastatingly attractive, and looking at him head-on made her heart feel crumpled up again. Made her feel like she was on the verge of tears. If he touched her…

Well, she didn't know what she would do.

Cry. Throw herself at him. One. Both.

One thing was sure, she was certain to make an idiot out of herself.

So she took a step back, putting the love seat between Gabe and her.

"I wanted to make sure you were okay," he said.

Jamie poked herself in the arm. "Yes. It seems like I'm okay."

"Jamie…"

"I'm fine. You're the one who was worried. I'm not worried."

"Okay." He took his cowboy hat off his head and pushed his hands through his hair. She tried not to think about what it had been like when she'd pushed her fingers through his hair.

It was a weird thing, standing across from a man she'd seen naked. A man she'd touched all over.

How did people *do this*?

They did all the time. Managed to be in the same room as people they'd been naked with. Hell, everyone in her family did it on a regular basis.

People in the Gold Valley Saloon no doubt stood in the room when strangers they'd been naked with were in residence. There were few enough people that the going out and drinking crowd probably had a lot of crossover when it came to bed partners.

Everyone did it. That meant she needed to be able to get a grip on herself, too.

"Anything else?" she asked.

"Yes," Gabe said. "Can I sit down?"

"Sure," she said, gesturing toward the threadbare red chair with the heavy, craftsman-style frame.

He settled down on it, his hat in his hands. "I got to thinking about what you said. About what the ranch meant to you, about how your dad made you feel cared for by how he cared for it. By making sure that you loved it, too."

"Okay," she said, crossing her arms and taking a step back.

He might be able to sit down and relax right now, but she couldn't.

Gabe hesitated, his blue eyes distant, his jaw tight. It took him a moment, but then he finally spoke.

"I don't like what I'm doing. Well, that's not really fair. I'm done with it. The rodeo… I'm done. I've taken home the big prize more than once. I have enough. At this point I'm just getting on the wrong side of the age bracket. Competing against a bunch of eighteen-year-old kids who don't have to go sit on ice for the rest of the night after they finish their ride."

"You don't really do that," she said. "According to Wyatt, it's nothing but drinking and debauchery after the night ends."

"That's how it starts," Gabe said. "Then you get old. And your big, sexy evening consists of a night alone on a lumpy motel room mattress with a tube of Bengay."

"You're exaggerating," she said.

"Maybe. But the truth is definitely somewhere in between Bengay and debauchery."

"Well," Jamie said. "I guess that is disappointing for you."

"It's never what I wanted to do," Gabe said. "But I fell into it. And… There was something about what you said that made me realize I wanted something that would last."

"Your father's reputation has sure lasted."

"It has. But the glory doesn't last. And no matter how many trophies you hang up in your house, no matter how many parades you grand marshal at, no matter how many women you take to bed, younger and younger as you get progressively older, you can't go back to where you were. I'd rather make some new glory than hang on to something that's fading."

"What did you have in mind?"

"Well, that's the thing. I'm not sure what I have in mind. I have a decent-size ranch, but the equestrian facility my father has built on his property is extensive. And I know that we could do more with it. Right now we're focusing on rehabilitating horses. But I really believe that horses can change people," he said. "I've seen it. I've…hell, I've felt it. Even with how it is riding saddle bronc, I feel it. I've seen people say the horse and the cowboy are fighting each other, but that's never been how it was for me. I was always trying to find the rhythm. Trying to get permission to stay on the horse's back, because it's his show. There's no sense fighting. If you can learn that, if you can learn to connect with an animal that powerful, learn to care for something other than yourself, you can't help but change."

And there was something in the fire in his eyes that sparked something deep inside her. And it was more than attraction, more than the heat that had flared between them when they had kissed. More than that combustion that had occurred when their bodies had come together.

Because that was what she believed, too. In her soul, she believed that her connection to the land, her connection to animals, was a deep, altering thing that went far beyond logic. It was something almost spiritual.

The Dodge family wasn't a churchgoing one. Not to say that Quinn Dodge didn't instill a sense of faith and gratitude in his children, he did, but it wasn't based in anything taught in a building.

Jamie's concept of God had come from riding through the mountains, had come sitting on the back of a horse.

Her peace. Her healing.

Her wonder and awe at creation.

"I know that there are a lot of facilities that rely on ranch work and equine therapy to help people in bad situations. I just want to do more research on it. And I want you to help me. Because you have the best instincts when it comes to horses. Of anyone."

This was strange. Because of course when she had first seen Gabe sitting in front of her house, she had expected he'd come here for more sex. And she hadn't been sure how she would handle that. But the fact that he wasn't here for sex was maybe even a little bit stranger.

And maybe a little bit wounding.

Then he stood up. "I should go."

She wanted to ask him to stay. But she couldn't. For reasons of pride, and also that her brother was somewhere on the same property, and she couldn't risk him coming by while Gabe was here. Staying. No. That would be horrible.

"Okay," she said, the word sounding flat and lame.

He looked down at his hat, then up at her. He moved over to where she was, the couch still between them, and pressed his knee down on the cushions, leaning forward and gripping her chin, tugging her to him, pressing a quick kiss to her mouth.

It was like a lightning strike.

When they parted, it left sparks behind.

Scorched earth and crackles that sizzled over her skin.

"I'll see you Monday," he said.

"Yeah," she echoed. "Monday."

And when he left and closed the door, he left a thousand questions behind.

Why had he joined the rodeo in the first place, really? If he felt this way about ranching, why wasn't that what he'd done? Gabe Dalton wasn't a pushover, and she knew it, but this whole conversation, which he'd come in and made all about her, had a layer to it that she couldn't quite reach.

But more shocking than all of those questions was how much she wanted the answers to them.

None of this was simple. None of it was what she thought.

She knew that her brothers—particularly Wyatt—had slept around, and they'd never acted like sex had left pieces of themselves embedded in the other person. She hated the idea that she might just be...inherently different when it came to sex because she was a girl.

She thought about Grant. Grant, who had never recovered from the loss of his wife. Not until he met McKenna.

If anyone *hadn't* treated sex that way, it was Grant.

So maybe... Maybe there were just some people who ended up feeling like this.

Or maybe everybody did, and some of them just put smiles over the top of it a lot easier.

More questions. More questions that she wasn't going to have the answers to.

She hated it.

She stripped her clothes off angrily and headed back toward the bathroom, toward the shower. She was dirty, and she needed to wash...everything off her.

She hadn't showered this morning. She'd been too cranky and messed up when she'd woken, and she'd had to get down to the mess hall. Which meant that Gabe was still on her skin.

Maybe this was the solution. Maybe she could wash him off.

But no matter how long she stood underneath the hot spray of water, she still felt him. She still felt changed.

And she was left with the depressing realization that probably only time would make it fade. And maybe, if she gave it enough time, her curiosity would fade, too.

But damn, working with him in the meantime was going to be tough.

Jamie looked at herself in the mirror and wiped away the steam that had collected there.

She looked younger to herself right now.

She frowned, squaring her shoulders.

Yeah, it might be tough. But Jamie was tough. And she could take anything that the world threw at her. A higher power that wrenched your mother away from you only two days after you drew your first breath obviously didn't care much for your tenderness.

So Jamie wasn't going to waste any time worrying about it, either.

She was just going to go on.

"Wipe the blood off, put a Band-Aid on it and get the hell over it," she said to her scrubbed-clean reflection.

It was what she'd always done. And it was what she was going to keep on doing.

There wasn't another choice.

CHAPTER FIFTEEN

GABE HAD TO laugh that when he'd asked his sister to have dinner with him, she had insisted on making it at Bellissima, so that it could be fancy, she'd said.

Especially since he was buying.

When he walked in, McKenna was already seated at the table, a scarred redbrick wall with vines climbing the side behind her, the menu spread out in front of her.

She stood when she saw him, and went in for a cautious hug.

"How have you been?" he asked, grabbing hold of her hand and looking down at her engagement ring. "I still can't get over this."

"I know. You didn't even get a chance to be an overprotective older brother."

"The Dodges are good people," he said, clearing his throat and taking a seat across from her.

"They are," McKenna agreed.

They made small talk until the waiter came to take their order, and when the bread came out, McKenna attacked it fiercely.

"So," she said. "To what do I owe the pleasure of a personal fancy dinner?"

"Does there have to be a reason for me to want to sit and have dinner with my sister?"

"I don't suppose," McKenna said. "But usually,

you're content to invite me over to the ranch so that I can see everyone."

He should have known he couldn't get anything past McKenna. It amazed him how much she was a Dalton, through and through, even having not been raised with them.

"I did want to talk to you," he said.

"Is it about Jamie?"

His stomach tightened. "No."

"I *know* something is going on between the two of you," she said. "I was at the bar that night. You're about as subtle as a couple of yowling house cats. It was completely obvious when she came back to the table that something happened."

Thank God she only knew about the bar, and nothing else.

"It's complicated. And Jamie isn't what I want to talk about. Though there are some things about Jamie that have me thinking…"

"If you hurt her," McKenna said, picking up a butter knife, "I will kill you. She is my future sister-in-law. And you're my brother. But she's younger, and my husband will side with her. Which means I have to side with her, too."

"How do you know she wouldn't hurt me?"

McKenna laughed. "Whatever. Okay, what do you actually want to talk about, since you're clearly not going to give me details about the situation with Jamie. Which I will weasel out of someone."

The glint in her brown eyes left him in no doubt of McKenna's ability to weasel. But he wasn't going to give her what she wanted.

He was about to talk personal with her. But *his* personal. Not Jamie's.

What had happened between him and Jamie wasn't something he could just go around talking about for a variety of reasons.

"The way that Jamie is with the horses... It reminded me of how things used to be for me. Before. I don't like to complain about this stuff to you, but you know growing up with Tammy and Hank Dalton was like living in a box full of rattlesnakes and live firecrackers. God help you if it all went off at once."

"I can imagine," McKenna said. "I've heard about how they used to fight."

"It was something else. They were like different people than they are now. I would escape. Go out to the barn, go for a ride. It was like I could finally hear myself think again. My horses were companions and they were therapy." He grimaced. "It sounds dumb but..."

"It doesn't. I feel that way about them now."

He sighed. "I used to want to do something with the rodeo. Use my money to make a difference or something. And then I lost that somewhere along the way. Just...being in it. I need that to change. Because I think that the ranch could be...therapy the way it was for me. Maybe for kids like me. And kids like...you, I guess. And I wanted to talk to you because... What could you have used? My dad left you to fend for yourself."

"Our dad didn't know I existed," McKenna pointed out, sliding her knife through the garlic butter that had come with the bread and slathering a thick layer on.

Gabe bit back the words that hovered on his tongue. McKenna was right. He hadn't known that she'd existed. He believed his dad on that score. But there were other kids. Kids that Hank Dalton had known about. No one else but Gabe knew it. Well, Gabe and his mother. And he didn't even know if Hank *knew* that they knew.

"He didn't," Gabe confirmed.

"I'm not angry at him," McKenna said. "You guys are the only family I have. I waited twenty-seven years to find you. To find him. And your mom has been... I'm not going to waste time being mad about things I can't change. There's no earthly reason."

"I admire that about you," Gabe said. "But... I want to take the ranch and make it something big."

"Are you atoning for Dad's sins?"

"I don't know."

"I think kids who have been in foster care like I was could benefit from knowing there's a home base. When you're done with the system, oftentimes you slip away. There are things in place to help, but there's not a whole lot of accountability, and it's easy to kind of walk off into the distance. There needs to be more training. A sense of belonging. I can't tell you what working at Get Out of Dodge did for me. Right away. Just the sense of...accomplishment that he gave me. Ranch work might have saved me."

"Well, you look like you're pretty intact."

She smiled and shrugged. "Yeah. I think I might have gotten this way a little bit sooner if I would have had something that I'd worked for and accomplished. I think the really hard thing about that kind of life is...the sense of futility. You can't control anything or change anything. Nothing is yours."

"That must be tough," he said, his throat tightening, overwhelmed by the differences that had marked his

upbringing versus McKenna's. It made him wonder…
It made him wonder if it was different for the other
kids that were out there. If they were struggling, too.

Well, it wasn't like any of them were kids. They
would be his age to a couple of years younger. At least,
based on what his mother had told him.

Right before she'd…

Right before she'd asked him to go into the rodeo.

"It was," McKenna said. "Here I am. All survived.
And I'm here with you."

"Yes, you are," he said.

As if on cue, the waiter brought their dinner.

McKenna looked down at her very expensive steak,
then back up at him with a big smile on her face. "Now,
can we talk about something other than my depressing childhood?"

"Sure," he said. "We can talk about mine."

"Hard pass."

"I'm still not telling you anything about Jamie."

"It was worth a shot. Okay…" She looked up as if
searching for something in the cracks of the pine plank
ceiling. "Have you ever broken your arm?"

"I have."

"And that is a story I haven't heard."

And so he spent the next few hours exchanging
stories with his sister, that they would have known if
they'd had a chance to grow up together.

And Gabe did his best not to think about *what if*.

GABE HAD RIDDEN his horse until he was saddle sore on
Sunday. And that was a hell of a feat for him. But he
had nothing else to do, and he had a feeling that if he
didn't exhaust himself, he would wind up at Jamie's

cabin sometime that night, begging her to give him another chance to kiss those lips.

She'd been reticent, and very, very cool with him when he'd first shown up at her place Saturday.

And he wasn't going to push. Not after the crying thing.

He'd never really been involved with a woman beyond a night or two before. And he'd certainly never had to figure out how to work with one that he'd had sex with.

Had sex with, held while she cried. Yeah, he wasn't familiar with the protocol for all this.

And Jamie wasn't exactly giving him a road map.

Jamie seemed perfectly happy to be unreadable.

A ball of prickles.

At least, until she was naked. When she was soft and sweet underneath his body. Responsive and pliant and vocal.

Yeah. His memories of that night were perfect.

Until he got to the crying.

He shook his head, shuffling the papers around on his desk in the rustic office. He'd been doing a lot of research and thinking a lot about his conversation with McKenna. And he was formulating some plans. But he wanted to talk to Jamie first.

He'd shot her a quick text this morning telling her to meet him in the office, and she was due any minute.

Jamie walked in without knocking, but it was less of a stride, and much more of a subdued walk.

It was a subtle thing, but her entrance lacked her usual… Jamie.

She was wearing her typical uniform. A pair of work jeans and a black tank top with a scoop neck. It didn't show off much of her body, not thanks to the sports bra she wore underneath it. Now he knew she wore sports bras. He thought it was a tank top layer underneath the other one, but he'd been wrong.

He knew what her breasts looked like, though. They didn't spill up over the top of her shirt, but they were a perfect handful when he got her naked. Firm and sweet. Better than any dessert.

He firmed up his jaw, not about to embarrass himself by getting hard for her in his office.

He had limits.

At least, he wanted to have them.

"Hey," she said.

"Hey," he responded.

"So what are we doing?"

"Jamie, I need you to help me. I need you to help me think bigger."

She frowned. "Why me?"

"Because you think big. Look, here I am. You're strong willed and you care a hell of a lot about these animals. You understand horses. I know you understand what they meant to people who are lonely. Who are afraid or aimless. I lost touch with that. For a long time, and you reminded me. And you're exactly the person I want to help work on this project, because you never forgot. Because you know. You understand."

"Can I ask you…" She frowned. "Why are you thinking about something like this? It's not like it's going to make you a lot of money."

"Because there has to be more than that. I already know what money gets you. And I have it. I was raised with it. It never made my parents happy. Frankly, it's never done a damn thing to make me happy."

Get Up To 4 Free Books!

Dear Reader,

IT'S A FACT: if you answer 4 quick questions, we'll send you 4 FREE REWARDS from each series you try!

Try **Essential Suspense** featuring spine-tingling suspense and psychological thrillers with many written by today's best-selling authors.

Try **Essential Romance** featuring compelling romance stories with many written by today's best-selling authors.

Or **TRY BOTH!**

I'm not kidding you. As a leading publisher of women's fiction, we value your opinions… and your time. That's why we are prepared to reward you handsomely for completing our mini-survey. In fact, we have 4 Free Rewards for you, including 2 free books and 2 free gifts from each series you try!

Thank you for participating in our survey,

Pam Powers

To get your 4 FREE REWARDS:
Complete the survey below and return the insert today to receive up to 4 FREE BOOKS and FREE GIFTS guaranteed!

"4 for 4" MINI-SURVEY

1 Is reading one of your favorite hobbies?
☐ YES ☐ NO

2 Do you prefer to read instead of watch TV?
☐ YES ☐ NO

3 Do you read newspapers and magazines?
☐ YES ☐ NO

4 Do you enjoy trying new book series with FREE BOOKS?
☐ YES ☐ NO

Please send me my Free Rewards, consisting of **2 Free Books from each series I select** and **Free Mystery Gifts**. I understand that I am under no obligation to buy anything, as explained on the back of this card.

❏ **Essential Suspense** (191/391 MDL GNQK)
❏ **Essential Romance** (194/394 MDL GNQK)
❏ **Try Both** (191/391/194/394 MDL GNQV)

FIRST NAME	LAST NAME

ADDRESS

APT.#	CITY

STATE/PROV.	ZIP/POSTAL CODE

"Well, *not* having it doesn't make people happy, either."

"Maybe *happy* is the wrong word. Maybe what I'm looking for is something deeper."

She nodded, and he knew she understood the deeper.

"I did some searching around," he said. He turned his computer screen so that she could see it. "I found a place called Revival Ranch in Montana. They do equine therapy predominantly for soldiers that have PTSD. I thought that was pretty interesting. I also found a few equine facilities that do therapy for kids with autism. And then..."

"What?"

"Well, I read the story about a ranch where troubled boys got sent. An alternative to prison, basically. For nonviolent-type offenders. To teach them a skill. Teach them work."

"Motherless and fatherless kids," she said softly.

Gabe had both of his parents, she knew that. But there was a loneliness in him, and she knew he identified with that loneliness in those kids. In her.

And he was right. Horses. Ranch work. It was the best thing. To fill a void with something that mattered instead of something that would just fade away.

"Yeah," he responded. "People who need to learn the honesty that you find working with your hands."

"I think you know what you should do."

"Will you help me? When... When you're not gone... I'd like you to help teach them to ride."

"Well, you'll be able to do that, too."

"I know. But you're going to know just how to teach them, I know you will. You'll know just which horse to put with which boy."

"It's going to take some work," she pointed out. "Where are they going to stay?"

"Well, there's going to be some building to be done. But I'm going to have a talk with my dad. I'm going to see what he's willing to invest. And then... I've got my own money."

"Can I ask you something?" she asked.

The fact that Jamie was asking for permission to ask him a question was strange in and of itself. Like she had suddenly sprouted some kind of nuance and sensitivity.

"Sure," he said.

"If you didn't love the rodeo, why were you in it? I mean, it's not an easy life. And mostly, it's not that lucrative or glorious. I mean, I guess it ended up being that way for you, but it isn't for most people. It's not like it's a...path to being a CEO or whatever."

"Yeah," he said. "And that's what my dad thought I should do. You know, not a CEO, actually. But he wanted me to go to school. Like I told you already. He wanted me to do something with a guarantee."

"So you didn't. And I guess that's what I'm having trouble putting together. You still work here with him. You're home all the time. You obviously love your family, or you wouldn't be here. And I assume that you include your dad in that."

"Family is complicated," Gabe said.

"Yeah," Jamie said. "I get that. I mean, I stayed at Get Out of Dodge for a lot longer than I should have. The relationship that I have with my brothers. With my dad... It's not straightforward. They take care of me. At least, that's what they think. That I need them. But I've always felt like maybe they needed me. I wanted to help, however I could. And I have. I helped Wyatt get the dude ranch changed and up and running. I'm part owner in it. I helped my dad with the chores when he was still there. I did my best to not let the fact that I was a girl be a drain. Not when they could have had another son to help out. Not when they could have had a mother."

"Jamie…"

"Whatever. I'm not trying to sound pathetic. I'm just saying, I understand that families are complicated. And that sometimes things aren't perfect, but that doesn't mean you cut them out of your lives. It doesn't mean that you quit going home. It doesn't mean that you cut off association. I'm just curious. Because you're one of the few people in this world that I've met that's about as hardheaded as I am, Gabe Dalton. So I would figure that…it isn't that you have a hard time telling your dad where to shove his edicts."

"I don't. I didn't. That was basically what I did when I joined the rodeo. What I wanted to do was something with horses. What I wanted to do was get the equine facility established here on the ranch. I think with more information… The idea that I have now is probably what I would have arrived at then. But I'm talking… I was fifteen. I was neglecting school. Heading straight out to ride as soon as I got home. I made it my life. I lived it. I breathed it. This land, those animals."

A soft smile came over Jamie's face. "Yeah. I mean, I relate. That was basically me. Being inside and doing school…torture. When I could be out riding. I'd always rather do that."

"And what did Quinn Dodge think of that?"

"He liked it. My dad and I… It's not like we talk.

It's not like we sit around and share our feelings. He's one of those men… He's filled with wisdom. But like, little pearls of them I think it takes a few years for him to cogitate on. They come out of strange moments, not in full conversations. And certainly not frequently. Mostly, he's that strong, silent kind of man. Confident in his opinions, and in the fact that the work he does is good. But opinionated."

"And the two of you connected over riding horses."

Jamie nodded. "Yes."

"Well, Hank and I didn't. He wanted me to pay better attention in school. He wanted me to get into a good college. He wanted me to have everything that he didn't have. And when it was clear to him that I wasn't going to fall in line, he took matters into his own hands."

She frowned. "What do you mean?"

"He sold the horses. All of them. I loved the horses, and I wanted to make them my career. More than that, they were the way I dealt with the shit going on in our family home. I wanted to make that life my life. And since nothing he could say would get me to do it, he took them from me."

CHAPTER SIXTEEN

THE WAY GABE spoke the words was almost mechanical. There was no emotion behind it, but Jamie felt something move through her, creating a rift inside her chest. The very idea of having a horse sold out from under you like that. She had loved the horse she had in high school. She'd been such a beauty. And she and her dad had spent hours riding together. When they couldn't connect any other way, that was it.

And... And Gabe's had...

"Wow," she said. "I mean, you know, Quinn didn't want Wyatt getting saddled with the ranch if it wasn't going to be profitable. We struggled when I was growing up. But it was complicated. A lot of it was linked to my dad's grief. To the fact that he was trying to balance being a rancher with raising four children. The fact that he ended up with me, all by himself, from the time I was three days old. But he would never have done that. Never."

"Hank is a hell of a character," Gabe said. "And yeah, it's complicated. But I had to let that go. I couldn't have back what he took from me. But I also didn't have to give him what he wanted."

"So you went into the rodeo to piss him off."

"Yep. I think...you know, I worried so much about being like him. I think he worried about it, too. In some

ways I think I did just what he did to make him see
how that looked. And then Jacob and Caleb followed
me right on when they were eighteen. I don't think they
did it to make him mad. I think they did it because they
were following their big brother. And that's... Yeah,
that pissed him off, too."

"What does pissed off look like with your dad?"

"Oh, stony silence. For about two hours of a family barbecue. After which he's drunk and forgets he's
supposed to be ignoring you, so he starts grumbling.
He didn't buy me a Christmas present for about three
years, but that was pretty hollow since my mom bought
me two and I didn't care."

"He obviously didn't stay mad."

"No, eventually he started coming to events sometimes. Mostly after I started winning a lot. The thing
about my dad is he does reckless things. But he's not
vindictive. He didn't sell the horses to get back at me.
He did it because he thought he was removing an obstacle." He shook his head. "I guess everyone just does
their best."

Gabe didn't look vulnerable, but Jamie could feel it,
down beneath that hardened exterior of his. Because it
reminded her a lot of hers.

And suddenly...

She wanted to take care of him.

She wanted to make him feel good. Wanted to reach
that place inside him somehow.

He'd left her with a thousand questions on Saturday
when he'd come to her house. And now a few of them
had been answered. But it hadn't simply satisfied her
curiosity about him; it had just made her connection
to him feel all that much more pronounced. Made her

want to know even more. To get beneath his clothes. Beneath his skin somehow.

And suddenly, it made her feel a little bit less vulnerable about the whole thing. Particularly because it made him more human.

In the fact that it was suddenly not just about her, not just about her embarrassment, or the vulnerability she'd felt when the two of them had made love, she felt…

She rounded the desk and came to stand in front of him. He was sitting in the office chair. It was an incongruous scene. This big, rough man who didn't belong indoors at all sitting in front of a computer, his hat tipped back on his head, his jeans battered and dusty, his hands dirty and scarred from hard labor.

She didn't care for the computer. The office. Any of the fancy things.

But she seemed to care a lot for him. She bit her lip, and then grabbed hold of the back of his chair, bending down and kissing him, the way that he had done at her house Saturday. Quick. Decisive.

She straightened. "Could we…? Could we maybe have sex again?"

He growled and pulled her down onto his lap. "Jamie," he said, "I thought you weren't going to ask."

"Well, I didn't figure I'd have to. I thought maybe you would take the initiative."

"I didn't know if you wanted to."

"Well, neither did I. So I guess that's fair enough."

"Tonight," he said. "Come to my place tonight."

"Okay…"

He cut that word off with a kiss. Deep and hard, his whiskers rough against her skin, his hand calloused and glorious as he cupped her cheek and took the kiss even deeper. When they parted, Jamie could barely breathe.

"Tonight," she said, peeling herself up off him, her legs unsteady.

"Yep," he said.

Jamie backed out of the room and headed down the center of the barn, making her way to the stall that contained the horse she was going to work with today.

Her head was filled with Gabe. Her body affected by his touch. By the way it had felt to be in his arms. It was like she could still feel it.

It was hard to believe that only a couple of weeks ago Gabe Dalton hadn't occupied much of her mind one way or the other. Now he was large. Just like he'd felt in her house.

The world around her head seemed foreign for quite some time now.

Her own self felt foreign now.

But Jamie Dodge only knew how to do one thing. To keep moving forward.

And so she would. No matter what.

CHAPTER SEVENTEEN

GABE HADN'T BEEN to see Jacob in a while.

The asshole's cabin was so difficult to get to that Gabe didn't often bother with the twenty-minute drive straight up the side of a mountain. Or maybe that was an excuse. Maybe what he was really avoiding was dealing with Jacob's dark moods.

Sometimes the idea of trying to draw Jacob out seemed like too much work. More and more while he was figuring out the direction to take the ranch. Figuring out his situation with Jamie.

But now he wanted to talk to his brother about this new ranch idea. He wanted his brothers on board with him before he went and spoke to Hank about it.

He put his truck in Park and killed the engine, walking up to the front of the modest cabin and knocking twice. He looked around at the barren landscape around the place. The rocky clearing he stood in that looked over the edge of a cliff face, the trees behind the cabin that shrouded the whole thing in shade. There was a maul and a log out front with split pieces of wood all around it. A stack of kindling up by the door.

Jacob was turning into a little bit of a hermit stereotype. Not that he didn't see him; it was just that he typically only came down for family gatherings. He seemed to avoid spending alone time with him or Caleb. Or at least, with Gabe. For all he knew, Caleb and Jacob continued to have the same relationship they'd always had.

He doubted it, though.

The door jerked open, and there was Jacob.

"How long has it been since you shaved?" he asked his brother.

"I grew a beard," Jacob said, touching his facial hair. "Shaving is kind of counter to that objective."

"Sure," he said. "Can I come in?"

"Why don't we talk out here," Jacob said, stepping out onto the porch. "Can't beat the view, anyway."

He gestured over to a couple of lawn chairs, one yellow and one red, set up and facing the view. Craggy, gray granite creating a jagged frame around the staggering layers of green beyond. The sharp edges of dark pine trees and the soft, feathered greens of the fields.

The silence was like a presence. Thickening the air and settling over Gabe's skin.

He preferred a little noise. Horses snorting and beating their hooves on the dirt. This silence seemed to create a buzz in his ears.

"Have you ever actually had anyone over to sit in these?" he asked.

"No," Jacob said. "I just thought that I should get two. It seemed like the thing to do."

There was a cooler sitting in between the chairs. "You have beer in that?"

"I do," Jacob said.

He went and sat, flicking open the top of the cooler and pulling out a couple of bottles of beer. Gabe decided to go ahead and sit down and accepted the cold bottle, popping it open using the plastic arm of the chair.

"I want to talk to you about something," Gabe said.

"Well, I figured, seeing as you drove all the way up here."

"How much longer are you figuring you're going to smoke-jump?"

Jacob took a long pull on his beer. "As long as there are fires."

Gabe bit back some irritation. "All right. Fair enough. But do you want any other work any other part of the year?"

Jacob looked around. "To help cover all of my living expenses?"

"I figure you're not going to stay up here forever."

"I actually figure that I like it up here. If you think this is some kind of temporary phase..."

"I think you feel guilty. I think you feel guilty about Clint, but you're not going to find an answer up here."

Jacob chuckled. "That's pretty rich coming from you. I think you're still looking for answers in the rodeo. Doesn't matter where you hide, it's still hiding."

Gabe rocked back in his seat. "Is that what you think?"

"Wouldn't have said it if I didn't."

"Well, as it happens, I'm quitting."

"You're quitting?"

"Yes. Because you're right. I don't want to do it. What I want to do is establish a ranch for troubled youths. I want to have classes and work programs. On-the-job training stuff. And I think that it would be good to have you around to help. You could help with horses, you could help with basic first-aid training and a whole lot of other things. I think it would be good to spend some time talking about what kind of jobs are available to people who might not have access to college.

Figure out ways to facilitate getting the older kids into work-training programs."

"What prompted all this?"

"A couple of things. McKenna, first of all. She's someone who could have used help. If we had known about her, we could have given it. Instead, she was left out on her own. Plus…this is what I always wanted to do. Something that connects to horses, in a meaning-ful way. I love them. And I loved riding, for as long as I can remember."

"Why didn't you?" Jacob asked.

"You know why."

"Because Dad didn't want you to?"

If there was a safe space on earth, it was Jacob's re-mote cabin. And Jacob himself. He was a fortress, and he didn't share shit with anyone.

For some reason that perversely made Gabe feel like it was the right time to share this. And like he was the right person to share it with.

His stomach churned. Yes. Yes and no. "I did it for Mom," he said.

He didn't elaborate. He'd never told anyone even that much before.

"She's proud of you," Jacob said.

But it was deeper than that. More than that.

"Yeah," Gabe said. "Either way, though, it's time to move on. I'd like you to help me."

Jacob looked around. "I'm hardly in a space to help myself."

"Maybe if you got off your ass and started thinking of even one other person in your life, you would." He realized that sounded harsh, but his brother was being ridiculous. He wasn't dead.

"You can't help anyone up here on a mountain," Gabe pointed out.

"I still go out and fight fires, every year. I go right into the smoke, Gabe. I know how it can end, and I do it, anyway. So you can come up here and run your mouth about how I'm not doing anything…"

"You haven't moved on."

"Clint can't move on. He's dead. And if I hadn't declined the call?"

"You would be dead. And we would be mourning you. I loved Clint. But you're my brother, Jacob, and I am damned glad I didn't have to say goodbye to you."

"I'm not a husband or a father. Clint left Ellie and Annabelle. Amelia won't ever know him. He never even saw his daughter, Gabe. Ellie was still pregnant…"

"I know. But this isn't fixing it. And there's some boys… There's some boys that could be fixed. You know what Clint's home life was like. The ranch was a refuge for him. We could make it a refuge for some other boys, too. I think he would have liked that."

That made Jacob stop, still, the bottle of beer frozen up against his lips. "Yeah," he said, settling the bottle down. "I expect he would have. Do you even know how to go about that? How to get funding?"

"I suspect we start by talking to some different agencies, figuring out what kind of certifications we need."

"Well, I'm not dealing with any of that shit."

"Don't worry about it. I'll handle it."

"What made you decide to do all this now?"

He didn't know how to explain that it had something to do with the fire in Jamie Dodge's eyes. And he didn't particularly want to talk about Jamie with his brother at all. Jamie, and everything that surrounded her, was his.

His secret. His pleasure.

And the crying really hadn't been that big of a deal, because she wanted to be with him again.

"Just an idea I had," he said, standing up, leaving half of his beer bottle sitting on top of the cool chest. "Maybe you can come out with Caleb and me sometime next week."

"Maybe," Jacob said. His brother's eyes were fixed on the expansive view of the valley below. And he knew that Jacob had no intention of going out with them.

"You know, it doesn't matter how long you sit up here. It isn't gonna change anything."

"That's not why I'm sitting here."

"Why are you sitting here, then?"

"Maybe I'm waiting for something inside me to feel different."

"Well, I doubt that's going to happen with you sitting here by yourself."

Gabe had been sitting with himself for a long damn time, and it had taken Jamie to make him see things a little bit differently. He had a feeling it was going to take something like that to reach Jacob. But up here on a mountain, he had no idea how he was going to find someone to do any changing.

"Well, I'll see you around, then," Gabe said.

As he drove away he had to hope that no matter how disinterested his brother was, maybe one of the things he'd said would appeal to him.

CHAPTER EIGHTEEN

"Want to just catch a ride back home with me?"

Jamie looked up and saw Gabe. She was just finishing up with the last horse, getting him brushed out and ready to get put away.

"I...I can't do that."

"Why not?"

"Because I...I should. I should have my truck. And I should probably go home tonight."

"Why?"

"I can't leave my truck here. Someone will see it."

"There are like twenty trucks here at any given time. No one's going to realize it's yours. Not that your Ford's not super original, Jamie. But it's basically what everybody has."

She shifted. She didn't know why she was resistant to this. Mostly because it seemed... Well, she wouldn't have her escape plan. Her exit strategy. She wouldn't be able to just jump into her truck and run back home. If things got real, she would have to stick it out. And she didn't know how she felt about that.

But also, she did want to go home with him. And she didn't really want to be weird about it. Really, she didn't want to expose her inexperience. They hadn't had a discussion about it, so she was kind of hoping he didn't know... You know, about the fact that he was her first. It would all be so much easier if he never realized that.

And, if he hadn't by now, he probably wouldn't.

She took some comfort in that.

"You can drive if you want to, Jamie, but I figured we could catch a ride over together."

She wanted that. Suddenly, she wanted that very badly. She had been skipping breakfast occasionally since she'd begun work at the Dalton ranch, so it wasn't like she would owe Wyatt an explanation. And like he'd said, there were tons of trucks here at any given time. Nobody would notice if hers got left behind tonight.

"Okay," she said, feeling breathless and a little bit giddy.

Giddy.

It was a strange, surreal kind of sensation. Being giddy over a man.

She wasn't sure if she liked it. But she felt it. So there wasn't much use fighting it.

They finished work silently, the only sound the metal buckles on the tack clinging against each other, and the shuffle of boots over the cement floor. Once they finished up, they both walked out toward his truck. Then Jamie looked around once before getting inside.

"You know, the only thing that makes this appear slightly suspicious is how shifty you look," he pointed out.

Jamie buckled herself, wiggling in her seat. "I am *not* shifty."

"You are intensely shifty."

She frowned. "I didn't know that I was submitting to be teased."

"You don't want to be teased?"

"Can't you just feed me toast and tell me I'm pretty?" She said that lightly, but in point of fact, she would really like it if he would feed her toast and tell her she was pretty.

She blinked. He was chuckling softly, clearly amused by the joke, but she was too busy grappling with that marked change inside herself. She cared if Gabe thought she was pretty. She really cared. She wanted him to think that she was beautiful. She didn't want to just win the battle over who got him in their bed for now with Crystal the beautiful blonde.

She wanted to be prettier than she was.

And Jamie didn't think there was a world in which she was, or could ever hope to be.

She really, really wanted Gabe to think she was pretty.

She had always been disdainful of things like that. Beauty, to her mind, was found in a mountaintop, and anything else was unnecessary. Was high-maintenance, temporary and insubstantial.

She wanted to be that. Just for a little bit. Just to him.

Something precious and special and...well, just pretty. She kept coming back to *pretty*.

"It bodes well for me that you like toast. Because that is about the extent of my culinary skill."

"There's nothing to *dislike* about toast."

"I share that opinion."

"Well, there you go. We have some things in common. Which will make the long hours of tonight go by much quicker."

Hours. That was the thing. They had hours together. She swallowed hard, her heart beginning to thunder faster, and faster still. What kinds of things could two people do naked together for…hours?

She had no idea.

She hoped that he wouldn't pick up on that.

It didn't take long for them to get to his house, and he didn't act like he noticed if she took a little bit longer to get unbuckled and get out of the truck than he did. But he did wait by the door for her.

His smile went wicked as they approached the door. "I'd say race you to the shower, but there's really no point. I don't mind sharing."

Sharing the shower. That seemed way above her skill level.

It seemed like you should have to compete in a few rounds before you went pro in an event like sex. A shower seemed like professional-grade activities.

In fact, if sex were barrel racing, she would basically need a Shetland pony, a lead rope and one water glass to go around in a circle. She was not ready for the real deal.

But she wasn't going to say that.

So instead, she simply followed him to the shower. And once they were in the bathroom, he turned the water on, then grabbed her and pulled her to him.

"It's been a long day of work. I figure we might need to get clean."

"I…"

"I'm going to go get a condom."

"I don't… I don't know how to do this," she blurted out.

"You don't know how to do what?"

Oh, well, she'd said it. She wasn't going to tell him, but then she'd said it. Because she didn't have any practice holding back the things that came in her mind. Because she usually just charged forward and said whatever, because she was always confident in her ability to handle things, to be right. To take on any fight.

But nothing about this made her feel confident. She knew that she wanted... She knew she wanted to be with him again. But she didn't think she could accomplish whatever he had in mind in the shower.

Not without falling and killing them both.

"Gabe, I didn't want to have this conversation. But I... The first time was my first time."

She'd said it. She'd said it, and her heart was hitting her sternum so hard she thought it might start breaking apart. She felt dizzy. She wasn't just admitting to being inexperienced at something. She was admitting to knowing nothing. Absolutely nothing. And as messed up as that was, that was one of the scariest things she could even think of. Having to admit that she didn't know anything. Having to admit that she was all talk.

That she wasn't really that tough at all.

That she cried because it had felt huge and scary and different, and she wasn't really different than other women. She was the same. Vulnerable and susceptible to all the same things.

And no amount of pretending, no amount of posturing and running around lifting hay bales that weighed a third of her body weight, would change it.

"What?"

"It was my first time."

"You can't... Jamie," he said. "Are you telling me that you were a virgin?"

She frowned. "I don't like that word. It's a stupid word."

"Well, were you?"

She sighed heavily. "I guess so. If you want to be technical about it. Or whatever. I guess I was."

"Shit," he said. "And that's why you cried?"

She spread her hands. "I don't know. Maybe I cry every time. I guess we'll find out. Unless I have completely freaked you out and ruined this for me, and for you."

"No," he said, pinching the bridge of his nose. "No, you didn't. Just… Come with me."

He took her by the hand and led her down the hall after turning the water off, and brought her upstairs, back to his room, and into the bathroom that was connected.

There was a large tub in there that was raised up on claw feet.

"I figure we can change tactics."

"Oh," she said.

He turned the tap on and waited a moment, testing the water temperature. Then, seemingly satisfied, he put a plug in the drain. "Go ahead and get undressed, and I'll meet you back in here in a minute."

Jamie did, awkwardly, after he closed the door behind him. She was shaking. Which was stupid. She'd already had sex with him. But she had no idea what he intended to do now.

She didn't…take baths.

They seemed silly. A waste of time. Just as well to rinse off.

Still, she couldn't deny that when she sank into the warm water, which went all the way up over her shoulders, she couldn't deny that it felt good.

There was a slight knock on the door.

"Come in," she said, sinking down a little bit in the water.

Gabe did. He was shirtless, wearing his jeans, belt and cowboy boots still. He had a couple of condom packets in his hand, but he set them on the counter. Then he walked over to the edge of the tub, and crouched down beside her, those blue eyes making no secret of the fact that they were looking down through the water.

"Is that all right?"

"I'm fine," she said.

"You're not fine. I upset you. And I didn't mean to." He sighed heavily. "My dad… I don't think he takes advantage of women. I think they throw themselves at him. I think they throw themselves at him because he's famous and rich. And for women who are into that kind of thing…it doesn't matter how old he is. Doesn't matter if he's married, has kids. But I think… I don't want to be like that. The kind of person who doesn't think. I don't think a man is any kind of man if he can't control himself. That's part of what it means to be a man. To be strong, and to never use it against anyone. To be able to take advantage of people if you wanted to, but to choose instead to care about their feelings."

"I think you do… I think you do a pretty good job of that, Gabe. Wyatt definitely has you wrong."

"Yeah, he thought I would take advantage of you." Gabe's mouth pulled down into a rueful frown. "I pretty much did."

"I think *I* took advantage of you. I purposefully withheld information about my virginity. Mostly because I was hoping it wouldn't matter."

"Have you ever not charged into things full on?"

He grabbed a bar of soap and worked it to lather over his hands, and then Jamie jolted when he stuck those hands into the water, rubbing them over her shoulders. She relaxed against him then, because his touch felt good, soothing to her aching muscles.

No one had ever done this for her before.

"Good?" he asked, his voice husky.

"Yes," she said.

He took his hands away for a moment, then took hold of the bar of soap again, slicking them up, before he returned his attention to her. This time he slid his hands down over her breasts, touching them, cupping them and teasing her nipples before sliding down her stomach and grazing that place between her legs.

She shifted, whimpering slightly and turning her head, burying her face against his forearm.

His touch felt…so good.

His hands were so strong, and the way they slid over her body… He made her feel soft.

And yet again, the feelings she normally associated with that weren't there. There was no fear. No sense of being weak. No, she felt… She felt wonderful.

He moved his hands back up to her shoulders, kneading her tight muscles with his thumbs, and she let her head roll back, resting on his arm as he pleasured her in an entirely different way now.

He moved his hand down again, and this time when he touched her breast he lingered there, sliding his thumb in low, slow circles around her nipple. Pinching her lightly, before circling again.

She turned her head up toward him and he dipped his head, kissing her in a rhythm that matched the way he was touching her breast.

She sighed and arched upward, into his touch, into his kiss.

This did not feel like it was beyond her. This felt easy. Natural. Felt right.

He removed his hands, and she made a small sound in protest until she realized he was taking his boots off.

He stood for a moment, shucking off his jeans and underwear before walking stark naked over to the bathroom counter.

She took a moment to admire his body. That broad, muscular back, the way his waist tapered in. His butt.

She had never been a big one for Wrangler butt. All the girls around her at amateur barrel racing events had gone on and on about it. Jamie had just been there to race.

She didn't know about Wrangler butt or not. But Gabe Dalton's butt was a thing of beauty. His thighs were muscular, and she had the strangest urge to take a bite out of one of them.

She didn't know why the idea of putting her teeth on him was arousing. But it was.

Maybe because everything about him was arousing.

He picked up a condom packet and brought it back over to the tub, setting it on the rounded lip carefully.

"Scoot up, princess. I'm coming in."

Princess.

No one had ever called her that before.

It was like Gabe was bound and determined to make a laundry list of firsts for her. Even when they were things she had never noticed or thought about before.

He pushed out her shoulders gently, and she leaned forward. Then he planted one foot in the tub behind her, then the other, sliding down slowly so that he was behind her, and her head was now resting against his muscular chest.

"This works for me."

He went back to massaging her, back to her breasts, where he teased and tormented her until she was wiggling against him.

She could feel his erection, firm and insistent against her back. Could feel how much he was enjoying this, too.

If he put his hand between her legs, he would feel just how wet she was.

And as if he read her mind, he slipped his fingers between her thighs then, delving between her folds and stroking her. Those calloused fingers creating just the right amount of friction and sending little ripples of pleasure through her body.

"Don't be quiet now," he whispered in her hair. "I like when you make noise."

He moved his thumb in a firm circle around that sensitive bundle of nerves there, and she bucked against his hand, an involuntary cry escaping her lips.

"There you go," he said, a smile in his voice.

He kept stroking her, whispering words of encouragement in her ear.

"That's good, that's good, baby," he said, pushing his fingers forward and pressing two of them deep inside her. She arched against his hand.

"That's right," he said. "Come for me, pretty girl."

Pretty girl.

She was his pretty girl.

Pleasure crashed over her like a wave, intense and blinding, and humiliatingly, she found tears in her eyes again. But this wasn't about the intensity of the orgasm—though it had been off the charts.

Pretty girl.

He made her feel fragile.

He made her not hate that fragility.

And she didn't know what to do with that except roll over onto her stomach and slide herself on up his body, kissing his lips and taking it as deep as she possibly could.

He wrapped his arm around her waist, sliding them down in the tub just a little bit and positioning her so that her knees were on either side of him, so that the thick length of his arousal was resting right there where she needed him most.

Their bodies slid together, their breath mixing, harsh and broken as they continued to kiss. As she rolled her hips against him, as she felt the build of another orgasm, impossibly soon after the last one.

And that deep, wonderful pleasure took away her thoughts. Took away some of that unwieldy emotion that she wasn't ready to deal with. Some of those questions inside her that she wasn't ready to have a conversation with.

He grabbed hold of the condom packet then and tore it open, shifting her to the side and rising up out of the water just enough to slide it over his body and protect them both. Then he settled her back over his lap again, prodding the entrance to her body.

She bit her lip, lowering herself on him slowly, the water making her buoyant, but making their skin slick.

She clung to his shoulders, dug her nails into him to keep hold as she rocked back and forth against him, building the sensations between them until they were both shaking.

"Quit messing around and ride me," he said, his voice rough.

A smile touched her lips. "I'm an expert rider," she said.

"That's what I hear," he said, moving his hand down her back, cupping her ass and squeezing hard. "I'm looking forward to a demonstration."

She rolled her hips upward, then back down, gratified when he let his head fall back, when his eyes closed.

But they didn't stay closed for long. No, he opened them again, looking at her with those blazing blue eyes that she was sure could see right into her soul.

She rode him until her thighs hurt. Until she thought she would die from holding back one more moment. She needed to come. She needed to... She needed... He slid his hand deeper between her legs then, worked his fingers around where their bodies met, the intimate contact so shocking, so intensely pleasurable, that Jamie forgot to hold anything back at all.

Her fingernails went right into his skin as she screamed, burying her face in his neck while her orgasm overwhelmed her.

When it was done, she was limp, boneless.

Lying against his chest, her hands splayed over his muscles, feeling the intense pounding of his heart between her hands.

His eyes were glassy now, and he kissed her, holding on to her chin as he did. Taking it slow, taking it deep.

He tightened his hold on her as he slipped from her body and maneuvered himself out of the tub.

He turned away from her, taking care of practicalities before grabbing hold of a towel and holding it out for her.

She let him wrap it around her when she got out, let him carry her back into the bedroom and deposit her on the bed.

She didn't know who she was, letting a man do these things for her.

But right now she was a little bit too tired to keep on fighting it.

She was really tired.

It suddenly crashed into her. And it had nothing to do with today.

It might just have to do with her life.

And right now the towel was soft, the bed was soft and Gabe was just the right kind of rough.

He dried her off, took the towel from her and settled her beneath the blankets before joining her, fitting her up against his body and pressing a kiss to her shoulder.

"Do you want to eat?"

"No," she mumbled. "I just want to go to sleep."

"Well, if you want some toast, just say the word."

She didn't say anything. She just smiled. And then she rested her head back against his chest and closed her eyes.

CHAPTER NINETEEN

JAMIE WOKE UP in the early hours of the morning. When it was still dark outside. The stars were weak against the velvet gray, fading away to clear the path for the sun.

And Gabe Dalton's very naked body was pressed up against hers.

She'd never shared a bed with another person before.

Those realizations, those *first times*, were playing on an endless loop in her brain. A single one couldn't pass without her notice.

And why not?

She was having an *experience*. And she'd never really been someone who was interested in having experiences just for the sake of them.

But she also didn't back down from things when she wanted them. No matter how big or how scary. And even though she knew this wasn't going to be… anything other than whatever this was—this strange, naked friendship where they talked about their lives and worked together, slept together.

Shared the same air.

Yeah, she knew it was never going to be more than this. But it was quite a lot as it was. And she wanted to memorize each and every detail of it.

She rolled to the side, looking at his profile, pressing her hand to his chest. It was well muscled and hot.

There was hair there and she didn't know if she'd ever tire of running her palm over it and feeling the difference in texture between his own skin and hers.

There was something exhilarating about this. About being in bed with him. Not just having sex, but *being*.

Under the covers. Against each other.

She took a deep breath, trying to ignore the pressure in her chest.

She felt another pressure—pressure in her bladder—and wiggled away from him. He grunted, a very masculine sound, and rolled over onto his back. She got out of bed and stood, facing him. There was just enough light in the room to make out the outline of his masculine form.

His arm was thrown up over his head, the blankets down around his waist, exposing his body.

He had a beautiful body.

A whole different kind of beauty than she was used to seeing. She enjoyed a view of the mountains as much as the next girl. But she didn't usually want to press her face against it and lick it.

That was what she wanted to do to Gabe's body. Every time she looked at it.

She shivered slightly and tiptoed into the bathroom, still completely naked.

They'd woken up a few times during the night, and he'd reached for her, and she'd gone to him willingly. At about two in the morning he'd made her toast and hot chocolate, and they'd both eaten in bed, before going back to sleep.

Just remembering it made her feel tingly all over. Then made her feel very tender in her chest.

She looked at herself in the mirror, looking for dif-

ferences again. She didn't look different. It was the
strangest thing. She expected to see some vibrant, clas-
sically beautiful woman staring back at her. Someone
who looked a lot more like Crystal from the bar. But it
was just still Jamie. And she couldn't deny that there
was almost a comfort to that sameness. Gabe was re-
sponding to her.

Whether it made sense to her or not, that was the
truth of it.

There must be some power inside her she couldn't
see. Some kind of feminine appeal in her slight curves,
her athletic body. She doubted there was any in her
stick-straight hair.

She stepped away from the mirror and went to the
bathroom, and then returned to it, washing her hands
and looking around at the items on the top of the counter.

She dried her hands slowly, taking inventory of what
was there. A razor. Aftershave. A bottle of cologne—
which was funny, because she didn't think she'd ever
smelled cologne on Gabe. Not that she was overly familiar. But her dad and brothers were the same. They
had it, even if they didn't wear it.

It was funny to be around all these masculine items,
which were so familiar to her but felt so different when
they belonged to Gabe.

Seeing them, seeing the brand of soap that he used,
the kind of razor that he shaved his face with, the scent
that he probably saved for only special occasions… It
seemed intimate.

Somehow, these very familiar things became foreign, strange and wondrous.

She took a deep breath and moved away from the

sink, leaving all of his things behind, and then she went back into the bedroom.

He was sitting up, the lamp on the nightstand turned on. And suddenly, she felt a little bit more embarrassed about her decision to roll out of bed naked.

"Good morning," he said.

"Good morning," she responded.

"Don't get all shy on me now."

"I'm not," she mumbled, edging toward where her clothes were.

"Yes, you are."

She held her hands out wide. "Well, I'm naked. Go ahead and look."

"I am," he said.

"What time do you want to head over to the ranch?" she asked.

"Sometime after breakfast. And coffee. And maybe…"

"Oh, surely not in the morning, too."

He demonstrated then, very thoroughly, that yes, he did mean in the morning. They were so occupied with that, in fact, that they barely had time for coffee, much less breakfast, before heading over to the Dalton ranch to start the day.

He treated her to one last, lingering kiss before they got out of the truck and went their separate ways.

Jamie finished up with all of her assigned work pretty quickly, and decided to move on to running the barrel racing course a few times with Gem. Though she knew she was going to have to text Gabe and see if he wanted to come and evaluate the situation before she did. Considering she hadn't been on the horse since she fell. Her bruise was looking okay. A mottled purple that wasn't her most attractive feature, particularly since she was now intimate enough with a man to have him see it, but whatever.

It was funny, because a couple of days ago—it was impossible to believe it had only been a couple of days—she would have kept fighting Gabe on the whole him checking everything out thing.

She didn't want to fight him. Mostly because she just didn't want to have a fight.

Why?

He could come and watch her and he would feel better, and he wouldn't be upset. Then they wouldn't have to waste angry words when they could be exchanging something far more pleasant. And just like that, she felt like she understood a concept she never had before. It was a strange thing. But it seemed like a minor mystery of the universe had just clicked into place for her. Sometimes you didn't fight, because it didn't matter if you were right. Because there was something bigger than right. A relationship between you and another person that you wanted to keep on steady ground.

Again, it was a way that her relationship with Gabe was completely different from any relationship she'd ever had with family.

That was different. She and her brothers were mean to each other, because they always had been. It was a right of birth, and they had to love each other, anyway. It was difficult to be strident with Beatrix because she was so soft herself, and going too hard at her made Jamie feel mean. Though she knew that she had definitely bulldozed her on more than one occasion in the past.

She just never thought about it. It was her knee-jerk reaction to try to prove that she was tough and she could handle things. To make sure that everybody knew she had a firm idea of who she was, and that she didn't need to be babied.

She supposed one of the big differences here was that she didn't mind the way that Gabe babied her.

She paused, setting the barrel up on its end and resting her forearms on the top of it. She thought about last night. And she couldn't help but smile.

"Getting ready to ride, cowgirl?"

McKenna was standing against the fence, her arms draped over the top rail, almost mirroring Jamie's current pose.

"Yeah," Jamie said, feeling a little bit embarrassed that she'd been caught fantasizing about her friend's brother.

Of course, all things considered, it was fair enough, seeing as McKenna slept with Jamie's brother.

Jamie frowned. That was a little bit of an intense connection.

"You know," McKenna said, "not that long after I first came to the ranch Grant took me to watch you ride. You were going around underneath the covered arena, getting ready to do a demonstration for some of the guests. It was freezing, and we barely had very many people there. But you were ready to go. I've never seen anything like it. I've never been to a real rodeo, or anything like that."

"Grant hasn't fixed that yet?"

"He assures me that we are headed up to Sisters to see a good one in a couple of weeks."

"That will be great," she said, her heart aching a little bit, because she wished that she could be there. Wished that she could be riding at an event like that.

Maybe next year.

She would hold out for that.

It was strange, though, because while her heart ached

when McKenna mentioned the event, and while Jamie definitely longed to be a part of it, the primary image in her mind was of Grant and McKenna together. Of them experiencing the rodeo with each other.

She sighed heavily. "Anyway. That will be fun."

"Yes," McKenna said, smiling. "Did Gabe tell you that I had dinner with him the other night?"

"No," Jamie said, her face getting hot. "Why would Gabe tell me that?"

McKenna squinted. "You're gonna play it that way, too?"

"What which way?" Jamie tried to make her expression innocent. But she didn't think she had an overly innocent face at any time, let alone when she was being deliberately obtuse.

"Gabe wouldn't tell me anything, either." McKenna looked irritated.

Jamie gave thanks for Gabe Dalton's circumspect mouth.

"There's nothing to tell." She shrugged. "I'm not entirely sure what you're aiming for."

"He kissed you," McKenna said, sounding incredulous. "He kissed you at that bar, and now you're trying to tell me that nothing happened after that?"

"He was drunk," Jamie said.

"No, he wasn't. He drove home. And Gabe is way too much of a stickler to do anything idiotic like driving home drunk from the bar. He was sober, and he kissed you. *I* was drunk, and I advised that you go have a little fun with him."

A little fun.

She supposed that sex with Gabe was fun. There wasn't much point denying that. In fact, right now, if given the choice between barrel racing—which was the most fun Jamie had ever had until recently—and sex, she would choose sex.

So that, she supposed, proved Bea and McKenna's points.

She schooled her face into a serene expression. "I just don't know what you're talking about, really."

It was safe to say that while the sex she was having with Gabe was fun, they weren't really having *a little fun*. It felt too deep for that. Too big. And so, she felt like technically, she wasn't lying.

"You're infuriating," McKenna said.

"A constant in a world of change," Jamie returned, grinning.

"I'm going to make Bea give you a pet rabbit."

Jamie wrinkled her nose. "You will not. I don't want a rabbit. I thought I made my position on rabbits perfectly clear."

"She'll give you one, and you won't be able to return it because you will feel bad. You'll make her cry if you refuse the rabbit."

"I don't fear Bea and her animal-related generosity."

"You should," McKenna said, squinting. "I might tell her to give you a raccoon."

The very idea of that filled Jamie with horror. But she didn't show it. "Bea only has one raccoon. And she would never give Evan away. She loves him. Possibly more than she loves Dane."

"That isn't true. She's crazy about Dane. Being in love is not like loving a pet."

A dreamy smile crossed McKenna's face, and Jamie knew that she was thinking about Grant. Likely thinking about sex with Grant.

And Jamie had to wonder how many times that same look had come across McKenna's face before, and whether Jamie just hadn't noticed. If she'd been too blind to see. She probably had been.

She hadn't understood that.

"Did you...? Did being with Grant make you like things you didn't used to like?"

She was thinking about Beatrix and the beer.

McKenna blinked. "I... Is that a sex question?"

Jamie's mouth flew open. "No. I have no sex questions about you with my brother. None at all."

"I didn't think so, but I thought in the interest of sharing information, I should check."

Except now Jamie was curious. Against her will. She was not going to follow that on. "No. It's just... Beatrix mentioned that Dane had gotten her into drinking beer. Beatrix didn't used to drink beer at all. She obviously does it because of him. You're going to the rodeo with Grant. So I guess that kind of answers my own question."

McKenna laughed. "I moved to a ranch to be with Grant. Well, I guess I moved to the ranch first. But I'm staying on the ranch because of Grant. He's definitely changed me."

"Does that bother you?"

"No," McKenna said. "Being with him has... My life wasn't easy before I came here. I mean... Everyone's life is hard, so I'm not trying to be all sob story about it, but it was tough. I had a pretty thick sheet of armor all wrapped around me. Nothing could get in and hurt me. But nothing could get in and heal me, either. And until him... I didn't care about that. But I wanted to let him in. Because I wanted to be the kind of woman that was worthy of a man like him. Honestly, Jamie...you have no idea what a strong, wonderful man he is. And he would never want me to go talking about all that. Because of course he doesn't like attention and recognition, either."

"Do you have secrets with him, too?"

"That's the nature of intimate relationships. I mean, that is the thing about sex, Jamie. It's intimate. I spent a long time pretending that it didn't have to be. But it doesn't just move things around in your body. It shifts them in your soul. For better or worse. It's kind of a mirror of what happens in a real relationship. You want to do things that you would ordinarily think were crazy, because it's…him. Physically and emotionally, those things are true."

Jamie blinked. "Well, love sounds overrated."

"I would say that it's not," McKenna said. "In fact, I would say that we as a culture have bizarrely underrated it."

"I have to take your word for that."

Letting someone under your armor. That was the most terrifying thing Jamie could think of. And even though McKenna was happy now, Jamie couldn't think of anything she would like less.

She had absolutely no inclination toward that.

But even as she rejected it, what McKenna said made a strange kind of sense. Because she thought about the way that Gabe touched her, and how when she was with him, when she was in the moment, it didn't just seem sexy, it seemed necessary.

And if she were told cold, when she was just standing in an arena with no tingle between her thighs, that it would feel good to have a man touch her between the legs, and suck on her breasts, she would have crossed her arms over her chest and recoiled slightly.

But Gabe made her crazy. A special brand of it. And whatever he did…it seemed right.

Gabe seemed right.

But the armor thing didn't.

"Hey," Gabe said, loping up to the fence, his cowboy hat pulled low over his eyes, his movements mesmerizing for Jamie.

McKenna shot her a glance, and made a skeptical sound. "Yep. Nothing?"

Jamie treated McKenna to a wide grin, stretching straight across her face, with no curve at all, and a whole lot of teeth. "Hi," she said to Gabe, pulling her focus off McKenna.

"Are you ready to ride?"

"Yes," she said.

"You should give McKenna a show, too."

"Hopefully, it won't be a show of me falling off the horse again."

"Definitely," Gabe said, his expression suddenly getting stony.

"You're going to rush into place and catch me if I start to fall, right?" she asked. "Because I seem to recall that last time you felt that had you been here, you would have prevented it."

"Get your smart ass up on the horse, Jamie," he said. Then she went off to do just that.

GABE FELT HIS sister's gaze burning into the side of his face.

"Don't bullshit me, Dalton."

He kept his eyes on Jamie, and resolutely not on McKenna. "Why not, Tate?"

"Soon to be *Dodge*," McKenna said. "And don't forget it. The same last name as the girl you're currently fooling around with."

He looked off in the distance where Jamie was tightening the girth on her horse's saddle. "I'm not fooling around with her."

"You *are* sleeping with her, though."

"Why do you think that?"

"Because I'm clairvoyant." He drew back and looked at her, his eyes wide. "I'm not clairvoyant, you idiot. But I know Jamie. She seems different. In the way she looks at you… You two have secret smiles. Secret smiles between men and women tend to mean there's been nudity."

"First of all, I didn't believe you were clairvoyant, not for a minute. I was a little concerned you might believe you were. Second, I'm not messing around with her," he reiterated.

"I believe you," she said. "But what are you doing?"

He lifted a shoulder. "Enjoying myself."

McKenna responded slowly. "And I can see that she's enjoying it, too."

"I think so."

She assessed him and didn't speak, but there was a funny smile playing around the edge of her mouth, and he wanted to tell her not to get ideas.

Jamie got up on the horse, then went to the edge of the entrance to the arena. And when she and the horse let fly, it was incredible to see.

Jamie practically stood, working her legs up and down in time with the horse, her incredible control around each curve amazing. And he knew exactly how all those muscles in her body felt. How it looked when she was naked.

She'd earned all that athletic, toned beauty, and it was on display here. And giving him a hell of a rush.

Jamie finished off the course, and Gabe stuck two fingers in his mouth and whistled.

McKenna clapped next to him, shaking her head. "Even if I didn't know Jamie so well, I would know there was something going on, because you can't handle yourself watching her like that. You're so into her it's hilarious."

His knee-jerk reaction to that was anger. She was being nosy and she didn't have the right to be. What was happening between him and Jamie was between him and Jamie.

"Look, you can be judgmental if you want. And you can talk about how predictable I am, and how Wyatt was afraid this would happen, and his suspicions were unfounded, or whatever. But whatever you think... McKenna, being around Jamie reminds me of what it was like to care about things."

He hadn't meant to say that. It was more revealing than he'd have liked it to be.

"Because you're older than she is," McKenna said. "So she reminds you of being young."

He scowled. "Maybe." Hell, maybe that was it. Maybe she reminded him of his twenties. He didn't think that was it, though. "Also, I'm thirty-three. I'm eight years older than she is. That's not that insane."

"All right, I'll quit making fun of you."

"Thank you," he said.

"Great job," McKenna shouted as Jamie approached where they were standing.

"Thanks," Jamie said.

"I haven't gotten to the reason I'm here yet," Mc-Kenna said.

"And that is?"

"Wyatt wants to do a little rodeo show for the guests. Even Dane is going to do something. Next weekend."

"Oh, yeah?" Gabe asked.

"And, well, he figured Jamie would barrel race. But he sent me to ask you if you would provide us with a steer wrestle and a saddle bronc ride."

Gabe was surprised by the invitation. "Yeah, I can do that. Dane doesn't want to ride the bronco?"

"Dane is going to do some steer wrestling. Grant is going to team rope with Dallas. Apparently, that's Grant's one rodeo skill. I'm very much looking forward to seeing it."

"It's not that impressive," Jamie said. "There's a reason he never competed."

McKenna lifted her brows. "I don't know. I think your brother has pretty good rope skills."

"Can you not?" Gabe said, his tone dry. "Please."

She grinned, and he knew that Jamie had missed the inference she was making.

"Well," McKenna said. "I will leave you to the rest of your...chores. See you around." She patted Gabe on the shoulder and sauntered off, setting herself like a cat in the sunbeam. Likely over the fact that she had managed to pry the truth out of him, even if it was all through implication.

"What's with her?" Jamie asked.

"She knows," he said.

Jamie swore violently. "She's nosy."

"Yeah, she is. And way too damn perceptive. I'm not bothered by it."

Jamie blinked. "I'm not bothered by it. Especially not if you aren't."

"Nope," he said.

"Well, that's good," she said.

"I'm not worried about McKenna. And this rodeo thing will give us something fun to work on over the next couple of days."

"True. Hey, I bet you can use one of the horses here for steer wrestling. That would probably be just about right."

"What do you think about Gus?" he asked.

She considered it. "I think he'd do fine."

"As long as I'm not an idiot?"

A softness touched the corner of Jamie's mouth. "Yeah. Especially then."

"You'll have to help me."

"I think I can handle that."

CHAPTER TWENTY

GABE HAD SPENT the better part of the week training with Jamie for the rodeo, which had been more fun than he had doing any kind of rodeo work for a long time. He wasn't thinking about his own enjoyment, about winning. He was thinking about putting on a good show for the guests at Get Out of Dodge, and enjoying honing his steer-wrestling skills, which were not great.

But Jamie had said that he looked sexy holding a rope in his mouth, so it had given him a little bit more impetus to try more rounds than he might have otherwise.

It had all been going well. Jamie didn't spend the night at his place every night—her rationale that her family would get suspicious—but every so often he was able to entice her to stay into the early hours before she sneaked back home for breakfast.

They had also been working on figuring out all the logistics for getting permits, certifications and various assorted licenses they would need to bring the kids on board.

Fortunately, Ellie had some insight into that kind of thing as a teacher who had often worked in special programs. And now all that was left was to talk to Hank.

Gabe wasn't sure how ready he was to have the conversation. Not with the strange anger he felt toward his father so close to the surface of his skin these days.

All these changes in him, changes that had started months ago, changes that had gotten stronger, more pronounced because of Jamie, were propelling him in strange ways that he didn't understand.

The issues with his dad were just a part of that.

So he wasn't exactly sure of what was going to come out of his mouth, not even as he knocked on his dad's office door.

His parents' house was truly something else. With longhorns from big-ass, Texan bulls mounted above the doorways, scarred wood framing them in, reclaimed pieces of barn every which way, and framed belt buckles, rattlesnake detailing and carpets made of cowhide and leather with brass detail everywhere you looked. He knew exactly what he'd see in his father's office. More of the same, and then some. Cowboy kitsch like you wouldn't believe.

Poor man's luxury. Basically.

And really, it was Gabe's reference point for luxury.

He'd remembered thinking that his father's office was the coolest place in the world. And when his dad told him to come in, and he opened the door, he could remember being a boy.

He could remember idolizing his old man. And not really understanding the screaming fights that he and his mother had.

He could remember looking up at that weathered face as he sat behind his desk, doing God knew what. Managing endorsements and things, Gabe supposed now, but at the time he hadn't known, and he hadn't asked.

There were old lariats hanging on the wall with labels, braided rawhide and leather. Each one carrying a hefty price tag. And a jackalope with antlers and bird feet.

"What brings you by?" Hank asked.

"I came to have a talk with you. About the future of the ranch."

"Well, don't you sound grave?" Hank pushed his hat back on his head and gave Gabe a speculative look.

"I'm not meaning to."

"You've had a tone with me for the past few months now. Care to share what that's about?"

Gabe closed his eyes for a second. And he lost that sense of how he'd seen his dad as a boy. Lost that image of that larger-than-life cowboy who was everything a kid could ever hope to become.

Hank had been such a mythical figure when Gabe was young, traveling for a lot of the year. It had only added to that intense sense of pride and awe that he had felt whenever Hank looked his way.

And then he'd started realizing why his mother was crying after she and Daddy had a fight.

And he'd started to understand the ways that Hank had hurt her.

Not with fists. No, Hank Dalton would never leave bruises on a woman.

Because Hank Dalton would never hurt anyone on purpose.

And sometimes… Sometimes Gabe found that much harder to deal with.

An asshole who went around using his fists on people…that was easy.

You used your fists right back, and added a steel-toed boot for good measure. It was easy to deal with someone who was a bully.

But a man with a ready grin and an easy wink? That was a whole different situation.

A man who killed your dreams to get better for you, not just to hurt you, he was hard to hate.

"I want to turn the ranch into a school," Gabe said, not making small talk.

"What?"

"I want to give troubled boys a place to work, a place to learn skills. I want to work with CPS to find homes locally for them to stay at, and we can have a work and school program here. We can get grants from the state, and from the Fed. And we can also get funding as an alternative school. It's something that Ellie is looking into. It won't be a moneymaker, but it's what I want to do. And if you don't support me doing it here, you'll have to find someone else to run the ranch...or I'll buy you out."

Hank thought for a long moment, then looked up at Gabe with faded blue eyes. "I don't know why you think you have to come to me presenting ultimatums," he said.

"Because I know you don't support me doing this."

"What exactly is...this? We've never discussed using the ranch as a school."

"You never wanted me to be a rancher. You didn't want me to work with horses. But it's what I am. I believe in the land, and I believe in the animals. I believe they have the power to heal people. To give people a sense of purpose. I'm not going to hold that in. I want to share it. I can go out there and I can compete...for how many more years? I don't even know. Not many. And it's empty. The only thing it fills is my wallet. And I'm done with that. I'm done with that kind of living.

Maybe you can't understand that, but I don't need you to understand. I just need for you to not be in my way."

"This is about me selling your horses?"

"Selling my horses. In general, being an unsupportive tool about my choices."

"That was a long time ago," Hank said. "It would be nice if you didn't assume I'm still who I was then. I've changed a lot in the past decade and a half, and you know it. I've done my damnedest to do what's right. To do what's right for this family, to do better by your mother. I'm trying to be a better man, Gabe. And at a certain point you have to let me. Your mother forgave me. You can't just punish me forever. And if you want to do that, then maybe you should just cut me off. Do your ranching somewhere else."

"I don't want to *not* have a relationship with you," Gabe said. "I think that's pretty clear. I could have gone off on my own a long time ago."

"You want to be angry at me about all kinds of sins I've committed, and I get it. But I've changed who I am. I have. What I did to you back then? It was a shitty thing to do. I'm sorry. I don't blame you for running off to the rodeo angry with me. But you did well. So I never went after you. I thought you were happy."

Gabe opened his mouth to tell his father that he hadn't been, but that was a lie. He'd found quite a bit of happiness at the rodeo, the attention, the sex…the money. It was all good. And he felt guilty about the enjoyment because of what he thought it symbolized. Especially when he was only supposed to be going out there to punish his dad.

"I found a way to be. But only after going through a lot of shit. And I still didn't do what you wanted me to."

Hank shook his head. "I know. It's why I never… why I never pushed again. Gabe, I felt bad about what I did."

Gabe looked up, his eyes clashing with his dad's. "You did?"

"But I didn't know how to take it back. I didn't know how to make it right after I broke it like that. And I lost you. I knew I did."

"Why didn't you tell me that?"

Hank shook his head. "I've spent a lot of my damn life asking why I did anything. And it's only been with counseling I've gotten some of the answers."

Gabe could have gotten knocked over with a damned feather. "Counseling?"

"Yeah, your mother and I started counseling when I retired. When she demanded I change. We had to figure out how. Because God knew I wasn't going to figure it out on my own. Even with that… I'm not good at making amends. I like to ignore it and pretend it didn't happen. I'm sorry, Gabe. I've been sorry since I hurt you. I want you to have the life you want."

"So…you don't have an issue with me doing this?"

"No. Whatever sins I committed… I just wanted what was best for you boys. I struggled. I was uneducated. I didn't have any money. I married young, had a family that I couldn't take care of. I don't think you remember it much."

"I remember."

"I wasn't proud of that trailer. I wasn't proud to have you boys there. I wanted better."

"I remember being happy there."

"Because you didn't know how much we struggled just to keep us in that little place that was run-down and molding. Dammit, kid, I was afraid you were going to fall through the floor one day. I'm glad you didn't know. I guess that's something I did right. Then I got successful, and I let things get to my head. And sometimes I think I forgot why I was doing what I was doing. It became more about me and less about you. But you have to understand that even when I did the wrong thing, it was because I wanted to do right by my children."

"Dad…"

It was on the tip of his tongue to talk about the one thing they never talked about. To bring up the one subject that had always been taboo. Now that he knew what he wanted, now that he wasn't lost in that rodeo haze, he felt like it was time to have all this out.

If he was going to be here, he needed to be here. And that meant no more holding on to the resentment. It meant having it out.

He'd discussed it once, with one person. And never again.

"It's true," Hank said. "For all my sins, I love my boys."

And then he couldn't hold it back anymore.

"What about the other boys, Dad? What about your other sons? The ones that you refuse to acknowledge? The ones that you chose to ignore? Because apparently, illegitimate children were one sin too many for you to acknowledge. I know you didn't know about McKenna. But there are others. What about them? How can you look me in the eye and tell me you just wanted what was best for us, when you didn't want anything for them?"

Hank said nothing. Instead, he went deadly still. And he looked up at Gabe with pale blue eyes, his expression one of confusion. "One of the other boys?"

"Don't fucking lie to me," Gabe said. "I know that there were at least two others. I know there were. Mom told me about them. She told me about them right before she told me to go into the rodeo and make you miserable for what you did. To not let you win after you took those horses from me. Because you *deserved* it. Because it wasn't just me whose life you controlled. You control mine by giving me everything, and then those boys… You did nothing."

"Gabe," Hank said, his voice strangely calm and even. "I don't know what the hell you're talking about."

"Are you lying to me?"

"No," Hank said. "You're right. It would be stupid for me to pretend I didn't have illegitimate children when I got caught sticking my dick into other women all the time. I admit to what I am. I was a philanderer for a good long time, and I had no business making vows to your mother when I couldn't keep them worth a damn. But among my sins was not ignoring children that I knew about."

"I don't understand that."

"Obviously, I can add to my list of sins occasionally not using a condom."

"Dad," Gabe said.

"What? There's no point dancing around it. No point pretending that's not what we're talking about. I was shit at controlling myself. But… Gabe…there aren't other sons. At least not any that I know about."

CHAPTER TWENTY-ONE

JAMIE WAS JUST finishing up with the last of her duties, which had included checking on the motor she'd installed earlier. She checked it off on the main roster, and just resisted drawing a hand with its middle finger waving in the air. She didn't want to leave any kind of public clue that her relationship with Gabe went anywhere beyond professional.

So she initialed it, and then suddenly found herself being hauled backward into the office.

Gabe shut the door behind them, locked it. There was something terrifying in those blue eyes of his. Fury, but something else that she couldn't read.

"Gabe..."

"I need you," he said, his voice fractured.

"You...what?"

"I need you."

"What's wrong?"

"I don't want to talk."

He reached over to the desk and swept all the papers that were on the edge of it on the floor, then picked Jamie up and deposited her on the edge, stepping between her thighs and taking her mouth in a searing kiss.

His heart was pounding hard, and it wasn't just desire, or anything like that. It was beating like he was afraid.

And she didn't want him to be afraid. So she clung to his shoulders and kissed him back, offered him everything he had taught her to give. He needed her.

His strength was failing him, and he needed her. Needed her to be strong now so that he could break.

She didn't need to know why to know that.

At the same time it frightened her to be entrusted with such a thing.

Because when a man as strong as Gabe needed you to hold on to his strength for a moment, you had to be strong.

You're strong. You've always been strong.

She'd taken care of her brothers, hadn't she? Her dad?

Except, as Gabe wrenched her shirt up over her head, as he planted raw kisses on her neck, fractured sounds escaping him, she realized that in her family, they didn't do a very good job of depending on each other at all.

Because what they really did was keep everything as tight inside as they could. That was their version of caring. Making sure they carried all the burdens on their own without handing them over to anyone else.

Gabe wasn't doing that, not now. He might not be sharing with words, but he was demonstrating with feelings now.

There was no guard up. There was nothing but pure, raw need.

He dispensed with her bra next, setting her back on the ground for a moment while he helped her shed her jeans and underwear, before setting her back up on the desk.

The wood was cold against her ass, and it felt pretty weird to be sitting naked on a piece of furniture like that, but any sense of strangeness was quickly taken from her as he returned to her, kissing her, her bare breasts brushing against his fully clothed chest. The denim of his jeans was rough against her tender skin, but she didn't mind.

He undid the buckle on his belt, unsnapped his jeans and drew the zipper down, and she pushed the fabric out of the way, exposing him to her hungry gaze.

She wrapped her fingers around him, squeezing him tightly.

His body had become more familiar to her over the past week and a half of being his lover. But there was still something she hadn't tried yet that she really wanted to.

But she had a sense that this was the right time. That this was what he needed.

She wanted to... The way he had come to her, with those walls down, she wanted to give back to him in that same way. They'd been naked together, but she was always protecting pieces of herself. Not wanting to get things wrong or look inexperienced. And that was what had held her back from this. But it wasn't about her right now. She shifted, sliding gingerly from the desk and onto the wooden floor, totally naked, while he remained clothed, with only his erection exposed. She leaned in, sliding her tongue over his length before taking as much of him into her mouth as she could. He groaned, moving his hand to her ponytail and wrapping his fist around it, holding on to her tightly as she moved forward, experimenting with just the right way to tease him with her tongue and slide of her lips.

He didn't protest, ever. His hold on her was firm, and he directed her, with her hair, and with his hand held around the base of himself, guiding her in how to please him.

And pretty soon, she forgot that there was anything to it other than want.

Other than giving.

Her own heart was hammering hard, an echoing pulse between her legs as she allowed herself to be consumed with the experience of pleasuring him.

His scent, his taste. And pretty soon, he was shaking, his hold on her no longer so firm, his breath coming in short, sharp bursts.

"Not like that," he said, wrenching her away from him and lifting her back up to the desk. "I have to have you."

He reached into his back pocket and took out his wallet, pulling out a condom and chucking the billfold on his desk before tearing the packet open and protecting them both. He hooked her legs up over his hips and slammed himself inside her.

Jamie gasped, pleasure piercing her like an arrow as he moved within her, his thrusts desperate and intense. Everything she could have hoped to want.

There was something wonderful about him being clothed while she was totally naked. The same kind of wonderful that he needed her right now, in the office, and without waiting to get home.

And it underlined the fact that this was for him. That she was there for him.

And it made something shift inside Jamie. Made her feel like another half to a whole.

Because so many times over the course of the past week and a half, he had been instructing her. Carrying her. Bolstering her.

He had given her a whole list of firsts, and he had taken cracks and broken spaces inside her and filled them.

Called her his pretty girl.

Made her toast and hot chocolate when she cried.

And that she could give to him now… It was an essential part of this thing between them, and she hadn't even realized it. His movements became even more fierce, more fractured. The look in his eyes wild. And she knew. Knew just what he needed from her.

Pleasure uncurled in her stomach, and she stretched up, pressing her lips to his ear. "Come for me," she whispered.

His body shuddered, and he slammed against her, pouring himself inside her.

His release set off a reaction inside her, created her own sense of intense, driving need that broke her open and satisfied her, left her shivering and spent against him.

"Let's go home," he said, rough.

He pulled away from her, and sighed heavily, looking at the papers on the floor. He threw the condom in the wastebasket and covered it with the papers.

She nodded, collecting her clothes. "Are you going to tell me what's wrong?" she asked.

"It's nothing."

"So *nothing* that you jumped me in your office?"

He sighed heavily. "We'll talk at home."

Home.

He kept saying that.

And earlier, she'd thought of his house that way.

She didn't know why that felt so easy. Didn't know why it didn't seem scary or strange.

They were silent in the truck on the way back, and

when they got inside, he went straight to the kitchen. Began slamming cabinets open and shut and Jamie shooed him away. "Go sit down," she said.

He looked angry, but complied, sitting in a chair at the breakfast nook in the corner.

Jamie grabbed a saucepan and poured some milk in it, putting it on the burner while she got some bread and stuck it in the toaster.

"That isn't exactly dinner," he pointed out.

"No," she said. "But I thought this was our upset food?"

A smile tugged at the corner of his mouth, even though he seemed determined not to let it show. "Thank you."

She bustled about the kitchen easily, marveling at how she knew where things were. She spread butter across the toast after it popped up, and put one on each plate, setting a mug of hot chocolate in front of Gabe, and another in front of herself.

"Are you ready to talk yet?"

"I told you about my dad selling the horses. But I didn't tell you about the other piece of it."

"I'm all ears," she said.

"My dad was my hero when I was a kid. I think your dad is always your hero."

Jamie nodded. "Yeah. Definitely."

"To me, he could do no wrong. He was like a larger-than-life figure. A real cowboy come to life. And I didn't understand the conflict he and my mother had. I just knew they fought. I didn't think… I didn't know why. It wasn't until I got a little bit older that I realized he cheated on her. A lot. They separated for a while, but then they got back together. They actually divorced at one point. But then they got back together. And she was never… She was never not with him. Not really. Their relationship is one for the ages, with a dose of toxic that I could never understand. She just… She loved him so much. No matter what he did, she could never leave. And so he really had the power to hurt her. And I…I'm the oldest. I started taking it on myself to protect her. Because if I didn't, I didn't know who would. My dad wasn't doing it. So I had to. She was enraged at my dad when he sold those horses. Because she knew. She understood that sometimes logic and love don't come into each other. She didn't care what I did with my life, as long as I was happy. She felt like anything else coming from the two of them was hypocrisy. And that was right when she found out the thing that had betrayed her most deeply. That my father didn't just cheat, but that there were children. That he had other children with other women and had covered it up. She wanted to hurt him, and I did, too. For her. For me. So I didn't let him win. I didn't let him have me. I didn't let him have control over who I was going to be. That was why I joined the rodeo. And it's why when McKenna came… It's why it was so easy to embrace her. Accept her. Because I'd known about those other kids, and I had felt guilty about it for as long as I could remember. It wasn't like it was their fault."

Jamie didn't know what to say. No one had ever really sat and spilled their guts to her before. And she wanted him to. She wanted more of it, more of him. She just didn't quite know how to comfort anyone. There was no real right or wrong. It wasn't a question. It wasn't even a request for her to fix anything.

She swallowed. "My brother has a kid, you know.

Bennett. He really didn't know about him. Maybe your dad didn't…"

"He didn't," Gabe said. "At least, that's what he's telling me. My mom said he did. And so either… Either none of it was true, and she was manipulating me… I don't even know what else to think."

"Have you talked to her?"

He barked a laugh. "No. I came straight to you."

Jamie's heart twisted. "Oh."

"I don't know what the hell to do with this, Jamie. My family is dysfunctional. We love each other. We always have. But I…I wanted to take care of her, no matter what. She didn't have to lie to me."

"I'm sorry," she said. "I don't know what to say. But I know that secrets are toxic. Wyatt and my dad had their share, and it nearly destroyed them. I also know that family is complicated. Because the relationship Wyatt had with Dad isn't the relationship that Bennett had with him. Or the relationship Grant had. Or even me. All the stuff is just… It's complicated. And it doesn't mean you don't love everybody."

"This is testing it," he said.

"I'm sorry," she said.

She reached across the table and put her hand over his. She'd never been in a situation where touch was required for comfort.

Stand up, wipe the blood off, move on.

But she didn't want to tell Gabe to wipe the blood off. She wanted to make him feel better.

The desire made her feel both softer and stronger. More than a little bit vulnerable.

But what struck her most of all was how much she wanted this. To help him carry that burden. And it had her thinking about her own life, and the way she had tried to act tough, and what she'd assumed her brothers and father wanted from her. She swallowed the lump building in her throat, because it wasn't really the time to think about that or talk about it. This was about him.

"You're going to have to ask her," she said.

"I know," he said. "But not now. Not for a while."

"Those siblings... Those ones that you found out about back then. They're one of the reasons you want to do this last chance ranch thing, aren't they?"

"I've always felt guilty. Because I never asked my mom if she knew how to get in touch with any of them. So that concern that I felt...it didn't really mean much of anything, did it?"

"How old were you?"

"Seventeen. Old enough."

"No," Jamie said. "Not really."

"What would you have thought about that? If it were you?"

"Oh, even a couple of weeks ago I would've told you that seventeen was old enough to make those kinds of decisions. Old enough to handle yourself. But it's a strange thing... Having two weeks of firsts. You realize all of a sudden, when you know a little more, how little you know at all."

"I'm not sure I follow that."

"No, well, I guess you wouldn't. You know, considering that you probably lost your virginity—" she squinted at him "—when?"

"High school sometime," he grunted.

"Right. Like you don't remember the exact moment." Not that she wanted to think about other women touching him. But while she might be in a more emotional place than usual, she was a pragmatic soul. He'd been with other women. So what? He'd be with other women after her, too. She'd be with other men. She liked sex. She wouldn't want to go back to being celibate.

That little line of thinking was supposed to make her feel better. Instead, she felt hollow.

"Fine. I was seventeen. Her name was Trisha. In the back seat of her car."

"Okay. So that's my point. I thought because I knew about sex that I knew all about it. Because at my age it's not like… It's not like being seventeen and the wonders of sex feeling mysterious. I figured I knew. But I didn't. Because knowing isn't the same as doing. I understand that suddenly on such a fundamental level that it makes me aware of everything I don't exactly get. So now I would say no, at seventeen, you wouldn't handle all that exactly the way you should. You can't hold yourself responsible for that. The only people you can hold responsible are the adults involved."

"And if my mom is one of the adults involved?"

"I guess you have to figure out who you are if you're not rebelling against your dad or pleasing your mom."

The words were strange, and echoed inside her in an odd manner.

It made her wonder. Who was she? If she wasn't trying to protect her brothers and her dad from having to worry about her. If she wasn't living every moment in reaction to a loss she couldn't even remember.

A loss she kept insisting wasn't hers to claim, because she hadn't known her mother. But every moment in her life was shaped by it. Was a reaction to it. And it made her wonder things.

It made her wonder if the Jamie that spent nights with Gabe Dalton, and made him toast and hot chocolate right back, was a lot closer to the woman she would have been if…

No. She didn't let herself think of that.

There was no point to it. She was who she was. And if she could feel some different things with Gabe sometimes, then that was fine. It didn't need to be anything else.

"Are you ready for bed?" she asked.

He looked up at her and grinned, looking a whole lot more like the man she thought he was, before she'd actually known him.

"Yeah. For a while. And then I'm going to want steak."

"I don't cook steak," Jamie said.

"I do."

"You said toast was the extent of your skill."

"I didn't want to overwhelm you. I have a few things yet left to show you, Jamie Dodge."

He spent the rest of the evening showing her a few of those things.

CHAPTER TWENTY-TWO

GABE WAS AVOIDING his father and his mother. If Hank had gone and had a conversation with Tammy after their talk, Gabe hadn't heard about it. And if there was one thing Hank and Tammy Dalton did not do quietly, it was fight. Hell, they didn't do anything quietly. So if something had happened, Gabe would have known. His dad's shit probably would've been on fire on the front lawn.

That thought was a strange one, because he'd always thought of his dad as being reckless. Selfish. And everything his mother did was a reaction to that. Which was reasonable. Because his father didn't deserve to have quarter given to him if he was going to treat his vows so carelessly.

But whether or not his mother had just cause, in that moment he could see…the vindictiveness. When she was hurt, she wanted to hurt back. She wanted to get her own. Not that he could judge, necessarily, but something that changed his perspective on a few things.

And it all sat heavily in his gut. But he didn't have time to worry about it. Not now. He had just rolled into Get Out of Dodge with two horses in a trailer, ready to take part in this demonstration for the guests at the ranch.

Jamie had already been there. She had offered to come over and help him get Gem prepared to go, but he had figured it was probably best if she stayed the night at her place and got up the next morning and had breakfast with her family.

Mostly because Gabe had the feeling that Wyatt might be able to see down inside him, and maybe guess that he had slept with the other man's sister. And that was basically the last thing on earth that Gabe wanted to be contending with right now on top of everything else.

Of all the things happening in his life, Jamie was the sweet spot. The steps he was taking with the ranch were good, but they were complicated. The issues with his parents were...

Hell, he was pissed.

He hadn't even talked to Caleb or Jacob about it. He probably should. But he didn't want to. Not till he had everything settled.

Either way, Jamie was the one thing that was fun. Working with her to get ready for this had been about the only thing he'd enjoyed the past few days. Well, except holding her in his arms every night. Taking her in his office whenever he could find a moment.

He knew that she had some concerns about that, considering she was supposed to be on the clock, but he'd waived that by virtue of being her boss. Which she had said was not less problematic.

But she had also kissed him enthusiastically and locked the door behind them. So he figured her protests were pretty empty.

He pushed those thoughts to the side as he parked near the covered arena, moving around to the back of the horse trailer.

He looked up and saw Wyatt walking toward him.

"Morning," Wyatt said.

"Good morning," Gabe responded.

The other man stuck his hand out for Gabe to shake and Gabe took it.

"Glad you could make it out."

"Thanks for inviting me."

"No problem. Jamie thinks the world of you," Wyatt said.

The words made the hair on the back of Gabe's neck stand up. "Well, that's always nice to hear."

"She practically lights up when she talks about working at the ranch."

"She's great with horses. And the work that she's putting in to help me figure out the way forward with this new endeavor…it's great. She's great."

"Yeah," Wyatt said, his eyes searching. "She is."

It was safe to say that Wyatt was suspicious. That wasn't overly ambiguous, but the strange thing was that Wyatt seemed not at all very interested in punching him in the face.

"This is Jamie's horse?" he asked, gesturing to the trailer. Wyatt started getting ready to open it up.

"This one," he said, gesturing to Gem. "She's hers. Soon enough, she can have her back here if she wants."

"She told me. That she's planning on taking off and racing pro."

"Did she?" Gabe asked.

"So," Wyatt said, assessing him closely, "you knew about it."

Gabe shrugged. "She mentioned it to me when I hired her on. When I was asking how long I would have before she left."

Suddenly, the words felt like they might have two meanings, and Gabe wanted to stay well out of that territory with Wyatt.

"Jamie is a tough nut to crack," Wyatt said. "I don't know how long she's been planning it. But she certainly didn't let me in on it until it was all final in her head. To be honest, I'd rather not have my sister out running with that crowd."

Yeah, if Gabe thought about it too deeply, he didn't particularly want Jamie out with that crowd, either. Considering he had been part of it until recently, he knew a little bit too much about the guys who were still there for his own good.

"But you know, she's a Dodge. Once we put our mind to something…"

"Jamie particularly," Gabe said.

And he realized that that had probably been a little bit too far, considering Wyatt was looking for tells that Gabe knew things that he shouldn't.

"Yeah, she's hardheaded, that girl."

He cleared his throat. "More than that, though. The way that she's helping me out with the ranch is proof of that. She's compassionate. She's had lots of ideas of what we could do for the boys that we'll be bringing in."

"Well, that's good. I'll help you get the horses out."

He worked with Wyatt getting the horses unloaded, and then tacked up and in their pens for before the event.

It was a fun group of people that had turned out. Jack Monaghan was there from Copper Ridge with his wife, Kate. Kate did barrel racing professionally off and on, and Jack was retired from bull riding. Jack was holding a toddler on his hip, and Kate was standing next to her horse, clearly ready to do a run. Sierra Thompson was there, too, another barrel racer from Copper Ridge. Along with Dane, Wyatt, Grant, Bennett and Dallas, Bennett's son.

The barbecues were fired up, the whole party being made out of the little mini rodeo event that had been included with the stay of those who were at the dude ranch this weekend.

It had also pulled in a small crowd from town. In spite of the late notice.

A testament, he thought, to the unwavering popularity of the Dodge family. The Daltons were revered, but they were whispered about. It wasn't quite the same as it was for the Dodge family. Whose patriarch had earned the unending sympathy of the town, along with his four children, when he was widowed. Quinn Dodge was a salt-of-the-earth man, and if his sons had ever raised a little hell, it was all because of what they'd gone through way back when.

The Dalton boys were born hell-raisers, from a family that people admired, but also envied, because they had done the uncommon thing of rising up above themselves. From trailer park to house on the hill. All in the same few square miles. It made people talk. It made them wonder. It made them jealous.

And given that Hank was more sinner than saint, it didn't seem like particularly great karma in the end.

Gabe couldn't much argue with that.

Still, now wasn't the time to be thinking about his family. He walked over to the group of cowgirls, standing together now and chatting near the end of the arena.

"Good morning," he said.

Jamie looked up at him, her face getting pink. "Good morning."

Kate and Sierra gave him an enthusiastic hello, Kate treating him to a hearty handshake. The other two women couldn't be more different. Kate was that practical cowgirl, dark hair in a braid, much like Jamie. Sierra had that big rodeo hair, all wild blond curls teased as big as they could get beneath that white studded cowgirl hat of hers. She had on shocking pink lipstick and glitter up by her eyes. "The kids helped with my makeup," she said, smiling and gesturing back toward the stadium, where her husband, Ace, was sitting, along with their two children.

"Looks good," Gabe said.

Sierra smiled. She was the exact kind of rodeo cowgirl he had typically had a great time with over the years, though never Sierra specifically. But as beautiful as she was, as sparkly as she was, his eye kept being drawn back to Jamie. In fact, there were plenty of beautiful women in attendance, but he acknowledged them much the same he would as jewels in a museum.

They were lovely, but he didn't *need* them.

Jamie wasn't like a jewel. She was like water in the desert to a parched man. Like so much more than want. Before long, Wyatt came out and began to emcee, and then Violet Donnelly came out to the center of the arena and sang the national anthem. They all faced toward the flag that was on the Dodge property, Gabe putting his hat over his heart. When they were finished, he went back to where the rovers were getting ready.

Dallas elbowed his uncle. "Who was that?" he asked Grant. "She was pretty."

Grant guffawed. "Cain Donnelly will kill you. Keep it in your pants."

Dallas looked intrigued, and not at all dented. He kept on winding rope around his hand, an introspective look on his face.

Just a few months ago the kid had been fascinated with Beatrix Leighton. But now Beatrix was with Dane. Teenage hearts moved on pretty quick. But one thing was for sure. Dallas seemed to have a thing for older women.

The air was thick with dust and pine, with the sweet smell of cotton candy and kettle corn being popped up by a local outfit called Hillbilly Kettle Corn, that traveled around to all the local fairs and parades and things.

Lucinda was here from The Mustard Seed with a big pot of chili, which she would be serving up to all the attendees after, and Ace Thompson had brought beer all the way from Copper Ridge, since his wife was riding in the event.

There was no pot of cash to be won at the end of this event—this was all for the enjoyment of ranch guests and the townspeople—but Gabe figured chili, beer and Jamie Dodge was a whole lot better of an incentive to ride well than money ever could be. Jamie had never watched him ride.

He would be damned if he was going to embarrass himself.

The roping event was first, opening with Grant and Dallas, who took off like a shot behind the calf, with Grant getting the rope solidly around the calf's neck, Dallas jumping off the horse and rushing to get three of the four feet tied as quickly as possible. Gabe stood back, his arms crossed, and laughed, banging his boot against the bottom rung of the fence. It wasn't any kind of record-breaking time, but not bad for a sixteen-year-old kid.

Next, it was Bennett and Wyatt, going out for team roping, and Gabe had a suspicion that father and son had a bit of a bet.

Bennett crushed his son's time, proving that age and experience triumphed over youth in some things.

As a veterinarian Bennett handled wiggling calves all the time. So while he might not be a rodeo pro, he certainly knew how to get an animal into the position he needed it in.

Wyatt was going right back in rotation for the steer wrestling, and Gabe was going to follow up behind him. The calf was released, but Wyatt was too close behind him. Gabe pounded the side of the fence. "You broke the barrier, Dodge!" he yelled.

The judges—Sheriff Eli Garrett, Connor Garrett and Cain Donnelly—clearly agreed with Gabe's take on what had happened.

Wyatt had failed to give the calf the appropriate head start, and because of that, he had earned himself a ten-second penalty. And he wasn't gonna come back from that shit.

Of course, he still had Dane Parker to try to best. But Dane still wasn't in top form. And Gabe wasn't too proud to take that advantage.

It was an unfamiliar event for both of them, after all.

But Dane posted an ass-kicking time, getting his body off his horse and to the steer with incredible speed, and getting the animal down on the ground and tied with the dexterity he did not usually associate with bull riders, whom he considered the blunt instruments of the rodeo world.

Dane walked back over to where Gabe was, a hitch in his step. "Let's see how you do, Dalton."

Gabe took his position, getting on the horse and getting situated in the pen. And once it was time, he was off. He threw the rope, and the damn steer jerked sharply to the left. He had missed completely. He slowed his horse to a stop and shrugged, looking back at Dane and Wyatt, who were laughing their asses off.

He looked over at Jamie, who was covering her mouth, likely to keep him from seeing her smile. He shook his head, smiling at her right back. When she put her hand down, and he saw that brilliant grin, his insides lit up like fireworks had been set off. And he'd just lost an event. Spectacularly. He had no time. Even Wyatt's penalty was better than his.

But he'd won Jamie's smile. So that was good enough for him. He got off the horse and brought it back around, where one of the ranch hands took him away, and Gabe started to worry about his next position.

"You gotta quit flirting with my sister long enough for her to get set up to race," Wyatt said, giving him a sideways glance.

"Tell her to quit flirting with me," he said.

"I might."

To his surprise, Wyatt sounded more fascinated than angry. Damned if Gabe knew why.

Then the barrels were all set up, and the course was ready for the three barrel racers to have their run. Sierra went first, off like a rocket, and glittering like a lure through the course, her blond hair flying in the wind as her horse turned sharp around the barrels.

But too sharp around one. The horse's hoof caught the side and tipped it over. In spite of the penalty, Sierra kept on grinning all the way back in. The crowd gave her some hearty applause, and then Kate was set up to go.

Kate attacked the course with a lot of ferocity, and a lot less smiling, making every turn with precision, and racing in to the gate, posting a very respectable time.

Then it was Jamie's turn.

Gabe put his foot on the bottom rung of the gate and hoisted himself up. "Come on, Jamie," he said.

He knew that she was good. And he knew that Gem was good. But this was a whole different test of their skill. A competition, even if it was in her brother's backyard.

He took a breath, and then suddenly, Jamie was off like a shot. Her horse kicked up clumps of dirt. One of them hit him in the shoulder.

Jamie was all intensity, her mouth in a grim line, her brows lowered as she flew through the course, and back across the line, her time better than Kate's by half a second.

Gabe threw his hat up in the air and cheered, not caring if the response drew attention. "Thatta girl!" he shouted.

The crew came out into the arena and started to take the barrels away in the back of a flatbed truck, and that meant that he and Wyatt were up. They were doing the only two bucking animal events.

"You ready?" Wyatt asked.

"Ready. Age before beauty," Gabe said, gesturing to Wyatt.

Wyatt raised his middle finger and climbed over the metal fencing, into the pen and on the back of the horse.

The horse was kicking against the side of the pen, and the handlers had him restrained.

And then it was time.

The gate opened with a clang, and Wyatt's horse burst out, bucking in place, up and down, up and down.

That was child's play.

The horse wasn't even going to give a decent ride.

But suddenly, he turned the other direction, and he sent Wyatt Dodge flying. Wyatt managed to land on his feet, the momentum walking him forward, and the horse trotted away, doing half a lap before turning and going back out through the gates.

"No score," Gabe said, clapping his hands together and rubbing them.

It was his turn.

He climbed up behind the gate. Exhilaration fired through him.

It didn't matter how many times he did this. It was a rush. Because you never knew what you were going to get. If you were going to get that pansy-ass pop-and-turn shit that Wyatt had just done. Or if he was going to get the real deal.

Judging by the barely leashed energy from the horse underneath him, he was in for something. Although, sometimes those horses surprised him. Spent all their energy in the lead-up.

But not this one.

When the gates opened, the horse burst forward, and Gabe's mind was blank of everything but the pitch and roll of the animal beneath him. The horse threw him forward, then back, and Gabe moved with him, one arm held back to balance.

He had a mental clock going off in his head but soon

he let that fade away, too. All that mattered was the horse. That he find its rhythm.

That he hang on tight.

There was a hell of a lot of skill involved in this event. No lie about that.

But some of it…some of it was just down to pure grit.

Sometimes grit was the most important part.

Then the buzzer went off, letting him know he'd gone to the eight-second mark, and he waited until there was an easy opportunity for him to jump down onto the arena, planting both boots firmly in the dust, the momentum spinning him forward about two steps.

The cheers that erupted for him felt different than the cheers on the circuit.

He had enjoyed that. There was no denying it.

Whatever anger he had let get twisted around him since coming back…

He had enjoyed the glory. He had enjoyed the women.

He had found himself sinking into all the things he had judged his father for wanting more than he wanted home.

But in front of the home crowd, Gabe found something different. And when he turned and saw Jamie, not clapping at all, just leaning over the fence, staring with an expression of pure adoration on her face…

Yeah, the home crowd was the best crowd he'd ever been in front of.

He lifted his hat and waved it, then walked out of the arena.

"Show-off," Wyatt grumbled.

"That's the entire point, Dodge. To show off."

"Hell," Wyatt said. "If we had a bull, I could've shown you up pretty good."

"Maybe. But you have to admit, the bronco's harder than you thought."

"It's tough."

"To my mind," Gabe said. "Bareback, saddle bronc, bull... On some you lean backward, on another you lean forward. It's all just a different kind of back pain."

Wyatt laughed. "I guess that's how you know you're getting old."

"I don't mind it," Gabe said, looking around again at the crowd that was meager by the standards he and Wyatt were used to. And then back at Jamie, who was grinning like a fool. "Yeah," he said. "I don't mind it."

JAMIE HAD POSTED a record time for herself. One that was definitely competitive in professional circles. One that meant she was ready. As soon as she could go, she was ready. She didn't have to wait a year or two, as long as she could get the money together.

And for some reason, her heart was pounding into overdrive having just watched Gabe complete that ride. It was the sexiest damn thing she'd ever seen in her life.

She suddenly understood why women flung themselves at cowboys.

But she only wanted to fling herself at one cowboy. And she honestly wanted to do it so badly she was concerned for her health.

Right now the only ride she wanted to complete was a ride of Gabe Dalton. Naked. In his bed.

Hey, against a wall would work.

She wasn't picky.

She clenched her thighs together.

It was so strange, now that she had her ticket out. And part of her felt like she had never wanted to stay so badly.

"Good job," Kate said, clapping Jamie on the back. "You, too."

Sierra gave her a hug. The woman managed to smell like perfume, even after a run like that. "Great job," she said.

Then the two women went off to their families, and Jamie was struck somewhat dumb by the sight of it.

They had families. They raced. She knew that Kate still did it professionally when she got the itch. Sierra never really had, but Jamie had always had the impression that Sierra had been more involved in amateur events, and had never had a real aspiration toward professional riding.

But they had it all. They had it all in a way Jamie hadn't ever let herself imagine a woman could.

Sierra even had it all with glitter.

Suddenly, McKenna and Beatrix bounded over to Jamie and pulled her in for a hug.

"You did great!" they both said, overlapping each other.

"Thank you," she said. "I'm surprised."

"I'm not," Bea said, smiling.

"Gabe was pretty amazing," McKenna said.

"Yeah," Jamie said. "So were Grant and Dane."

She inadvertently realized that she had compared Gabe to McKenna's and Bea's fiancés. As if it was the same thing.

McKenna smiled. "You really like him."

"I don't know," Jamie said.

Except she did know. She didn't really like him. She

liked him in every way a woman could like a man. She liked him clothed and talking, and eating toast, and naked and not talking and eating her.

"He's a good guy," Beatrix said. "I had my doubts, but I can see it in the way he is with the animals."

"Is that your gauge for how you feel about everyone?" McKenna asked.

"Not everybody likes animals," Bea said. "I figure that's because they haven't met the right one. But unless you've given animals a reason not to like you, they should. So a lot of it is how animals react back."

Jamie absolutely believed that that was how Bea decided who was worthy of being considered good, and who wasn't. Everyone was getting chili and beer now, and Jamie should have been enjoying the festivities more than she was. The problem was, she wanted to spend them with Gabe. In the way that they could be when they were alone together. But... Even though it seemed like they were a pretty poorly kept secret, she didn't feel comfortable wandering around touching him. Making some kind of claim on him like they were a couple, when they were... She supposed they were friends.

Friends with a particular affinity for each other's bodies.

Jamie went and got herself a bowl of chili and a cup of beer, and sat down on the bleachers. Gabe followed suit, sitting next to her, but with a respectable distance between them.

"You were incredible," he said.

Those simple words ignited something in her chest. "Thank you," she said.

"You're going to tear it up out there. When you go pro."

"I guess... I mean, it should be pretty quick for me. Not two years, even."

"I wouldn't think," he said.

"I'm going to help get your ranch set up, though. That matters to me. I don't want to leave until that's established."

"Well, if all goes according to my plan, it should be good to go before you need to worry about anything for next season. So I appreciate it. But I don't think the plan should delay you. Especially since I'm committed to that now, and I'm not going back. Hell, I'd gladly trade out my spot for yours, anyway. You're the one that should be doing it."

She shifted uncomfortably. "That's very nice."

"I'm not trying to be nice. It's just true."

Everyone had cleared out of the arena area, most people going to sit at the picnic tables that were all around the property, and around the firepit, where there were marshmallows.

It made them feel isolated over there, even though Jamie was sure that Wyatt knew exactly where she was and who she was talking with.

"Hey," Wyatt said, wandering over to where they were.

"Hey," Gabe said back.

Jamie had known that her brother was around.

"We're all going out to the bar later. You want to come, Dalton?"

"Yeah," he said. "I'll be there."

"Just don't hug Jamie the whole time," Wyatt said.

And if she had needed an indication that Wyatt was pretty aware that something was happening between them, she had just gotten it.

She wasn't sure why he was being okay, when he'd

been a bear about it for the months leading up to her taking the job.

But then...

She hardly recognized the girl she'd been. The one who had stormed up to Gabe on the first day of the job and given him hell. The one who had fought with Wyatt at every turn, all prickles and insisting that she was tough enough to handle anything.

It wasn't that she was less tough. It was just that... she felt like she had uncovered some things that had been hidden for a long time.

Jamie bumped her boot against his. "I guess I'll see you tonight, then, too."

"I was kind of hoping I would either way," he said, bumping her boot back. "But it'll be interesting to go out with your family."

"Yes," she agreed. "Yes, it will."

CHAPTER TWENTY-THREE

JAMIE KNEW THAT she was taking kind of a risk exposing herself this way. That her brothers were going to have commentary, and that...that the whole town would.

But she was thinking about Sierra Thompson more and more. And even about Kate. And how though they definitely had different senses of style, both women didn't seem afraid of femininity. Kate had a child, and a husband, and still did barrel racing.

Sierra did, too. Plus, the woman was cowgirl Barbie.

And Jamie was sick to death of feeling like there was one more thing she'd missed.

Gabe loved her body the way that it was. He could barely seem to keep his hands off her. And he never seemed to care when she showed up in a sports bra and plain cotton panties.

On the contrary, he seemed perfectly happy.

But this wasn't about changing for a man. Not even for Gabe specifically. This was about her.

And maybe she would hate it. She might hate it.

But she wanted to know.

And that was how she ended up at McKenna's place, with Beatrix in tow.

"What are we doing?" Beatrix asked.

"You'll see," she said.

And then when McKenna let them in, and confirmed that Grant was not home, Jamie told them her mission. "I want you to make me look like a girl."

McKenna looked her up and down. "You definitely look like a girl," McKenna said, "so was there something more specific to that or…?"

"You know. Like a girl like you two look like girls. Like a *girlie girl*."

McKenna laughed. "I don't think I've ever been accused of being a girlie girl before."

"You are compared to me."

"I have been," Bea said. "I am one."

"Yes, you are," McKenna agreed. "But with rodents as your accessories."

"I'm complicated." Bea sniffed.

"Complicated, girlie or not, you both dress better than I do, and your hair does—" she waved her hand "—things."

"What do you mean *does things*?" McKenna asked.

"It…it moves. It stands up away from your head."

"That's called volume," McKenna said.

"And that's just because I have curly hair," Bea said.

"Well…couldn't mine do more than—" Jamie grabbed the limp end of her ponytail and lifted it, then dropped it heavily "—this?"

"What's causing this?" McKenna asked. "Is it related to Gabe? Did he say something about you not being feminine enough?"

"No," Jamie said. "Gabe… He doesn't care. But I want… I want to look like that woman that he would've crossed the bar to see. He knows me. And he…" Her face felt hot. "I don't know why, but he wants me. And that's kind of amazing. But I'm definitely not anything like that woman he was trying to pick up that night."

Bea blinked. "So he... Have you slept with him?"

"Yes," Jamie said, squirming a little bit.

"I knew it," McKenna responded.

Bea just squealed.

"Details!" McKenna crowed.

Jamie could not share details. What she and Gabe did together was...raw and personal and she wasn't ashamed of any of it. But it was *hers*.

His body was hers. And what it made her feel.

She didn't want anyone having details.

"Don't get excited," Jamie said. "It's not like it's... anything big. He's working on this new endeavor, and I'm helping. And then I'm going to go pro next year. It's not... It's not serious."

"You want a makeover."

"I always thought that I chose to be what I am," Jamie said. "But I've been realizing the past few weeks that I am what I am by default. I never wanted my dad to feel guilty that there wasn't a woman in the house. I never wanted to seem like I wasn't every bit as tough as the boys. But I had to go buy myself my first bra when one of the boys at school said something about how my T-shirt looked when I was about eleven, so I went and found myself a sports bra at Big R and smashed everything down as flat as I could."

She ignored how large Bea's eyes had gotten. And how protective McKenna's stance had become. She didn't like people feeling sorry for her and sometimes that was a barrier to her talking about her life.

But they were her friends.

She had told them she was sleeping with Gabe.

She was asking them to help her do makeup.

They could hear this story.

"Thank God for school health class," she continued, "because if not for that, I don't think I would've known what was happening when my period started for the first time. There was nobody to talk to about that. Not ever. And it's not really their fault. Because I didn't say that I needed help. I just decided I didn't. And that if I didn't care about it… If I didn't care that no one was around to talk to me about those things, that no one was around to give me makeup tips, or anything like that…then I wouldn't miss her."

Beatrix wiped a tear off her cheek. "Oh, Jamie."

"I don't have the right to miss her," Jamie said. "Not the way the boys do."

"You have every right to feel the way you do," McKenna said. "Nobody can decide that or change it."

She let those words glance off. She couldn't bear to hear them.

"Well. Whatever about feelings," Jamie said, taking a breath. "I just want… I just want to look hot."

"Oh, I think we can do that," McKenna said, her words a little bit shaky as she opened up her closet. "Yes, I think we can definitely do that."

By the time McKenna and Beatrix were finished, Jamie thought she might have miscalculated. Because the dress she was wearing clung to her body like it was another layer of skin, and her hair—still not curled at all—was hanging loose and shimmering around her shoulders. And thanks to a quick trip to town, courtesy of Beatrix, Jamie even had lacy underwear on.

She had cleavage. Minimal though it was, it existed.

And she was about to parade it all in front of the town. She'd already spilled her guts to McKenna and Bea and she felt like a wrung-out disaster. Now she felt like a wrung-out disaster that would be very easy to tip over.

"I'm staying home." She sat down on McKenna's bed.

"No!" Bea said. "I just put eyeliner on another person's face. That isn't easy. I might be blind now."

Jamie flopped back onto the bed, her arms spread wide. "Well, Evan can be your guide raccoon."

"You're a *terrible person*," Bea said.

Jamie sighed and sat back up. She looked in the mirror, stunned by the woman looking back at her. She was a stranger. A stranger with very large eyes and glowing skin. Rosy cheeks.

It was like someone had put on a very glossy Jamie suit, and was trying to imitate her motions and facial expressions.

"What?" McKenna asked.

She watched the unfamiliar-familiar mirror face contort. "I just don't know if I can go out like this."

"Why not? You are the one who wanted to do it."

"I know but I feel…like I'm basically going to be walking into the barn naked. And everyone's going to know that it has to do with Gabe."

"So what?" McKenna asked.

Bea wrinkled her nose. McKenna gave her a baleful look. "You don't agree with me, Beatrix?"

"Not especially," Bea said. "It's not that easy when you've lived somewhere all your life. What people think about you and the way they see you feels more… magnified. People don't know you well enough to be shocked by you turning up at the Gold Valley Saloon in…a Care Bear costume."

"I am pretty sure people would be shocked if I turned up in a Care Bear costume."

"Still not as shocked as they would be if it were Jamie," Bea pointed out.

"You look amazing," McKenna said, not taking on anything Bea or Jamie said, rummaging around in her closet and producing a pair of strappy, high-heeled shoes. "And this will complete it."

Jamie just stared at the shoes dumbly and McKenna sighed, getting down on her knees and putting them on her feet.

"Ready for the ball, ma'am?"

Jamie stood, feeling like she was up on stilts. She took a couple of steps forward, surprised at when her heel hit the ground, versus when she'd expected it to.

"Your *ass*, though," McKenna said.

Jamie turned around and tried to look at her own butt. "Really?"

"Ass for days," McKenna said.

"It looks very nice," Beatrix agreed.

"This is the problem," Jamie said. "Now everyone's going to look at my... And like I said, everyone's going to know that..."

"Your brothers already know. The way you and Gabe were staring at each other all through the rodeo today was ridiculous. You can keep your hands off each other, I'll give you that, but you can't seem to keep your eyes off each other. They know."

Bea nodded. "They do."

"But Wyatt didn't kill him?"

"I mean... I suspect that Wyatt doesn't want you to know how reasonable he is because he would like you to heed his warnings. But he's a guy. And he went out and sowed all kinds of wild oats. He must expect that you'll want to."

Jamie felt subdued. "I'm just not sure about… making announcements about how I've changed for him. Because of him. Not really for him. But that's what everyone will think…"

"Yeah," McKenna said. "Everyone will. But being with someone changes you."

"It's not a forever kind of thing…"

"It doesn't matter. He's changed you. He's making you want to be different. That's real. And it matters. And whether it lasts or not…"

"It's like the beer," Jamie said, looking over at Beatrix. "That you drink beer because of Dane."

"It turns out I kind of like beer," Beatrix said. "I wouldn't drink it if I didn't."

"Yeah, well. Gabe is making me have feelings. A diverse array of them. And it's just… I used to think there was only one way to be strong. I used to think there was only one way to protect people. But he makes me realize how much I hold everyone away from me. I don't want to do it anymore."

Beatrix stretched her arm out and leaned in, curving around Jamie and squeezing.

"Are you ready?"

"I think so," Jamie said.

"You are going to knock him on his ass," McKenna said.

"Good. But if Wyatt tries to attack him, promise me one of you will shoot him with a tranquilizer."

"Will do," McKenna said dryly.

"I actually have tranquilizers," Beatrix said. "Sometimes they're necessary at the sanctuary."

"Well, you may need them handy," Jamie said. She looked down at her boobs and then pushed them up slightly. "I have a feeling there might be trouble."

GABE WAS ALREADY seated with the Dodge family that was present when Jamie arrived.

At least, he was reasonably certain it was Jamie. But then, *his* Jamie didn't seem the type to wear a red dress and heels out to the Gold Valley Saloon on a Saturday night—or any night.

A dress that was practically painted on that body he knew so well, with cleavage he'd never seen on her before.

Her hair was loose and silky, straight as ever, but shiny as it fell over her shoulders in a glossy brown waterfall, rather than being corralled by a rubber band. And she was wearing makeup. Her eyes large, her lips bright red.

She had every head in the bar turned toward her. McKenna and Beatrix were looking extraordinarily satisfied on either side of her, and it didn't take a genius to figure out that this was their handiwork.

Jamie bit her lip, her hands held up against her chest like a frightened mouse. She looked uncertain, and his Jamie never looked uncertain.

He wondered what in the hell had inspired her to do this.

She walked over to the table, her movements unsteady, and sat down beside him. Across from Wyatt.

"Well, you look...different," Wyatt said.

Jamie's dark lashes swept downward. Then she looked back up. "I thought I would celebrate my win by looking a little fancy."

"Okay, then," Wyatt said.

"You look beautiful," Gabe said.

Wyatt's sharp gaze caught his, and Jamie looked over at him with wide eyes. "Thank you," she responded.

"Don't mention it. I'll buy you a drink," Gabe said.

"You don't have to do that," she said, looking over at Wyatt, a little bit nervously.

"This round is on me. For everyone," Gabe said, getting up and heading toward the bar.

It took a moment for him to realize that there was a clicking sound coming from behind him. And that the clicking sound was Jamie.

She was tottering on the heels, as fast as she could go on them, as quickly as she could move in the tight dress.

"You don't have to do that," she reiterated.

"I want to," he said, touching her arm.

"Do you really think I look pretty?" she asked, breathless, gazing up at him from behind her lashes.

Gabe swallowed hard. "If your brother wasn't here, I would take you in that bathroom and screw you senseless against the wall."

"Would we get to carve our names in there?" she asked, suddenly looking keen.

Her response surprised him. "You know about that?"

She shrugged. "Yeah. Everyone knows about that. I mean, my brother's name is in there. I asked him about it. I didn't like the answer."

"And Luke Hollister's name, too, I hear."

"And Olivia's now," Jamie pointed out.

He blinked. "Now, that is a surprise."

"People are surprising," she said, tugging at the hem of her dress.

"I would say so," he said.

They walked over to the bar together, and she leaned against it. He looked behind her, at all the male gazes currently staring at her ass. Meanwhile, her brothers were exchanging looks around the table, all of them a little bit grumpy.

"You're getting attention," he said.

"Am I?" She looked up at him, so comically uncertain.

Her eyes looked larger than normal, and she had such a vulnerable expression on her face now it only exaggerated it.

"Yeah," he said. "None of these men knew you had an ass like that, Jamie. Only *I* did. That was my secret."

Just saying that thrilled him in ways he couldn't explain. He was a total damn caveman when it came to Jamie.

"Are you upset that I shared it?" she asked, her tone overly innocent. He wouldn't be surprised if she would enjoy the idea of him being upset. Apparently, their relationship stripped them both back to some pretty elemental basics.

And he couldn't say he minded.

He had to think seriously about her question, too. Because there was definitely something to the fact that the men around here didn't understand how damned beautiful Jamie Dodge was.

But he did.

Of course, there was also something to be the envy of every man in the bar. And Gabe had never minded that.

"Not upset. Just as long as they look and don't touch."

"That's kind of possessive," she said.

"I'm feeling a little possessive."

She clicked her tongue, her eyes darting every which way, before settling at his throat. "Well, I might be in the mood to be possessed."

"If you keep looking at me like that, I'm going to expect a kiss."

"I *want* to," she said.

"We should maybe talk to Wyatt before we go making out in front of him, don't you think?"

"He can handle it," she said.

And without another word she stretched up and pressed a kiss to his neck. He groaned, fire moving through his veins.

Just then, Laz walked up to the bar, and Gabe fired off a rapid order, making sure that he chose damn expensive whiskey, because Jamie had just announced to her big brother that Gabe was sleeping with her, so Gabe figured getting Wyatt buzzed on some of the good stuff couldn't hurt.

As they headed back to the table, the drinks on their way, it occurred to Gabe that it was probably also helpful that Wyatt's wife, Lindy, was sitting right next to him, her hand on his forearm.

Wyatt probably wouldn't get in a brawl with Lindy there.

Wyatt's gaze lingered on his sister for a moment before traveling back to Gabe. He cleared his throat. "I'd like a word with you," he said to Gabe.

Jamie went stiff behind Gabe.

"It's fine," Gabe said, patting Jamie's hand. He stood, and Wyatt followed suit, gesturing toward the door. Gabe followed him outside onto the sidewalk, unbearably conscious of the fact that it was right around the corner that he had first kissed the other man's sister.

"Look, it's obvious that you have something going on with Jamie, and I don't need to have the details. Any more than she needs to have the details about my life. I had a talk with her a little bit ago, and I realized some things. I've babied her when it made me feel like I was protecting her. But I'm not sure that I ever really took care of her. I let her pretend that she was fine when I know that she wasn't. I took care of her like she was a brother. Until I wanted to get overprotective on her like she was a little sister. That wasn't right. And yeah, I was up in her face about you, and all of that. But I can't... I left. I went into the rodeo, and I didn't look back. I was so mired in my own shit that I didn't care that I left her behind. I can't be overprotective now. So look, whatever's happening between you two, you don't have to hide it. I mean, you're not doing a good job of it if that was your goal."

Gabe nodded slowly. "We were. But I got to questioning what the point was. Anyway, it's a little bit too sticky, what with my sister being one of her best friends. And also being engaged to Grant. It just doesn't work. It was never going to stay quiet. And then... I'm not ashamed of it. And I would never want her to think that I was. That I was hiding her."

Wyatt's expression was grim. "I appreciate that. I know that Jamie isn't looking for a forever kind of thing. I'm not going to demand that you marry my sister. Hell, I'm even going to try to be enlightened and say that I get why a person needs to...have experiences and whatever."

Gabe laughed. "You look thrilled about that."

"Oh, I'm horrified. Unto my soul. I don't want to be thinking about any of this. But I want to be there for Jamie in a way that's real. And not in a way that's just me making myself feel better about what I didn't do for her all those years ago."

"I don't think she feels deprived of anything."

"Well, that's nice of you to say. But I'm not looking for reassurance. Not from you. Make no mistake," Wyatt said. "I'm not going to intervene in what's happening between the two of you. I'm not going to make Jamie feel bad about it. But if you hurt my sister, Dalton, I will fucking end you. Cadaver dogs won't be able to find you because the pieces will be too damned small, you got that?"

Gabe got it. And he believed it. Gabe could hold his own in a fight, but Wyatt Dodge was built like the bulls he rode, and the last thing on earth Gabe wanted was to be in a fight with him.

As much as he didn't want to be in a fight, he appreciated that Jamie had not just one brother—but three—who would willingly beat him to a pulp to protect her.

He didn't want to pose that kind of danger to Jamie. The last thing he wanted to do was do any damage to Jamie at all.

"I don't want to hurt her," Gabe said.

Wyatt nodded slowly, his cowboy hat shading his eyes. "See that you don't. Because the Dodge brothers travel in packs."

Wyatt clapped him on the back and headed toward the saloon. And Gabe stood for a moment, watching him go in.

He looked around outside for a moment before deciding to go back into the saloon. He looked at Jamie, sitting there with her family. Looking so unlike Jamie, and somehow very like her at the same time. Then he made his way to her. "Do you want to dance?"

CHAPTER TWENTY-FOUR

JAMIE LOOKED OVER at Wyatt, and then back at Gabe. "I don't know how to dance," she said.

"Well, I'm bad at it. But we might as well."

He took her hand and pulled her to him, up out of her chair, and over to the small dance floor that people occupied in front of the jukebox. There was a country song playing, a slow tune about how God must've spent a little more time on a certain woman, and when Gabe pulled her up close to his chest and began to sway with her, she thought she might pass out.

"So, I take it Wyatt is one hundred percent clear on the fact that we are sleeping with each other?" she asked, looking up at him.

A muscle in his face twitched. "Yes, he knows," Gabe said. "Now, I didn't put it quite like that. Because I like my extremities where they are, thank you."

"Well, I would hope not," she said. "What did he say to you?"

"We have his blessing. Kind of."

"Can I cut in?"

She looked behind Gabe's shoulder and saw Wyatt standing there. She wasn't sure it looked like they had Wyatt's blessing. But he wasn't punching Gabe, so that was something.

"By all means," Gabe said, stepping away.

Wyatt took hold of her hand, his hold keeping her at a distance, but still moving in time with the music.

"You're dancing," she pointed out.

"So are you," he replied.

"You're not mad?"

Wyatt shook his head. "No. I was never going to be mad at you, Jamie. I worry about you. Do you know that? Do you know that I worry about you?"

"Yeah," Jamie said.

"No, I mean really. Not that overprotective stuff. That's for me. It's to make me not feel so…guilty."

Her heart twisted. "Why do you feel guilty?"

"Because I left. I left when you were a little kid. Because for a while I had a hard time dealing with our family, and with the situation. Because I let my relationship with Dad, and the mistakes I made there, affect everything else. And because for a moment… For a moment I did resent you. This red, screaming thing that was left behind after…"

"After your mom died," Jamie said softly. Her throat tightened. "I know. I mean, I know that you had to have felt that way. I don't know why you wouldn't have."

"That went away, though," Wyatt said. "And you were…the brightest sunshine that we had. I think if it weren't for you, Dad would have lost himself completely."

"Yeah, but the thing that I always struggle with is that if it weren't for me you wouldn't have lost her at all."

"I can't think of it that way," Wyatt said. "It wasn't a trade. And you know what? Life is just random sometimes. There's no explaining it. It could have easily been a car accident, a blood clot caused by…anything else. Or nothing at all. No one can guarantee what would have happened. In the end, it doesn't matter. The way that things went… We lost her. We have you. I'm so damn thankful for you, Jamie. But I also didn't do the best by you."

"That's not true," Jamie said.

"No. It is. Because you acted tough, so I treated you like you were tough." He cleared his throat. "And so did Dad. So did we all."

Her heart suddenly felt heavy.

"I *am* tough," she said.

"Jamie, someone should've been there for you. To make sure that if you wanted a dress you got one. To make sure that you got makeup if you needed it. Or… whatever else."

"I handled it," Jamie said.

"You shouldn't have had to."

Those words cracked at something inside her that she had tried to ignore for a long time. That on some level, she had wished that someone would do all those things she said she didn't want, no matter what she told them. It wasn't fair. Not at all. But it didn't stop her from having those feelings.

She couldn't expect somebody to guess. She couldn't expect older brothers who were busy with their own lives, and a father who was contending with everything that Quinn had been through, to guess at what she needed.

But a part of her had wished that they would. A part of her that had done its best to stay hidden away. But it felt exposed now, and it hurt. She didn't want to hurt. This was a nice moment and Wyatt was being nice. She didn't want to bring bad stuff into it.

"It's okay," she said.

Because it was. In the sense that it had to be. The way that she'd always had to be.

There was no sense in telling Wyatt that no matter how tough she acted, he should have damn well kissed her boo-boo.

She hadn't had enough insight into herself to know that was what she wanted. Why should her teenage brother have known?

She was finding all this out for herself now. And she had to find out a way to move forward with it, not just tie it all to the past. It was part of that same realization she'd had about Gabe a few weeks ago. There could be a fight. And the old her would have gone right in for it. But…she didn't want to fight. She didn't want to be right. She didn't need desperately to prove a point. She wanted closeness. She wanted it in a way she hadn't ever had it. And the only way to do that was to take a step forward.

Not steps back.

She wrapped her arms around Wyatt and gave him a hug. "You made me who I am. The way that I ad-mired you, the way that I looked up to you, is why I'm here. Don't waste any time wishing it could've been different. I don't."

Mostly.

She released her hold on him and took a step back. "Now, can I have my boyfriend back?"

"Boyfriend, huh?" Wyatt's lips lifted in a rueful smile, a heavy sigh shifting his shoulders up and down.

Jamie shrugged. "He's never called himself that. I don't know. But I didn't want to say like…*lover* to you."

Wyatt's face contorted. "Please don't ever say it again. I'll go get him."

Gabe returned to her, just in time for the finish of the song, and for the beginning of an up-tempo one, which saw Jamie tripping over those high heels, braced only by Gabe's strong hold.

She was dizzy. Dizzy from his touch. From the strange, surreal fantasy that seemed to wind itself around them tonight.

She was in a dress. She felt beautiful.

"Do you want to get out of here?" he asked.

"Yes," she responded, "I do." They said their good-byes, and when her other brothers exchanged confused and somewhat stony-faced glances, Wyatt stood up and shook Gabe's hand, making it clear that the thing between them had his stamp of—if not approval—resignation. And she could only be thankful for that.

They walked outside into the cool evening, and Jamie shivered. She wasn't used to having so much of her body exposed to the elements.

"Let's go for a walk," Gabe said, throwing his jacket over her shoulders.

A smile curved her lips, her heart thundering a little bit harder. "Okay. I'm not really sure how long I can walk in these heels, though."

"Well, I can either carry them or you if it comes down to it."

She ducked her head, her hair falling in her face, her heart so full it almost ached. She felt like a different person tonight. Like for just a moment, she wasn't sad Jamie Dodge, or anything remotely familiar. Like she was something made completely new. And oh, she would gladly take it.

That conversation with Wyatt had felt good, and she'd made a lot of decisions to set some things aside.

But it was nice, for a while, to not have anything to set aside at all.

To be a beautiful woman walking with Gabe Dalton, with his jacket thrown over her shoulders.

And then he took her hand, his fingers laced through hers, and her heart gave a hard bump against her breastbone, feeling bruised and needy.

"You might want to take your shoes off," he said.

"Why?"

"We're going to go across the field."

They came to the end of the sidewalk, where it faded out into a farmer's field, and Jamie looked over at him. "Are you serious?"

"Yeah, I'm serious. I thought we would take a walk down by the river."

"I bet you do this with all the girls," she said.

"No," he said. "But then, you're not all the girls. You're Jamie Dodge."

And just like that, she was snapped back to reality, and she wasn't sure how she felt about it. About him having her name on his lips like that. But then... Then if he felt that way, if he felt like she was special, then maybe she could be Jamie Dodge, and this woman walking with him. Or maybe they were the same woman.

Her stomach knotted up, her whole body feeling just a little bit tense. She paused, bracing herself on his shoulder and undoing the ankle strap on her shoes, then the other strap.

"If I step on a sticker I'm going to punch you in the nose," she said. He laughed, and then she cursed herself for spoiling the illusion. Because she doubted any other woman in a beautiful dress, wandering barefoot through a field, would threaten her date with bodily injury. But Gabe didn't seem to mind.

The field was soft, thank God, and there was neither sticker nor cow pie to spoil the walk. When they arrived at the edge of the trees, Gabe swept her up off the ground, into his arms. He carried her over the part of the ground that was littered with sticks and pebbles, and set her down again on the sandy, damp riverbank. The water rushed loudly down the stream, the fine sand freezing cold beneath her skin. She stood there, barely able to see the water, glittering in the moonlight that filtered through the trees.

Gabe pulled his boots off, along with his socks, rolling his pant legs up and extending his hand.

"What are you doing?" she asked.

"I don't know. I thought you might want to finish dancing with me."

"In the river?"

"I'm not that great at romance," he said. "But I'm trying."

Considering she thought her heart might go ahead and beat right through her chest, she thought he did a damn fine job at romance, but she wasn't going to tell him that. But she did take his hand, and let him lead her into the ankle-deep water. She shrieked, not even caring that freaking out over the cold was not a very tough-girl move.

"It's cold," she said as he took both hands in his.

"I can warm you up," he responded, pulling her up against his body and kissing her, before dipping her backward and bringing her back up against him. They swayed in the water, the rocks slippery beneath her feet, but also softened by the moss that covered them. Then he spun her, the water swirling up around them as he did. And she laughed.

Because she didn't think the evening could get more absurd or wonderful. She'd gotten a makeover. And now she was dancing in the river. With the man that she...

Her heart gave another bump.

She was pretty sure she loved him.

And part of her wanted to say it. Desperately. To tell him exactly how she felt, so that he would know. Because she'd been hiding for so long, pushing everything down deep and pretending she didn't feel things she damn well did for an awfully long time.

They stopped moving, and she looked up into his eyes, the word echoing through her body with every beat of her heart.

Love.

Love.

Love.

But what if you're wrong?

And she didn't think she could face that what-if. Because there was every chance she was wrong. Every chance that whatever this moment was, it wasn't love. Not for her. Not for him.

What did she know? She had been a virgin until a couple of weeks ago. And he had given her a lot of firsts. A lot of changes.

It would be easy to mistake that for love. And she wanted to barrel race. And if she barrel raced, she wouldn't be here. And if she wasn't here...then love didn't much matter. So she stretched up on her toes and kissed him, because she knew that was right. And she knew it was true.

"Let's go home," she whispered.

"Okay."

CHAPTER TWENTY-FIVE

GABE KNEW THAT he had put off talking to his mother for longer than was reasonably possible. He was only surprised that his dad hadn't gone in there already. And he assumed that his father's reaction was by design in some way. That he was going to make Gabe be the one to start the fight.

Hank Dalton had never been confrontational. His style was to slink around, then dodge the fire he drew from his wife when the time came. And while he'd changed in some ways for the better, when it came to dealing with Tammy he trod even more carefully than he'd used to.

Last night with Jamie had been like a surreal break from the reality of his actual life. He felt like a dick, using her for that.

As a distraction.

As this beautiful, soft thing that kept him from having to cope with the reality of his situation as long as it suited him.

He sighed heavily and walked into the family house without knocking. He might not live there anymore, but all of them moved freely in and out of the house. Including Ellie and her daughter Annabelle.

And in fact, when he arrived, Tammy was in the kitchen with both Ellie and Annabelle, and they were up to their elbows in making biscuits. Little Amelia looked like a doll, as always, her hair up in a ponytail with an oversize bow over the top of her hairband, her blue eyes large, and mirroring those of her mother. Ellie was standing back, drinking coffee, her golden-blond hair cascading over her shoulders in waves. She looked up at him and smiled when he walked in. "Hi," she said. "I have some more information for you on grants. And ways you can work with the school district."

"Thanks," he replied. "I actually came to talk to Mom."

His mom looked up, brushing flour off her apron. His mom was blonde, too, but hers came out of the bottle, her makeup painted on, her clothes fittingly sparkling. She was nothing if not bedazzled at all times. The Dolly Parton of rodeo wives.

He'd always thought she was the most beautiful woman in the world.

"Sure, honey. Talk away. We just need to get the biscuits in the oven."

"No, Mom," he said. "We need to talk alone."

She frowned. "All right."

She didn't argue, or reiterate the need to put the biscuits in the oven, because of course she had recognized that Gabe was serious in a way he normally wasn't. She rinsed her hands and dried them on a dish towel full of chickens before gesturing out of the kitchen.

They walked into the living room, where there was a large cowhide rug in brown and white spots spread over the floor, a chest masquerading as a coffee table and a massive leather couch with another cowhide rug thrown over the back of it.

Gabe cleared his throat. "I had a fight with Dad."

Tammy frowned. "I hope it wasn't serious."

"It was pretty serious. Just about…my entire adult life. And some of the stuff that went down when I was a teenager."

His mother's face softened. "The horses. I know that hurt you badly when he did that. It hurt me, too. We were going through an awful lot right at that time."

"I know. And that's what I need to talk to you about. Remember when you encouraged me to go into the rodeo… When you told me to do it… You said you'd found out about Dad's secret kids. Boys, you said. You didn't know about McKenna."

"No," his mother said slowly. "I didn't. No one knew about McKenna."

"But you knew about the boys. And you told me that Dad did, too. That Dad was the one who had sent them away. Told their mothers that there was no place for them here."

"Yes," Tammy said, closing her eyes. And that momentary break in her typically smooth composure told Gabe more than anything else ever could.

"I asked Dad about them. The kids. The kids who are my age. Caleb and Jacob's age. He told me he didn't know what I was talking about."

Tammy sank slowly down on the couch. "Did he?"

"He did. So I'm going to ask you, and I need you to tell me straight. Did they ever exist? Or were you just using that to get me to do what you wanted? To get me to hurt him the way that you wanted me to."

"They exist," she said.

"So is Hank lying to me?"

She shook her head, tears filling her eyes. "No. He's not. He never knew about them, Gabe. He never knew about them because the mothers—there were two of them—came to see me while he was gone. They told me my husband was a cheater and they'd had his kids. Kids who were teenagers, and that they wanted money."

"Did you believe them?"

"Not at first. The part where they said your dad was a cheater I knew already. But I couldn't figure out for the life of me why they would've waited all that time to come and try to extort money out of us if they'd known they'd had his kids that whole time. But in both cases, Hank wasn't famous yet. It took them both quite some time to realize the man they'd had one-night stands with all those years ago was the same man winning big pots of money in the rodeo, and landing big endorsement deals. By the time they did, they were strapped for cash." Her lips thinned. "I don't blame them for doing what they did, Gabe. They were protecting their kids. But I had to do the same."

Gabe was unmoved by that. "And you never told him?"

"No. I gave the money and sent them on their way. Money that I had from him. I managed his career, and I managed that, too. I was not going to have those women come in with their bastards and undermine what you boys had."

His mother's words didn't surprise him any particular amount.

"They're my brothers," Gabe said. "It doesn't matter how they got made. The fact of the matter is that he has a responsibility to them."

"I didn't see it that way," she said. "I just wanted things to be fixed."

"That's bullshit, Mom. You didn't. You didn't just want things to be fixed, because then you used me to get revenge on him. You used me to make sure that he would be punished for what he'd done. And you lied to me. You let me think that he ignored his own children. He didn't even know about them."

"And I feel bad about that," she said. "Why do you think I let McKenna into our house so easily? I almost wish she had been one of those boys. So that it would… erase what I did. But that was when everything fell apart, and I was so angry. And when we got back together your father promised me that things would be different. And they have been. How can I tell him I'd done that? *How?*"

Her eyes shimmered with tears, and she moved, giving Gabe a strong hit of that heavy floral perfume she always wore that made his heart ache with the familiarity of it. Because his mom didn't feel familiar right now.

"What about me?" he asked. "You let me… You used me to hurt him."

"He hurt *you*," she insisted. "He hurt me."

"Yes, but if you're going to use me to hurt him back, don't you think I should know the truth?"

"I don't know," she said, her voice trembling. "I don't know what right is in the situation, Gabriel. I don't. I wouldn't do it the same way now. I didn't. When the opportunity came again, I made another choice."

"You and Dad make a lot of choices. A lot of choices to control and manipulate the people around you. And Dad doesn't seem to be able to make the choice to wear a damn condom."

Tammy closed her eyes again, bringing her hands

up to the bridge of her nose and pinching hard. "I'm sorry," she said.

"Yeah, I'm not sure it's going to be enough. I'm going to find them. My brothers. I'm going to find them, and you're going to help me. I need the names of their mothers."

"I don't know that I still have that."

"Bullshit. You have them memorized. You might play a dumb blonde when it suits you, Mom, but we both know you're not. You are a hell of a redneck woman, and you're ruthless when it comes to making people pay, and you don't miss a trick. And the problem is, I know you too well to believe now that you don't have everything planned out in that brain of yours. How did this all get to be such a mess?"

"We are a mess, son," she said. "And over the past fifteen years I think your father and I have tried our very best to atone for some of that."

"I just don't understand. You had no problem having Clint over all the time, basically taking care of him. And I had half brothers out there…"

"Well, your father didn't sleep with Clint's mother."

And that was right there. The heart of it. The worst, ugliest parts.

When there was love involved, it all got crazy. And it got toxic. And his mother, who had a heart big enough to spend her days making biscuits with Clint's widow and his little girl, to treat them both like family, had turned a blind eye to other children who had been in need because she'd been scorned. She'd even been willing to push her son in a direction he didn't want to go to satisfy that need for revenge.

"You know I didn't want to go into the rodeo," he said.

"But you ended up being a champion," she said. "And look at all the money you made. Now you're able to start up this ranch for troubled boys. And if you're so worried about all of that then how can you regret it?"

There was the tough part. He was standing here, the man he'd been molded into by all these years, and he wasn't sure what changing the past fifteen years would even look like.

"I guess I can't," he said. "But I can be as angry as I want to be about the method. And I am. Trust me on that."

He turned and walked out of the living room, walking quickly past the kitchen without saying goodbye to Ellie or Annabelle.

He felt… He felt like a damned fool. And like barbed wire was being twisted around his gut. His mom was the one he'd trusted in all of this. And he'd been so damned vulnerable at the point when all this had come to pass.

Fresh off his breakup, which had taken what he'd believed about himself and turned it on its head. He'd thought he was capable of loving a woman. That he was different than his parents, than his father. He'd thought he was stronger, more mature, more capable of a relationship than either of his parents.

And he'd found out how untrue that was.

How much you could lie to yourself. How much decay you could miss inside your own soul.

And he'd been in desperate need of a chance to prove himself.

And he had to wonder if really he, Caleb and Jacob had always just been pawns for Hank and Tammy to manipulate in their game. Their relationship, which mattered above all else, and somehow mattered more than right, wrong or their own children.

He pressed his hand to his chest and rubbed, and he knew that it was past time to meet with his siblings and have a discussion.

Because the steps they were taking next, from the ranch to the situation with his parents and with the half siblings they didn't know they had, were going to have to include them.

EVEN JACOB CAME down from the mountain. But Gabe had figured that if he had called a family meeting, his siblings were likely to take him pretty seriously.

He told Jamie that he had some things to take care of tonight, and he hadn't elaborated. She'd seemed subdued, which was strange, because Jamie was rarely subdued. It was one of the things he admired about her. But in this case, she had seemed oddly so, and because it was what he had needed from her, he didn't push it.

"Thanks for coming," he said.

They were all here. The Daltons. Such as they were right now. Jacob, Caleb and McKenna. It was going to change, though. It was inevitable. After this everything was going to change.

But he already knew which side McKenna would stand on firmly. And while he didn't know what Jacob's and Caleb's initial reactions would be…it wasn't a discussion. Not really. There was only one right thing to do.

What happened after they did it was up in the air, but reaching out was the only appropriate response in his mind.

And his brothers were never going to be able to stop him from doing it.

"I suppose you're wondering why I called you all here today," McKenna said, her expression comically serious.

"Unfortunately, it's serious," Gabe said.

"You're not dying, are you?" Caleb asked, the tone of his voice indicating that he didn't actually believe Gabe might be dying.

"No. No, that would mean you'd have one less brother. And we're here to talk about the fact that we have two more."

"What?" Caleb asked.

"I'm going to be straight with you, and tell you that I've known about them for a long time."

"You knew?" McKenna asked. "Wait a second. There's two other random kids. Two other random kids that aren't me?"

"Yes."

"And you knew about them all this time, and you didn't…"

"I didn't have any information on who they are or where to find them. I didn't. But I got it today. I got some contact information, not for them, but for the mothers."

"From Dad?"

Gabe gritted his teeth. "From Mom. Dad didn't know."

"What the fuck?" Jacob asked. "You mean, Mom knew that Dad had two other kids? And he didn't?"

"They came to the house to try and get money. Dad was traveling. Mom gave them cash and sent them on their way. They took it and left, and signed an agreement saying they wouldn't come back and ask again."

"Seriously?"

Gabe held up his hands. "I didn't know all that. I knew about the boys. But I thought Dad knew. And

Mom was hurt. And I...I wanted to protect her. I wanted to protect her, because you know how bad he hurt her," he said, directing that at Jacob and Caleb. "You know what it was like for her."

"I'm sure she was hurt," McKenna said. "But those kids..."

"I knew you'd take it hard," Gabe said, looking at McKenna. "I know it feels personal to you."

"Yeah, the only way it could be more personal is if it was actually me. Because it basically was me. Only a year ago."

"Well, Mom would handle it differently now, and she did. She feels... She's not proud of what she did. Not at all."

"Well, she did it. Whether she's proud of it or not."

"Yeah," Gabe said. "But I think it's safe to say that she did change."

He didn't know why he was defending her. Not when he was so pissed off about it himself. Not when he was the one who had been used as a weapon against his father.

"I needed you all to know. Because... I'm going to contact them. I'm going to find out who they are, and I'm going to make sure they know..."

"What? That they're welcome here? That we have room for them?" Jacob said it dryly, but McKenna looked at him with ferocity in her eyes.

"Didn't you have room for me?"

"It was different," Jacob said, not having the decency to look shamed. Because Jacob never did.

"How?" McKenna pressed.

"You're a sister," he said. As if that explained everything.

"It *does* feel different," Caleb said, nodding.

"That's not fair," McKenna said.

"Fair doesn't come into it, McKenna," Jacob said. "Life's not fair."

"How's preaching to the choir going?" she asked dryly.

"I'm not trying to. I'm just saying it feels different. It doesn't mean I don't support Gabe's decision."

"Well, supported or not," Gabe said, "it's what I've decided to do."

"What do you think is going to happen?" Caleb asked. "We are all going to end up one big, happy family taking care of troubled boys on your ranch?"

"Dad's ranch," Gabe said.

"Why? Because…"

"Because I feel damned guilty," Gabe said. "Because I probably could've gotten more information. And you know…if they'd been younger, I probably would have."

"How old are they?"

"Our age."

"Oh, wait a second. Dad was cheating before he had money?" Caleb asked.

"Yeah," he said. "That's the size of it."

"Damn," Caleb said. "I like to pretend that all that went to his head. But even when he was just a regular ranch hand he was out fucking around."

"Yeah," Gabe said. "Pretty much. And that saved them from coming after the money for a while. That and the fact they were married at the time. But eventually they realized they had a potential cash cow on their hands having Hank Dalton's kids."

"Well, that's something," Jacob said, his tone bitter.

"They may not want to be part of this, anyway," McKenna said. "Let me tell you, I had to make a choice not to be angry. So that I could be a part of this. Because I love the three of you, idiots though you are. I'm getting to love Hank, too. And your mom… She's been good to me. This isn't a normal family situation, not by a long shot, but it's the family I have. They may not make that same choice. They may have stepdads that they are just fine with. They might be married and have kids of their own."

"And that's fine. But it needs to be their choice." Gabe shook his head. "I mean, who knows how much they know."

"Yeah, I guess that's true." His brothers cleared out quickly, but McKenna lingered.

"Are you okay?" she asked.

"What kind of question is that?"

"You're changing everything. I mean, your whole life. Don't think I haven't noticed. Deciding to leave the rodeo, establishing this place for the boys. And now contacting half siblings. I just… I guess I want to know why. Is it because you're thinking about settling down with…with Jamie?"

His head snapped up. "No. Jamie's not looking to settle down with anyone, least of all me.

"But if she were?"

He chuckled, but there was no humor in it. "Look at this tangled mass of shit that Mom and Dad have created. Why would I want any part of that?"

"Then why are you…? Why are you doing all of this?"

"Because I need something to do that isn't just being like him. Because I need something to do that isn't just something I did to… Hell, McKenna. Part of today was finding out that Mom pushed me into the rodeo to hurt Dad. She told me that thing about the half brothers to push me into doing that. Children Dad didn't know about. So now I'm going to build a life. One that I'm choosing for myself."

"Do you hear yourself? You want to build a life for yourself, but you don't want to get involved too deeply with Jamie because of Hank and Tammy, and the way they've acted. Is that actually living for yourself?"

"Some of it is about knowing what you are, and what you're capable of. What you're made of."

"Well, in that case, I'm made of a terrified woman who abandoned her daughter, and a man who can't keep it in his pants. So what does that make me?"

"I'm not here for a heart-to-heart, McKenna. Your relationship is yours. And it's unique. And I'm happy for you. But it's got nothing to do with me. Anyway, Grant is a relationship guy. Jamie is not…"

"Well, it's good you know her in her heart and all," McKenna said, her words hard, her expression scrutinizing.

"I'll see you later," he said.

"Oh, I'm being shown the door," McKenna said.

"You know I love you," Gabe said. "I'm sorry if the way I handled this whole thing with the half brothers makes you feel differently."

McKenna shrugged. "It doesn't. Look, people really do change. They do. I've changed a hell of a lot in the past year. I'm not going to hold something against you that you didn't pursue when you were seventeen because you were trying to protect your mom."

"Yeah, I tried."

"It's just a shame they didn't protect you better," she said.

He thought of the conversation he'd had with Jamie not so long ago. When he'd said that his mother hadn't needed to be told to take care of him. When he really stepped in it in terms of sensitivity.

Yeah, Tammy had made him hot chocolate and toast and chicken noodle soup when he was sick.

But she'd done this, too.

And dammit, he didn't understand why people had to be so complicated.

Because on the one hand there was manipulation. And on the other hand there was chicken soup.

And it was difficult to mesh those two things into one person and make it all make sense. But it was all one person, and he called her Mom. And at this point, he didn't know what the hell to do.

CHAPTER TWENTY-SIX

JAMIE FELT LIKE she was having trouble nailing Gabe down. He had gotten weird the day before, saying that he had something to do that evening. And then he had been scarce the couple of days since at work. She'd spent the night at her house, which was reasonable enough; it wasn't like she lived with him. But usually they talked a little bit more.

And so today Jamie was planning an ambush.

She might have experienced a small bit of reformation over the past few weeks, but she was still her. And when she wanted something, she was more than happy to go and get it. Whatever that might be. And so today she was packing camping supplies and a plan. She was going to propose an overnight trip, of the trails they had ridden on earlier. And sex in the woods.

Anyway.

It was her birthday. So she supposed she could probably get him on her team by playing that card.

She never did much for her birthday. It was a strange and complicated time of year and always had been. What with her mother's death happening two days afterward and all. Wyatt and the others would give her a party this weekend. Which would fall after the anniversary of her mother's death. That was the way they usually did it.

It was an unspoken thing.

And she really didn't mind.

But she wanted to do something this year. Because it felt different. Because she felt different. And because she wanted to find a way to connect with him, in spite of the creeping strangeness that she had a feeling pertained to his family. At least, she hoped it did. Because if not, it might have something to do with her. And she just... She didn't want his uncertainty; she didn't want any of that to be about her.

In some ways she'd been happy to let him have his weirdness. Seeing as she'd been wrestling with some things of her own.

That whole love thing.

She really very much didn't want to be in love. Not right now. She was finding herself in so many interesting ways. But the problem was, he seemed to be inextricably linked to it. It wasn't as if she thought all these newfound pieces of herself would go away if she didn't have him. It was just that she thought—no, she knew—that these experiences that were so magical and healing with him wouldn't be the same with anyone else. Wouldn't be the same alone. He was an important part of her life. A catalyst to her self-discovery. She'd lived with her own self without him for nearly twenty-five years, and she hadn't found any of these things. She would never be able to separate that from him.

She tightened up her backpack and walked toward the office, strolling in. He looked up from behind the desk. "Come in," he said dryly.

"Oh, I already did," she said, grinning.

"Yes. You did. And you have a backpack on."

"I do," she said. "And that's not all. In my truck I have a few other things."

He narrowed his eyes. "What other things?"

"A tent," she said.

"A tent," he repeated.

"Yes. Because I thought that we would go camping."

"You want to go camping?"

"Yes," she said, speaking as if he were incredibly slow.

"And what brought this on?"

"I haven't seen you in a few days," she said.

"That's not true. We see each other every day."

"It is true. Because we might see each other every day, but we haven't slept together. And we haven't talked to each other. And it's different. It's been different. Anyway, I missed you."

"Sorry," he said. "Just a lot of stuff going on with… the ranch."

The words that he spoke sounded so heavy that she knew there was more to it, but if he wasn't going to tell her, there was no point badgering him.

She blinked. Well, usually she wanted to badger people endlessly. Whether there was a point or not. But with him, she knew it wouldn't work. And he would only get annoyed. So she had to figure out another way.

"It's my birthday," she said.

"Is it?"

She grinned again. She could only hope that the slight alteration she made in her appearance today made her as adorable as she felt when she left the house this morning. She had put on mascara. She had put her hair into two braids, which she thought looked a little bit fancier. She had also put on ChapStick. Which she sometimes did before her makeover. But it did make her lips kind of shiny.

"Yes," she confirmed, "it's my birthday."

"And the birthday girl wants to go camping?"

"Yes," she said.

She could sense the moment he relented. She'd suspected he wouldn't be able to be stubborn about her birthday. And she had been correct. "Okay. And what do you want for dinner?"

"Fish. And you have to catch them for me."

He laughed. "I didn't realize you were going to put me to work."

"Yes. You have to prove that you're man enough to take care of me. You have to catch me trout."

"Okay," he said. "I assume you have backups with you?"

"Peanut butter and jelly," she said. "But if there's trout, we can have Rice-A-Roni and salad. And rolls. And beer."

"Okay. You convinced me. I think I can take time off work to go up into the mountains with a beautiful woman, go fishing and eat bread."

"Excellent," she said.

"We don't even need to put in a full day here. Let me finish up what I'm doing in the office. There's a spot on the property that will be ideal."

By the time she and Gabe were headed up the mountain in his pickup truck, with all the camping supplies in the back—the ones that she had brought, and a few that he had rounded up—Jamie felt lighter than she had in days. More connected to that moment they had down by the river, which had been so perfect and wonderful.

Except for the inner turmoil it had given her. But she supposed you couldn't have everything.

The spot that he led them to was perfect. A vast field covered in a carpet of purple flowers, with taller yellow ones mixed in. The mountains surrounded them, great, misty-green guardians with a forest spread out before them like soldiers. There was a little path that led down to a small lake, where Gabe expressed confidence there would be trout.

"I'm not eating birthday catfish," she announced as she began to get the necessities out of the back of his truck.

His face contorted. He was still handsome. "I'm not going to catch a catfish."

"In a lake you can't really be sure."

"Well, if I catch one, I'll throw it back."

"That seems mean."

He rolled his eyes. "Do you want birthday catfish or not?"

"*Not.* But I figured maybe you could eat the catfish if you caught it."

He sighed heavily and got out the tent.

"You're pitching a tent for me," she said, barely able to hold back her grin.

"In the metaphorical sense, that's nothing new, Jamie. Glad to set up a literal tent for you, too."

He set the tent out in the middle of the field, next to a cleared-out patch with a fire ring that had clearly been used for camping many times.

"Do your brothers take women up here?"

"You're hoping that *I* don't take women up here," he said.

She shrugged. "Maybe."

"I don't. My parents come up here sometimes. My brothers and I have come up here. I'm pretty sure our friend Ellie and her husband, Clint, used to come up here."

"Ellie's the one who lost her husband," Jamie confirmed.

"Yes."

That made Jamie's heart squeeze tight. She had always known, in a philosophical sense, that her father had lost his wife. But it wasn't until Gabe that she understood what that might mean. They didn't even have children together. She never said that she loved him. He never said he loved her. They weren't married. And yet...

Losing him would devastate her. She would feel like she'd lost part of herself.

She swallowed hard. "Poor thing."

"Yeah. She's strong. She's doing better."

"What about her daughter?"

"She never knew him. Ellie was pregnant when he died."

"Oh," Jamie said, a black hole opening up in her chest. She started hunting around the back of the truck for fishing poles, the rods clattering around against the metal bed.

"I'm sorry," he said. "I didn't mean to say it like that. Like it was easier."

"It is," she said softly.

"Is it?"

"In the sense that I don't know what I'm missing."

He looked at her for a long moment, but didn't press the issue. Then he grabbed the white disposable container of worms and his pole, and she took hers, and the two of them began to walk down toward the lake.

They set up on some rocks a ways from each other and cast out as far as they could. It would've been better to have a boat to fish in a lake, but since they didn't have one, this would do. The place they were standing was a pretty decent drop-off, and Jamie really was concerned that all that she was doing was dragging the bottom and snagging catfish. She reeled back continuously, trying to make sure that her bait didn't snag the bottom.

Her dad had taught her to fish when she was a tiny child. Something she learned that was a part of her now. Muscle memory. Same with horse riding. Same with shooting a gun.

If she'd had a mother, would putting on makeup have been second nature? Would all that have been her secondary skill set? Baking pies, making biscuits.

She would never know.

She sighed heavily.

"What?" he asked.

"Nothing." As soon as she said the word, she wished she hadn't. She'd spent her life not sharing. Holding it all in. She'd never had to do that with Gabe, and she didn't have to do it now. The realization made her feel like a small weight had been lifted from her heart. She didn't have to pretend to answer. She could answer. "Except…the really hard part about losing a parent you don't even remember is that you wonder all the time. What would your life have been like? Who would you have been? That's what I wonder. And I didn't let myself wonder it for a long time. I didn't even let myself think I might want any of the things my mom might have been able to give me."

She reeled her line in, then cast out to the center of the lake again. "I know all the things my dad taught me," she continued softly. "But what would she have taught me? All of us, really. What would have been important to her to have us know? And who else might I have become? Amelia will probably wonder that. She will probably wish that she knew what his voice sounded like. That she could just once know what it was like to be held in his arms. People talk about that. A mother's love. A mother's touch. What it's like to be cradled by your mom when you fall down and get hurt. I don't know what it feels like. I don't know... I don't know what that kind of love feels like. And sometimes I wonder if it means I'm missing something. If I have a hole that can never be filled by anything else."

She turned away from him, and her pole jerked. She yanked up hard, making sure the hook took purchase, before beginning to bring the fish in.

"Fish on," she said as her pole wiggled and resisted against her emotions. She brought him in, a tiny rainbow trout that was barely legal. She dispatched him quickly, and cast her line back out. Before long she and Gabe had caught the daily limit, enough to have themselves more than a decent supper. And some breakfast. They worked in silence, cleaning the fish, and then Gabe got the fire started, and they began to panfry the trout and the rice. Jamie left the cooking to him while she put the salad together and wrapped the rolls in tinfoil, placing them next to the coals to get them warmed up.

When it was done they sat together, eating what

Jamie thought might be the best damned birthday dinner on the face of the planet.

"I know how to do all that," she said, taking a bite of fish and grinning.

"And you do it pretty damn well," he said.

"My dad wanted to make sure that I was never going to go hungry. So I learned how to be self-sufficient." She blinked, unexpected emotion pressing down against her eyes. "I learned how to be self-sufficient. I'm not sure I ever learned how to need anyone. Or...how to be comfortable needing people. And sometimes I...I feel like I really do need people and I don't know how to tell them."

Suddenly, Gabe's arms were around her. She set her plate down on a stump by her feet and let him hold her. "You said earlier you felt like you had a hole. Like you were missing a certain kind of love. But I think... Jamie, I think love is pretty much love. And there's a whole lot of people in your life who love you."

"I wish I had hers." Her throat tightened all the way to closed, and tears started to pour down her face.

She never cried for her mother like this. Because there had never been anyone to answer those cries. She let him hold her, and she cried.

She cried like a motherless child, because that was what she was.

Tears that she'd never allowed to exist, coming from a grief she had told herself was pointless to have.

But maybe, just maybe, some things didn't need to be fixed. Maybe some things just needed to be felt. And this needed to be felt. With all of her. From the deepest part of her soul. And it was like that hole she'd been talking about was filled with tears, filled with pain, but filled. And Gabe's arms held her, rough and tight and comforting. "I need you," she whispered. "I really do need you."

She'd been afraid of this. Of this need. Needing another person. But she needed him, and she'd admitted it. And the world hadn't fallen to pieces. The world was just fine. And she might be a little broken in it, but he was holding her together, so she wouldn't fall apart. Not totally. He angled her head and kissed her, and she let him kiss her. She let him comfort her. Let him see her. See how wounded she was. How badly in need of healing.

She wasn't going to get up and wipe the blood off.

She was just going to bleed for a while. With him.

When Jamie finished crying, they finished dinner in relative silence. They worked together to get everything cleaned up, to get everything that might attract a bear dealt with. Their sleeping bags were already unrolled inside the tent and zipped together, because his mother—though a problem for him right now—had not raised him to be a fool.

He hung a Coleman lantern up in the center of the tent, the light raining down in strange, wavy lines.

While he'd been out making sure the fire was dead, Jamie had changed into soft-looking pajamas, which covered a bit much of her body for his taste, but also looked soft and made him want to touch her. So as far as he was concerned, that was a decent enough trade-off.

He had not brought pajamas. He didn't own pajamas.

He kicked his boots off, pulled his shirt up over his head and stripped off his jeans. She looked up at him, her eyes still a little bit red from crying earlier. "She died two days after I was born," Jamie said.

His gut seized up tight. He had known she died when Jamie was a baby, but he hadn't known it was so close to her birthday.

"I'm sorry," he said.

"Me, too. Really sorry. And I think I've been sorry for a long time, and didn't really let myself feel it. I was afraid because somewhere in all of that I've…I've blamed myself. And I…I feel like I can deal with it all better now. There's something about you that makes me want to…feel things." She laughed, a watery sound. "That sounds really cheesy. But…it's true. It's weird. Nothing like I thought it would be. This whole thing. This whole physical thing."

"Yeah," he agreed.

He didn't know why, but the way she said that made his stomach get all tight.

"Is everything all right with you? With your family?"

"Yeah," he said.

He brushed that off, and she looked hurt. And it made him miss the Jamie she had been a few weeks ago, who would have probably just taken him at his word, and not notice that he was holding anything back.

He had liked that about Jamie. That she seemed invincible.

She didn't now. And she was blaming him for that. And he wasn't sure he was up to the task of handling the responsibility of Jamie when she wasn't made of Teflon and bravado. But then she was crossing the space between them and kissing him, and he couldn't think. This woman… She knocked him on his ass.

She wasn't like anyone or anything that had come before her.

"You're like Annie Oakley," he said.

He felt her mouth curve against his. "Straight shooter who never misses?"

"Yeah. Like some kind of strange that only comes around once every hundred years. Some kind of magic."

She looked dazed, and again, he had to wonder what the hell he was playing at. Same as he had wondered when he'd taken her down to the river. Danced with her in the water.

She made him feel like he had just been introduced to a part of himself he didn't know existed. But he knew it was alive. All that romance and shit wasn't in him. Not really. Not sustainably.

That was the problem. He knew better. Knew people didn't change without putting themselves and those around them through a lot of broken glasses, sweat and tears.

And that what was in your blood… Well, it stayed.

His father might have changed, but his mother was a liar.

He didn't know what the hell his life was.

Then she stripped her shirt off, and he couldn't think.

Her breasts were small and perfect, so close to his chest, he wanted to crush her to him so that he could feel her body in that way.

He didn't know if he'd ever get enough of touching her. It didn't seem to be possible.

She pressed her hand to his chest. Her hands… They were all Jamie. Just like her. Delicate in their way, but strong. Soft skin, but calloused in places, from all the work that she did.

A true kind of cowgirl who didn't shy away from any challenge.

Who rode horses better than anyone he'd ever seen. Who sensed what the animals felt.

Who'd brought him back to a place where he did, too.

Who looked beautiful with her hair and her makeup done, and knew how to catch and clean a fish. Who looked beautiful without makeup, and with nothing at all.

Strong as steel and hard as flint. And wept in his arms.

And somehow gave him the feeling it was the only place she cried.

And that should terrify him. But it didn't.

Because there was just no damned way to be terrified when Jamie Dodge had her hands on his body.

He kissed her and captured her hands in his, laying her back on the sleeping bags, the motion rocking the tent, rocking the lantern above them, stripes of white dancing over her body, teasing him, giving him glimpses without revealing all. He lowered his head and sucked her nipple deep into his mouth. She was beautiful. Was it possible she hadn't always known that? He could barely believe it.

And he certainly didn't deserve any kind of adoration or credit for that. And yet she seemed to give it to him. And he didn't want her to stop, because he wanted all that adoration.

The way she looked at him...

Like his hands were magic and like his mouth had

told her the secret to life… Well, no man was ever going to want that to stop.

He moved his fingertips slowly down her stomach, to the waistband of those flannel pajamas, and he made quick work of those, leaving her naked before him, watching as the light painted shapes over her skin. And then letting his hands trace the path. Tasting her, touching her. Listening to every sigh, every moan, every sound she made. She was a revelation. And he wished…

He wished that he could be the man that she seemed to think he was. The way she looked at him… He didn't know a man that deserved to be looked at like that.

He couldn't have her forever. And he knew it. But he could have her tonight. Bathed in light and nothing else, and he would damn well take it.

She was different. His hard-riding girl who didn't mind if things got sweaty, didn't mind if things got rough.

Tonight she was soft. Open.

And it made his knees weak.

It made him weak all through.

And when he thrust inside her body he was lost. And found, all at the same time.

It was a fitting thing, because it was just like Jamie herself. That soft, strong creature made of contradiction and glory. She was a woman who might wonder what she could have been, but in his mind, there was no doubt she knew who she was. And for a man who had lost that anchor, who had no earthly clue what tethered him to his life anymore, what the hell choices had brought him to where he was, it was a beautiful, terrible thing.

Jamie was almost ten years younger than he was. But she was so much more grounded in many ways.

He had done what he'd done to protect his mother. To get back at his father.

But part of him wondered…just for a moment…if what he'd really been protecting was himself. But that revelation got lost on a tide of pleasure, on a whole ocean of longing that pulled him under and made him its slave. She arched against him, crying out, her body pulsing around him, her orgasm drawing his own out. This time together had been making love, and it had been remarkably different from anything else he'd ever done.

But this orgasm wasn't gentle. Wasn't a calm, easy pulse of pleasure. It was fearsome, and it was deadly, savaging him down to the bone. Leaving him less than he'd been before, and somehow more.

Like she'd stripped every last ounce of bullshit right out of the way, and left behind nothing but him.

And he was desperate to hold on to it, to hold on to her. Because this was the closest thing to a glimpse at certainty he'd had in days. When they finished, he was spent, and after taking care of the protection, they both fell asleep wrapped around each other.

When he closed his eyes all he saw was a woman, riding her horse through the field, her hair blowing in the wind.

CHAPTER TWENTY-SEVEN

WHEN JAMIE WOKE UP, she was warm, nestled against Gabe's body. Her face was cold, thanks to the biting mountain air, though.

If not for that, she might have forgotten that they were camping.

Well, that and the hard ground. But she was so comfortable with Gabe that she barely registered it. She sighed heavily, sitting up and rubbing the sleep from her eyes. Then she leaned forward, unzipping her tent, revealing the broad expanse of field and mountains before them, the sun just cresting over the trees, creating a rose-gold ring that lined the ridges there.

She took a breath, looking all around them, and then back at the man still sound asleep in her tent. Her aspiration suddenly felt flipped. Because somehow, life right here felt complete. And she could imagine existing here. Just here. With him.

This was all that love-changing-you stuff, she imagined.

It wasn't that she didn't want to barrel race anymore. Of course she did. She wasn't just going to change her thoughts on that because she...

Well, she loved Gabe.

She snuggled back down in the sleeping bag with him, enjoying the view, and enjoying touching him.

She supposed everybody who was stricken down with love had that thought, though. That they could be completely happy, out in the middle of nowhere, removed from the reality of life.

It was life that worried her.

She turned over onto her side and examined his face. When he slept, the lines in his face weren't as deep. As if some of the tension and pain he carried around with him when he was awake lifted when he dreamed.

He was such an intensely beautiful man.

The strong slash of his dark brows, his dark lashes. That mouth. She wanted to lick it. All the time. She'd never understood the giggling obsession girls around her in high school had had with boys.

She felt like giggling around Gabe. She felt obsessed.

He stirred, opening his eyes, those blue eyes hitting her somewhere deep in her soul. "Good morning."

"Good morning," she said. "Thank you for yet again holding me through another emotional breakdown."

"Sorry that there wasn't any hot chocolate."

"The trout was pretty good. And anyway, we can have some campfire coffee this morning."

"Can we?"

She stretched. "Yes," she said, some of the stretch lingering in her voice. "But one of us has to go out in the cold and start the fire."

"I think that falls under the purview of pioneer woman."

"No," she said stubbornly. "I think that's men's work."

"No, pretty sure men chop wood, and women stoke fires. The wood has been chopped. So…"

"That's not chivalrous," she pointed out.

"Oh, I didn't know you wanted chivalry. I thought you were a strong, independent woman."

"I'll bite you," she said.

"I don't think you—"

She sank her teeth into his shoulder and he growled, before climbing out of the tent, stark naked, and heading outside. "I'll light the fire. But only because you're crazy."

She smiled, enjoying the view. Who would have ever thought that she, Jamie Dodge, would someday go camping and get to watch the most perfect male specimen she had ever seen start a campfire in the buff. It was a triumph that she hadn't even known she might want to achieve.

"Be careful," she warned as he got a flame going. "You have some very extreme exposure happening there."

"Don't worry," he said. "I promise to protect all relevant parts of me. There is no way you can be more concerned about it than I am."

"Hmm," she said, "I think I can give you a run for concern there."

"Yeah, I don't know," he said.

Silence fell between them for a space, and Jamie decided she couldn't let it go, not anymore.

"Are we going to talk about what's wrong?" she asked.

"What?" he asked, getting the flame lit, and getting the blue-and-white-speckled pot placed over the flame.

"What's going on with your family?"

The lines in his body went hard, all of his muscles tensing up. "There's no need for us to have a discussion about that."

"I'd like to."

"It's all related to the bullshit with my dad."

"Yeah," Jamie said. "I'm not all that surprised to hear that. But...I would like to know what exactly happened that's kept you so busy that you couldn't see me over the past few days."

"It's nothing."

"Did you talk to your mom?"

"Jamie, it doesn't matter."

"It matters," she said. "It matters because I...I care about you. And we've been sharing all this family stuff. All of it. I just...cried a trail of snot on you yesterday over a plate of trout. I think that you can say that I'm a safe space for you to tell me whatever's going on with you."

He laughed. "I don't need a safe space."

"Everybody needs a safe space," she said.

"Okay," he said. "Yeah, I talked to my mom."

"And?" He turned to face her, his broad, naked back toward the mountains, his...everything facing her. There was something incongruous about the picture.

Gabe naked in the open air like that, as if he had nothing to hide, when she could feel the walls going up between them.

"I understand if it hurt you..." she began.

"My dad didn't know about the kids. She did. She hid it from him. She used me. Does that satisfy your curiosity?"

She frowned. "No. I mean, I guess. But there's nothing satisfying about that. Gabe, I'm sorry."

"You don't need to be," he said. "I mean, it is what it is."

"What are you going to do?"

"There's only one thing to do. I'm going to write some letters. I'm going to see who I can find."

"Well, that's...good. That's a good thing to do."

He made a grunting sound.

"I'll help you," she continued.

He shook his head. "You don't need to help me."

"Why not? I'm helping you with the ranch. I'm helping you get everything set up to bring those boys on. Why can't I be involved in this, too?"

"McKenna, Jacob, Caleb and I are handling it."

She was so frustrated she wanted to scream. She wanted to take care of him. She didn't want to do that strong, silent Dodge thing and ignore the pain. Cover it up, and pretend that it was being self-sufficient. Pretend that that was the way a family should take care of each other.

"Secrets and dividing lines are the ways messes like this start," she said.

He frowned. All those lines that had seemed lighter in sleep seemed more pronounced now. "What the hell does that mean?"

"It's all about keeping things from each other. And not being able to talk about feelings."

"You just started talking about feelings two weeks ago, and now you're lecturing me about mine?"

She shook her head. "Every problem I've seen in my family has come down to secrets. Sure, there were things we couldn't control. Things like my mother's death. But everything else... The reason that Wyatt left, the reason that Bennett didn't have his son... Secrets. But you have to break the cycle somehow."

"That's what I'm doing," he said.

"While also building walls between you and me."

"You're not my family."

The words hurt. So damn bad, and she couldn't for the life of her figure out why, when they were true; she wasn't his family. She was just…the woman he was sleeping with. And maybe for him that really didn't mean anything. Even now. It had been tempting for her to make it into something, because it felt like a hell of a lot to her. But he'd never promised anything more than this, and she was the one who had changed. She was the one whose feelings had changed.

"I know," she said, the words muted. "But *I'm* something. I'm something, and it feels like that should matter."

"You can't help me with it," he said.

She was tempted to shut her mouth then. Tempted to let it go. Because that was what she'd always done, when she'd been a kid. She'd shut her mouth, and let it go. She'd picked herself up and told no one she was in pain.

She let the anniversary of her mother's death go by without saying anything. Had dealt with getting her period. And not told a soul.

Had watched her brother grieve his wife for eight years, without pushing into that pain.

Had let Wyatt carry the burden of the rift between him and their father, and let him stay quiet about it.

Had never pushed into Bennett's facade of the perfect life to find out why control was so important to him.

Because that was how the Dodges had cared for each other.

Giving each other space.

And it hadn't helped a single one of them work their shit out. In each and every case it had taken a person busting into their lives and pushing.

So Jamie was ready to push. Not just to be right.

Some things in the world couldn't be fixed.

But some things could. And she had a feeling that wisdom was all about knowing when to push on what could be healed.

She could only hope that in this moment she had some wisdom, and not just stubbornness.

"Your mom lied to you. None of that's fine. None of this is okay. And if you're not okay with it, that's to be expected. Why would you ever just accept this?"

"There's not another choice."

"Let me help you. I might not be family, but I'm here now."

"How are you going to help me?"

"I don't know. I could always just be with you."

As offers went, offering herself was a damn scary thing. Because there was every chance that he would just laugh at that.

"Whatever you need to do," he said, shrugging. "Coffee's on."

She had won the argument, more or less, but she didn't particularly feel like she had, seeing as his acquiescence wasn't in any way cheerful.

"We gotta have that coffee," he said. "So we can get going."

Jamie nodded slowly. "Okay."

If there was one thing she knew how to do, it was clinging to something with tenacity.

She didn't always feel like she had the best set of skills when it came to dealing with this man. But she sure knew how to hold on. And right now holding on might be the best thing she could do.

CHAPTER TWENTY-EIGHT

IT TOOK TWO days for him to find an address for Leonora Caldwell. She lived two hours down the five, to Cottage Grove.

Close enough that Gabe thought it might be the thing to do to pay her a visit.

He knew that when Jamie found out about the whole thing she would want to go with him, but he was struggling with the point of including her. She wanted to, but there was no reason.

What they had was temporary. Temporary was all he was good for.

And all those things he'd done with her lately, the things that went beyond sex and a good time, he was concerned that they'd muddied the waters. He'd hardly been able to say no to her birthday camping trip idea, but this… Yeah, he wasn't going to tell her about it. And she would be pissed later, but well, he'd deal with that when he had to deal with it.

He hightailed it out of the ranch before running into her that morning, stopping for coffee at The Sugar Cup before getting on the road. And when he pulled his truck up to the dilapidated house on the very end of a dead-end street, fury ignited his blood.

Whatever money his mother had given to this woman clearly hadn't been enough.

And then there was ,ury at himself.

That he hadn't done anything for them when he had been told of their existence. Sure, he might not have been given a name, but that didn't fully absolve him.

Of course, fifteen years ago, it hadn't been quite so easy for someone to just look up an address at home, but that was beside the point.

He put his truck in Park, grateful that there was a run-down car in the driveway. It meant that someone might be home.

He walked up to the front door, his hands stuffed in his pockets, and then he knocked, rocking back on his heels while he waited.

It took a few minutes, but then the door opened, a thin, young-looking woman answering. It surprised him how young she looked, though he supposed she could be his mother's age. Her hair was dark and neat, her frame slim. She was tiny, only coming up to the bottom of Gabe's chin. She had no makeup on, which added to her youthful appearance. "Can I help you?"

"Are you Leonora Caldwell?" he asked without preamble.

"You're not going to serve me papers or anything, are you?" There was a glint of steel in her eyes. And it let him know that no matter how young she looked, she was a woman who'd done a lot of living.

"No," he said. "I'm not going to do that."

"I'm Leonora Caldwell."

"I'm Gabe Dalton. I'm Hank Dalton's son."

A parade of emotions went through those dark eyes. Disbelief, hurt. Anger. Then she made a scoffing sound. "Oh, you're his real son, then."

"I'm his son just like any other he's responsible for. I'm looking for my half brother."

She straightened, tilting her pointed chin upward. "Why are you looking for him?"

"Because I figure it's time someone in my family tried to do right by the both of you. And if that has to be me, then it's me."

"Well, don't stress yourself out none."

"You should've been treated better than you were."

She looked around. "You're not going to yell at me for having an affair with your father?"

"My father had more than one affair. As you well know. And he's responsible for his own behavior. He's the one who made vows to my mother, not you. And ultimately, while I don't blame my mother for trying to keep you away from him, trying to protect what little she did have, it wasn't the right thing to do. She shouldn't have done it. We should have had the chance to get to know our half brothers. And so, I want to make sure I fix that. And I want to make sure that…when it comes to inheritance, and all of that…he deserves a cut when the time comes. Because if the money is Hank's, and not ours, and it's going to his children… then that should include all his children."

"Well, aren't you an honorable one," she said, her voice tight. "That's a surprise."

"I'm not honorable. I'm Hank's son, through and through. But I'm trying to do the right thing here."

"Well, he doesn't live here anymore. He's in Texas. I don't have his current address, but if you want to try to get in touch with him his name is West Caldwell."

"Can you get in touch with him?"

She shook her head. "We are not on speaking terms."

"I'm sorry to hear that," he said.

"Family," she said. "What are you going to do?"

"You're telling me," Gabe said. "Here's how you can contact me. If you need anything. You're right. Family's complicated. But in a way, you're part of mine."

Gabe was glad he had the whole drive back to the ranch to get a handle on himself.

JAMIE HAD TAKEN every single horse out for a brief ride—very brief—but every single one, and was getting antsy by the time Gabe's truck pulled into the property. She didn't know why, but she had a strange feeling of intense anxiety over his whereabouts. The fact that he hadn't answered her texts hadn't helped.

It wasn't like she didn't expect him to have other things going on, but normally, he would have just answered the text and told her where he was, rather than ignoring her, or being all cloak-and-dagger. Which was what this felt like. The fact that he hadn't been at the ranch when she had arrived that morning had seemed... Well, it was weird. And she had no real reason to think that, except that her gut was telling her it was a little bit messed up. And she was going to have to go with her gut on this one. She put Gus away, and then walked out to the front of the barn, hands on her hips. "Where have you been?"

"I went to talk to Leonora Caldwell."

She frowned. "I don't know who that is."

"The mother of one of my half brothers."

She blinked. "I thought you were going to... I thought I was going to help with that?"

"I found her easy enough, and I didn't see the point to trouble you."

This was all becoming unbearable. All of this intimacy had been built between them. And it had... It had changed her. On a fundamental level. It had altered who she was, and how she felt about things. It had opened up the door to a piece of her she hadn't known was there, and with it, she'd been flooded with all these new desires, hopes and dreams.

And now he was pulling away, and it was killing her. And there was only one thing she could think to do, one thing that had been tugging at her for at least a week now. And she'd been avoiding it. Avoiding it because she was afraid. Because she was afraid of being wrong, afraid of being hurt.

But she... She'd cried on Gabe. On her birthday.

And she'd let herself hurt for her mother. And she hadn't worried much about whether or not she deserved it. She had just let herself have it.

And that Jamie—that Jamie who had found a way to crack open all that armor she spent a lifetime building— she thought that the risk might just be worth it. That no matter what happened...

That honesty with vulnerability was different than shoving your opinions out on everyone and insisting you were right.

She considered that honesty for years. But it wasn't. It was layers and layers of steel with some true things placed over the top of it, but there was no softness for anyone else's pain to land on. There was no crack so that their response could find any purchase inside her. Her version of honesty had been something that went in one direction.

"I wanted to help you," she said softly.

"Why? I didn't need it. There wasn't any point."

"There doesn't have to be a point," she said, looking up at him, dirty from the day, sweaty and clammy beneath her tank top. It was the worst possible time to be having this conversation, but she didn't know what else to do. And she didn't know when else to have it.

Because unless something changed, things weren't going to get better. He was slipping further and further away from her. Like all of this intimacy that had happened had been an accident on his end, and now that he realized it he wanted to make sure that it stopped.

"I love you," she said.

He looked at her, those electric-blue eyes gone hard. "What?"

"I love you. That's the point. When you love somebody, you just want to be involved in their lives. And you know what? I haven't let myself do that. I love my brothers, and there was still a wall between us. There's been a wall between me and my friends, me and my father. All because… All because I couldn't deal with the loss of that first love, that I wouldn't even let myself grieve. It's all self-protection, and it's bullshit. It doesn't protect you from anything. It just keeps you lonely. I don't want to be lonely. I want to take care of you, and I want you to take care of me, because that's how you love people. Because that's how you find some closeness. That's how you erase some of the loneliness that we all carry around in our souls. Believe me, I'm a champion at figuring out ways and reasons to not let people close. But I just can't do it anymore. I can't."

"Jamie, look at the shitshow my family is. I am not in any place to love someone, and, honey, that's not what you want, either."

She wasn't sure what she'd expected, but it wasn't

that. That paternal, ridiculous tone. Him telling her that she didn't want to be in love.

And regardless of the other changes that had taken place inside her over the past few weeks, she still didn't like being told what to do.

She never would.

That was one thing she was sure about.

"No," she said. "I'm pretty clear on the fact that I'd like to be in love with you."

He pinched the bridge of his nose. "You want to barrel race."

"Kate Monaghan barrel races. Sierra Thompson barrel races. Nothing stops them from it. Having a husband, even having children, doesn't stop them."

"Yeah, and it didn't stop my father, either. But then, having a wife and children didn't stop him having affairs."

She blinked, trying to process the meaning of his words. "And you think I'm going to have affairs?"

He sighed, the sound tired, weary. The sound of a man much older than thirty-three. "I believe that at some point, my genetics are just going to catch up with us. Look at my family. My mother lied to me, manipulated me. My father deserved basically everything he ever got."

"They made bad choices," she said. "Your blood doesn't make you go out and cheat on your wife, Gabe."

"I don't know about that."

She was stunned just then, by the unfairness of it. Of him acting like there was no choice. They were alive. They were alive and well and they could be together. And God knew what was up ahead, but they could have *now*.

Except he was a damned coward.

"You know what your blood does?" she asked. "Sometimes it makes a clot after you have a baby. And that clot travels into your lung and kills you. You don't have any choice over that. My mother didn't have any choice over that. That's something you can't fight. That's something real. Blood doesn't make you cheat."

"Then maybe it's all about what you learn," he said. "And I sure haven't learned how to be a husband. I sure haven't learned how a relationship is supposed to look."

"And I have? Look at me, learning all of these things."

"You don't understand, Jamie. I am like my dad."

"Right, as evidenced by the trail of broken hearts in your wake? You even told me that the first time we had sex, how you have this act and you only sleep with women you can't hurt and..."

"I had one girlfriend in high school. After Dad sold the horses. I put all that feeling into her, and I made her promises. I was going to make a life with her. The life we wanted. Her parents sucked, and she wanted— She dreamed of making a life with me. I thought I was immune to acting like my dad. I hated my dad right then. And then what did I do? I had unprotected sex with her."

Jamie's breath felt like it had been sucked from her body. "Oh... I..."

"And then her period was late and she thought she might be pregnant, and do you know what I wanted to do? I wanted to run. As far and fast as I could."

She swallowed hard, trying to collect herself. "Gabe, anyone would want to do that. I would want to do that if I found out I was... I mean, let's not even talk about that. But I think everyone gets scared when something like that happens."

Her heart was pounding hard and she was fighting against the fierce need to demand the details of what had happened.

She felt scarred and battered from just hearing he'd had unprotected sex with someone else. She knew he had a past, but he was hers and she didn't like thinking about it.

"Well, I sure as hell didn't get down on one knee. A few days later she got her period. False alarm. And I was so damned relieved. She was devastated. The fight we had... That girl kicked a dent in the side of my truck that someone her size shouldn't have been able to accomplish. I screamed at her because she was being crazy, and before I knew it, I was...standing out of my body looking at my parents. And that was when I knew. I was just...I was just gonna be part of that cycle. I'm not different. I'm not better."

"You are, though," she said. "You are. Look, you made this whole life for yourself..."

"Because my mom told me about my dad's other kids, and coming off what had happened with Trisha, I wanted to make him pay. Because you hate the ugliness you see in yourself most of all, don't you? I'm not any better than he is."

"Yes, you are, but you're bizarrely committed to the idea that you aren't. You're scared," she said. "So I want you to just be honest about that. You don't want to do it because you're scared. And I understand that, Gabe, because it's a whole hell of a thing. But pushing me aside isn't going to help you. Not in the long run.

Hiding from it all… It's not going to make anything better. Believe me. I know."

"You're going to lecture me with the best wisdom of your twenty-six years and one lover, Jamie?"

That hurt. Stabbed her right in the heart and made her eyes sting. "How dare you use that against me? You experienced all this with me. How dare you minimize it? And make me into…just a twenty-six-year-old virgin, or whatever. It was more than that. This is more than that. And you know it. And you never saw me as somebody beneath you in experience, or silly because of my age, and you never acted like I was. So don't go pull it out now when it's convenient for you. I want… I'm so tired of this. I'm so tired of living a life that makes me feel alone. I just want… I don't want to stay the same. I want to change. You changed me. And that's what I want. And I want…I want to change *you*. The way that you did me. It's not fair. It's not fair for me to have lost all my armor. To be all cracked open, and crying all the time, and for you not to have changed at all."

"It's like you said," he said slowly. "When you haven't experienced things before, sometimes you don't know all there is left to learn. You have more to learn than me, Jamie. That's just a fact. I've lived more. That's not me insulting you, or using your inexperience against you. It's just how it is. It's how it is, honey, and I'm not trying to be a dick about it. But it's life."

"Don't you dare," she said, her voice shaking. "Don't you dare lecture me. You…you coward."

She was firing on all cylinders now, and she could feel it.

Could feel the old her rising up inside like granite,

but this version of her was different still. She was full of sharp edges and pain, and she wanted to use those edges to hurt him back.

Because she was Jamie Dodge, and she didn't want to cry for a man, not one she'd cried for so many times already. She had given him every damn thing.

Everything.

And he was just going to stand there and stare at her with those blue eyes. He was just going to stand there and let her brother be right. About the fact that she was just going to get her heart broken. And she was going to have to face the fact that at the end of the day, she was vulnerable to it just like everyone else, and she hated it. She hated it, and she didn't want to let it be true.

"You don't know what you're doing right now, any more than you knew how to handle Gus when I first showed up at the ranch. You're being…you're being an absolute ass!" she shouted, her heart thundering, her hand shaking. "You're afraid to make a damn choice. Because then it might be your fault if you fail. It was easier to go into the rodeo to piss off your old man, and then blame him for all the success that's been thrust on you over the years. *Poor you,* Gabe. *Poor fucking you.*"

She could feel her emotions completely spinning out of control, and there wasn't a damn thing she could do to stop them. He was protecting himself, and so she wanted to hurt him. Wanted to hurt him the way he was hurting her.

"Both your parents are involved in your lives, and they're not perfect, but you could talk to them, and you could deal with it," she continued. "My mom is dead. And that's it. There's nothing I can do about that. There's no way that I can have that back. I think of it every time the anniversary comes around." He looked stricken by the mention of it. "There's no way I can have it at all. And you can have me. You could. But you won't, because you're too damn scared. And you're hiding again. Behind all these excuses. You're a big, tough guy. Big Mr. Alpha, out riding the rodeo and banging groupies and starting a ranch for troubled boys. Help your damn self. You're the most troubled boy around here."

She spun on her heel and started to walk away, and he grabbed hold of her arm and pulled her toward him, pressing a kiss on her mouth.

And oh, she wanted to sink into it. Into him. Let that kiss swallow up all the words that they'd spoken. Even her words of love. To go back and pretend that the past few minutes were nothing.

That this kiss was everything.

The only thing.

But she couldn't do that.

She struggled against him, hitting his chest with her closed fist. "Don't kiss me. Don't kiss me if you don't love me. Don't touch me if you don't love me. Hell, don't even talk to me if you don't love me." She was shaking, rage pouring through her like a river. "Because I deserve better than that. Because I had to figure out what giving everything meant. And then once I did I offered it to you. I changed. And I dug deep. And I found pieces of myself I didn't even know were there for you. And you want to stand there and tell me everything I don't know. Want to tell me what I want, and how you have less growing to do. That's bullshit, and I'm not here for it."

"If you really did it for me, Jamie," he said, his voice

rough, "that was your first mistake. Because I didn't ask you to."

"I didn't need you to," she said. She lifted her chin, her expression defiant. "Some people don't need to be asked."

"Jamie, you're going to be a hell of a lot happier if you go do your barrel racing, live your dream, and then when you're finished, find a guy your own age."

"Oh, you think that I want your advice? Is that what you've been thinking this is? I give you advice about horses, you give me life advice that I didn't even ask for? That's not how this is going. That's not...that's not what this is. I love you. You big, stupid, scared... asshole idiot."

"If that's what you think I am, what you know I am, shouldn't you be happy to let me go?"

"No, jackass. I love you knowing that you're all that. *I love you*, and it's not about life experience. I thought... When we were out camping I thought that I could have happily stayed out there with you forever. And then it hit me—that's the problem. I think anyone could be in love for life if they were just separated out of the real world. Away from family. Away from problems. Away from work. Conflicting schedules, and all of that. But I love you here. I love you even though I'm mad that you didn't include me when you went to talk to your half brother's mom. Because I would've helped you. And even if I couldn't have helped you, I would have been there for you. Because that's what you do when you're in love. When you're really in love."

His lip curled, a growl rumbling through his chest. "How do you know? How do you know it's real? Because let me tell you, Jamie, I think my dad thought it was real. But he never kept it in his pants once. My mom thought it was real, but she's let herself stay in this…toxic, ridiculous relationship. She's had fifteen good years with him. These past fifteen. In thirty-five of pain. So you tell me, how do you think you know it's real?"

"Because I'm choosing. Believe me, when you're as protected as I am, when your heart is as hard as mine… you have to choose to fall in love. And I did. Because I could see what was over there. I could feel myself… I could feel myself. *Me.* And not this person that I forced myself to be who was brave and strong, and didn't need anybody. I *want* to need someone. I want to need you. Because…needing you has made me feel more things, deeper things, than I even thought were possible. And I don't care if it hurts. I mean, I would rather it didn't. But it's better than feeling nothing. It's better than feeling alone."

The terrain inside her seemed to shift, and as it did, her rage seemed to shift, as well. A sense of heaviness, of sadness, joining it now. "You make choices, Gabe," she said, the words softer. "And if you *can't* make choices, life will make a few for you, but then you can't bitch when you wake up one day all by yourself, realizing that your glory days are behind you in every sense of the word. All because you didn't reach out and grab better when you had the chance."

She waited. She waited for him to say something. She waited for him to step forward and kiss her. She waited for him to tell her to stay with him. She waited, as her anger drained away and a sense of futility filled her body, her limbs getting weak.

She waited, and he didn't speak. His blue eyes had

gone glacial, and then something shifted in them. A dawning realization, and she knew, in her gut, that it wasn't one she was going to enjoy.

"I went into the rodeo to hurt my father," he said. "But do you know what I actually found out?"

"What?" she asked, the word whispered.

"I *am* my father. I wanted to be different. I thought I would choose something different. Ranching. It's inevitable, though. I ran from the frying pan to the fire. From the potentially knocked-up girlfriend to the rodeo. Once I got a taste of glory, that's all I wanted. Do you think I said no to any women who threw themselves at me? Because I didn't. On the night you found me in the bar, I would've slept with that woman, Jamie. Even though I wanted you. It didn't matter. Sex has been cheap for me for as long as I can remember. And that's… I'm not different. I'm never going to put myself or any woman in the position that my mother is in. I'm standing here hurting you right now, and you would be signing up for a lifetime more of that. And I just don't want to do it. You shouldn't want to do it, but you don't know better, because you didn't see it. So I'm going to be the one to tell you. To tell you that you don't want it. To tell you what you do want. And that might make you mad, but you have to understand. I watched it. And I will never be part of putting someone through that."

"So choose not to," she said.

"That's what I'm doing. Whether you can see it or not, that's what I'm doing."

"Well, from here it looks a whole lot like running," she said.

"You can think what you like."

"You have to tell me you don't love me," she said, facing him head-on. "You have to tell me."

"Why?"

"Because I'm not going to let you take the coward's way out. I'm not going to let you try to make this about me not knowing what I feel. I'm not going to let you talk all around it. You better look me in the eye and tell me you don't love me, Gabe Dalton. Because if you can't do that then why should I walk away?"

"Love doesn't mean anything. My dad tells my mom he loves her all the time. He did it before they were married. When they got married. When he would come out of the bed of another woman. What the hell does love mean either way?"

"Say it," she said, crossing her arms. "I dare you."

"I don't love you, Jamie. I'm not the kind of man who falls in love."

She steeled herself against the words, let them glance off her like a blow. She swallowed hard, her hand shaking. "Then I think we're done here."

"I think it would be best. It was good working with you, Jamie."

"You don't need me anymore?"

She kept a sharp eye on his face. "I'll manage."

"You either could have managed without me before, or not. So which was the lie?"

"Just go, Jamie."

She turned, feeling strangely numb, her feet feeling disconnected from the earth as she walked on. And in her head, that refrain rang on.

Stand up. Wipe the blood off.
Stand up. Wipe the blood off.
Don't cry. Don't cry.

She got in her truck and closed the door, starting the engine and heading down the road. She didn't look back, her shoulders held straight, her body stiff. And it wasn't until she made it a few miles down the highway that the first tear rolled down her face. And another. Then another.

She pulled over to the side of the road and put the truck in Park, burying her face in her hands, a sob breaking through her body.

She couldn't stop. She couldn't get up.

She couldn't just wipe the blood off and go on. There was no Band-Aid for a wound like this. There was nothing to stanch the flow of misery that was pouring through her. She cried, cried and cried, and the whole time she kept thinking about the realization she'd had on the camping trip. Some things couldn't be fixed. But they had to be felt.

And losing the man you loved… You had to feel it.

She had always thought that something like this was a weakness. Something that she would never fall prey to.

But she realized as she sat there on the side of the road, the highway on one side and a wall of pine on the other, that this was the strongest damn thing she'd ever done.

She *felt* this. And it was terrifying.

Because what if she never felt okay again?

This was what she'd been protecting herself from all of her life. She hadn't wanted to feel the grief of the loss of her mother, because it might never end. She hadn't wanted to be soft because then she might be easily damaged.

She hadn't wanted to be in love, because she might lose it.

But she couldn't stop this, and she couldn't cover it. So she had to live in it. Pain broke over her like a wave, as intense as any pleasure that Gabe had ever given her.

This, she realized, was strength.

Opening your heart even when it might be wounded. Feeling all this, even when it might bring only pain. It was the one thing that Gabe wouldn't allow himself to do.

He was a coward.

But at the moment she envied him just a little bit. Because he was still standing, and she was the one crying by the road.

But in the end, she was the one who was strong. And he was still hiding.

Though at the moment that was cold comfort, indeed.

CHAPTER TWENTY-NINE

GABE DIDN'T HAVE any time to overthink the way Jamie had left earlier. He had shit to do...

Ellie came by his office with a folder filled with information and program ideas.

"I talked to some people down at the district, and they're very supportive of the program. They have some suggested students already. Meanwhile, I've put inquiries out elsewhere and there are some parents and officials who also have kids they'd like to have here. Rather than doing detention, what they would like to do is get the kids who earn what would typically be referrals into doing ranch work for two hours after school. They would bus them over, and what you would have to do is basically do work training. An outdoor art class is another thought, working with various mediums. Eventually, when you have kind of a halfway house set up, I would be able to teach classes. The boys could go part-time to Gold Valley High and to the middle school, and they could go part-time here. What we would do is kind of a hands-on project-based learning. Alternative education."

"Hell, I would've liked that better than school," he said.

"I think it will work great. This is the funding avail-

able through the grant that I got to hire an art teacher."
She presented a figure that made Gabe's eyebrows rise.

"Not bad," he said.

"I'll say. So we'll have to find somebody that's well
versed in various mediums. I also like someone who's
not completely unfamiliar with these kinds of kids. It's
going to be a lot of back talk and possibly harassment."

"Well, we'll make sure whoever we choose has been
sufficiently warned. They'll definitely be well com-
pensated."

"Yeah," she agreed.

"Thanks for doing this," he said.

"No problem. It's nice to have something to do
again. I've been... I don't know. Amelia and I have
sufficient money to live on for a while, thanks to the
insurance settlement we got. But I need more. Right
now a traditional teaching job isn't the most practical."

"I expect not."

"This is great, and she loves to come here and visit
your mom."

"Yeah," he said, tenseness creeping into his voice
at the mention of his mother.

"You guys had a fight when I was there that day.
Didn't you?"

"What makes you think that?"

Ellie smiled. "Oh, just the yelling, and you storm-
ing out."

"It'll be fine," he said.

"Well, I would hope so. You've been the best family...
You're the only family I have."

"Your parents and Clint's really never come and
see Annabelle?"

She shrugged a slim shoulder. "Clint's parents mean

well. But they're distracted with their own stuff. Then I think Amelia and I are a reminder. A not particularly happy one. I know we wouldn't be for some people. But that is not how it works for them. My parents... They've been disengaged for a long time. Hank and Tammy, you, Jacob. Caleb, of course. You're the reason I'm standing strong. You're the reason I was able to be so strong for Amelia. Because you helped me."

"Why do good people do such terrible things?" he asked of no one in particular. But since Ellie was the one who was sitting there, she definitely seemed to think it was directed at her.

"I don't exactly know what you're referring to... But... I think very few people are wholly good or wholly bad. I guess what makes it balance out differently in the end is how many times you choose to do the right thing instead of the wrong thing."

"I guess."

He thought about Jamie. And choices. Jamie seemed to think that everything came down to choices.

He ignored the cracking feeling in his chest.

Ellie stood and got her things together, stuffing her binder into her pale pink shoulder bag and sweeping her blond hair out of her face. She turned, and the door opened, Caleb walking inside. Ellie brightened visibly. "Hi, Caleb. Will I see you later?"

"Uh...yes."

"I have to go grab Amelia now." She walked by him, her fingertips brushing his shoulder, and for just one fleeting moment, an expression of intense pain crossed his brother's face.

It was so acute, and so apparent, that it left Gabe

shaken. And it echoed against something inside him, something that recognized that kind of pain.

A kind of pain he wanted to pretend he didn't recognize at all.

"Bye, Ellie," Caleb said, his voice gruff.

Gabe's eyes met Caleb's, and the expression there was so closed off, Gabe knew that there were no questions Caleb would answer.

"You wanted to see me?" Caleb asked.

"Yeah. It's about West Caldwell."

"I don't know the name," Caleb said, leaning against the wall.

"He's our half brother."

Caleb nodded slowly. "You have a name."

"Yeah, and an address in Texas. I'm going to go ahead and send a letter."

"Good," Caleb said. "Have you talked to Jacob?"

"Couldn't get ahold of him. I assume he's up out of cell service somewhere."

"Probably."

They let that settle between them. Neither of them knew what to do about Jacob. Or the fact that his reclusiveness was getting a bit more pronounced, and not less.

"Ellie's getting us all set up here. We're going to hire an art teacher."

"Really?" Caleb asked.

"Yeah. And Ellie is thinking she can maybe teach some general education classes once we get up and running and have people here residentially."

"Great," he said, though there was an underlying emotion in Caleb's voice that Gabe couldn't read.

"So why is it that I saw Jamie Dodge getting the hell off the property looking murderous earlier today?"

"I don't know," he said. "Because Jamie always looks murderous?" He gritted his teeth against a wave of pain.

"No, she doesn't. What's going on between the two of you?" Caleb asked.

"Nothing," he said.

"Right. That's why you look like you want to murder me right now."

"We had a little fling. That's it. She's pissed off that it's over. She'll get over it. She's young. She'll bounce back."

"Really?" Caleb shook his head. "That's some denial."

"What?"

"I haven't seen you around her much, but I'd say what's between you is more than a little fling."

"It doesn't matter. I like her. I do. But like I'm going to get married and have kids? Anyway, that's not what she wants."

"That's not what she wants? Or it's not what you want her to want?"

"Jamie is headed in for a big barrel racing career. She doesn't want to settle down with me. Maybe if I were still going out and riding..."

"So you have an excuse for everything?"

"Caleb, don't you dare come in here and lecture me on what you think well-adjusted looks like."

Caleb's face went hard. "You have something to say to me?"

"You're an ass," Gabe said. "You act like you have everything together, sitting back and judging Jacob for being up in the mountains and not dealing with his grief, and you're…playing husband and daddy to Ellie and Annabelle, except you have none of the physical perks of it."

"Are you suggesting that I have sex with our dead best friend's wife?" Caleb's jaw was hard as granite.

"He's dead."

Caleb's lip curled up into a sneer. "I'm taking care of her because it's the right thing to do. Do you not understand that?"

"I'm just saying. You can stand there and call me out for having excuses… Doesn't mean you don't have the same."

"I'm not the one letting a woman I obviously care about walk away. Hurting someone that I obviously care about."

"I admit, that one is much more Dad's MO than mine, usually," Gabe said. "But then, that's kind of the point."

"Sorry, I missed the point. Can you elaborate?"

"Come on. The way that Mom and Dad have always been with each other, the way that Dad is… Can you even imagine getting involved in that willingly?"

Caleb barked out a laugh. "No. Not *that*. But you know, there's plenty of marriages that aren't bad."

"Sure. But my concern is the likelihood of that being mine. Of me being Dad."

"I don't believe that," Caleb said.

And it was the second person in only a couple of hours to look right at him and tell him that he was a liar. He didn't know quite what to do with that.

Caleb held up his hands. "Look, have whatever narrative you want, but you don't actually know everything about my relationship with Mom and Dad. It's just not simple enough for us to have all gone through the same thing. All this bullshit is complicated. So whatever issues you came out of our childhood with...

"If I had a woman who loved me, staring me in the face and telling me she wanted to be with me, and I loved her back, I'd take it."

"How do you know that's what happened?"

"Because she had the look on her face of a woman who'd had her heart smashed to pieces. And I figure that's about the only thing that'll do it."

A wave of physical pain washed over Gabe and he kept his face stony. He'd ridden bucking horses for years. Had all kinds of cuts and bruises, minor stomping, that he had to stand up and walk off. Because there was a crowd of people. Because a champion didn't show pain. Because you got up again, no matter what.

You didn't cry when your dad sold your horses.

You didn't fall apart when your mother was crying in your arms and telling you about your father's bastard children and the way you could get back at him.

You stood up, and you moved on. It was what you did.

It was what he'd always done.

Except...

Except now it was all crashing into him.

He had done it for so long, and it had taken him to a place where he wasn't sure how to do it anymore.

He met his brother's eyes. "Unless you have something else to say, you can go now. I have a lot of work to do."

"I don't have anything else to say," Caleb said, turning away. "No, just one more thing."

Gabe gritted his teeth. "Of course you do."

"If you're so angry about the way Mom and Dad railroaded you into choosing the path they wanted you on, then at some point you have to quit letting your life be their choice."

"Why do you think I'm here? What do you think I'm doing now?"

"Just enough that you can pretend what you're doing isn't a reaction to them. Just enough."

And then Caleb walked out of the room, closing the door behind him, and Gabe didn't let any part of the conversation replay in his head. Instead, he wheeled his chair over to the fridge and took out a bottle of beer.

It was one in the afternoon. And he figured he better start drinking now.

JAMIE DIDN'T KNOW how to be sad. Not for a prolonged period of time.

But she'd had a pretty solid twenty-four hours of sadness. The dull edges of pain from the grief over her mother were still there, along with the sharper, biting pain of losing Gabe.

She didn't know what to do. She didn't know what you were supposed to do when your entire body hurt, and your eyes were dry and painful from having cried out every last tear in your body.

She was pretty sure she was in danger of being dehydrated.

And she was *hiding*.

Buried deep in her cabin, where no one could see her having such an obvious meltdown, because there would be no way she could hide the fact that she was in the throes of heartbreak.

Heartbreak.

She looked up at the ceiling and started to count the wood planks there.

She supposed she could look at it as an experience. Being heartbroken. She'd never been heartbroken before.

"Another damn first from Gabe Dalton," she said to herself.

Yeah, she could have skipped this one.

The bastard.

She felt spiky, and harmed. And she didn't know whether she wanted to find someone and fling herself into their arms, or hide for the rest of her life.

At the moment she was exploring the hiding-for-the-rest-of-her-life option.

There was a heavy knock on the door, and she cringed. She supposed that depending on who it was, her hiding option was about to be taken from her. If it was one of her brothers, she could always say she was sick.

Or maybe that she had cramps.

That would probably make them go away.

She crawled out of bed, keeping her blanket wrapped around her shoulders. She paused as she walked by the bathroom and looked at herself in the mirror.

Oh, for the love of God. She had not considered this as a potential problem when she had begun wearing mascara on occasion. But there it was, her sadness tracked down her face in telling, black lines. Being a woman was dumb bullshit. She tightened her hold on the blanket and went to the door, jerking it open.

Then looked down slightly. Because it was Bea, her expression determined.

"Hi," Jamie said.

"Hi," Bea said. "Can I come in?"

"You're going to come in whether I tell you you can or not."

"Probably," she said cheerfully, walking inside behind Jamie. Jamie shut the door and looked at Beatrix, who was wandering the perimeter of the room as if she half expected to see Gabe somewhere in the cabin.

"I was worried about you," Bea said.

"Why?"

"Because we had a little barbecue last night, and Dane and I came over. And also, Dane and I came for breakfast this morning. You were at neither thing. That's not like you."

"Well, here I am." Her friend just stared at her. Jamie sniffed dramatically in response. "I'm not feeling well."

Bea narrowed her eyes. "Is that a euphemism for Gabe broke your heart?"

Jamie swallowed hard, turning away from Bea and trying to collect herself. "This is stupid," Jamie said. "I haven't cried so much ever in my entire life. Probably not even when I was a baby."

"Yeah, love is like that."

"Well, it shouldn't be," she said. "You were talking about how fun it was. When you and Dane were sleeping together. *Fun, fun, fun*, you said. McKenna said *go have some fun*. You told me sleeping with Dane was... What did you say? *Athletic*. And *fun*. This doesn't feel fun. And unless weeping is cardio, it's not exercise, either."

Bea had the decency to look moderately guilty. "Yeah, that whole no-string sex thing is only fun as long as you can lie to yourself about it." She sighed.

"Eventually, you have to start dealing with the emotions. And if one of you isn't ready for that..."

"Did Dane do this to you?"

Beatrix grimaced. "I did it to him."

"You...you broke Dane's heart?"

"I did," Beatrix confirmed.

"That doesn't sound remotely like you."

"I'm just a person, Jamie. And I was scared. Because I'd never felt that way for anyone else. And the idea that someone like him might love me, all of me... it didn't seem real. I wanted to protect myself.

"I never fit in with my family. I never felt right. And I just couldn't believe that this man that I thought was so perfect...thought I was right."

"I'm not sure that Gabe thinks I'm so perfect," Jamie said.

"Well, I don't think he broke up with you because he feels nothing, either," Bea said.

"How can you be so sure? Maybe he doesn't. Maybe I felt so much because it was so different for me. Because it was such a change. But for him... For him it wasn't."

"I've seen him with you," Bea said. "Believe me, Jamie, if he wanted sex, he could have just gone home with that blonde that night. That would have been easy for him. But he chose you."

"I feel like you're not trying to compare my beauty to that woman's, but it is feeling a little bit that way."

"That's not what I mean at all. I'm not saying he could have picked a more beautiful woman. I'm saying he could've picked someone he wouldn't have had entanglements with. Someone whom he wouldn't have had to see later. Someone he didn't work with. Someone whose older brother wasn't looming around the corner waiting to punch him in the face. If he didn't have skin in the game, he would have gone with simple. You and he are a lot of things, but you're not simple."

"No. This isn't simple at all. It's just awful."

"Well, what are you going to do about it?"

"I can't do anything. He said no. He said he doesn't love me. He doesn't want to be with me. I can't…I can't fight my way through this one. I don't know what to do, Beatrix."

"Jamie…"

"I was wrong. I thought that maybe if I told him I loved him that it would make everything okay. That it would fix him. That it would fix us. But I was wrong. Because I don't know…anything about this. Less than a month ago I thought I knew everything. And now I think I don't even know myself. I don't even know… I don't know anything. I've never felt so sad or small in my whole life. I don't know what to do, Beatrix. He showed me all of these wonderful things, and he made me feel all of these hard, complicated feelings, and now he's taking himself away from me."

"You're going to do what you've always done, Jamie. You're going to fight your way through. You're going to carry over all those things you learned from him. Because that's the kind of woman you are. You're strong, and you're scrappy. And you never let anyone tell you how it is. So why should you start with him?"

"Because I can't exactly—" she waved her hand "—make Gabe love me."

"No. But you can choose whether or not you let

him make all these things you learned about yourself mean nothing. You can take it forward, and you can build yourself something good. Build yourself a life. It's terrible. But you can… You can choose what to do with the pain. We talked a little bit about my…my dad. And how the man who raised me isn't my biological father. How getting rejected by the man who was my biological father hurt me. It was the reason that I couldn't face Dane. The reason that I almost destroyed everything with Dane. But you learned something real here, with Gabe. And your feelings are real, too. But you can choose what you do with them. With this hurt. And then, when the right guy comes along, you won't hide from him."

"I don't *want* another man," she said stubbornly. "I want *that* man."

"Yeah, and I expect that will be true for a while."

It would be true forever, and Jamie knew it.

Maybe there would be another man eventually. Because that was just how life seemed to move on.

But it would never be like it was with Gabe.

He was her first. He was her firsts. Sex. Love. Being told she was beautiful. Eating toast and hot chocolate in bed. Heartbreak. Longing.

The first of so many firsts.

"In life, the only thing we can control is our own choices," Bea said, the note of pragmatism in her voice making Jamie feel murderous.

"Funny, I pretty much said the same thing to Gabe. It didn't seem to make a difference."

"It might someday. You don't know. I had to go and sit with my fear for a while. Maybe that's what he has to do, too. In the meantime, don't forget who you are. You're strong as hell, Jamie Dodge."

"I'm a lot more fragile than I thought, too."

"But I think being able to admit that shows me that you're even stronger than I thought you were."

CHAPTER THIRTY

GABE HAD DECIDED not to keep drinking, because the only thing worse than being sad was being a sad drunk.

By the time he got into bed that night, he was regretting it.

He could use a little oblivion.

The absence of Jamie in his house was so pronounced it was surreal. She hadn't lived with him. She'd spent a handful of nights with him. And yet his house felt…

It felt wrong somehow. Like it had lost the most important piece.

And a strange, matching emptiness echoed in his chest. He refused to think about what that might really mean.

That the missing piece might actually be in him.

He didn't know how the hell he'd gotten here.

He was a successful man. A man who'd gotten everything he'd set out to get. But he was a man who hadn't set out to get anything he loved.

And that was a strange realization.

And as he sat there in his bedroom, filled with things he bought with his money from the rodeo, memories of that life flashing through his mind, it felt…empty. An empty pursuit. Something that had fed his bank account and nothing more.

Something that had fed a desire for revenge against a man who had hurt him.

And that thought brought about anger. Anger at his mother. For the part that she played in that. For the way that she'd manipulated him.

Who are you really angry at?

He gritted his teeth. He didn't know what to do with this damn life. This life that had so many wonderful attributes. That didn't have a damn thing that he could even complain about, really. He hadn't thought meaningfully about choices. Not really. He thought in terms of the way that his father hadn't wanted him on one path, and his need to protect his mother had put him on another.

And it all made it sound like some big hand was reaching down from the sky and moving him around. But if that was his concept of God, it was a bad one. Particularly since he'd never thought of it that way before. And he wasn't a man who had ever given much credence to fate, either.

And that meant that he had to acknowledge, with all honesty, that the choice had been his.

He might have done it for his mother, but he made the choice to go into the rodeo.

He made the choice to stay.

Just like he'd made the choice to tell Jamie that things could never happen between them. Like he made the choice to turn away from that.

Because it would be hard.

Because it was what he wanted.

Yeah, the rodeo had been easy for him. That was the bottom line. Because he hadn't truly cared whether or not he failed. Because it meant nothing to him. And if he'd fought tooth and nail and stood against his father and told him that he wasn't going to accept the old man's edict to not join the ranch and he'd failed, then he would have...

Well, he'd have had no one to blame but himself.

Damn.

He built a life for himself, made entirely out of materials he didn't give a shit about. And then he wondered why he felt nothing. Nothing in triumph, nothing in failure. He made it that way.

Because he never wanted to...

He'd never wanted to be like his mother. Broken and crying and destroyed over caring so much about something that didn't love you back.

He was a coward. Jamie was right.

He'd ridden damned bucking broncos, so it had never occurred to him that he might be living life afraid.

Oh, he wasn't afraid to have his bones broken. Wasn't afraid to get stomped on and ground into dust in an arena. No, he wasn't afraid of that.

But he was afraid to love.

He was afraid to put his whole self into something and have the return come back broken. Damaged and mangled beyond repair.

He was afraid of wanting someone who would never want him in quite the same way. Who would hurt him. Again and again.

He got out of bed, his feet making contact with the cold floor. And his thoughts kept racing, even as he started moving. As he put his boots on, grabbed his truck keys and headed out the door.

He wasn't afraid of being his father. He was afraid of being his mother.

And he wondered if part of him had chosen to behave just a little bit like Hank Dalton, so that he would never find himself in Tammy Dalton's shoes.

He could see himself, seventeen and being told he might be a father. And the real terror he'd felt. Not just that he couldn't do it, but of all the pain he'd be opening himself up to.

Marriage. A child.

It had terrified him even then.

Fuck.

He was just so very fucked.

And Jamie…

At that moment that dull ache in his chest turned into something more. Something deeper. And it fractured. Pulling his whole chest apart, and he bled. He bled for this. Bled for her. Bled for them.

He was, in a metaphorical sense, selling his own horses out from underneath himself. So that he couldn't try and fail. So that he couldn't try, and end up wounded.

It was that moment when he realized he was headed to the Dalton ranch.

He had given himself a mediocre life that he didn't want any part of, and he had blamed his parents. He had blamed his circumstances. He had blamed his need for the rodeo money. He had blamed every damn thing in the world except for Gabe Dalton. But Gabe Dalton was the only one who could answer for these sins.

It was easy to make it about the sins of his father. Easy to make it about the sins of his mother.

But all had sinned. And he sinned against himself more righteously than anyone else ever had.

And Jamie… Jamie had loved him, anyway. Jamie had demanded he look her in the face and say he didn't love her, and he was such a coward he'd looked her directly in the eyes and spoken those words. Lied right to her. Lied right to himself.

Because the scariest thing in all the world wasn't getting on the back of an angry animal. No. The scariest thing in all the world was opening himself up to love. To the potential for pain. Real pain.

Not physical pain that might leave you with a limp, but emotional pain that would live with you for the rest of your life.

He pulled into the driveway and drove to the barn. Sitting in his truck for a moment before turning the engine off. He walked outside the barn, and he went into Gus's stall. He put his hand on the animal's neck. And he closed his eyes. It made him think of Jamie. The way that she connected with horses. The way that she loved them. The way that she loved this life. In an unbridled way. A way that hadn't been harmed by it.

She was what he might have been. If different choices had been made.

And he could no longer put the blame at anyone else's door but his. He swallowed hard, a strange amount of emotion rolling around in his chest.

Then he brought Gus out of the stall and began to tack him up, not sure what he had in mind. Or where he might be going.

He hadn't ridden with no purpose in longer than he could remember. He'd started this project because he believed in the power of animals, of ranch work, to heal. And he'd withheld the healing from himself. Because he hadn't wanted to go back to those feelings he had, to that pain that he'd experienced as a boy.

That loss.

Oh, he was a coward.

He mounted the horse, rode him out of the barn. The night was clear, the full moon providing ample light for both horse and rider. He guided him up a path that led to a broad, open field. He maneuvered him into a run, a trot that transitioned into a gallop, and Gabe let his hands fall to his sides, and then wide. With nothing but the moon and the stars to witness what was the equivalent to an emotional breakdown in his world.

And the only thing that could have made this moment better was to experience it with Jamie.

There wasn't another woman, another person alive, who understood his connection to this. The connection he'd been denying himself for so long. He didn't even have to explain it to her. She'd been born with it. He had found a woman who made him laugh.

Who made him hot chocolate and toast.

Who got him hotter than any other woman ever had. And who understood the most fundamental emotional avenue he even had. His connection to the horses. His connection to the land. And he'd sent her away.

Because of fear.

He wasn't worthy of Jamie, and he was overwhelmed by that thought right then.

Because she had faced him on earlier today, her eyes blazing with anger. She had demanded he tell her he didn't love her. She had dug in and made him answer for himself. And she had stood her ground.

She was a hell of a woman, and he wasn't worthy of her.

But he could change. He could choose.

Because if he let this go to hell, he'd have no one to blame but himself. It wasn't the sins of Hank Dalton that had made him the man he was. It was his own fear.

And he had to choose now. Love or fear. And as he looked up into the stars, at the moon, swollen with light, even in the darkness, he knew the answer.

Because fear wasn't the greatest, and it never would be.

No, the greatest was love.

And for him, the greatest was Jamie Dodge.

And he was going to have to do whatever it took to have her in his life. No matter the cost.

And just like that, as soon as he accepted it, all the things that he feared seemed small. Like stardust in the sky.

And he knew exactly what he was going to do.

"I NEED TO talk to you both," Gabe said as he looked between his mother and father and saw the tension there. But it wasn't his job to fix that. "I need to talk to you both, because we need to sort some shit out."

"Well, if you didn't know, we're kind of in the middle of sorting something out ourselves," Hank said.

"I do know," Gabe said. "But it doesn't separate from me. It doesn't separate from us. And that's the thing. All of the stuff between the two of you…it affected us. It always did. And it still does."

"I don't know what you expect anyone to do about the things in your life you're unhappy with," Hank said. "You've been pissy with me for months. But I can't change the past."

"Neither can I," Tammy said. "But you're doing an awfully good job of hanging on to my mistakes, when I just had to put up with yours for the past thirty-five years."

"You hid the fact that I had other children from me," Hank said.

"I was trying to protect *my* children," she said. "Those children were a mistake, and you shouldn't have had them. I accepted McKenna. I did it without question."

"That you did that because you felt guilty is hardly my problem."

They were acting like children, and Gabe didn't have the patience for it. Not now.

"I wrote to West," Gabe interrupted. "West Caldwell. That's his name. One of them. I have yet to track down the other brother. When I do, I'll let you know."

Hank looked pale. "Have you heard from him?"

"Not yet. I don't know if I will. He may not want anything to do with us, and I can't say I would blame him."

"Don't say that," Hank said. "Don't make it sound like it's our entire family. Like our whole lives together is nothing but a mess for you. We had good times."

"We did," Gabe said. "And what I did or didn't do with my life…that was my choice. That's actually what I wanted to talk to you about. Dad, I was angry at you for years for the way that you tried to manipulate me into going to school instead of ranching. And I get what you were trying to do. I even understand that it came from a place of caring for me. But it was caring for me in the wrong way. About what you wanted, and not about what I wanted. And I let that anger I felt make my choices for me. And, Mom… When you admitted that you told me about that situation because you wanted me to hurt him…I got angry at you. You shouldn't have lied to me. You shouldn't have kept that from Dad. But nobody chose my life for me. I chose it. The same, Dad, as you chose not to honor your vows. The same as you chose to stay, Mom. How angry can we be, for how long, about our own choices? I can't blame other people for the shit I've done anymore. I've got to take responsibility."

"So what are you saying?" Hank asked. "What does that have to do with us?"

Typical of his father, that he immediately wanted to know how it all boiled down to him. "I'm choosing to stay here. And to use your property to run this ranch with these boys. I'm choosing it to try and rectify some of the mistakes of the past. I'm choosing not to be angry at you both."

He turned his focus to his father. "Dad, I thought I was scared I'd be like you, but that's not it. I was afraid I was going to grow up and be like Mom. And stay, and stay. Let someone hurt me. But I won't. I'm not going to let fear dictate who I am. And most of all, Dad, you were right. You have changed. You've changed, and Mom forgave you. I'm going to choose to do the same. I've got to set aside those things you did back then. Because otherwise…none of us gets to move forward. But I think you have to do the same for

Mom. Otherwise, there isn't a point. You can't hang on to someone that you're that angry at. It gets in the way of everything else. It gets in the way of being family." Gabe shook his head. "We're not a perfect family. But I think sometimes we're more good than bad. I want to make my life more good than bad."

Gabe stood up. "I have somewhere to be."

"Where you going?" his mother asked.

"To get my life."

Gabe Dalton had spent more than fifteen years believing that the restlessness inside of him could never be fixed. But now he knew.

He'd been searching for peace. For a reason to stay home. To make a home.

He'd found it.

In Jamie Dodge.

And he wouldn't rest until he had her back.

JAMIE WAS HOT, sticky and feral by the time she got back to the barn after what had been an arduous trail ride. Not because the ride itself should have been arduous. It was for inexperienced guests, after all. But it was the dumb-ass rider she'd had on the trip that had made it a pain in the ass. There had been a bachelor party, which was unusual. It was much more common for groups of women to come to the ranch than groups of men.

But she had herself a pack of frat burros, who hadn't listened to anything she'd said, had been intent on using bad language in front of the family on the ride, and who had gone off course and forced Jamie to go after them, and get into a screaming match with drunk douchebro best man.

She was sick of everything, and the next person who got in her face was going to end up savaged by her teeth.

Plus, everything just kind of pissed her off right now.

A side effect of heartbreak, she was realizing.

Heartbreak she was no longer able to hide. She'd been the recipient of pitying glances, threats to Gabe's body and three pies in the past forty-eight hours. She had to admit, the threats and the pies were nice.

But they didn't exactly fix anything.

That was what she was going to do. She was going to go shower and eat a pie. A whole pie.

She was stomping out of the barn when she nearly ran into another person. She stopped and looked up, her heart catching when her eyes took hold of an intense blue gaze that she would know anywhere.

"What are you doing here, Dalton?" she asked.

"I have some things to say," he responded.

He looked beautiful, wearing a black cowboy hat and T-shirt, tight Wrangler jeans that made her want to get her hands all over him.

She wanted to stab him with a pitchfork.

"We don't have anything to say to each other. We're not friends. We're not friends and I'm never going to make you toast again."

"I deserve that," he said. "But the trouble is, Jamie, we are friends. We're friends, and were a hell of a lot more. In fact, I didn't know one woman could be so many different things. It was news to me."

"Why are you here?" Emotion rose close to the surface. She was ready to cry again. She wasn't even ashamed. "I told you that I love you. I put myself out there. I exposed myself, and you know that nothing in the world is scarier to me than that. You know that I spent my whole life protecting myself. Because I told you. I gave you all that information about me. You know things that no one else does, and you...you abused that. You really, seriously wounded me."

"I'm sorry," he said. "I was a coward—you were right. I was blaming my actions on everyone but the person who's really responsible. Me."

She narrowed her eyes. "Go on."

"Really?"

"You can keep on telling me how you messed up. I'm okay with that." She crossed her arms and cocked her head to the side.

"I messed up. You did all this work, Jamie. You figured out how to deal with the things that scared you, and fall in love, anyway, and I...I couldn't do that. Not fast enough. You're right. I let myself think that I was the experienced one. That I was the one who didn't have growing to do. But I did. I blamed my parents, but I let that go. I can't blame them, not for my choices." He took a breath. "Jamie, I have consistently aimed beneath what I truly want for most of my life. Since that first obstacle. That first time I lost something I cared about, I haven't tried for anything I loved again. Because I didn't want to keep putting myself out there and keep hurting like that. Because I watched my mother do it for so many years. I buried it all. Pretended that I was like my father. Like I just didn't care about much but me. Like the rodeo and success and anonymous sex was enough for me. But it never was. That was never me. But a coward… Yeah, that I always was. But not you. You were brave. You were brave enough to cry."

And that was when the emotion broke inside her, and Jamie felt tears streaming down her face again. She threw her arms around him and held him close. Because whatever he said next, it was what she wanted to do. And she wasn't scared. She was strong enough to handle whatever came next.

"I love you," he whispered. "I love you. And I'm going to cheer you on when you barrel race, and travel to every damn one of your events that I can make it to. I want to build a life with you. I want to marry you. I want you to live with me. And, Jamie, I'm going to choose to be the best damn husband ever. I'm going to choose you, and only you, every day for the rest of my life."

The rush of love, of relief, of pleasure, that washed over her was so intense she thought she might faint. And wouldn't that be a thing. Jamie Dodge literally swooning over a man.

But this was the right thing to swoon over, if she was going to.

Her life.

Her love.

Her man.

"Okay," she whispered. "I choose you, too."

"People like us, people with so much protection, we don't fall in love. Honey, we have to hold hands and jump in. We have to do it on purpose. Because there's too many barriers in the way for it to happen on accident. And I am so damn glad you chose me. Because it gave me the strength to choose you back."

"Gabe, so many things in this world are outside of

my control. That you would choose me, that you would take one of those few things that you can choose, and make it me… That's the most powerful, wonderful thing I can even think of."

"So do you love me?" Gabe asked.

"Yes." She flung her arms around him again. "Yes, I do."

"Will you marry me, and travel all over and become a barrel racing champion, and come back home to me when it's time?"

"Yes," she said, through tears that she wasn't afraid to let fall.

"Will you eat toast with me and drink hot chocolate?"

"If we don't have it at our wedding I'll start a riot."

"Perfect. I can't wait."

"Me, either," Jamie said.

"Are you going to wear jeans to the wedding?" he asked.

"Hell, no!" she said. "I'm going to be a princess. I'm going to get the biggest, fanciest wedding dress you've ever seen, and I'm going to wear it. Because I don't need to put on armor every day anymore. And I don't need to pretend that I'm one of the Dodge boys. I don't need to try to keep the town from thinking I'm poor, sad Jamie Dodge. I can just be me."

She kissed him, and she never wanted the moment to end.

Because right then, Jamie Dodge felt all the pieces of herself join up together. Completed by this man. And she was whole.

They were whole.

Together.

Jamie Dodge had always taken care of herself. When she'd fallen down, she hadn't cried. Not even once. She stood up, wiped the blood off and moved on.

But she wouldn't have to do that anymore.

Because in Gabe's arms, she found a safe space to cry.

Now when she fell down, he would be there to pick her up.

And that made her feel strong.

* * * * *

SPECIAL EXCERPT FROM

HARLEQUIN *Desire*

*When Reid Singleton buys the beautiful stranger
a drink, he doesn't realize she's actually his best friend's
little sister, Drew Fleming—until after he sleeps with
her! Will their fledgling relationship survive...as even
bigger family secrets threaten to derail everything?*

Read on for a sneak peek at
One Night, White Lies
by Jessica Lemmon!

London-born Reid Singleton didn't know a damn thing about women's shoes. So when he became transfixed by a pair on the dance floor, fashion wasn't his dominating thought.

They were pink, but somehow also metallic, with long Grecian-style straps crisscrossing delicate, gorgeous ankles. He curled his scotch to his chest and backed into the shadows, content to watch the woman who owned those ankles for a bit.

From those pinkish metallic spikes, the picture only improved. He followed the straps to perfectly rounded calves and the outline of tantalizing thighs lost in a skirt that moved when she did. The cream-colored skirt led to a sparkling gold top. Her shoulders were slight, the swells of her breasts snagging his attention for a beat, and her hair fell in curls over those small shoulders. Dark hair with a touch of mahogany, or maybe rich cherry. Not quite red, but with a notable amount of warmth.

He sipped from his glass, again taking in the skirt, both flirty and fun in equal measures. A guy could get lost in there. Get lost in her.

An inviting thought, indeed.

The brunette spun around, her skirt swirling, her smile a seemingly permanent feature. She was lively and vivid, and even in her muted gold-and-cream ensemble, somehow the brightest color in the room. A man approached her, and Reid promptly lost his smile, a strange feeling of propriety rolling over him and causing him to bristle.

The suited man was average height with a receding hairline. He was on the skinny side, but the vision in gold simply smiled up at him, dazzling the man like she'd cast a spell. When she shook her head in dismissal and the man ducked his head and moved on, relief swamped Reid, but he still didn't approach her.

Careful was the only way to proceed, or so instinct told him. She was open but somehow skittish, in an outfit he couldn't take his eyes from. He hadn't been in a rush to approach the goddess like some of the other men in the room.

Reid had already decided to carefully choose his moment, but as she made eye contact, he realized he wasn't going to have to approach her.

She was coming to him.

One Night, White Lies
by Jessica Lemmon,
available July 2019 wherever
Harlequin® Desire books and ebooks are sold.

www.Harlequin.com

Get 4 FREE REWARDS!

We'll send you 2 FREE Books <u>plus</u> 2 FREE Mystery Gifts.

Both the **Romance** and **Suspense** collections feature compelling novels written by many of today's best-selling authors.

YES! Please send me 2 FREE novels from the Essential Romance or Essential Suspense Collection and my 2 FREE gifts (gifts are worth about $10 retail). After receiving them, if I don't wish to receive any more books, I can return the shipping statement marked "cancel." If I don't cancel, I will receive 4 brand-new novels every month and be billed just $6.74 each in the U.S. or $7.24 each in Canada. That's a savings of at least 16% off the cover price. It's quite a bargain! Shipping and handling is just 50¢ per book in the U.S. and 75¢ per book in Canada.* I understand that accepting the 2 free books and gifts places me under no obligation to buy anything. I can always return a shipment and cancel at any time. The free books and gifts are mine to keep no matter what I decide.

Choose one: ☐ **Essential Romance**   ☐ **Essential Suspense**
    (194/394 MDN GMY7)   (191/391 MDN GMY7)

Name (please print)

Address   Apt. #

City   State/Province   Zip/Postal Code

> #### Mail to the **Reader Service:**
> **IN U.S.A.:** P.O. Box 1341, Buffalo, NY 14240-8531
> **IN CANADA:** P.O. Box 603, Fort Erie, Ontario L2A 5X3

Want to try 2 free books from another series? Call 1-800-873-8635 or visit www.ReaderService.com.

---

*Terms and prices subject to change without notice. Prices do not include sales taxes, which will be charged (if applicable) based on your state or country of residence. Canadian residents will be charged applicable taxes. Offer not valid in Quebec. This offer is limited to one order per household. Books received may not be as shown. Not valid for current subscribers to the Essential Romance or Essential Suspense Collection. All orders subject to approval. Credit or debit balances in a customer's account(s) may be offset by any other outstanding balance owed by or to the customer. Please allow 4 to 6 weeks for delivery. Offer available while quantities last.

Your Privacy—The Reader Service is committed to protecting your privacy. Our Privacy Policy is available online at www.ReaderService.com or upon request from the Reader Service. We make a portion of our mailing list available to reputable third parties that offer products we believe may interest you. If you prefer that we not exchange your name with third parties, or if you wish to clarify or modify your communication preferences, please visit us at www.ReaderService.com/consumerschoice or write to us at Reader Service Preference Service, P.O. Box 9062, Buffalo, NY 14240-9062. Include your complete name and address.

STRS19R

The countdown to Christmas begins now!
Keep track of all your Christmas reads.

September 24

- ☐ *A Coldwater Christmas* by Delores Fossen
- ☐ *A Country Christmas* by Debbie Macomber
- ☐ *A Haven Point Christmas* by RaeAnne Thayne
- ☐ *A MacGregor Christmas* by Nora Roberts
- ☐ *A Wedding in December* by Sarah Morgan
- ☐ *An Alaskan Christmas* by Jennifer Snow
- ☐ *Christmas at White Pines* by Sherryl Woods
- ☐ *Christmas from the Heart* by Sheila Roberts
- ☐ *Christmas in Winter Valley* by Jodi Thomas
- ☐ *Cowboy Christmas Redemption* by Maisey Yates
- ☐ *Kisses in the Snow* by Debbie Macomber
- ☐ *Low Country Christmas* by Lee Tobin McClain
- ☐ *Season of Wonder* by RaeAnne Thayne
- ☐ *The Christmas Sisters* by Sarah Morgan
- ☐ *Wyoming Heart* by Diana Palmer

October 22

- ☐ *Season of Love* by Debbie Macomber

October 29

- ☐ *Christmas in Silver Springs* by Brenda Novak
- ☐ *Christmas with You* by Nora Roberts
- ☐ *Stealing Kisses in the Snow* by Jo McNally

November 26

- ☐ *North to Alaska* by Debbie Macomber
- ☐ *Winter's Proposal* by Sherryl Woods

Harlequin.com

XMAS0319BPA